Misfit Toymakers

Author's Edition

Written by Keith T Jenkins
Edited by April Love
With help from Brook Phillips

Cross & Hammer Publishing
San Antonio, Texas 78228

Cover design by Keith T Jenkins, San Antonio, Texas

Original Photoshop: Levi Jenkins, San Antonio, Texas

Completed Cover Artwork
   Photoshop Work – Eyenegho Dickson
   https://www.fiverr.com/galesackss

C&H Pub

Cross & Hammer Publishing
354 Consuelo Av
San Antonio, Texas 78228

https://www.facebook.com/CrossAndHammerPublishing
http://www.crossandhammer.com

Misfit Toymakers
Book 1 Misfits Made
ISBN: 978-0692445907

Published by Cross & Hammer Publishing January, 2015

Because of the dynamic nature of the Internet, any web addresses or links contained in this book may have changed since publication and may no longer be valid. The views expressed in this work are solely those of the author and do not necessarily reflect the views of the publisher, and the publisher hereby disclaims any responsibility for them.

Table of Contents

Part Two First – Opening My Eyes

Keith T Jenkins

.

The Crash and Recovery

I wasn't always this young, you know? More than a lifetime ago, there was screaming tires! Headlights to my right! Shrieks of terror from the front seat, with blood lacquered on my hands and a BANG of glass exploding all around me. Pain and the dark of night envelop me as a car door is shoved against my head with a BOOM. Airbags inflate and pop like paper bags, somewhere out of sight. My feet stop bracing from the crash, and soon, yelling in the distance and the crackle of burning, something . . . everything. Even with the flames all around me, and while my bleeding or burning to death is on the menu, there is still a small, quiet voice in the back of my head saying, "Hmm, that happened." And though I am flailing about in the dark of night with flames all over my body, I can't help but see through the smoke and screaming pain, that there is a head, shattered and splattered, on a car window opposite me with only a singular crack running up and down the window, and I'm so ADD that somewhere in the back of my reeling mind I am thinking, "That's some impressive glass." That's where this story really begins. The cold wind blows over me through the window, and outside there are shouting voices getting closer and the door being torn from the car . . . tears flow, cooling to my face, even as parts of me are crunching in their hands. I'm fading from consciousness . . . sirens sound . . . people shouting to me, at me, for others to come. Fading, "But . . . !"

I want to scream, but nothing happens. I am trying to flail, to put the fires out, to shout, to cry, but nothing comes. My eyes are so watered up that all I can see are pools of darkness followed by a blob of colour, then colours, undulating one among another, and then I'm blinking, the tears run down my cheeks, as I realize that the colours I see are not the colours I had seen, they're brighter – whiter – cleaner – daylight – indoors. "Where am I? What's going on? Who are you, and why are you doing this to me?" I try to say it all, but nothing comes out. Still, I'm not burning – I'm cool and not in pain, so there's that.

There's a guy in a doctor mask with his hands on my face. He must have seen the terror and confusion in my eyes because he replied. He removes his mask and his lips move as if to say, "Just a moment," but it sounds like Charlie Brown's mom, and everything was gone. I didn't realize what was happening then. Really, it would be days – even weeks and months – before any true understanding of my reality would arrive.

I just wake up and I can't move. I can't scream for help. I can barely blink my eyes and think, and more than anything else I am worried about what I am thinking. I am thinking that it seems like weeks since I did anything, and I can't remember what that was. I can't remember if what I did last was work or play or spend time with my wife and kids. What is my wife's name? I can't picture her face at all. Do I have a wife and kids? I try to think about what I do for a living, and it simply will not come to me, and then I realize, "Wait a minute, who am I? Holy crap! I can't even remember my own name." I close my eyes hard and try to think, but even my face won't come to mind. Who am I?

I begin to panic, but that doesn't help, and no one comes to see me. I hear some beeping and quiet whirring noises around me and realize that these are the sounds I have heard on TV when someone was in an ICU – I think, "I'm hooked up to some doctor junk." Hard as I try, I can only look around as far as my eyes can move, and that ain't much. Just on the bottom edge of my field of vision, I can see a breathing tube of some sort, and I hear the slow and steady "whish . . . whoosh" sound from a respirator. I'd heard that before, but I can't remember where or when or why. I start feeling a panic going on and hear the beeping of my EKG or EEG or something getting faster and very shortly, a nurse comes in. She sees, she glares, and then she shouts.

"He's awake." I hear, but the words are garbled. It is like my head is under pillows or like I am laying down in a shallow bath with my ears covered by water. A small, red light in the hallway begins to rotate and flash quietly as a stream of people dressed in scrubs flood into the room, finally followed by an authoritative looking woman and a man with a lab coat. It seems like a dozen others are mumbling around me as if my ears aren't quite working; everything still garbled. Lab coat guy comes close beside me and leans down saying, "Looks pretty good." And that's all I recall from that visit. I must have passed out or something.

"Wanna take it for a ride?" I had asked someone – I don't remember who, but he looked hesitant. "We can stretch it out this weekend if you want. We can take it to El Paso and back and see what she burns." He said that this sounded like a "capital idea," and we made the arrangements. He was going to meet us at the Exxon on I-10 near UTSA at five o'clock on Friday morning.

We made the trip from San Antonio to El Paso and back. We exited 10 to 410, then Callaghan to Evers, which turns into Benrus. We turn left into the ANG store on the corner of Culebra to fill 'er up. It was 538 miles to our stop in El Paso from the Exxon, then 550 back home on 28.4 gallons of gas. That's a little over thirty-eight miles to the gallon, on a one ton van, carrying 1600 pounds of cargo for a third of the trip, plus the riders, using only existing technology and inventing nothing. "What could happen," I asked, "if we were to improve the battery situation and change the generation motor to something not off the shelf, but something designed to keep an even speed, under load, while being tuned and tweaked for efficiency? And, what if we put it all under the hood and into the body panels of the vehicle? What if we apply some serious imagination?" Where did that come from? I have to quit nodding off, not knowing where I've been. Thirty-eight mpg?

I was away for a while, and again, I don't know how long. I wake again and try to look around once more, and strangely, my head has a little play. I can see some of the gadgets that take my vitals. I am pleased that they look like scenes from a hospital room instead of scenes from any of the medical examiner shows I used to watch. What were those shows? Really? I can't remember a single show, cast, name, but I can recall that a crushed hyoid bone is a bad thing! There's so much I don't remember. There's so much I do. How can that be? I remember *I Love Lucy* and *Gilligan*, but who doesn't? Strange, my head now has some range of motion – up and down and left to right – but no leaning side to side. I can make a "yes" or a "no," but just by a couple of degrees, and no more movement, anywhere. Wow! That is a busy day. Yes, no, and Lucy. From time to time it strikes me: why do I keep thinking about petechial hemorrhaging, and who the hell is

Jordan Cavanaugh? She flashes into my mind, and all I can remember is, "She's hot!" but that's all I've got. And then there are moments when I am asking myself, "Who is that Armani suit that keeps peeking in the door?" Whoa! This has been another long day, or at least it seems so; though I can only recall about two minutes of it at a time, and then, all of a sudden, things spin for a moment, and I am heading for a nap again.

It feels as if I have been asleep for only about twenty minutes, or maybe an hour, tops; but the suit has changed his suit. Still? Who is he? He is a medium sized man that I guess from my angle is about 5'8" and 150, about fifty something with graying temples, round metal glasses, and the smoothest looking dark green suit I have ever seen. Why are the lights going out again? Everyone looks so calm? Nope, I'm . . . G'nite.

I hear a snarfling noise and suddenly wake. I was snoring. He sees that I am awake, if that is the word for it, and he comes over to the bed. He tells me that his name is Gerhardt, and he works for the . . . ah . . . hmm, what was it . . . some word, not too big, it means organization, business or company . . . consortium . . . that's okay . . . and that Joshua Danz is my name. To be clear, Joshua Danz is the name that was chosen for me by the . . . Enterprise. That's the word! Enterprise! He says that I am to worry about nothing but getting better, that all else is being handled quite well, and that he would be back in a few days to discuss everything. The word "everything" rolls from his tongue like a magic carpet, but at the same time, it seems somewhat ominous, fraught with danger. Maybe that is just his manner, and I am not some sort of endangered international agent. Oh, God! Don't tell me that I'm a spy. That would be something, huh?

Over the next few days, I wake up six or eight times a day and work my way up to staying cognizant for as much as an hour at a time. Gerhardt stops by and clears the room to explain that I really am not a spy and that there are no reasons to worry about anything, even the bills, as they have all been paid, that no one wants to kill me, and I am not going to jail. He also confirms that I have no wife and kids, or girlfriend; not even a puppy. No one is looking for me and no one is missing me; no one is waiting for me. It's kind of a glad and sad thing all at the same time. I am relieved to know that I am not being hunted or haunted, but saddened to hear that there is no one waiting to hug me, hold me . . . yeah.

Ethyl

There is this one nurse named Ethyl. It's a strange and old fashioned name, Ethyl. Still, she seems familiar. Over the next few months, she will be the one taking most of my vitals and checking me over for bed sores or rashes. She speaks to me gently, in a warm and friendly but still professional tone. There are a few nurses that pass my way, that get a little too friendly, and as soon as they bat their eyelashes at me, or give the wrong smile, that's the last time I see them. I like Ethyl, and I trust her.

I am still on my back when I first meet Ethyl, and she is leaning over me with a small flash light in my eye, and I think she was checking my optic reflexes. She sits me up a little bit, so we can be more face to face and she mouths the words, "Can you see me?" I nod my head. Then she says, "Can you hear me?" I nod again. She says, "Can you talk to me?" I shake my head from side to side to indicate I cannot.

Then she says, "Close your eyes." And I do. There in my vision, scrolling from right to left are the words, "If you can read this nod your head." So, I nod my head. The scrolling words say, "Can you see the words with your eyes open?" and I open my eyes to see that I can. They scroll by about three quarters down my field of vision. Ethyl tells me that my eyes are replacements. "Do they work well?" I nod back to her. My vision is really excellent, as near as I can tell. She is holding a tablet in her hand that she is using to feed the data directly to my eyes. "Check this out," she says, then crossing the room and facing me, with the tablet covering her mouth, through the tablet she says, "Peter Piper picked a peck of pickled peppers." It is not a sound from in the room, but audio being fed directly to my ears, almost as if I have a Bluetooth in my head, but she is much clearer than any Bluetooth I have ever heard. She says that if I think about a reply to her messages the switches are established to allow a response to be sent. "Try it," she types, "I not . . . cert . . . out . . . dis," was on her tablet when she turns it around for me. What I tried to push was, "I'm not certain about this at all."

Over the next several weeks I would learn to send and receive on these devices whenever I wish and, more importantly, how to turn them off when I wish. Once the listening system is engaged, it allows me to hear things from distances that would have gone completely unnoticed before. I can hear Ethyl whisper, "Lights out," from outside the room. When I learn to turn off all the input, I can get a great night's sleep.

She tells me that in the accident my eyes and ears had been severely damaged and my jaw had been almost destroyed, so they made a new one of those, as well as a full set of teeth. I asked if there was more that I needed to know, like if I had bionic speed and strength, and she said, "No, the only other part that I know was replaced was a joint near the top of the spine that keeps your head from falling off." But I think she may be kidding about that part.

There are times when Ethyl comes in and reads to me, classics mostly, and children's books. I can't get enough of Dr. Seuss and his worlds of wonder. I love the "what-if-i-osity" of those kinds of things; still do. She reads from *There are Rocks in My Socks Said the Ox to the Fox* and then *The Hitchhiker's Guide to the Galaxy* to me, even though it is not her cup of tea. Many days, her reading is the main reward for the work of rehab, and endless education by Gerhardt.

School

Gerhardt stops in almost daily to "school" me in my new personal reality. Each time he comes, he will first make certain that there are no medical procedures or activities that have to be done, no rehab or med management. This becomes easier once they have unplugged me from all the liquids, and I am eating real food.

It is nearly six months of just healing and endless hours of physical therapy, continuous education by Gerhardt and I have been having glimpses of events that I assume are parts of my life but also might have been bits of my favorite films for all I know, because they are all a jumble. Some are of a fairly modest life and some of blatantly greater opulence. When I have these flashes, they might sometimes be in direct conflict; like I have memories of two different twenty-first birthdays. A person remembers some of their birthdays better than others; twenty one is usually one of them. The theory of it all being parts of different films makes more sense of everything though, at least more sense than I can otherwise make of it now.

For the one birthday, I spent the afternoon with a girl, a fairly pretty girl, tall, profoundly freckled and redheaded, with a slim, athletic build, whom I believe I loved. I held her hand through a movie about a music writer, madly in love with his girlfriend, distracted by a woman who was extremely beautiful – and as it turns out later, totally bangable and even fairly easy – but he learns how useless a woman like that can be, especially when he has a "10" at home. It is fairly good, but after the movie, we went back to her place where I was hoping that I was going to get lucky, like the little composer in the movie had, and, SURPRISE!!! It is a birthday party. Somehow I knew everyone there, and most of them I remember by name. At about midnight we left her place, leaving the others to clean up everything. We went home to my place, and I was right. I was about to get lucky . . . very lucky.

The other birthday has less details and less people because in this birthday I say goodnight to a stunning woman – obviously and professionally well coiffed, as my dad would say, polished to the nines – dad would have said that? And we go to what I believe is a combination birthday and bachelor party. I leave with a guy that has one of those names that said, "I am manly and rich," like . . . oh, yeah, it's Judson, I think. And we drive to a private club where about a dozen of us, all guys I know, have a very expensive meal and large quantities of Macallan 26 that someone found in the basement of some castle. Why do I remember this? But after a bit of drink, we are joined by a bevy of buxom beauties that might have come from any gentleman's magazine with a long page in the center. I remember looking around the room and thinking, "Wow! She's a regular 'Marilyn.' And there's an awesome 'Pamela' and a dead ringer for 'Sophia Loren.' I'll take them all." And that is exactly what I do. We leave the club in a cab and go to a really swank hotel, and they do amazing things . . . together . . . to me.

The strange part of it is, when I remember it all, this last party feels more like watching a movie, and making love with Diane – that was her name . . . her name was Diane – she is remembered more as something very special and very, very real. I close

my eyes, and I can almost smell her perfume. I don't get it. Maybe later it will make sense. Maybe later I will remember the name of the movie too.

I get these little pictures of work – sometimes with my hands, sometimes on what looks like a short con or a scam, sometimes I'm in an office wearing my own Armani suits, and sometimes I am working in a restaurant. Gerhardt continues to pop in from time to time and fills in a few of the blank spaces, but not many. He says that if he tells me everything I might suffer a mental collapse, and possibly die. There are doctors standing around when he says it, and they are nodding in wise-looking approval, and I really don't seem to be in a hurry to go anywhere, so I take the trickling stream of information as it comes. There are some frustrations though. I would like to know what happened to Diane.

I think about raging against the machine, so to speak, and demanding to know what had happened to me and what is going on, but in reality, I am just so grateful that so many people have been doing so much for me; and with very few exceptions, every one of them is extremely pleasant, hardworking and seems genuinely concerned for my wellbeing. It was almost like being watched over by a well-trained and loving family. But what do I know? I don't even know if I have a family. With all these holes in my memories, I could be an orphan. Hell, I could be a tyrant . . . I hope not. All these people are being so nice; I hope I'm not an asshole.

After a couple of months, I am able to move my arms and legs fairly well, but the strength is not enough for me to go anywhere by foot. After about four months or so, I am able to wheel my own chair, though I did just have the cage on my head removed, and I still have a rather rigid collar severely limiting my head movement, but they explained that due to the accident and the healing still needed in the upper spine, it would be best if we didn't monkey with their program. I am determined, however, to overcome this medical business as quickly as possible.

Since I can move my arms and manipulate my hands in gestures, Gerhardt brought me a pair of what I call my "Learnin' Goggles." These are a virtual education system made up of a pair of goggles that will present a 3D rendering of whatever it was fed, and it has ear buds built in that gave astounding sound quality. Along with that comes a set of "tips" – three point gloves that covers the tip of the thumb, index finger, and middle finger on each hand. They have proximity transmitters in them that allow me to manipulate the images and pages of what is in front of me. I can zoom in and out, rotate an image, and slide it left and right, up and down, but I can also control a video that I am watching so that I can stop, pause, rewind, and fast forward, jump to a point on the timed progress indicator, etc. I can even manipulate some of what he called 4D videos to where I can spin them around and see the action from another angle. The system also allows me access to hundreds of thousands of books, magazines, news recordings, and movies from before the accident. But only from before.

The facts of my case, which Gerhardt spools out as we go, are that apparently there was some sort of accident, which he doesn't discuss yet, from which I was retrieved, rescued and although I was quite damaged, burnt mostly, I was also very wealthy, and apparently I still am. Because of the healing needed on my spine at the base of my skull, everything had been shut down or disconnected as it were. There had been burns and grafts and nerve work done before I woke up that first day, but after almost nine months of my work and rest, since that first day of panicked awakening, I am easing into the memories that I have, even though there is a strange pattern and non-pattern of disconnection.

Also, in these memories – these ever growing, sometimes diametrically opposed memories – I have begun to see my face in mirrors, and it doesn't look like it does now. But neither does it look like it did then. It is like I have two faces, plus the one I'm wearing. Or, more accurately, it is like I am watching two different movies of my life played out by different actors. It's like *Frankenstein* played by Boris Karloff and Lon Chaney, Jr. Somehow, they're both Frankenstein, but different, and somehow, still me. Also, I understand that I have a new face. According to Gerhardt, mine was so badly damaged that they had to do a whole face transplant from a guy that I later learned was an out of work actor/model. Good looking guy too, and I wear it well, if I do say so myself, though it may have fit him just a bit more perfectly. On me I think it may have had to be tucked here and stretched there, but on him I bet it looked amazing. Of course, it may also be that the reason he was an "out of work" model was that he was only this good looking. Still, I gotta say, I like it, and when I hear Gerhardt tell me about the work done, I tell him, "I'm just grateful to look better than Ernest Borgnine." Seems like only old film buffs still know who he is anymore. Hmm.

I have been at it pretty hard and the work has paid off. The doctors say that they really expected the process to take much longer. I heard someone say they were expecting to keep me around a couple of years. But what else do I have to do? That's okay; I don't mind making room for some other Joe. I couldn't wait to see the outdoors. Seems to me that I spent a lot of time outdoors, and some of the memories I have are working on construction sites, framing to finishing. I feel like my hands may still know how to do the work, but Gerhardt paints a very different picture of me as an office magnate of some sort. Today is officially the day. I am going to Gerhardt's office, expecting to have the last of the blanks filled in by him and the secrets of all the bodies and where they are buried, so to speak. I hope that isn't an accurate statement.

A driver has come to pick me up, and I am checking out of the hospital, finally. I realize that I don't see any other patient rooms in the place. There appears to be my room, the nurses' station, an office and through the door, an elevator. Beyond the nurses' station is where we rolled to get x-rays and where lab work disappeared. And that is all I can see of the place. The elevator area doesn't look like a hospital elevator area, but like an office space. As I wait for the elevator to arrive, I look into the little windows on the door at the other end of the vestibule, and there is another office with a reception counter and beyond that, what looks like a dentist's chair and a wall full of hard drives. Hmm.

I am wearing a fine suit. On the one hand it feels right at home, and on the other hand it is almost as if I have never seen anything like it. Weird, eh? I notice that everything seems to be a bit more tech than I remember it, and the fashions are somewhat unusual, but a fine gentleman's suit hasn't changed much. I exit the car, which reminds me a bit of the cab in *The Fifth Element* – some old film – and I walk into a tall glass building that seems to cover four blocks of what I believe used to be something else, someplace else – I can't really place it, but there is a large, familiar looking sort of sporting arena across the street – across Cherry Street – but that doesn't make sense, does it? Still, here I am, there it is, and I am going up.

The elevator arrives on the 137th floor in about twenty seconds, and I didn't even notice the acceleration much, but for a moment there the elevator was counting floors by tens. Cool!

Office

Is that the nurse? As I exit the elevator, I can swear it is Ethyl, the nurse from the hospital. "Ethyl?" I say.

She turns quickly and walks right up to greet me, as if we'd never met before, but she knows who I am. "Good to meet you Mr. Danz. May I get you anything?" Strange . . . different hair and style of dress, no uniform, but still her, I'm sure of it, but I have nothing to say. "Mr. Gerhardt will be with you in a moment. He had some finishing up to do on the information he was getting for you. Would you follow me, please?" Her voice seems a bit softer, yet more formal, and still, she is quite pleasant with me as she leads me to a small conference room with glass walls and a table for about a dozen people. Her hair is an almost electric red – magenta – and in a big sort of poof, with a bun on top, held in place with chopsticks, pencils, or something like that. I had not really noticed the freckles 'til now, at the hospital or here. She has a pronounced patch of freckles from below her eyebrows, to her temples, to halfway down her cheeks. She is magnificent to see and womanly in every way. She gestures me to be seated at the far end of the table in the largest chair in the room and pours a glass of water, which she sits down in front of me, then she pushes a button for the glass walls to become frosted white in about three seconds time. "I have received word that Mr. Gerhardt has just arrived and is coming down from the helipad. It only takes half a minute to get here. I'm Ethyl," she says as she shakes my hand, firmly but gently, "and I will be your Administrative Assistant." Then she turns and leaves.

She is scarcely out of the room before a man in a pinstripe suit, with a very large briefcase enters, followed directly by Gerhardt. I rise and he says, "I'm sorry I'm late, but I wanted to have as many ducks in a row as possible for this meeting, and we are about ready." I am wondering what we have to be ready for. I haven't even seen a newspaper for over a year, I have no idea what has been going on in the world, much less why there had to be ducks lined up for me. Still, I have learned to trust Gerhardt in the last nine months or so. He has taken complete care of me, in every non-medical way. Even the trip over here was arranged by him, including the car that brought me, the suit I am wearing and the socks, shorts and shoes that he had delivered to my room in the hospital. However, the biggest surprises are still to come.

"As you can see, Mr. Danz, we have done pretty well at taking care of your estate in your absence. Even with an adjustment for inflation, we have managed to follow your instructions and principles, as best we could, though without your direction, advice, or consent. Your fortune and holdings, in your absence, have increased nearly sixteen thousand percent." He says this with a little pride, but still in a rather matter of fact way, as if it was common knowledge.

"So, what you are saying is that I am really well off?"

"No sir, what I am saying is that you were very 'really well off' when you died, sir. But, now, you own almost everything worth owning. Quite simply sir, it will take weeks or maybe months to even go over it all."

"Died? What the hell do you mean, 'died'? You mean 'died?' 'Died' as in dead?" All of that other stuff about being rich kind of fell away from view. "Died?" The young man's head is tilted slightly, like a dog that has just heard an odd sound.

"Sir," says Gerhardt, "the formalities first." The younger man comes across the room with the briefcase and opens it. "Don't mention the near-death experience to anyone, understand?" he says to the young man with him, who nods knowingly. The case has a computer of sorts in it with a small black glass in the middle, about ten inches by ten inches, and a small light under the glass. "Sir, if you will first place your right hand on the glass, then your left, then the photos of the eyes, and a signature, then, we can effect transfer to your possession and Mister Bernard can be on his way so we may talk." He gestures to the case, "Please sir."

I put my hand on the glass and a bar of light passes under it; and again with the other. There is a small camera inside a cup on a stick that rises from the case and I put each eye to the cup. The computer makes a "bink" sound. "Sign here sir, three times please, sir," the young man asks, and I sign. The signature looks perfect of course, without hesitation because of all the practice and familiarity. Since Gerhardt told me my name, I have been practicing my signature, many times a day. He had said that it would make everything seem more familiar, more 'matter of fact,' in daily use. The young man closes up the briefcase, gestures a zipped lip and a thrown key and departs. Gerhardt closes the door behind him, and we are alone.

"Yes, sir! Your body was retrieved from an auto accident, badly burned, but with a slight pulse and very shallow respiration, in San Antonio on Halloween back in 2015. We had your life signs monitored, from the moment the ambulance picked you up, and when we saw that your body was failing, we had them divert to our facility where your body was put into cryostasis immediately. You were frozen until we could figure out how to 'unfreeze' you safely. Since the ambulance was able to get you to us within about two minutes of your last heartbeat, we were quite confident that your brain would survive the ordeal, so we planned a contingency for it. And here you are."

"What do you mean, 'and here you are?' Is it really that simple to put a man back together?" I can't help wonder about the technical aspects. "Is this just an ordinary *Six Million Dollar Man* kind of day for you?"

"No. Mr. Danz, we didn't just pick up the pieces and reassemble them. We were prepared. You were prepared. It was, after all, your idea." He explains, "Even the day before the accident, we had completed a download of your entire mind."

"What?"

"It may take a while before all of the memories come online again, but you arranged every bit of it, sir. You bought all of the stock in the cryogenics companies – every bit. You had them moved to San Antonio and hidden in the closed subway tunnels that you had purchased. You invested in over three dozen frozen food companies from around the world to develop the thawing processes. And you created the 'If-Then' investment guide that we have used all these years. You founded the nerve treatment centers and advanced the brain mapping and more. Your acquisitions of technology, logistics, and petroleum ventures expanded your wealth."

"Wait a minute." I say. "There are about a dozen things you just said that I am trying to wrap my head around, with no success at all. 'All these years?' It sounds like a long story, but how long could it have been? I'm, what, about forty?"

"Your body – that is, this body – was thirty one when we took possession of it." With a lot of back and forth between us, mostly with Gerhardt telling the story and me interrupting and asking a lot of questions, in the end it seems that I had made a lot of money in car-tech adventuring and back door investing in casinos, movies, and tech companies. Apparently, I own as much as 30% of over 200 small oil companies, and at least 5% of all the big ones. I have a small to medium sized piece of over 400 moving, shipping and air freight companies, including Fed-Ex, UPS, DHL, and the USPS, which had bankrupted and been privatized about twenty years ago or so. As mentioned before, there are frozen food companies, private medical practices, and research operations, and there is tech. Along with a diversifying bite in Microsoft and Apple, I also have my hand in almost every gaming company, both software and systems, and every cell phone maker from HTC and Samsung to Oppo and more, and that turned out to be the tide turner. I also have stock in Google that was enlarged over the years so that, having gotten out in the nick of time, I am one of the wealthiest unknown men in the world. I am the world's richest nobody because no attention is drawn to me in any way. I don't make many public appearances – hell, I didn't make any, being dead – and because of what had been done to the Koch brothers in the media, I don't really dabble in politics much either. Though I did sneak a dozen million or so into the Texas secessionist movement; I can't wait to see how that turned out. But that was then. This is now. Between the office – and make no mistake, this is my new office – and the helipad on the roof, there is my apartment, three floors, with a gym. Gerhardt's office is on the floor below my office. Welcome home. Today is July 12th, 2052.

Who What Where

He had told me of the destitution of Detroit and the decimation of the car industry because of the absolute crap product they made, and how there hadn't been a decent movie out of Hollywood in ten years or more, saying that he and Helge, his wife, never went to the cinema anymore, but watched things on digiview from way back when. Washington is nothing but vipers and neophyte Socialist Democrats, communist wanna-be's, and hangers-on to the power brokers, which are the money people that wanted to impose socialism on the rest of the masses, so long as they could keep using the money and masses for their own purposes.

I am suddenly abused by the memories as I remember seeing a 'pretty boy' actor, back in the day – married to Angelina someone – on an interview program saying something like, "I don't see why all these people are upset about Socialism. I've worked in a Socialist country, it worked fine."

Stuck in my memory is the thought of, "Would it have worked 'fine' if he didn't have millions of his capitalist dollars backing him up? Would it work as fine for him if he lived and worked from a Socialist or Communist country and ended up keeping only $50,000 a year? That's where reality occurs." These arguments stay in my mind forty eight hours a day, because I am stuck in two sets of thoughts and memories, as if I'm possessed, or maybe schizophrenic.

"Well, they certainly have screwed this place up," I say.

"Oh, no! Not 'this place.' This place is Texas," he says with determination, "or more precisely, the FreeNation of Tejas." I think for a moment that he is about to snap to attention and salute. "And, we're not very screwed up at all." He looks at me with my deer-in-the-headlights look and says, "When Texas became the FreeNation we kept the same government in place and made a few changes in the following years. We quit paying into the US federal funds nightmare that was costing us so much, and we later sued for recompense of what had already been sent to DC, within limits of reason. We don't have an Income Tax and it is constitutionally illegal here. Our property taxes went down and our sales taxes went up, from 8.5 to 13%. Socialism and Communism, in every form, is illegal here, even unions. Entitlement fraud in our country is estimated at less than 4%, whereas the US has nearly 30% fraud – and another 30% is just unneeded – according to Texican standards. Just the drug testing qualification cleared out a bunch of them in Texas; most of whom moved to Illinois, California, and New York. No, Toto, you're not in Kansas anymore; although, Kansas is now part of the FreeNation."

"The primary reason we brought you back now, besides the fact that we now have the reliable ability, is that although we have been able to get this far using your If/Then, we are uncertain as to how we should proceed. We have run to the end of the political projections, as we understand them, and figure that you can set the stage for the next century of growth. If we can bring the Enterprise it to this level of success without you, just using our interpretations of your methods, how much better could it all be, if it is led by the man who developed those methods?"

Bad Business

Gerhardt tried to overview all of history since I was out, and this is what I got. With the media and the number crunchers firmly against him, Mitt Romney was soundly beaten by Barack Obama, who came back as the press reinstated their messiah. In 2016 the press was so enamored with Socialism and sticking it to the rich, that they adopted Barbara Boxer as their candidate. She endorsed President Obama's views on pretty much everything and in reality, for the Democratic primaries it came down to the fact that she was a woman, and a more than slightly attractive woman, who could complete sentences without seeming racist or putting her foot in her mouth too badly. Simply put, she had out-glammed Hillary, and no one had to think of turning Bill lose on the White House staff without a keeper of any kind. Boxer was still totally disrespectful to the military, but the military were not in vogue any longer. For her first VP, she chose Joe Biden again, thinking that if he could be the bulletproof vest of Barack Obama, he could do the same for her. After all, one of the key reasons why no one ever took a shot at Barack was that they knew they would have Joe in the Oval Office. Joe was getting well on in years, so her second term, she took the young socialist and friend of the unions, former Mayor Julian Castro of San Antonio, recently employed as a strategist/spokesperson for the DNC. Most of San Antonio was glad to see him go, but he had made many friends in Chicago some years earlier. In his bid for mayor of San Antonio, he sought and apparently received ample funding and support from the Chicago Machine, the Mob, and the Unions – so that in 2012 he was connected enough to be the keynote speaker at the Democratic National Convention. In the election, they got only forty percent of the vote in Texas even though Texas was Castro's home. Part of the reason was that his "PreK4SA" initiative was such huge financial boondoggle, without any educational value, and that was discovered rather quickly. Still, since the media was solidly in the tank for any Socialist Democrat, which they now called a "Social Democrat," the failure was completely dismissed whenever it arose with little more than a raspberry by any noteworthy member of the press. If you pressed questions about PreK4SA, you were labeled a racist. Then, together with a grossly Democratic Senate and House, they passed FRIA, and it was a speedy road downhill.

It was called the Federal Re-Investment Act of 2019, but it was far more of an "act" than it was an investment of any kind. By the Federal Re-Investment Act, or FRIA, the government formally realized the power that they had leveraged in the GM "bail out" of 2009, as well as the power they had failed to leverage, along with the opportunities they had missed out on there, and they proceeded to "bail out" every major company they could, under the auspices of investing for the common good of the common people of the nation. They claimed that the federal government was investing in these companies as a means of generating revenues, allegedly for the expansion and surety of Social Security and the propping up of Medicare and Medicaid, and the general fund to reduce the overall tax burden. But in reality, no taxes ever went down, but the investments allowed the government to get their claws into the board rooms of these companies and expand their stock percentage, not by purchase, but by union leverage, fines, and fees, and promotion of "Social Justice" so that, eventually, these companies became tools of the State. And, "eventually" meant, in many cases, less than three years from the government's initial buy in date at a company.

Google was the most compelling story because of the sheer enormity of it all, and the unmistakable mass of calamity that followed. In 2011, Google broke ground on their plans for super-fast internet connectivity, the "Gigabit Connection." Their service was begun in Kansas City, and in just over ten years' time, they had over thirty million customers in just over fifty markets. The beauty of Google was that they offered several dozen free services and products, but they also offered hundreds of low cost, low maintenance services, plus their internet packages and Android operating systems. Google didn't seem to care if you were an individual buying their services or a dental office that wanted a connection. It didn't matter to them if you were a dozen lawyers or a factory – a single internet connection was a single connection, and it had the same price for everyone; commercial or personal. This forced the cable companies and phone service providers to rethink and remodel their businesses. But it also made Google the most valuable company in the world, eventually surpassing Apple more than four times over. And that was when they sold 97% of my holdings in it. I had bought those shares for a total of about 315 million dollars over a twenty year period, some of which was when they were fairly new, and part of it when I was dead. Then it split several dozen times, and we sold it off for several hundred billion. Google had become an "indispensable" company, too big for anyone to do without. According to my "If-Then" guide, that was the time to get out, so we did.

Specifically, Gerhardt tells me, "According to your schedule, we saw that your projections of government takeovers were happening. We also saw that Google was, as they used to say, 'too big to fail.' So we put our plan in play to liquidate all but a few holdings so as to keep us on the board. It took nearly four months and over a million trades in bites of between 25 and 3000 shares per trade. We didn't want to spook the market. And then it happened."

"Four months later, in 2032, they brought the Federal Re-Investment Act to Google and they eased their way in. They made a relatively modest investment into Google, of about a quarter of a billion dollars, forced their way onto the board, leveraged all the employees into unions, even though they did not want to be in a union, forced the pensions and insurance packages to comply with the model presented by the United Auto Workers in the GM takeover, and the amicably hostile takeover of Google was complete." It would take about five years before the full effects of the takeover would really play out, and when I heard about it later, I was glad we had gotten out and even somewhat glad to have been dead at the time.

With federal oversight of everything in virtually every major enterprise and no one "on the ground" wanting to be culpable for making decisions and spending the money of the company for unscheduled repairs and maintenance or for additional stockpiling of supplies and equipment, they got to where everything they needed to install for these purposes had to wait until it could be ordered and delivered on a per project basis. Each job and each operational failure or breakdown had to have purchase orders for all the parts needed. It used to be that in a cable company or any outside service operation (such as plumbing or TV repair services), a service truck carried around as much as $80,000 worth of connectors, equipment, supplies, parts, pieces, and tools. But now it was down to just the tools (and usually, not all of those) and a barely minimal collection of parts or pieces. Whenever there was a problem with connectivity or speed of data transfer or e-mail management – or anything really – it took many times longer to resolve it, if it was resolved at all. Sometimes the customer was just told, "Sorry, but that's just the way it works now." The only thing that kept it from falling totally into the abyss was the Operational Mandate Act for Federal Agencies and Government Sponsored Corporate Entities. This act – more like a royal decree –said that everything had to work, under punishment of law. By "punishment" they meant that the government would take, as a fine for failure, percentages or additional percentages of the corporation in question. Their descriptions of "working" were so vague, that it didn't take long for the government to own Google outright, just as they did most things, including Sam Walton's dream which was now called Fed-Mart. Mussolini would have been proud. Fascism was reality, except in Tejas. But that's another story.

Trains all arrived late. Airlines became stripped down in staff and crew. Luggage disappeared almost more often than it arrived, and delays were a constant instead of the exception, or even common. Metropolitan bus services became the domain of the Administration of National Transportation Organization and Management, and soon after that happened, the term "organization and management" became code words for "failure and distress." Month after month, buses broke down on the roadside with passengers baking in the summer sun and freezing in the winter with little or no relief, even in spring and autumn. The price of a fare had doubled and tripled in some cases, and the services just got worse in every single enterprise.

Long ago, the electric companies of big cities had sold their customers the idea of being the customer being able to manage their electrical usage remotely, on their tablets or phones. They said that it would save a ton of money. A lot of people signed up, partly because of the savings, but partly because they had become addicted to apps on their tabs and phones that do everything. But the apps required the power company to come by and install a manager on the house electrical systems, which was now connected and controlled over the web. Five or six years later, the companies would be offering the service of managing it for them, and laziness set in, so people allowed that. Then they started managing the customers' energy use to "more adequately administer the public good." Still, even though they could manage your account, once the government ran it all, they couldn't manage their hardware in the field any better than the trains, the buses, or the cable company.

Brownouts became common in every major city, and people began dying in droves because of heat in the summer and cold in the winter and from allergies due to lack of filtration in the meantime. There were policies put in place that provided for the replacement of transformers and switches, etc, but the authority to actually approve the replacement of any materials worth over a thousand dollars still remained with someone further up the food chain than the field tech, but he dared not violate procedures. After all, if he went against the protocols of the system, he would get fired. It didn't matter after a while that it meant saving the lives of people who would die of heat or cold or something worse because the service tech's family and their children would be taken from the list of the "haves" and put on the list of the "have-nots" by his losing his job. As it was, almost every employee of every company was working part time hours because if they employed full time workers, there were serious government penalties and taxes that went into play. So, a guy that fixed a transformer would only be losing a part time job, but that was all he could get to put food on his family table. If you think that was a bad deal, what happened when a person in management made too many decisions to replace transformers or switches or ordered too much alloy wire to replace the copper that was being removed? He lost his job, and his was actually a good job to have. He may have had a full time job, with extra hours to be sure, and on salary, along with paid healthcare and dental benefits, all of which would dry up and die if he lost his job. He would be reduced from the upper crust to the down and outs in a very short period of time. Everyone wanted everyone to think they were doing okay, but the reality was that most banks had little savings in them from their customers. College plans for children had to be used to pay the bills. Most life insurance plans had long ago been converted from annuity to term life policies, and there was no cash value. Most of the nation was living hand to mouth; it's just that some had better looking hands. They had prettier houses and nicer cars, and it took a little longer for the reserves to be eaten up. But many were eaten up all the same.

That was when things had to change. Gerhardt says, "It began right here in Texas, just like you said it would in the If/Then. Thank God Texas had its own self-contained power grids," he says with a gentle smile. "This is the world you have inherited from yourself. Tejas! Not that other thing."

Controls

I spent a few weeks learning my way around the office and my apartment, right above the office. Gerhardt dropped in each day for between one and three hours to show me a bit more about what was happening in the Enterprise, my "empire," and take care of another detail or two. It seemed like I spent a thousand hours boning up on the history of the life I never lived as Joshua Danz, so that I could "recall" the details of my life in case someone had thoroughly studied me. There were reams of reading on my life and hundreds of gigabytes of electronic info as well. We spent some months after this working inside the tower, meeting with department heads and presidents and vice-presidents of the various subsidiary companies letting them know that the "Hermit King" was returning to civilization and that it was all just part of a process. There were a few more months visiting our own locations around the city and the central area of Texas inside the FreeNation, within an hour's drive or so. Everyone had been told that after a life threatening accident . . . an experimental airplane crash . . . that I had a change of mind and heart, wanting to rejoin the world.

In between being educated by Gerhardt and working with insiders, I also had to do lots of homework made up of just a little contract law, some extensive review of my *If/Then* and *Art of War*, as well as some "study" of movies that embodied excellent negotiating principles, and those that embodied the opposite. Gerhardt said that I should be re-educated and familiar with what was doomed to fail, so as to avoid it. In that few months I must have watched nearly a hundred movies and read fifty books. While I was in the hospital, Gerhardt brought me a constant stream of things to watch and read too. He later explained that it was what he liked to call "the *Karate Kid* teaching method." He said that by carefully selecting what went into my head he was helping me to become "what you have always been but never known." Wax on, wax off!

Apparently, it was all part of the process that I had devised for myself many years ago. There was always the expectation that everything may not come online perfectly and that I may wake up a bit fuzzy, or even completely blank from the experience, and need to be "sorted out" in some way . . . reprogrammed. So, I had come up with the first fifty or eighty books and movies, and Gerhardt and the guys came up with the rest. There was also every foot of film or video from my previous life to watch again and again.

More than a year has passed since I arrived in the Tower, and it is time for my "coming out" and my first meeting with others, with outsiders – with non-employees. I am feeling a bit like Eliza Doolittle at the races, in a rather exciting and decidedly terrifying way. Gerhardt makes it very clear that they must never know the truth of what has happened to me. "If anyone knows any of the details of what has been happening, the confidence in the company would falter, the value of the stock could collapse, and then tens of millions of people would lose everything they have invested in us." Gerhardt is adamant about this. "It is much more than our money that matters here. Remember, there are more pensions and retirements tied up in our company than there are fortunes of the rich, and that is why we MUST always do what is best for the Enterprise, for all of us, not just you and me." Wow! I had never thought about that. But Gerhardt had. He is a fascinating man, Gerhardt.

His father had worked forty years, winding up his career as a CFO in what would later become a subsidiary of Danzig, and as a part of his retirement package, he had invested in the company, and taken matching stock for his savings incentive, much as many of my co-workers had when I worked for Time Warner Cable. Did I really work for them? But in the forty years since, the stock had split many times, and since my death, as Gerhardt said, it had increased 16,000%. That's a multiplication in size of 160 times. That was easy to do when I started out with a few thousand dollars in saved up starter cash. I had made that increase in the first two years. I went from 5000 to 800,000 in personal wealth. In three years, I had more than done it again – double, and then some. In that same time frame I had gone from about a million bucks to well over a billion, even ten billion soon after. And I was on track to make much more. But for a single company like Danzig to continue to grow in this way is unheard of. Still, that is exactly the point. We aren't actually a single company, and we are not in the business of being "heard of." We are the ultimate multi-national, multi-functional, and multi-cultural conglomerate. We are mostly unseen, and we like it that way. Even the building where I live is not called "Danzig Tower" or "Somebody Enterprises," but, rather it is "Dancing Stag Tower" and we offer "Luxury Living and Corporate Office Leasing." Just pull the car up to the correct side of the building, Cherry Street for Residential Parking, Hackberry for Corporate.

When she hears about our upcoming adventures – Eliza at the Races – Ethyl finds herself adjusting my tie as we wait for Gerhardt. When she is done I barely realize that her hand is inside my jacket, sliding slowly from my chest to my waist. She is telling me, "Don't worry. I have all confidence that your big boy pants will fit just fine." Every time she gets close – physically – she seems less professional and more personable; maybe more personal as well. Her eyes glance slowly up, then down, then up again, almost like she is closing and opening her eyes, slowly, to take in the complete view of me as she steps backward. I can see her breathing.

Gerhardt arrives, and on this occasion he brings new toys. "Here is your wallet, Mr. Danz. Please, look inside so that if you need it you are familiar with its contents." It just now dawned on me that I have not carried one for . . . well, as long as I can remember. I open the wallet and look; there is a driver's license, with a motorcycle stamp, several credit cards, and all of them are either gold or silver in colour, and one of them, the Tex-Ex card, looks as if it is actually made with gold and silver. There is a collection of photos of me and some supermodel looking woman, Gerhardt and his wife, and some older photos of a couple of strangers, "Those are your parents, in case anyone should ask. They were Mikael and Genevieve Danz, and they were murdered in 2039." But that has already been covered in the education about me. He continues, "The driver's license is a year old as you can see. We had it electronically generated when they began working on you to bring you back. The photo was inserted after your healing. And your record of driving goes back until you would have been sixteen. All of the corporate credit cards have a $250,000 limit, except the Tex-Ex which has no limit. You could literally buy anything with it; as long as it's for sale and the price is under fifty million, you can swipe the card for it."

"So, there IS a limit."

"I guess, if you think of fifty million dollars as a limit on a credit card, then, yes. It has a limit. You will also see a proof of insurance card in the money pocket, and there is a flat grey coloured plastic card with an intelligent chip inside. Don't go anywhere without that, or you are nobody."

He sees the expression on my face as I ask about being nobody, so he explains, "It is an ident-locator chip. It has to be in physical proximity of the point of sale for any of these other cards to work; even the driver's license is attached to it. On most people, it is implanted under the muscles of the neck, and they don't even know that it is there. With it, the police of any city can locate any citizen that is above ground or not in a vault of some sort, shielded from signal reaching the network, and that location will be accurate to within a half meter."

"That's crazy! Who would want to have the government tracking them 24/7?"

"That's why they don't know it is there. Back in 2012, a school district in San Antonio had similar chips in cards that students had to carry around, but a few students refused. There was a lawsuit, and the requirement to carry the cards was removed. Then an appeal, yada-yada. Then an incentive was applied to encourage voluntary carrying of the card. It was supposed to be an attempt to hedge truancy. They said that any student that was not absent for an entire school year, making allowance for medically supported excused absence and death in the near family, could receive a ten percent discount on all four years of their state university tuition. This being the case, they would receive a discount for each year that they kept that record, so that they could actually save forty percent of their Texas college tuition cost. At first they told everyone that they wouldn't work outside of the schools, and to a certain degree that was true, but only because the sensors had only been installed and activated inside the schools. In ten years or so, they had begun to install the censors in every master tower, cell tower, and boosting array in America. And almost every police department was willing to pay a premium for that kind of tracking capability. The kids kept carrying them because they found that there were incentives at bars and restaurants around colleges that would offer discounts that were automatically triggered when your 'Ident' was present and in agreement with your registered credit cards. They did it, not only because it would get them more business, but also because it reduced the number of fraudulent sales which were rampant in a college area and which often came with charge-backs. This notably bumped their sales and saved them tons of money."

After another eight years, the government took over the big tracking companies, first by investing in them, then by creeping and fining – the usual things. But the big companies were only a small part of the ident card picture. As a whole, it was not the typical large and public company, but several hundred lesser entities that were of little interest to the public – almost like mom and pop grocery stores, that were the bulk of the industry. Many of them had been launched to serve one school or a few closely located schools or small school districts, such as in a single small city or county. But the government would even get around to latching onto them after a while, thanks to the IRS. In a combined effort of the Department of Labor and Statistics, the FBI and several government supplanted credit bureaus, in coordination with the American Medical Association, the chips were miniaturized, made to run off body heat and blood sugar exchange of energy, and implanted in every child born in any hospital in America. If a chip was not found on a child when he came to a doctor for a checkup or medical attention, as children are likely to do, they are injected with a chip. Failure on the part of a doctor to either find a chip, or place and record a chip, could result in loss of license to practice, and even prison, but no one knew about it because of an even bigger threat. After all, everyone has someone they care about.

But now Red-Light-Cameras finally have real power. The long past argument that they could not confirm who may be driving the car is no longer an issue. The camera can record the car's images, as well as who is in the car, and in which seats. As for the Constitutional inconvenience of having the legal right to face one's accusers, that was done away with by the re-stacking of the Supreme Court to dismiss more and more of the individual's rights, just as they had under FDR. After all, those individual rights generally get in the way of the things governments want to accomplish. It is made even easier when one of the conservative, Constitutionalist judges was killed in a car crash with a trash truck. And of course, as we all know, governments always seek to do what is best for its people . . . as they see it.

I learned about the Ident chips because we were going into what Gerhardt called "enemy territory; the central belly of the beast." At first I thought we were going to a foreign capital to visit an enemy nation, like Moscow in the 1960's or Teheran in the 80's and beyond, but as it turned out, we had to go to New York. He was right. We were in the very heart of evil, or so I thought, until we went to LA the following year.

We left out of San Antonio on a five year old Gulfstream G-Z1 with all the new ideas in air travel technology. As we board, there is a part of me that is all "business as usual," and yet as the jet accelerates to flight speed on take-off, another part of me (deep inside) is jumping up and down and shouting, "Whoa baby! This thing is cool." I feel like a little boy the first time riding a tilt-o-whirl and forever leaving the slow and circular up and down motion of the carousel behind. This aircraft is amazing, but how amazing I would learn in New York. On the way I read our prospectus for the meeting and browse the web getting more and more grist for my mill.

The flight from San Antonio takes about an hour and a half and everything about the landing feels and looks strange. I can remember from my youth all the sensations of take-off and landing, and this was not that. I find out soon that we are not landing at the airport, but on an office tower. I didn't see that coming. It is like a landing from *Star Wars I*. The jet, which had been traveling at nearly Mach two, slows to under a hundred miles an hour as we enter the city air space. A few minutes later, it slows to thirty, then zero, rises up on the rear, rotates about ninety degrees left, sits the rear down, and lowers the nose to a standing stop. We are on a platform which is about a hundred feet across and approximately circular, with a small twenty by twenty foot building standing in front of and to the left of the plane. As we get into that room, I realize that this is a VTOL pad, for Vertical Take-Off and Landing, for planes and helicopters. On the other end of the plane, but still on the same side, is a panel with a large yellow box with a red "X" painted on it. The little room we are in is about one third air lock, to stop the wind, and two thirds elevator. Just before the doors close, I see the red X lower and slide open to reveal another elevator that is for the cargo, in this case our luggage. The whole thing is sort of a Buck Rogers kind of moment. I put on my best poker face so that no one knows that I have never seen anything like this outside of a movie before. It is tough. In trying to not look surprised, I probably look grumpy . . . or maybe constipated. Hard to say. But, we have come to sell some sugar, more or less.

The Texas Secession

The United States is not what she used to be. For starters, in 2024, Texas and Texans, fed up with the previous sixteen years and seeing what was on the horizon, seceded from the US and began forming a new union . . . a more perfect union, called the FreeNation of Tejas.

It began with the presentation of the "Resolution of Secession" on the 4th of July, 2024, followed by a lawsuit from the Holder Division, along with threats to suspend Posse Comitatus, and invade the state, but they were met with an unimaginable reality. The entire Texas National Guard and nearly 85% of the reserves in every branch inside of Texas joined forces with the new "National Militia," made up of sworn, volunteer, gun-owning citizens, and together they numbered over 7,000,000 men, women, seniors, and youth. The guardsmen and reservists gave an option to the personnel of the US Army, Air Force, Marines, Coast Guard and Navy to either become Texicans or receive $2000 in travel cash and safe passage to the United States at the exit point of their choosing. Many of them would leave, under contract to the US, but return to enlist in the Texican Armed Forces when that contract was up. In the end, the result would be that the FreeNation would have the fourth largest standing military on the planet.

The same offer to stay or go was made to every US federal employee of any kind inside the new republic. One hundred thousand of them left. About ten to twelve thousand of them remained – the rest just walked away from their desks. And on July 4th, everyone who was willfully and legally inside the borders of Texas or who was born there or who already met residential requirements commonly used for "in-state tuition," were all declared "Free and True Citizens of the FreeNation of Tejas," if they wanted to be. No one would be forced to become a Texican. Conversely, if you were legally registered to vote in Texas the year before, you would likely still be registered. However, if you had not been registered before, you were not allowed to vote in Texican politics for a period of ten years. We had learned our lesson with all the Californians moving in over the past few decades. So, if you had moved from outside the state within the past ten years, but had been registered to vote the previous year, you would not be allowed to vote until the tenth anniversary of your arrival. Like I said, we had learned . . .

As for the Austinites; even they had awakened and begun to smell the caramel macchiato, as weird as they were. The town motto had been, "Keep Austin Weird," which is fine, as long as that didn't mean keeping it foolish, which it had become. At one point there was a petition to the White House to allow Austin to secede from the state of Texas as a separate political entity, but it was never given a hearing and, lucky for the Austinites, they got to see, for the most part, what "Tea Party Thought" really looks like, right before the secession from the USA. The reason? Money! Even Austin could understand that you can't tax a fortune from a people that doesn't have one. They had seen California get further and further in debt and beg for relief from the nation, and they had seen Michigan fall into virtual receivership because of the failed policies of Detroit and the surrounds, having been run by Liberals, Democrats, and Unions for over sixty years. Some had seen what had happened when in San Francisco, people put down their toys and their artsy-fartsy shops with no income and opened businesses that actually sold products that people wanted and needed. The actual commercial businesses began creating wealth and tried to make improvements in the area, but the hyper-libs shut that down in short order by putting up picket lines in front of the hardware shops and electronic stores, and whatever else didn't tickle their "flower powered" thought processes of nonsense and incense-abilities. Austin is still weird, but they are no longer Democrats, Socialists, or liberals of any kind – at least, not openly. There will always be holdouts against truth and reason. If not . . . ?

Texas had finished their portion of the Southern Border Fence years before, partly with the federal money they had been promised and partially provided under the Bush presidency but which was later cut off by the second Obama administration, but that didn't matter because the rest had been funded by private contributions, church fundraisers, and corporate sponsored activities such as bowl-a-thons and marathons and more, and much of that money came from Yankees who "got it."

In the years that followed, before another fence could be erected on the north, several things happened to make that unnecessary. For starters, the FNT – FreeNation of Tejas – suspended all non-essential government in March of 2025 for six months. The Department of Public Safety and Texas Rangers, as well as the Military, continued to function, as did every utility service and the other things that people just cannot do without. But the Railroad Commission and a hundred other operations were closed, except for the boots on the ground. State Parks and Rec was shut down, except for the people who actually worked in the parks. The payroll and benefits services were continued with a guarantee to pay all current employees for at least the next year, whether their jobs were continued or not, but the supervisors and managers and professional department leaders were given leave, with pay, while the government was reorganized.

A new Office of Transportation and Energy Management was created to replace the Railroad Commission and much more, and their purpose was to regulate who got a permit to drill for oil, build refineries or nuclear power plants and the like, and to regulate – that is to make regular or consistent – transportation and cartage of all kinds. The thinking was that less people could do more at running a single organization that replaced what had been several organizations, especially since they so frequently overlapped. They also served as the taxing authority of the energy industries inside the fledgling nation. It was a simple system of taxation of profits at 9.5%. When the Office of Energy Management was created, it was endowed with this percentage of taxation ability, and it is built into the Constitution of the Nation that a change of this rate would require a three quarters vote of the FreeNational Congress

To drill a well takes a $500,000 deposit that will be held against clean up after the well is either successfully connected to a pipeline or shutdown as a failure. If they do the cleanup, they get the money back. If they don't do the cleanup they will lose their deposit, the FNT would cover the cost of the cleanup, and they will not be permitted to work in the oil industry in the nation for a minimum of ten years. In the first ten years, Texicans opened 1500 old wells and nearly 2000 new wells. And, with an 85% success rate, this meant over 3000 newly operational wells.

A license to build a nuclear power plant cost $5,000,000, and the first five of them were built by large companies, but after they had figured out how to do it, they began selling kits. In a "Nuclear Power Kit," someone could buy the materials and equipment to build their own nuclear power plant and even get nuclear materials supply contracts. The city of Kerrville was among the first to get its own municipal power plant. It was, essentially, the same piece of equipment that powered an aircraft carrier, but on solid ground.

A man named Joshua Jenkins came up with a plan to merge a private company with the Bandera Electric Cooperative and put a nuclear plant under the property his Amah Nita had left him, his siblings and cousins, which was a retired dance hall called the Silver Spur, on top of a cliff known as Rugh Hill. He acquired the land across the river which had once held cabins that had been flooded away back in seventy nine and converted it into the parking, construction staging, and security offices for the facility, and after it was all built, that land became a company park for employees to enjoy the river. The power plant was dug into the side of the granite cliff nearly 300 feet and housed a four plant system that provides power for almost everything for 20 miles east and a 150 miles west and south, and 45 miles to the north. He donated the money to replace not only the bridge across the river and into the plant, but also every bridge in the city. With the plant under sixty feet of natural stone, it is one of the most secure plants around. It also expanded the entire economy of Bandera.

He called it the "Rockin' J Energy Corp," after his Grandpa Bill's registered brand, and had put it together by getting all his Land Family relatives to agree to put up the family property in Utopia as an incentive which made all the descendants of his Opa, Clifton Land, equal partners in the first part of the plan. The second part was to leverage his parents' wealth and his Amah's property into an impressive enough package for selling "stock" in the idea. But the time was right. He got a total of about two thousand people, mostly from the US, to invest by buying lottery tickets for $100,000, which would get them a half of a percent, of a percent in the venture, but also a chance of ownership of one half of the property in Utopia, a quarter or one of two units of an eighth. There was about sixty acres so it was broken down as 30, 15, 8 and 7 acres for the winners.

The OST – Old Spanish Trail Restaurant was the oldest restaurant in town – had an increase of well over a hundred customers at each meal of the day, and the ability of the customers to pay increased as well. Two excellent and enterprising waitresses, Crystal and Jessica, had the foresight to strike out on their own, and with their tip increases for a year, they had saved up enough to buy the buildings across the street, including the Silver Dollar Saloon, and turn it all into a giant cowboy style restaurant and saloon complex that is still in operation today. The US now buys about 60% of their petroleum products and 30% of their electricity from the FreeNation, or, more precisely, from FreeNation companies. The government doesn't get involved in these businesses.

If an outsider had Texican property ownership of over five acres and valued at $500,000 or more, or if he owned more than 10% of a business which employed fifty persons at "regular wage" or more, this would allow someone to gain citizenship in Tejas in five years instead of the usual ten, but voting rights would still wait for seven. So, you could own a shack, but employ twenty full time employees at one hundred twenty-five percent of average state menial income, and you were in. Another way to become a citizen is military service for six years. Lots of people from all over the world choose that option every year.

There is also a whole new underground market running in the north, in the old US, which interests lots of new millionaires, and even a lot of old money. They are moving investments into the FreeNation and later joining them. Tejas has become the new Cayman Islands of the age, and thousands of people each week visit and open an account and then, one day at a time, they begin to move their money, in amounts of less than $3000 a day into those accounts, from individual accounts in the US, so as to stay under the DHS/IRS radar since the "Re-Nationalization and Repatriation of Funding Act of 2020" which severely limited what percentage of anyone's money any citizen could have outside the US. But many people found a way around it and did so.

It took years for the feds to catch on because; there were people who were 20 to 90 years old, creating American bank accounts for their children and grandchildren, even if they didn't have any. They would buy previously held National Retirement Account numbers (like Social Security), from people who were current citizens of the FNT for $10,000, and open up "scholarship" accounts for these fictitious kids in Tejas. Then they can "contribute" as much as a thousand dollars a day to each of the American accounts and go unnoticed. They can then log into each of these education fund accounts and send almost everything to their accounts in Tejas every day or once a week or whatever time frame they preferred. If you were in any of fifty countries, including the United States, and checked the balance of a debit card originated in the FNT, the maximum balance it could show, due to the Texican Financial Protection Act, was one hundred thousand dollars. That would still allow you to swipe your card to purchase a car, even a house worth ten times that, if you had the money, but would not allow the US government to get into your Texican accounts.

The permit to build an oil refinery cost $10,000,000, which would be eighty percent refunded at the end of two years of mess-free operation. In five years, the Texicans built an additional fifteen refineries, five of them on the northern side of the nation and one just north of Oklahoma City. All of them recovered their original deposits.

Another aspect of the secession that was expected by many insightful Texicans was that some of the rest of the Union would want to join them in their liberty. When the other states saw that Texas was returning to First Principles, and that the US did not have the will to do anything about it but sue; several of them made the same move, switching their allegiance to the FNT.

First to join, in 2025, were Arizona and New Mexico, as a unit. With the exception of Albuquerque, Santa Fe, and a few minor liberal locales, they were tired of the US imposing their will without providing their protection from southern invasion. Phoenix had become a veritable war zone, and since the passing of Sherriff Joe and the murder of his successor and many of his trusted deputies and friends, the state was in serious peril. But several factors would soon make a very real difference. When they joined the FNT, the Texas Rangers re-established their more forceful policies in the region with Rangers on horseback and motorcycles and the new Hummers, and the law was enacted to charge all coyotes with human trafficking, and the penalty for that became death. People caught entering the Nation in groups of more than five were considered invaders and were arrested, interrogated, prosecuted, or redistributed, which meant dropped by parachute – if fit enough for the experience – into a nation south of Mexico. If they were not fit enough for the drop, they could be delivered by boat. Very few ever returned to Tejas after that. With all this cleaning up going on and the fact that life became safer for the new Texicans, even the people of Albuquerque got to be fairly well on board pretty soon.

The next annexation was Mexico in late 2025, as a provisional territory, followed by Louisiana, Arkansas, and Oklahoma in 2026. All the good that Governor Bobby Jindal had done in education with Charter Schools and vouchers was destroyed by the "American Educational Liberties Act," which required that all education be standardized across the US by the federal government, and it was managed and manned by Union Teachers, employed directly by the Department of Education. They said that "in this way, every student would be guaranteed the same educational opportunity." But many knew that it was guaranteed to be bad because they had watched public education since the 1960's and had seen it sink into the abyss that American Public Schools had become. Under Jindal, Louisiana had become the third ranking educator in the country, but the US under Obama had become the forty-fifth in Math and Science among the fifty most advanced nations and no better than thirty-fifth in any other area. That was the straw!

An enterprising gentleman named Harold Willettsen had created a very innovative Charter School District that operated in New Orleans, running on monies granted by the Jindal administration, and it worked in a very different way. They did use an exit test for graduation but never taught or trained or prepared in any way for the test itself. They just taught the materials. If you took the test and got an eighty or better, in each category, you passed and graduated. The teaching staff was made up of predominately non-teachers, but people who were experts in their field. For teachers in computers, he employed people who were already working in the tech industries, specializing in what they were teaching, usually wanting to retire from their labors in the industry. For American History and Military Studies, and everyone had to have at least one semester of Military Studies and two of American History, he used retired military men and disabled veterans using a comprehensive curriculum with materials provided in books and online. Many courses could be taken online, in real time, or in virtual class time, and that also allowed a lot of people that didn't already have their GED to get one or actually graduate from High School. For Sex Ed, which was an elective decision of the parents, which had to opt-in not out, the instruction was done by team teaching. Part one was taught with a team made up of a Baptist minister, a zoologist and a born-again ex-prostitute. Part two – Preparing for Marriage and Family – was taught by a collection of long-married Pentecostal ex-courtesans from India. Three quarters of the instructors of the district were retired seniors, and much of the rest were ordinary everyday parents. The American Educational Liberties Act totally destroyed this operation, in one fell swoop, without any grace or opportunity for redress. Harold found himself in violation of hundreds of new laws, and when he tried to continue doing something . . . anything . . . even just teaching . . . the criminality of the act . . . he was imprisoned on numerous charges that were incredibly bogus, but valid within the context of the American

Educational Liberties Act. After the secession, it was only about six months before Harold Willettsen and friends were back in business and kids started learning again.

The US Congress was about to enact such stringent regulations on oil, natural gas, fishing, and crabbing that Alaska had to make a move in a hurry. In private negotiations, the leaders of that state went "on vacation" to Tejas and offered free fishing and hunting expeditions to all Texicans that would be willing to provide their own supplies. Alaska would cover the cost of transport if Tejas would cover the means. Hunting and fishing permits would be free to any and all Texicans as would the first four hundred rounds of ammo and any needed bait. The US was surprised to learn that 300,000 Texicans were in Alaska, armed, on "hunting and fishing expeditions" of indeterminate duration, the day the "Declaration of Transfer of Annexation to the FNT" was presented to the US Congress. On that same day, all US military inside the borders of Alaska were offered the same deal they were offered in Texas not so long ago. This time only a hundred or so left, but most did so with provisional transfer papers allowing them to return with their families to the FreeNation as citizens any time within sixty days. Kansas was next in 2028.

In 2029 The FreeNation of Tejas was petitioned for adjoining by Hawaii, Utah, Nevada, California, Colorado, Wyoming, Idaho, Montana, Nebraska, Iowa, North and South Dakota, as well as Missouri. They said "no" to California outright, along with a "don't ask" being sent to Oregon and Hawaii which were considered, like California, to be "too far gone" to be brought back by Texicans.

Close examination of the books revealed that Californians had been amazingly well lied to, especially as regards their debt load. It had become over $65 Billion since they started strategically lying, saying the amount of debt was going down in 2010. If they really wanted to join the FNT, they would have to get their own entitlement society under control, reduce their debt almost completely, and get their wasteful spending under control to find a balanced budget. Show Tejas these things, and considerations could be made. Never happened!

In 2010 someone reported that they stopped at a California Rest Area near the border on the way to Las Vegas and had learned that there were shifts at all times of four persons working at that one rest area, twenty four hours a day, seven days a week, fifty two weeks a year, all of whom had pretty good incomes, full state benefits, and a pension package to die for. All together, it came to about $1,700,000 in payroll and benefits for a single rest area. That didn't include water usage, grounds keeping, building repairs, and plumbing or electrical work. In Texas, we just build them really well and have someone – one or two someone's – stop by once or twice a day if busy to clean it up. But we also try to teach people to not be pigs, always messing up the rest room. That is what we in Tejas would call wasteful spending.

Illinois tried to buy their way in, but the Texicans knew the level of corruption there and declined every offer, even the one that included paying off California's debt. The money was, it was later discovered, coming from several slush funds of some politicians and mob, who were expecting to be able to get away with whatever they wanted in the land of innocents called Tejas.

When they asked, Colorado was admitted to the FreeNation only after they disbanded their government, which came after they replaced 70% of their public school teachers and all of their school administrators, and then they removed tenure from all of their educational institutions from Kindergarten to Universities, dis-contracted their public sector unions, and a few other things. It was a ten year process, but to the people, it was well worth it. In 2035, they became full members of a genuine republic, and it was good. They got to vote for the first time as Texicans in 2045.

The movement to Tejas had become too big for the US to resist in many ways. The Dakotas, Montana, Idaho, Wyoming and Iowa simply filled out the paperwork and pretty much submitted their letters of intent to the Senate of the US.

Another thing that was submitted to the US in 2031 was a suit demanding three and a half trillion dollars from them on behalf of the new states of Tejas, who had been defrauded of taxes for services and protection from invading forces previously known as "illegal aliens" – some called them "undocumented Amercians" – and drug cartels. Since the then current Administration of the US was so fond of the World Court, that is exactly where Tejas sought redress, filed suit, and won. Well, they won the judgment, but the awarded amount was only one point six trillion. And, the US credit rating was so bad that the deal had to be struck that a vote would be taken in the potentially affected areas. After the deal and vote, Tennessee, Virginia, South Carolina, and Kentucky – including Fort Knox – were admitted to the FreeNation. The gold from Fort Knox was deposited into the FreeNational Treasury to offset legal fees, and for partial compensation to the repayment of the collection of taxes from the ex-states.

A Bigger Contract Means Something is Hiding

Does anyone wonder why these places would vote to join a new nation? Well, the FNT was offering to license moonshine stills for $200 each, with a one dollar tax per pint Mason jar, two per quart, and six per gallon, and no "revenuers" stomping about their mountains. And, thanks to a new supplier in Africa, those Mason-type jars could be had for about half the cost they had previously paid. Texicans offered to give privately funded, low interest loans to re-open the thirty five coal mining operations that had previously been shut down by the Obama EPA, then the Boxer-ites, using an unknown provision on page 2274 of the "Silkwood Act," which was supposed to be about nuclear power inspections, but seemed to have tentacles into almost everything. This little provision that no one had previously noticed said that an amount equal to 20% of the payroll and benefits of a coal company employee working in a mine had to be paid to the government as a separate tax for health and potential separation protection, even though health care coverage was already taxed and insured and more. It also said that 15% of the market value of any machine weighing over fifty pounds had to be paid annually in fees to the government for "environmental damages" and for a recovery process that was never defined even though recovery and repurposing of the lands had to be provided for by the mining company to an also undefined "federal standard," or they could be fined up to a million dollars per acre. That had shut down most of the mining operations in Appalachia. When West Virginia saw a chance to get off the dole and go back to work, they took it. For South Carolina, it was simple. They were already tired of the intervention and regulation and knew that they could do better. They had no idea how much better it was about to get, but they were ready for anything that would be better at all. But that caused a problem that was coming from the beginning.

When Texas left the Union, it was 10% of the economy of the nation, but only 4.5 to 5% of the national expense in services provided. The net loss of revenue versus the aggravation and expense of trying to stop the secession were decidedly in favor of allowing the state to leave the Union. With Arizona and New Mexico joining Tejas, that was financially acceptable to the US due to the ratio of taxation versus services and expectations. Besides, those states were getting to be a pain in the collective national ass, thanks to southern border issues, but that all went away for the Union when those states went the way of Texas. There was a bit more pain as the Mountain States and Plains States joined in. And let's face it; the states to the Northeast of Texas were bound to go.

Still, the national economy of the Union had lost over 30% of the tax base and only 20% of the expenses of the nation. That meant they were left with less than 70% of the income and 80% of the outgo; they were already writing checks they had no means to cash. Because the states that went before and after the lawsuit were predominately "working" states that had lower unemployment rates and higher productivity rates, and if need be, those states could be, pretty much, or entirely, self-sustaining, the risk to the new nation was small; the loss to the old Union was great.

In Tejas, thousands of micro-farms began popping up all over the new nation and started growing food that was traded and sold locally with no government intervention at all. Local bartering became a national phenomenon of the fledgling enterprise. Some even got sold to the neighbors and families and friends that lived across those imaginary lines called "borders" and across the rivers as well. The local productivity of these states went crazy. The Union was insane about what they called "Interstate and International Commerce." But the Texicans didn't have that problem, and they built co-ops of all kinds. If you owned a membership in a co-op, you could pay your annual or monthly dues, and you had the opportunity to buy your provisions of the products or services from that co-op. There were vegetable co-ops and bread co-ops, and there were also shine co-ops and beer co-ops. There were water and electrical co-ops that worked in new and interesting ways that included "energy investment co-ops" that were like little companies that expanded energy operations and returned profits to investors, first in unlimited free energy for their households in the areas of expansion, but then in dividends, and this forced the need for a new national cash denomination. We had been using American Dollars but things had to change because those dollars were becoming useless, and the Texican economy was booming. Our first hundred dollar bill had Sam Houston on it.

The most important thing about the expansion of these co-ops was the simplicity of dealing with the new federal and state governments. If you wanted, for example, to build power generating windmills on someone else's private property, you had to provide a copy of the bill of sale or minimum twenty year lease of the land the mill would occupy. If the land was to be fenced the owner had to agree, and be compensated at least a thousand dollars a year – in gold, silver, cash, or tangible trade, and the land for a single mill could not exceed a quarter acre. The owner of the mill would also have to carry insurance on the mill for liability that would be sufficient to cover the replacement of any structure within a distance of three times the height of the top most tip of the blade of the mill. This was called a "Good Neighbor Energy Insurance Policy." Since there hadn't been any notable property damages from broken or fallen mills in a long time, this was fairly cheap insurance. In ten years time, there were nearly 180,000 high efficiency mills across the FreeNation, built by private citizens installing Danzig Industries pre-packaged mills, made in Somalia.

Another aspect of the FreeNation that made things more profitable, and to be honest, a bit more pleasant and fun, was the legalization of marijuana. When the FNT was born, it got rid of several hundred laws that were deemed unnecessary, and weed restrictions were on the list. Anyone that was a non-violent offender in a Texas prison for growing, selling, or buying marijuana was released with a $20,000 apology or the opportunity to remain in prison and complete their time. They were encouraged to use their money to setup green houses right away, and they were connected, via e-mail, to tobacco companies that were starving for something to replace their lost income since the shame and subsequent outlawing of their tobacco weed.

RJ Reynolds was first to build a processing plant in Tejas. And the Tejas deal was much sweeter than the cigarette industry had ever had because it was simple. There was a fifteen percent packaging tax on every pack before the standard taxes. That's it. Even though there was no income tax in the FNT, there was a national sales tax of 12%

on what was deemed as "non-essentials" and did not include food and drink, the first thousand dollars per year of clothing per person, Scripture, ammunition – up to three thousand rounds per person per year – and utilities. The utility companies paid a tax to the FNT equal to ten percent of their total income on a monthly basis. Simple! Everything is as simple as it can be, and whenever possible, nothing is as complicated as it can be.

Another law that we dismissed when found was the law restricting a woman weighing more than two hundred pounds from riding a horse while wearing shorts. She was allowed to ride in jeans, but not shorts so; it was assumed that the issue was a lot of visible, jiggling womanhood, not contained by the shorts, rather than compassion for the beast. It did not, however, take into consideration if the woman was four foot nine or six foot three or her physical condition overall. Also, it did not take into consideration if it was anyone's business how attractive she may or may not be while astride her steed in shorts.

Conversely, there was a statewide ban on boys or men, in particular, but people in general from wearing their pants in such a way as to notably display their undergarments – usually boxers – or their bare behinds. It was determined that the purpose of one dressing in such a manner was nothing more or less than a personal intent to show one's ass, which is a military expression for one's willingness to display one's ineptitude or foolishness, and that is what became illegal. Some enterprising civilian decided to help the police out by creating a website called something like "drooppinpantz.com" where the name and a photo could be uploaded to it from any licensed phone, which meant any police phone or school administrator's phone. Then, if a person was caught in drooppinpantz, they could be charged a ten dollar upload fee, photographed for uploading to the site, and directed to the nearest Wal-mart, where they could be issued a free belt, and if they were caught again with their face on the website, they were deemed a repeat offender and arrested for three days minimum and assessed a fine of up to $300. A second "willful offense" of this nature, validated by the website, could bring a jail term of ten days and $1000 fine. After that, it could double every time within a three year period. If you had been charge free for three years, you could pay the site $100 to remove your name.

In 2031, there were nearly 10,000 doctors that did the grand-child shuffle, moving nearly $60,000,000,000 into Tejas, along with setting up new offices and moving their staff and records into the FNT. They came almost predominately from big cities in California and New York City, about 2000 of them from the Philly/Baltimore/DC area, another 700 from New England and nearly 3000 from Europe. The result was that although the US had ObamaCare 2.0, they were desperately short of medical staff to fill those needs. And in the FNT, medical staff was so plentiful that it was not quite as profitable to be a doctor, due to a glut of competition, however, it also cost considerably less to live here, so it still worked out okay for everyone. After all, a house in California costing $295,000, in a similar neighborhood, was $115,000 in San Antonio or $140,000 in Phoenix and KC. A jug of milk in NYC was sixteen US dollars, but in Dallas it was about four.

By 2042, the new union of the FNT also included Georgia, Mississippi, Alabama and Florida. Florida was only last because the Texicans didn't want to have a state join for long without having supply lines and direct commerce opportunities without having to cross the US if at all possible. South Carolina had been admitted because of the profound desire on the part of the citizens and the access to ports on the Atlantic, which could be protected by the Tejas Naval Marines. Once South Carolina was admitted and the ports were re-designated as FNT, there were two destroyers, a small aircraft carrier, and seventy of the new model PT boats securing the shores of that sovereign state.

In the FreeNation, every state is exactly that – a State, which is to say, a sovereign, political entity, equal to a nation, which agrees to enact commerce and politics with the other Sovereign States in the agreement, and in accordance with the Constitution of those States. They are, none of them, property or subservient to the greater collective of States in any way.

Carl and Terrance

About fifteen years ago, a company called "SweetUS" had created a sweetener that had one calorie per serving and no cancer effects, even when tested with Canadian lab rats. It rose to the top of the heap even though there was one unnoticed side effect. I say it was unnoticed, but not by everyone. The people conducting the tests didn't get it because they were looking at something else. Their big worry was that, like other sweeteners, there would be an association with cancer, bone destruction, or blindness, and that didn't happen, but the most politically handy thing did happen. For over a hundred years, the NEA, the teachers unions, and the Deweyites had been trying to do something that finally happened with a sugar replacement – people were losing the ability to reason. The side effect that SweetUS had was that it impaired neuron functions related to critical thinking and comparative analysis of things.

The people who discovered it were not the scientists doing the research, but the minimum wage clerks of the studies who admitted the subjects for testing and questions each day. They discovered it by a very simple means: they talked to them. It wasn't in the questions that they asked for the purposes of the study, but in the conversations that took place throughout the processes of each visit. In the time that their debit cards were being refilled, while they were walking to the scale to be weighed, at the counters confirming their next appointments, sometimes in the waiting rooms between shifts, and at all these times, there were simple, personal conversations, like ordinary people. And as time went by, some of the clerks noticed, and some even reported, that the people seemed to be getting "dumber" – but that was impossible. It wasn't like they were showing symptoms of Alzheimer's or dementia; their memories were just fine. They were simply less mentally capable. The technicians and scientists may have noticed it earlier, but they already thought that everyone was dumber than they were so they were already looking down their noses at the subjects . . . what did it matter how far?

Then came the important part: the business model. They never even attempted to sell it to the consuming public or the canned and bottled products industries. After all, sweeteners go in everything from soda to ketchup, from coffee, to candy, to canned yams, and the only agencies that touched on all those markets belonged to the government. So, they sold it to the government, who imposed it on everyone else under what had been lovingly called "Michelle's Dietary Health Initiative." This allowed the government to impose "better" health ideas on industries that provided food services to federal employees, and by now, that was just about everyone. And if you failed to comply, then they would fine you mercilessly and then "invest" in you.

The guys at SweetUS came up with the perfect business model for the times, and it involved every aspect from creation to management, sales and payment. They got the feds to fund their development of the product as a research grant when they were seniors at Cal Tech. Carl and Terrance got $20,000,000 in total research grants, and the actual costs of that research was nearly $6,000,000. Needless to say, they had made a little money. Having come up with the product, they had to thoroughly test it, so they moved to Berkley for their post-graduate studies, and for their credits, ran a study on the product known as "sugar13" using students as taste related lab rats, rigging the test questions.

When attempting to qualify students to be guinea pigs, they tended to choose students whose preferred aperitif was a dry wine instead of a sweet wine like ripple or a beer or the forbidden sweet soda. Since they were surveying people that did not like the sweetness in the first place, the sweetness became less of a factor in the results, as did the purity of that sweetness. After all, the sweet taste would soon be overshadowed by something the subject thought was far more pleasant. Also, on the surveys of those subjects as to the flavor of the products, they shifted the scale to where they were asked questions that were like: "On a scale of 1 to 10, where 1 is black coffee and 10 is a sugar cube, how would you rate the sweetness level of this product?" While that may not seem loaded to some, realize that in our Starbuckified world, almost no one but old-timers ever drank black coffee anymore, and by law, no one had access to pure sugar. The respondents consistently gave a solid eight rating to questions of that ilk. They had the actual rat tests done in Canada, like everyone else, because Canadian lab researchers still had no qualms about killing some rodents in product testing.

The product testing at Berkley cost the government nearly $60,000,000 more to Carl and Terrance, who paid out nearly a quarter of that in "trial fees" and "minimum wage plus" in payroll to students to run and staff the project. The government also paid an equal amount to the University for facilities and utilities and oversight. The University contracted Carl and Terrance as an incorporated entity to do oversight.

Carl and Terrance then sold the wholesale/retail/distribution rights of their product to the government for $500,000,000 and agreed to produce the stuff for ten cents a serving, packaged in little bags for restaurants, or for nine dollars a pound in bulk, with a 29% reduction for packages over twenty pounds in size. This was a good deal for them because, after the primary factories were moved to Iowa and Kansas, it cost about two dollars to make six pounds, so the profit margin was astounding. But even that was not enough for Carl and Terrance. No, they also made a management deal with the government to federalize and unionize their plants and that they would run and oversee everything from quality control to logistics for twenty million a year . . . each.

For $5,000,000 a year total, they put offices in each of their six facilities and hired managers and secretaries and bought all the needed office supplies and equipment to run them, and Carl and Terrance moved to Mexico. Every six months, they would appear at each of the plants, do a walk through and go visit family nearby. Each of their parents had divorced, and Carl and Terrance each had an ex-wife somewhere with a kid or two. Each of the ex-wives was always hoping to get back on the gravy train, and the guys were not terrible as friends and lovers, so the visits tended to be very, VERY accommodating.

After about ten years, they were each worth over $33 Billion, and Panama had passed the Enhanced Marriage and Women's Defense Act, which allowed a man to have more than one wife so Carl and Terrance moved there and took their wives back in a group ceremony where each of the men got their original wife and another and another! Billionaires can easily afford the overhead of numerous wives.

Some Congressman discovered about a $2 Billion screw up that had found its way to the door of Carl and Terrance, and the double billing of the original arrangement, and that started a firestorm investigation because, to Congress, any businesses or industries that made profits were evil except as they served the needs of the government, er, um, I mean, people. With the US government breathing down their necks about an impending audit of the operations of their businesses, they gave all their labor employees a severance package worth six months' income, and the middle-management guys each got two months' worth, and they closed the doors . . . without notice. They filed bankruptcy in a World Court office in Belize citing "Fiduciary Hardship" and federal duress. At the end of the bankruptcy, the government bought the entire operation from them, formulas and recipes included, for seven and a half billion dollars in gold, delivered. But the books for the corporation, however, had disappeared. Belize really is a wonderful place to live, especially if you can afford to live well. The government never did figure out how to make sweeteners.

"There always have been and always will be profiteers in bed with government because − since the days of Alexander − government is no damn good at management, business, personal care, and self-control of any kind. Any oversight of even the simplest operation by the government virtually guarantees the generation of amazing amounts of graft. This is the only explanation for the unabashed negligence and wastefulness that fattens the coffers of all non-medical personnel involved in government medicine." This pirated YouTube video showed an old politician, and he said this in what appeared to be a drunken or stoned stupor after retirement to a foreign beach. "That's how tons of us old Democrats, and a few Republicans too, made our first hundred million or so." Wow. Still, that may even be a bit light considering that some think-tank did an audit of Medicaid and Medicare and found that by the end of the twentieth century, between them, there was over a hundred billion dollars a year disappearing. By 2020, with ObamaCare, that number had nearly tripled. It showed up on ledgers and records for services and materials that never existed and were never provided to anyone, but the money was paid and simply disappeared. No one even knew who to tax for all that income.

Welcome to New York

We are in New York to sell sugar, sort of. What we have is a nutritional additive that is made with natural cane by-product and tastes sweet, like sugar, but it couldn't actually be sugar because it has niacin and thiamin in it, and other nutritional additives, and besides, sugar is illegal in the US, and we wouldn't do that!

Our meeting is with an independent Suisse emissary that interfaces with the US government, from time to time, on behalf of outside corporations in matters of food imports. Since the secessions, the population of the US is only down about 30%, but the food production is down nearly 80%. That poses a problem, and one that we are here to meet . . . well, partly. It is our foot in the door, so to speak. We are here to provide a delivered, packaged product at a price, and a price that someone can live with. Since those Californians had made their deal, become ex-pats, and then quit, there is a need. Actually, there is a void.

Mr. Ardit Iselin is not a large man, but also not one that any would call small. He doesn't seem terribly officious, but rather ingratiating by nature. He is obviously from a more old-world culture though. In fact, the thing that strikes me first is that his tie is, for lack of a better word, perfect. I won't recall the colour later, but that it is absolutely what a tie should be in knot symmetry and depth. His suit, like almost every suit I see in New York, looks like it is five to ten years old. It has been well taken care of, but had been worn many, many times. He is fit, and the fact that his double breasted jacket fits him like it was tailored yesterday shows his fitness off with aplomb. When he shakes my hand, his heels are together, and he leans forward slightly at the waist as if giving a half-bow to show respect. I remember seeing Lawrence Olivier doing this in a movie with Marilyn Monroe; Sir Larry they called him later. It is a sort of formal familiarity that few Americans or Texicans practice anymore. It makes me remember, when I was a child in Georgia, how my grandmother told me, "We put salt and pepper on the tables to show our guests courtesy. But to use the salt or pepper would be an insult to the cook, so no one would ever do that." I like it, and I think I like him, too.

We meet right outside the elevator, and he makes casual conversation on the way into his office, "how do you like the weather?" and "I haven't been to Texas in ages; I mean Tejas of course." Tejas is the FreeNation, Texas is the primary state.

There is some general back and forth and some question and answer with Gerhardt about the deal. I examine the photos and chotchkies, trying to look inattentive. The lawyers have questions, and for the most part Gerhardt has answers, and we have a legal eagle or two in the room besides. All is going down the endless rabbit hole of boredom when the most important question of the day arrives. Ardit sits down at his desk, halfway back in his seat, hands together with the edges of his palms on the edge of the desk in front of him, and says, "What is the bottom line of what we can buy your product for . . . before putting it into the hands of the Americans?" He looks straight at me with a clear, blue eyed stare that is neither menacing nor angry, but confident. Gerhardt has been seated across the desk while I wander around the office a bit more.

"Nine and a half Texican dollars a pound, in ten pound packages," said Gerhardt. "If you prefer, we can have it boxed, bagged, or packeted to specifications, but that will cost a bit more." Gerhardt is establishing a bargaining position and finding a baseline in Iselin's demeanor. I have seen this done before. It is like "Negotiations 101."

"At that price, how am I going to make any money?" he replies. He is using the motivation of "need" to shift the dynamic from a straight up business arrangement to one of a more common type of late, but we aren't buying. He seems to plead insufficient profit for himself, "When I go to the US and try to sell them your product, they are going to want a much better deal."

"Let's get all the lawyers out of the room!" I say waving a hand like a king dismissing jesters, until all have gone, even ours, and the door is closed. "Ardit, you tell them," I say, and then paused as I sit on the corner of his desk beside him, fiddling with something from his desk, "You tell them that they had a 'better deal' with the Californians, and it went south . . . literally." I put my back to Mr. Iselin, and I smile at Gerhardt, but put my finger up, very straight, so that he can see that I want control of the conversation now, "But it was the deal that the Americans had made." Another pause, "The government got to set all the parameters in the deal, and they still got screwed. So, what you do is tell the Americans that they cannot have a great product with a good deal because a 'great' deal would be ten Tex to the pound." Having read the particulars of the deal on the flight, I know that we can actually make a small profit at $7.50 US, per pound, labeled and delivered, and the guys are hoping to get 7.95. Also, having run an UberSearch on Mr. Iselin, I know a few more useful things. "But we are going to package it in ten pound containers for $8.80 per pound, $9.20 a pound in two pound bags and $10.50 a pound in those little bitty packets." I hold my fingers up about an inch and a half apart. "And we are going to charge you a quarter less a pound for the bags, only a dime less a pound for the packets – because we hate to deal with those little bastards as much as anyone – and we will even import them with YOUR label on them, from Switzerland, or not, if you would like to make a few million dollars right now." I give him a kind and gentle, but strong and friendly stare right back. "Does that sound like a deal to you?" I stick out my hand.

He looks and sees no hesitation in my eyes, leans back in his chair, with his hands in his lap, and asks, "How do we do it?" I withdraw my hand.

"Well," I say, "we harvest everything in our fields in Africa. We have fields and processing plants in six countries, and we collect the cane – er, um, I mean, 'botanicals' – we do all the expression, shred the meat, and make pressed cardboard products out of that, much of which is used to ship the sweetener. The 'extract' is then treated in a traditional way except for the addition of some 'nutrients,' then it is dried and ground into a various standards of grit and powder and packaged as requested. For the hyper-wholesome set, we even provide a brown product that looks less processed. We are going to put your labels on the bags and crates so that you 'become' the originator of the product. We are going to 'lease' you the lands and the mills for $10,000 a month, and you charge us a consultant's fee of $9000 a month, which is paid to you in Burundi, where there are no income taxes. All of the payments from the US will be paid into an account, and your Burundi corporate office will receive an eNotice of the transactions of the month, and within twenty four hours of the receipt of money and the eNotice, we pay to you your worthy workman's wage."

"It does sound rather simple, all things considered." His eyebrow goes up, and he stands as he asks, "But I know that you are a very shrewd businessman who creates wealth where he does not work. Why should I trust you with something this big?" He walks around to the other side of his desk to distance himself from me.

"There are three things that make it impossible for you to not trust me, Ardit. First, you really want to make this deal so that you don't have to make any more 'bits and pieces' deals, ever again. You could quit brokering smaller deals with a smaller pay-off and enjoy these rewards for the rest of your life. This could be what puts you out of the deal making game and moves you toward that lifelong vacation you think you want. Second, I have checked you out at least as thoroughly as you checked me out, and I know that your assets and income are being drastically outrun by your expenditures." His ex-wife was taking it all in a divorce. "And finally, Mr. Iselin," I say as I sit in his chair, "we are willing to let you have it all for the first four months, as my good faith, just to let you get an idea of what you can do with it." His expression changes and I can see the stress and worry ease up off of him as he sits down across the desk. "If you check it out, over the first four months, and think we can all save some middle money by letting you run the program, and if you prove to us that you can, then move to Africa and take over. Can you have this contract drawn up and a logo delivered? Should I put my people on it? Or, did we come to the wrong man for this job?"

He looks at his lawyer sitting in the hallway, makes some hand gestures, and the lawyer nods back, "We can handle that. Would tomorrow be soon enough for both?"

"I would really rather wait about twenty days, if that's okay with you. You understand." I say with certainty as I smile; he nods in agreement.

"Good, Travis will be on that right away," he says.

We shook hands like gentlemen always have after an agreement is struck, and I ask, "Where's a good place for a chicken sandwich around here?"

"Give me a few minutes, and I will take you to lunch, if that is okay." We all indicate agreement, and he leaves the room with Travis, who had just stuck his head in. Gerhardt gestures for one of our attorneys to come inside. He lets them know that they are no longer needed, that we have it well in hand. They will find their way back to the hotel, or the airport, whichever they would prefer. We would see them back in San Antonio.

When all are well out of earshot, Gerhardt says to me, "Did you know, you brought that deal in at nearly seventy five cents on the pound higher than anyone on the board thought we could get?" I nod and smile, take half a bow, and lean on the desk. "That increases our profit margin on this deal by nearly sixty five percent."

"I'm glad you like it," I reply.

"So, you actually read the selling prospectus on the way up, eh?" I smile again and nod with pride and a small shrug. "Did you happen to read the Danzig Industries bylaws as regards corporate negotiations?" he says in a more disapproving tone. I could feel my smile disappear and shoulders droop as I shake my head this time. "And what is the business about waiting twenty days?"

"Yeah, that." I perk up a little, being a little bit proud of myself again, I say, "Well, I saw in one of the tabloids online that a woman, and a looker, with the same last name, Iselin, is getting divorced from her Suisse financier husband and taking him to the cleaners. The divorce is finalizing in the next couple of weeks. If we can keep this under wraps 'til then, well, she can't have any. Since she was on a beach somewhere with a man that looked like an underwear model and was called a 'dive instructor,' but who also had his tongue in her ear, I figured that Ardit would be okay with leaving her out of it. But, tell me about the bylaws of the company?"

He makes a very serious face, looks toward the floor, and shakes his head. "Whew! Very serious stuff, bylaws! The bylaws have a section that is intended to keep everyone voluntarily acting as sellers and income generators for the Enterprise, and it says that any person or persons who sell up to the reasonable expectations of a deal get a commission, but anyone going beyond those expectations will receive the full standard commission on the larger amount . . . and an additional 25% commission on the profits above those anticipated for the deal until the terminus of the deal or five years, whichever comes first."

"Okay, that actually sounds pretty good," I am relieved that I am not in some sort of trouble, "but in real numbers, what does that mean?"

"It means, Joshua, I think you probably just made yourself an additional thirty to fifty million dollars a year for the next five years. That's what that means." I hurriedly sit, or more honestly fall to a seat, just as Ardit comes in the door. I almost miss the chair.

"Ardit," Gerhardt says, "would you mind if we have these contracts drawn to reflect that this is a Burundi business venture, NOT originating in New York? It could save all of us from taking a 65% loss on the profits, by not paying any US, New York State or City income taxes on it."

"I see your point, Mr. Gerhardt." He nods to Travis who immediately folds and pockets the draft, "We will do this business in Bujumbura, Burundi, in three weeks from today, February 24th, 2054, before lunch, if that will suffice?"

"Yes, Mr. Iselin," I say, "and by setting it up for everything to happen in Burundi, you remove the Texicans from the appearance of the business activities. We will meet you there and then. In the meantime, what about that chicken sandwich?"

"It's a little out of the way, but I know the place to go. It's called A Voce and they make a Rosemary and Lemon Pollo Salmoriglio that is out of this world. It is their signature dish since the sea scare."

The "sea scare" was the latest nightmare enforced on US food commerce as a result of some study that said that 98% of all seafood had trace amounts, but still dangerous levels of mercury, leads, and other heavy metal toxins. The bans had not yet been fully lifted, even though it had been over a month since it was discovered that the samples tested were actually tainted by the equipment used by the FDA and the EPA to transport them. The containers they bought and used to store the seafood were actually emitting the toxins as soon as the food was placed inside them. If they had been transported in a plastic bag or a stainless steel tub, they would have tested clean, but the government was trying to save a few dollars and almost lost their fishing industry.

It was one of many follow up enforcement attempts after the failure to enact a Global Population Initiative touting overpopulation as the cause of all the problems in the world. Unfortunately for them, there were actually dozens of studies by Universities in densely populated places like London, Singapore, Dubai, Bangladesh, and more, which all revealed the same thing to various degrees. They all said that the planet had a capacity of between one 120 and 140 billion people, and since we were only eight or ten billion of us, overpopulation is not a reality. There are places that are densely populated, but there is a plethora of space that is nearly vacant.

The math works out to where we could transport the entire population of the world into what had been the "lower forty eight" of the old USA, and each person would have a fifth of an acre to live on. But, when we distribute those people into homes and towers for living, cities for manufacturing, leaving the country for farming, and applied just a little modern technology to the farming industries, they could all be fed by the food grown in the old space of the lower forty eight as well. That means that, according to these studies, there would be the space of the entire rest of the world into which people could grow. Also, there are other circumstances that make these worries smaller.

For example, even after states quit leaving, the population in the US is in a steady decline. The economic and political environment has become so depressed and depressing that university studies are actually indicating that people are having thirty to forty percent less partner related sex, depending upon their social class. Couple that with the social normalization of gay marriage, near constant masturbation as a symptom of the depression, free access and acceptance of abortion, a dearth of opportunities to get ahead, or have a better life, and there you go. It wasn't really a matter of the old saying from the previous sixties, "Who wants to bring a child into this world?" it was a matter of the world being such a bad place to live that even getting laid has lost a lot of its appeal.

The people that supported the sea scare were the same ilk who banned previously safe Styrofoam only to reinstate it, and an EPA that in December of 2012 had actually declared water as the pollutant of a stream in Fairfax County Virginia. They are the same groups that tried to foist their Global Warming religion on everyone, and then called it Climate Change because there wasn't actually any 'warming' going on for dozens of years, and still isn't. They were the spiritual great-grand-children of the folks that had banned DDT. They were really nothing more than Socialist control freaks that had to have their hand in everything possible. Truth is that food, the environment, education, industry and religion were just a means to the end, and that end was control. This was nothing new; just look at the history of the NEA, the EPA, the FDA, the ATFE, the IRS, the Democrats as a whole, about three quarters of the Republicans in the last sixty years, the United Methodists, the Southern Baptist Convention, and the Evangelical Lutheran Church in America – just to name a few. Each of those had, pretty much, gone the way of Demas. Odd expression! What does that mean? DDT came back in Africa and the death toll has decreased by nearly two million a year.

We take the elevator down to street level and go out to meet the car. We are in the West Bronx, and it takes about twenty-five minutes on the elevated streets to get to the restaurant at Madison and East 26th. It is a quaint place with a perimeter around an outdoor dining area as well as a very elegant dining room inside, with a couple of very pleasant alcoves, but we choose to dine al fresco today, since it is so nice outside – if you can call it "outside" under the thermal dome of the city. Besides, we have just flown over a thousand miles and had all of the closed-door meetings anyone needs in a day, followed by a cross-town drive in a closed car. Al fresco sounds pretty good to me.

The patio is surrounded by potted shrubs and has what looks like twelve foot glass walls to keep the street noise out. I am later informed that it is four inch thick PlastiGlas, which is also bulletproof and somewhat bomb resistant, just in case. The staff is dressed impeccably and all their clothing looks new, unlike the suits of the businessmen around. There are no frayed or worn edges on the wait staff and maître d'. Everything they wear is either a synthetic or a modified, and nearly indestructible version of denim.

We sit at a small square table with a view of the street. To my right is Gerhardt, our host sits across from me. Mr. Iselin suggests we all try the Zuppa di Anatra with a Shiner Bock and some very pleasant conversation before what would become the real highlight of my day showed up. We have just gotten our beers and we're speaking casually. Mr. Iselin is telling us about his soon to be ex and what she is doing. I tell him about the article I saw, and he says that he already knew about the "boy" but that the family of his soon to be ex has huge connections among the jurists' world of the Suisse, so he will be thoroughly screwed in this divorce.

I glance up to the sidewalk and see that Ethyl has arrived. I am unaware and pleasantly surprised at her coming. She stops at the maître d' and points in our direction. He gestures for her to go ahead, and she does. Her hair catches the breeze, as she strides across the patio, with just a little more swish and spring in her step than usual, her magenta mane in big loose curls, suspended and flowing on the air. She is magnificent as she walks straight over to the table, hands a manila envelope to Gerhardt, and steps toward the chair to my left. She says, as if to everyone there, "I hope you don't mind my dropping by. May I sit?"

I say, "I for one am glad to see you. Would you like a beer?" She sits, nods approvingly for a beer, and I hold my bottle up to show it to our waitress and point to Ethyl. In a moment, she is enjoying an ice cold Shiner too. Shiner is one of the world's best German made beers, imported from Texas.

"Some of the car guys stopped by and wanted your input," she says to Gerhardt as he shuffles through the packet of papers. "But I also needed a day out of the office, and the boss wasn't there to tie me down, so I thought I would drop it by instead of sending it." Then she turns her glance to me. "So what else have you got to do today? And who is your friend?"

I introduce her to Mr. Ardit Iselin who shakes her hand and tilts his head, again, almost as if bowing in respect, while seated.

Ardit says, "Well, to tell you the truth, we had pretty much concluded the business portion of the day and we're free to cast off the fetters, so to speak. Have you ever been to New York, Ms. Ethyl?" She shakes her head, sipping her beer.

"I am going to have to get back to the office after dinner," Gerhardt says, "but that doesn't mean that you can't have some fun, Mr. Danz. Ethyl can keep an eye on you, and Ardit, would you mind showing them around the town a little?" Then he turns his gaze to me. "Did you actually make a deal with some sort of gator boy from a science fair?"

"Yeah! Well, actually, since he's seventeen, I had to make the deal with his dad. It seemed like a great idea at the time. He's got this battery idea that looks to be . . . well, I thought it was devastating. Did something go wrong?"

"What kind of deal did you make him? How did you find him, and what did you promise?" He is hard to read sometimes, like when he had talked about the bylaws before. He tips his head down, looking at me over his glasses, he said, "I need some specifics."

"We had a recorded video chat on my phone; I can send it to you." He eases up a little bit but gently presses for a little more. I begin fumbling on my phone, and Ethyl pats my hand, takes the phone from me, to find and send the recording. "I agreed to give him a hundred fifty thousand Texican dollars to sign with us as a battery developer with double the income of a standard entry-level lab-tech's pay and percentages of profits from his work to be decided later by his dad and me. Why? Did something go wrong?"

"No! Exactly the opposite; something went right. He did it. If everything I read is true, we should have a new battery in very short order – maybe ready for production and sales by summer - and the car guys are going crazy with the possible applications, and legal wants to know who owns what and how we pay who, etc."

I ask, "How much are we talking here, Gerhardt?"

"Well, if these specs are correct, we will save over 150 million dollars a year in battery expense, producing twice as many batteries for double the number of cars this next year and maybe double that number the following year. This could make us bigger than Toyota, even after they bought out the GM bankruptcy. We may need to buy another car plant somewhere or build one."

Ethyl says, "Don't forget the applications in flashlights, make-up compacts, and emergency lights," she says, reminding us of the other markets that we – as manly men – might overlook. "You could make a million dollars just putting lights inside of purses and another million in laser targeting for pistols. And what about Tasers? It's just a thought."

I don't think I hide the fact that a good looking woman discussing weapons is a turn on. I realize that my eyebrow is up. Then I realize that her eyebrow is up too, and she is looking straight at me. Lunch arrives. "I took the liberty of adding the same as the rest for the lady. I hope that's okay," the waitress says as she begins doling out the meals. "Is there anything else I can bring you?" Ethyl wants lemonade with her lunch, and I think that sounds rather appetizing as well.

"How did you find him?" asks Gerhardt.

"I was surfing the web the other day and found a story about a boy that had been beaten by some of his classmates. The story said that they had been taunting him about his science fair project and how it was 'stupid' and that even though he only got an 'Honorable Mention,' his dad said that it was 'because the teachers just couldn't understand what he was doing. He's just way ahead of 'em all.' He said in a distinctly countrified Cajun sort of accent. By the end of the article, I felt empathy for the kid, and I was so intrigued I had to call the guy." I tell him how I had asked the dad to have his son try to put it into layman's terms, and he did. Then he transmitted me a copy of all the research, and like I told Gerhardt, I was hooked. "This looked like the greatest idea since anything I could remember, so I jumped on it. Besides, I figured that I was offering him so little and that it was far less than the cost of my apartment, so you would figure a way to pay for it."

"Actually, it is far less than the cost of the desk in your apartment," says Ethyl, and I am corrected.

Ethyl seems chipper and even a little glib outside of the office. The sun is setting, or just hiding behind the sky scrapers, and the outdoors is apparently doing her some good, as is her second Shiner. She sits back in her chair, relaxed and vulnerable, with her legs crossed at the knee, and one arm hung over the back of her chair. We talk for what seems like hours and Gerhardt doesn't exactly get out right away, what with the talk of the gator boy, and the sugar deal, time slips away. I can tell he needs a respite as well. Somewhere in the sunset, Ethyl waves her eyelashes at me, leans in close, caresses my hand, and asks me, "How do those big boy pants fit?" I let her know they fit just fine. She smiles a knowing smile, gently rubbing the back of my hand.

As the shadows fade and evening begins, the conversation is less business and more about nothing in particular – sports, news, and even the things the people in the restaurant are wearing. Some of that is a bit bizarre. One guy in the corner has his hair buzzed down to about a two with herringbones shaved into it all around the sides. He wears a very small baseball cap that looks more like a lunar blue yarmulke with a canary yellow bill. He also has a lavender faux leather waistcoat and Frankenstein looking boots that have eight or ten Velcro fasteners and a zipper. Everyone at his table looks like they were dressed partly in his collection but not all the way. He is obviously their trendsetter. At the table next to them is a group of people that looked like they are from a century before, with Harry Truman looking suits, and the women have pencil skirts and floral seams up the backs of their stockings, open-toed stilettos, and broad brimmed, race day hats. The whole place is a puzzle of contrasts. Then there is us . . . the modern business folk in the latest from the Armani world, and some of those with ten years use on them.

Prowling Cat

As the sun goes fully down and the street lights come on, Gerhardt says it is time for him to take off, and Ardit suggests we go to another venue for further libations and entertainment. Ethyl and I smile, shrug, nod, agree, and I shake hands with Gerhardt promising to see him soon. He says, "You guys have a wonderful time, but, Ethyl, watch over our golden boy. He may have made a billion dollars today, but he still needs a keeper. Keep him company no matter what and make sure he gets tucked in safely. I am leaving him in your capable hands." He shakes everyone's hands, nods one last time to Ethyl, and strokes his nose at her as he disappears into the night.

Ardit takes the bill, and I notice that he adds a tip of eight hundred dollars to a three hundred dollar tab, but I say nothing. After all, I am feeling like a jungle cat that has just brought down a huge prey. I am having an amazing and wonderful day. I have taken my first Star-Wars-like flight and landing, taken control of a very important business meeting and succeeded like a champ, found a new business venture that looked to be on track for another success, and I am out on a new town with a new friend and my very beautiful assistant; what could be better? She puts her hand in mine. It's better.

We take a short tour of the park. Ardit says if we have never been there, we have to see the park. We drive through what is almost like countryside, but through the trees, we can almost always see the lights of the surrounding buildings. We have been driving around with the windows down because it is such a nice evening – warm air, breeze from the harbor, and no smell of trash or fish. The tour has been going for about thirty or forty minutes when, caught by a traffic light, we pause near a foot tunnel where we see a hooker plying her trade. She is leaned way over in the tunnel with the top of her head and one hand against the wall of the tunnel, an elbow leaning on a nearby trash can, and some guy has her from behind with her skirt up over her waist, going at her like a poodle in a hurry. We may not have noticed her had she not been shouting at him expletive encouragements about his manhood and strength. "Yep, Ardit, there's nothing like New York." The tour of the park winds down pretty quickly after that disturbing display of the nature of the city. Ardit assures us that this may seem common, but that New York is not all this bad.

We go to a club in the theatre district near what had long been called "Times Square" which Ardit has recommended; though it is a bit noisy, with lots of flashing lights, and crowds of people everywhere, dressed in the Nuevo-Chic everything that almost looks painted on, and hairstyles that remind me of Tim Burton movies. It makes me think that I may need to update my style as well. But that will have to wait.

The club where we are had, in fact, been one of the theatres that, like so many others, had to be repurposed. Drinking, dancing, hook-ups and even brothels – though not as openly – were the mainstay of business in this area since the forties revealed partying as the best way to forget that one is in cultural despair. Gerhardt would reveal this to me later. Still, as a matter of truth, there are only two theatres in the district that are still functioning as theatres.

In the past fifty years, entertainment has moved from public to personal to such a degree that most of the theatres can't begin to stay in business, and the two that remain are almost entirely supported by the city government; so that ticket prices could remain low enough for "ordinary" people to attend. Otherwise, it would be unimaginable. It is already so bad I wonder how they think ordinary people can afford that. The overhead of the theatre is so huge, what with the taxes on the property, the workers, the insurance nightmares, then there's the unions, altogether making it so expensive to present a play, that a single ticket has gotten to be nearly a $1000 in the cheap seats. And there really isn't anything new since Webber's death so long ago. Add to that the fact that you can now put on a pair of glasses and ear buds and have a 3D experience of the theatre for a small percentage of a ticket price, and do it over and over if you wish. Also, for a few hundred dollars, you could get a "virtual suit" which would add all the other physical sensations, and for a few thousand dollars, you could get a holo-bed to go with it, which would allow you to experience almost anything from horseback riding, to a day at the zoo, a night at the theatre or an evening with a woman – or man – of pleasures, complete with the happy ending; again, and again, and again. There is also only one library in town. After all, what is the point of having all those physical books, full of dust and bugs, taking up space, and having to be cleaned and disinfected, when ten times their numbers can be put in an Amazon or Nook account and brought to your device and even audibly read to you any time you wanted? You can even have them anywhere you want, which is a real bonus, because it has been years since the library would let anyone actually take a book home with them.

With the help of an escort, who turned out to be our suite server, we ease our way through the acre and a half of crowded dance floor and writhing bodies to a distant corridor in the back. Down a dimly lit hallway, behind a black curtain, there are more private and somewhat quieter accommodations. After we get behind the multi layered, linen and polyurethane batted curtain, the noise level drops to where we can actually speak to one another without shouting. We follow the waiter about six openings down as he turns into a room on the left. Once inside our room, we can almost whisper, although the sound of the dance party continues to be present, exuding itself through the walls as an encompassing speaker cabinet. The card outside the curtained opening to our room says, "Reserved for A.I." We have a room that is about twenty feet deep by fifteen feet wide, with a small round table halfway back, eight chairs and two coat racks, which are fastened to the wall. As we sit down, Ardit gives the waiter a fifty dollar bill and says, "Thanks." The waiter reminds me of Joel Grey in *Cabaret*. He has dark red lipstick in the shape of a small valentine in the middle of his lips, slicked back hair, a powered white face, like a geisha. He wears a tuxedo t-shirt with an actual bow tie, black jeans and what appears to be patent leather high-top Converse All-Star sneakers. I am expecting him to sing, but he speaks instead. In a Frenchified-Brooklyn accent he says, "Bienvenu! Welcome! What may I get you, miss-your Smith?" His French accent is terrible, but his expressionless demeanor is excellent. And apparently, everyone is, to him, "miss-your" or "mumzelle" Smith.

"We would like four Dos Equis with lime and four Jaeger shots, tall and cold." The waiter clicks his heels and disappears behind the curtain. "Maybe this is where we should meet next time you are in town for business, Mr. Danz."

"Call me Joshua. There are no lawyers to impress here. And, yes, this could work out just fine the next time I'm in New York. It's not really that much less private than some office buildings, once you get through the crowd outside." I look around at the sparsely decorated room with its dark mahogany stained walls, chair molding and crown molding, all in a dark green, the black tablecloth, and the non-descript chairs. "I like it. How about you?" I say, looking at Ethyl.

"It'll do in a pinch, but for the long-term, I like windows, lamps, and clean lines in a meeting room." she says.

Ardit pipes up, "There's a room about three doors down that looks like the inside of a space ship . . . all glass, chrome, lights, and plastic. There's another across the hall that looks like a picnic ground, and another down the way that just has sand and logs in it for an outing on a beach. Also, there are overnights up above, where couples or groups can rent a room for the night."

"So why the four of everything, Ardit?" I ask.

"Because we are expecting my friend, Meredith," he says, checking his watch. "I expected her to be here a few minutes ago." The waiter comes in with the beers and beer glasses, but instead of shots he has a bottle of Jaeger and four frosted shooters, and he is followed by Meredith.

"Babe," Ardit says, as he kisses her. Then he introduces her, saying, "Joshua Danz and Ethyl, this is Meredith, my very special someone." It is the waitress from restaurant, but she looks even more lovely than before. She is wearing a black linen sheath skirt with a slit up each side for greater movement, showing rather strong looking thighs and calves that look to be carved of stone or forged of twisted steel, a button up blouse with some fairly conservative ruffles and simple black three inch high heels and dark brown hair, flowing freely, unrestrained by the hair net of before. She is a picture of elegance without the pretense of glamour. This explains the oversized tip. Turns out, Ardit took us through the park as a stall tactic allowing Meredith to close out her shift and go home to change on her way here.

"Drinks are on Artie" she says, "I saw the papers today, and it looks like the vampire is going to take it all. So, in defense of Artie, we should spend as much as we can. Don'tcha think?" Her logic is undeniable. We have to help keep some of it out of the hands of the "vampire." I notice that Ethyl was almost laughing out loud at the "Don'tcha think?"

Suddenly, I realize how truly beautiful Ethyl is tonight. She always looks well pressed and dressed for success, and I have never felt for one moment that she does not represent me and the company well, even standing before anyone that came to my office, or who could come to my office. But, tonight . . . wow!

She is still dressed for business in a skirt of coarse linen, egg-shell, half tight, down to her knees, and her matching double breasted vest with ten buttons and a genuine suede, long draped, light beige jacket that keeps her backside undercover whenever she stands. I realize that she is wearing no stockings of any kind, only those little nylon slip-on's for her shoes. Her black silk blouse with the cleric collar tops it all off beautifully, now with the topmost button open. Combined with her alabaster skin, gorgeous shape – narrow in the middle, round (and I presume soft) in all the right places – hair that always looks like Storm, from the X-Men, only in varied shades of dark magenta; she is

49

amazing. Her nails are medium length with dark blue lacquer, and her brows are perfectly plucked to look almost like an ingénue from the days of the Ziegfeld Follies. Her skin is as polished like that of a trophy wife, but without the paint job to maintain the look. Even though we are having a great time and laughter is to be had by all, she still has piercing eyes and a nose of character, like that actress from way back when . . . Anna Kendrick. Whatever happened to her?

Suddenly something occurs to me, and I say, "Artie, could I speak with you for a minute?"

"Absolutely," he says, and we go over by the doorway for a moment. The ladies keep talking.

"Artie, is Meredith a serious girlfriend? Or is she someone that will likely be gone soon?"

"I am not certain if this is any of your business, Mr. Danz!" he has his panties in a bit of a twist over my nosiness, to be certain, and without better explanation, I would have to conclude that he is justified.

"I ask because you are about to enter a new business arrangement while getting a divorce, and there is the 'vampire' to consider, and I was worried about who shares what info with whom over the next few weeks and what may leak out. You see, if the 'vampire' gets involved in what we are planning to do, it could ruin the fun for all of us – but mostly you – and we don't want that. Okay?"

"Okay, I understand," he says, "We met when I sat in as a guest lecturer in her business class. I had only found out about the beach boy my wife was banging about a week before because of my private eye. I spoke at the class and saw her afterward in the vending area, she liked my flavor choice, and we had a cup of Americoffee. She is studying for her BS in business. She is a serious person, and I really like her, and I hope she likes me. So, what does that mean for the sweetener business?"

"It means that we should be getting back to our women, and I should do another bit of business before we do anything else. Okay?" I say.

"Okay!" He wants to sound bold and assuring, but his eyes are looking fearful and worried about what may be about to happen.

We get back to the table, and the girls are sitting together on the far side now. I sit next to Ethyl and Ardit sits beside Meredith. I say to Meredith, "Can I speak with you about business for a minute?" Ethyl is a bit surprised, I can tell. "Artie tells me that you are a business student and a serious person, and I have a dilemma that I think you can help resolve."

"If this is something kinky, Mr. Danz, you're talking to the wrong girl," she says. "I really want to be in a solid, respectable business someday, and anything shady could ruin my chances in school and after."

"It's nothing shady, or kinky, Meredith. It's just business," I say. "Let me ask you a few questions and see if we can put our minds together and discover a solution to my problem, so we can get back to the fun part of the evening. Okay?"

"Sure. What do you want to know?"

"First, what do you want to drive? Second, how much do you owe for school? Third, how much did you make last year? And fourth, what is your last name?"

She thinks for a moment and looks into my eyes wondering if I am creepy or full of crap or for real, and finally she says, "First, I want to drive a Mercedes, one of those extra fancy, embassy class sedans with all the toys. Second, I owe about sixty thousand for school, and third, I made about $137,000 last year including tips, and my last name is McGill. So, how does that help you?"

"Well, Miss McGill," I say to her, "I want to tell you that in the next few days and weeks Artie will probably tell you some things about the business that we have arranged. He considers you to be an intimate person with whom he will likely want to share his day's events, and I want you to tell no one anything about it, ever! Artie's motives and interests in you are genuine; mine, however, are strictly business; so let's not confuse the two. You would be doing this for me and as a matter of my business. Understand?"

Her eyes laser in on me, and squint, just a little, as she says, "Sure. But if this is business, what do I get out of it?"

"Good point young lady. Spoken like an attentive young capitalist and student of true business. What you get out of it exactly, Miss Meredith is this;" I lean in to say to her, "you will get your college debt paid in full and three years of your last year's income – in cash without strings or taxes, all in about three to four months' time, provided that you tell no one anything at all about any of what you may or may not learn about our ventures. That will give us all the time we need to get everything up and running the way Artie needs it to happen. Does that sound good?"

"Yeah," she smiles, "that sounds pretty good to me. But, how do I know I can trust you? I just met you, and as I understand, Artie just met you today as well."

"That's a fair enough question, Meredith, and one that I am prepared to answer. As my bona fides – my good faith gesture – I will have that car delivered to you within the week if you agree right now and write down your address for Ethyl." I turn to Ethyl and ask, "Can we do this?"

Ethyl says, "If I may have access to your personal bank accounts, Boss," I nod my consent, "and if she says 'yes,' it begins happening right now." Ethyl holds her hand out to Meredith and says, "May I have your address, Ms. McGill?" It is then that I suddenly realize that my hand is making its way up Ethyl's back across to her far shoulder. The fingers of her right hand curl gently as if coaxing the address from Meredith, her left hand is on my leg. Meredith pauses for a moment, then reaches into her purse, takes out her driver's license and hands it to Ethyl, who takes out her phone, snaps a picture, and then puts it back in her jacket pocket. We all lean back, there is a toast to a day's work done, relieved that the complete business day has been concluded, and we have another shot.

A belly dancer comes in for a few minutes and makes her way around the table, showing her gyratory skills to everyone, up close and personal, and Artie and Meredith seem to be getting a bit up close and personal as well. I must confess certain exuberance for the feel of Ethyl under my arm too and the scratching that she is doing on my thigh.

"I've got an idea," I say, "Gerhardt left an empty suite at the Peninsula Hotel; why don't you two take it? And, Ms. Ethyl can take one of the rooms of mine." I lean toward Ethyl and say, "Did you bring any luggage?"

"No. We may have to go shopping tomorrow." She replies.

"How about some souvenir wear for the morning?" I suggest.

"That could be a good idea. I could also have a few things delivered to the suite once I know what suite we are in and if we are planning to be in New York for more than the morning. Otherwise, I can just wear sweats." I cannot help realize her being an almost overly organized thinker, and that is a serious turn on.

We are now head to head with her arm around my back and my hand gently coursing through her blazing hair when our waiter comes in. Ethyl and I turn our gaze to him. "Can I get you more Jaeger or beers?" he says.

"No sir." I reply, "But the check and a pair of the club sweats for the lady, size four, magenta, like her hair, and a thirty five percent tip for you and five percent for the dancer." I extend my Tex-Ex card.

"It would be my pleasure to get that for you right away, sir." He takes my card and leaves.

"Two things you may want to know, Mr. Danz." Ethyl says. "First, I am actually a size five, so it's a good thing those things are stretchy. And second, psychologists say that when a man has his hand, active and playful on a woman's head, or in her hair, he is actually thinking of what he can put into her mouth."

"First off . . . Ms. Ethyl," I say, with a pause, "I thought you'd wear a size five, but I also thought that you would look amazing wearing those in a size four, stretched just a little tight. And secondly, Ms. Ethyl, who can argue with psychologists? And, with such wise insight as that, who would want to," and I kiss her for the first time, a long, deep, and passionate kiss. It feels as if I am coming home from a long absence.

She kisses me back, and as we separate, she laughs a little, saying, "I made up the part about the psychologists, but you really don't care, do you?" I shake my head and laugh while the others keep nuzzling like new-found puppies. They are so cute, like high school freshmen at their first boy-girl dance. On our side of the table, Ethyl has one hand on my back, scratching, and the other is gently digging into my thigh. I will not complain, even when it gets just a little bit painful, and my hand never leaves her hair until I need it to sign the check.

The waiter returns with my card, the check to sign, a receipt, and a set of lady's sweats, including socks, and a long blue bottle. "I took the pleasure of including a bottle of the house vodka to go. I hope that is acceptable."

"I hope you added in a tip for the bottle as well." I say.

"Of course I did sir!" he replies.

"Then you have done well in taking care of us, and now, we bid you adieu." I tell him.

"Then you won't mind that I rounded the tip up to the nearest ten, because, if you prefer, there is a quicker and much quieter way out of here than across the dance floor."

"Well, that would be worth rounding the tip up to me," and we begin following him out. Instead of turning to the right, which would lead us back to the dance floor, we go left, and in just a few dozen steps we are going up a more dimly lit corridor, up a couple of levels of steps, and then exiting a back door that puts us out on the next street over. There is plenty of traffic, and we are able to catch a cab almost immediately.

Best Night Ever

We snag a cab, and we all pile in. The accommodations are tight and Ethyl is pressed right up against me, crossing her left leg over her right, and over my leg as well. My arm is behind her back and her right hand reaches under her left arm to hold my hand, fingers interlaced. We are kissing most of the way, but the journey ends too soon, because, in ten minutes we are exiting the cab, walking up to the Peninsula front desk. I show the clerk my driver's license and, "Joshua Danz," I tell the desk clerk. "And I will take Mr. Gerhardt's key as well."

"Yes, Mr. Danz. You are in 2301," he says, handing me one key-card, "and Mr. Gerhardt has 2303." He hands me the other, which I hand to Artie. "The master bedroom is to the right in each of the suites, and that is where your luggage has been unpacked. Is there anything I can send up for you?" The guy is so snooty I feel like calling him Jeeves. Is that racist? Or maybe it's classist? I'm sure it is something-ist, but I really don't care.

"I think I would like a bottle of house champagne sent to 2303, please, with some hot white chocolate and chilled strawberries."

"Right away, sir!" the clerk replies, and we head for the elevators where we are joined by another couple of people heading for their rooms. As the doors close, Artie and Meredith begin nuzzling one another like newlyweds while Ethyl and I remain in the rear of the car, facing forward. But then she grabs me! I don't mean that she put her hand on my waist or shoulder and took a handful. No! Her right hand reaches to get a full open handful of my left butt cheek and digs in her nails. I nearly squeak in surprise. Then her hand goes down to the inside of my thigh and I can feel my whole body vibrating like a cell phone. It is all I can do not to make a sound. The other couple gets off at twenty-one.

"G'nite ya'll," Ethyl says with her best and sweetest, stickiest Texican accent, pulling her hand from my backside to wave at them. They reply something simple that passes my mind like the words of my ninth grade math teacher, and the doors close as Ethyl takes my hand. The doors open again in a moment, and we follow the numbered signs to our rooms. "See you in the morning?" Ethyl asks Artie and Meredith.

"How about breakfast at eight?" Artie replies.

"How about breakfast at nine?" Meredith suggests, playing with Artie's hair.

"How about I'll call you when we're ready for breakfast?" I say, sounding like I am in charge of something, but wondering if that is true anymore. I open the door and gesture Ethyl through, "Ladies first," I say. As we enter the suite, she turns to kiss me, and it feels wonderful, and yet there are proprieties to be considered. Aren't there? I take her shoulders with my hands and push her back a half step even though both of us are reaching forward to continue the kiss. "I really don't know – care – see – know what we're doing. Everything . . . It has been so long since . . . I can't recall anything I was more uncertain about than . . ." I can't even finish what I am thinking, so I turn and go into my room without looking back. I leave the door slightly open and toss my jacket and tie on the divan and kick off my shoes. And that is when she storms in.

"Storms" really is the right word as she crosses the room in strides of at least three feet. She has already removed her jacket, vest, and shoes, and right after the door flies open, she tears open her blouse, and it floats like a feather to the floor, as the buttons strike walls and dresser. Before I can think of anything at all, she is standing right before me, wearing nothing but her skirt, ripping open my shirt, launching more buttons. "I am certain of what I want," she says. "And I have a good idea of what you want," suddenly reaching for my pants. "And I want it right now." Pushing me onto the bed, she lowers from view, and takes me like I have never been taken before . . . and in record time, then she lingers at her labor for an extra minute. I have let go so quickly because, for my body, it has been at least a year since there was sex, and for my mind, it has been decades.

I am amazed at what I have seen and now by what I feel. She always wears those vests and jackets as if it is her uniform at the office, and until today, I had not seen her outside the office, and barely imagined what she would be like without them. But now her sumptuous lips and lavish body are mine. She crawls up the bed till her hands are on the headboard, lowering herself onto my tongue, where she finds complete release in just a couple of minutes as well.

When she is done for the moment, she crawls down the bed, rests her head on the pillow, and I crawl into position to do the same. She pulls my arm up, above her and then under her head, so that I can hold her as she lies there, with her head on my shoulder and chest, and she kisses me, scratching gently at my chest and tummy, like a kitten preening its pillow. I am not thinking of anything else at this time; nothing but her.

The whole day has been a build up to this moment. The flight, the deal, the gator boy battery breakthrough, the waitress bribery, and the drinks were all just the overture. And this? This is the crescendo to the opera that is the very best day of my life as I know it. She kisses my face and lips, digging her claws a little less gently into my chest and belly. By the light from the next room bouncing through the bedroom door and the moonlight shining in, at the edges of the floor behind the curtains, she is magnificent. Her kisses on my neck and scratching wherever she will is getting me more than a little excited, and she climbs on top to begin again. It seems like hours go by with her there, staring profoundly into my eyes. It is the most intensely intimate moment of complete engagement of my entire, long, and complicated life . . . as far as I can recall. There are still copious holes in my memory, but right now, I really don't care. What follows seems like unbelievable fireworks, lighting the night from within, and a nearly comatose rest afterward.

It is nearly nine when I awake to the streams of sunlight and the smell of coffee. Ethyl has been up for a while, and has already had room service bring up some OJ, a large bowl of sliced fruit, and a pot of Joe; not the regular kind – she paid extra on my account to get actual coffee. She looks good in the sweats, with the word "Glamourpuss" – the club trademark – emblazoned across her fairly ample behind, in faux chrome, tumbling this way and that as she walks. There is a knock at the door and a voice from the other side, "Packages for Miss Ethyl." She grabs a twenty from my wallet, winks at me, and goes to the door where a porter has two boxes from Saks and a large, bulging manila envelope.

Ethyl extends the twenty to the porter and says, "Thank you," as she relieves him of this burden without him entering the room. She walks over to the dresser to drops off the boxes and then she walks to me and hands me the envelope. "I thought you may want to take this to Meredith yourself." On the envelope it says,

> Miss Ethyl Anders
> Peninsula Hotel, Manhattan
> Suite 2301

On the envelope in ink is written, "Parking Slot 354." I open it and pour it out on the bed. What slides out are three tech keys with colour coded cases (red, blue, and black) and a stack of papers that include a title on the car in the name of Meredith McGill, with no lien, and a stack of documentation on the vehicle telling about every option that is on the car, as well as the standard equipment and numerous upgrade packages. "I gotta get dressed," she says.

"Wait a minute! When did all this happen?" I ask as she flits about.

"I ordered it from the club last night, with delivery location pending. Having gotten Meredith's address the title work could easily be done." Ethyl says, "When I knew what hotel and suite we were in, it was added to the order." Considering the night I just had, and the fact that I did go to the restroom once or twice, it made enough sense for me to not care about the details, so I hit the shower.

My suitcase is on the dresser, and my suits have been hung, but I don't want to wear a suit today. I want to keep it more casual as a whole and spend some time with this disturbingly wonderful woman. Still, my wardrobe is a little limited, having planned for little more than a business meeting or three. I get a belt and pair of pants from a charcoal suit and a salmon shirt for the day and hope it will be warm enough. Then I think to myself, "If not, I can probably afford a sweater, I suppose."

By now it is almost ten as Ethyl and I knock on the door of 2303. Meredith answers wearing one of Gerhardt's shirts from the closet, and I can't help notice her undergarments and shoes are still on the floor. When she sees what we see, she giggles slightly before asking in a humorous tone, "What can we do for you today?" Her voice has a lilt and giggle to it that reminds me of Marilyn Monroe.

"If we may come in, it is a matter of what we can do for you, Miss McGill." I say in an equally silly but still somewhat formal tone. She swings the door away from herself and holds her arm gesturing for us to enter . . . she even puts her head down slightly, like a Hindi house boy. She is a bit of a clown. I like her.

I sit down on the sofa and empty the contents of the envelope on the coffee table. "Since you didn't indicate a colour preference, Ethyl took the liberty of ordering it with the Gun Metal Grey, metallic exterior, and the Molasses and Honey-toned Leather and Genuine Walnut interior." She sits with a thud on the floor across the table from me so hard I wonder if she may have hurt herself. She has not. The coffee table being glass allows me to see that she is wearing no undies, so I slip the envelope under the keys to cover my view. She looks at each of the keys like a child with a new toy, examining their colours and shape, even pushing all the buttons as if they would do something from right there in the room. She slides the physical key out of one of them and realizes that it could be used in the old way as well.

"Shut up!" she says, and her mouth will not close.

Ethyl picks up the invoice and says, "Check this out. Not only does it come with an amazing stereo, but it also comes with the Medical Rescue Package so that if you are in the car and you are hurt, in labor, or sick, you just say 'Rescue me' and the car will automatically go to the nearest medical facility. It is able to maneuver through traffic, stop, and start for lights, and the underside of the car lights up almost like a police vehicle, so people can see you coming. There are also some serious security measures inside as well."

"And this is mine?" Meredith asks.

"It is all yours, taxes paid, and title clear." Ethyl says, "All we ask is that you keep your end of our arrangement, by telling no one about your relationship with Artie, or any of the business that he may reveal to you until you are told that all is clear. Do we have an understanding?" She nods slowly and deeply. "Another thing that may be just a little awkward is that because the money to pay for it came from Mr. Danz' personal accounts; if anyone gets wind of this transaction, they will likely assume that you and he are having an affair . . . let them." I am taken aback by what she has said. This is not what one would think a "girlfriend" would say to another woman. Are we saying "girlfriend?" Maybe I am too old fashioned. "If they think that an eccentric multibillionaire and a waitress are illicitly engaged, that will help take their eyes off of what we are actually doing. Understand?" Meredith nods again with an "Mmm-hmmm."

"Damn, you're smart." I say to Ethyl. "That also means that if anything needs to be transmitted between Artie and us, we have a built in excuse for me to be in New York, or she can come to San Antone."

Ethyl says, "How about you drive us to breakfast in your new car?"

"But my clothes!" Meredith blurts.

"Yeah, me, too!" Ethyl replies, wearing clothes that had just arrived from Saks, "Let's stop in at the boutiques in the lobby. My treat! What do you say?"

"Oh, thank you. That would be so excellent," she says; confirming her buttons, she suddenly realizes she can't wear Gerhard's shirt into the world. "Now, where did I put those shoes? Oh, yeah!"

These women were faster than most, partly due to the fact that the staff of the store was so accommodating and genuinely helpful, but partly because everyone wanted to see Meredith's new car. It was about an hour from "Oh, yeah" to the blip of the disarmed alarm system of the car in space number 354. Both of these women are wearing jeans perfectly fitted to their forms, a white blouse for Meredith, and cobalt blue for Ethyl with matching red stiletto boots just like the ones that Meredith has in white. Each has a clutch, Meredith's is gold, and Ethyl's is magenta chrome, accentuating her wild flowing hair. Having the eye of a guy, I notice that the only undergarment on either of them is a thong. I am so glad it is not a typical winter. Still, I got an insulated windbreaker for myself while shopping.

As we arrive at the car, Meredith shouts, "Holy crap, it's real." And she keeps saying that same thing. "Holy crap, it's real," as she circles the car a couple of times and looks into the windows. She presses the alarm and lock on each blipper a couple of times and actually kicks the tires as well, "Holy crap, it's real."

"Which colour do you want to be your personal key?" Ethyl asks with Meredith holding out all three of the keys.

"I like the blue," says Meredith taking that one.

"Put it in your pocket or purse," says Ethyl, "then reach for the door."

Meredith puts the key in the top of her boot and reaches for the door. When her finger touches the sensor under the handle – "Click" – it unlocks, and she can open it. She sits down in the driver's seat and a voice comes from the dash – a very pleasant feminine voice – saying "What is your name, please?"

"Meredith," she replies.

"Meredith, would you please adjust your seat first so that the pedals fit your feet? Then adjust your height in the seat and the preferred tilt. The steering column is in adjustment mode so that you may slide it to the desired distance from you and the dash. Then, adjust the steering wheel up and down and then the mirrors." And when she is done, the voice asks, "What is your home address?" After Meredith has given that information, the voice says, "The preliminary configuration of your cockpit is complete. Additional configuration information will be added as we get to know one another. Welcome to your new Mercedes, Meredith. Good day!"

"Get in! Let's go." Meredith shouts with childlike glee. "I want to drive. I love to drive."

She does love to drive. We head south on Fifth Avenue, girls in front, guys in back, turn right, and go across the Lincoln Tunnel, and before I know it we are on the other side of Secaucus pulling into one of those classic round-edged, stainless steel diners that you see in the movies. It's a quarter 'til noon.

"I grew up about three miles down this road. I live a few miles up that one," says Meredith as we pull in the vacant parking lot. "Dad was a union pipe fitter; Mom cleans houses. I'm hoping that, when I get established, I can send them something to help out; especially since Dad got laid off. Well . . ." She stops speaking, sullenly, and I know it is not actually a "lay-off" that brought about her father's unemployment.

Ethyl chimes in with an update, putting her phone in her bag, "Gerhardt says that you have given him plenty to do, in a good way, and he suggested that you take a week off and experience some of the world. Of course, since I am your assistant, I will have to go along to keep an eye on you." Ethyl tells me as we are crossing the parking lot, "He also said that there is a corporate jet at the airport, should you desire to go somewhere besides New York."

"Have you ever been to Maine?" I ask her.

"Have you?" she asks back, and I realize that I don't know.

This is a Dinermite diner, and it is a magnificent example of off-site construction, even though it is nearly sixty years old. It has new chairs in the old style, but for the most part, it is original equipment and makes one expect to see James Dean come out of the restroom. Or it would if anyone knew who James Dean was. Well, that doesn't happen, but the waitress who comes to our table looks like she stepped right out of the 50's. She is snapping her gum, wears a pale pink poodle skirt, princess puff sleeves, pen in her hair, and a half apron, but her Converse All-Stars also have gel inserts, and the cook, who we could see at the pass-through, wears a paper hat, white t-shirt covered by a Fed-Mart, low cost, oxford shirt, further covered by an apron that has seen better days and many grease pops and splatters. He is between forty and fifty pounds overweight – according to the MO scale – and has a half cigar in his mouth that has never been lit. It is a picture from another day. It reminds me of my childhood in Columbus, Georgia. Wait a minute, I've never been to Columbus, Georgia! Have I?

She sits us by a window because almost every place is by a window, and the waitress with a big name tag that says, "Flo" comes over and asks, "Wha kin I getcha?"

We all want coffee and I want orange juice as well. She asks, "Do ya know what ya want, er do ya need anutha minute?" Almost without a pause, she says, "N'er mine, ah be back." And she disappears for a couple minutes and comes back with our coffee and my juice. While she is gone, we get to look at the menus so that when she returns, we are pretty much ready to order. Artie and Meredith will each have the "Hearty-Healthy HomeRun Double," which has two eggs (whites only), two slices of turkey bacon, two slabs of turkey sausage, and two pancakes with all the imitation maple syrup you could handle.

"I'll have just three eggs, over medium, and an English muffin." I say.

"Real eggs?" she asks.

"Yeah. What?" She caught me off guard. "Why?"

"Ain't nobody loud to have morn ONE real egg at a time. Itza law!" she tells me.

"In that case, my two friends that are on their way and I will each have one egg, over medium, but I will also take an English muffin from the waitress that is likely to receive an additional twenty dollar tip, if that's okay?"

"Dat sound jes fine, ta me suh." She replies.

"MY friends and I'll have the same as him and his," Ethyl says, "yokes runny, whites cooked, right?"

"Same tip?" asks Flo.

"Yup!" says Ethyl

"Za good day!" and she is gone.

"That really is a nice car, Meredith." I say, and everyone, sipping coffee, nods.

"When I was ordering it, it sounded wonderful, but riding in it was far better." Ethyl injects, "How is it to drive?"

"Like a rocket made of butter." She says in an almost dreamy, and school girl sort of way. "Wanna try it yourself?"

"That sounds like a ton of fun, but first we need to eat, and before that, I should go to the ladies. Excuse me if you will." With that, Ethyl rises, followed by Meredith.

"Meredith is quite a girl," I say to Ardit. "I haven't heard her say anything silly or goofy or waitress-like all night or day. And she has been funny at times."

"Yeah, that is one of the things that impressed me when we met. She asked real questions in the class and had real opinions as we got to know each other." He continues, "Of course, the fact that she looks damn hot doesn't hurt." He sniggers just a little. "And, what about that Ethyl? Looks like you two have been together for a long time, and she's drop dead gorgeous, and noticeably smarter than you."

"Hey!" He may be right. She is definitely prettier than me. And she seems to get everything done, even if I don't think about it. "Yeah, I gotta give her that."

Flo comes back with our orders on a tray and moves them to our places at the table and asks if we need anything more. I request another coffee refill and a hand full of creamers. "Could you check to see if the creamers have expired? They don't taste spoiled, but they don't taste the way they should either."

"Az cause dey made of soy. You from da souff, ain'tcha?" I nod, "Would ya like a glass of milk? I got two percent if you'd like. Or condensed if ya prefer."

"The two percent will do just fine. I couldn't help notice your accent; whar yaul from?" I ask her.

"My famleez Geechee, from da Cayolina-Joe-Ja lowlands. I sure does miss em."

"Waz bringz you t' Jersey?" I ask.

"I come fer da work but stay cuz I gots caught upn da helfcare."

"I don't understand," I say. I gesture for her to sit, and after she looks around and realizes that the place is empty, she does.

"Well, my husben, Bennie, he werk fo da big company from Flo-u-da dat sin him here, an we had da medical from his job. We live in Passaic, an' he takes the train into town ever day, 'til the bridge bus up, an da train drop into da Hackensack, an everbody die, even him. So, I gotsta gets a job and gots dis. But da helfcares from da Bama ting, and my son gots the cherible paulsy, an now we can't move home cuz ain't no Bama ting down dare. Can't afford da move." She told me a little more of her story as we waited for the ladies; where she comes from, who's her family, what kind of work Bennie did before he died, and how she'd run a café –well assistant managed – back home, before the move, and how the boss "fair well lef'me run da place."

Just then the ladies return, and I ask Ethyl, "Could you do me a favor?" I hand her my phone. "Could you take a picture of me with Flo? I likes me some good people." Flo permits; Ethyl agrees and takes the phone. I stand up, and so does Flo and we take a picture of us standing in front of the kitchen with the counter behind us, and the cook-manager in the background looking unhappy about every bit of it.

"So," starts Ethyl, "Mr. Danz and I were talking about taking a few days off. Are there places to go and things to do that would be better than a few days on the coast of Maine?" I like the idea and let her know, but it turns out that Ardit has to get back to the office, in the late morning, and Meredith will be working tonight; don't count those chickens before they hatch. But tonight, she will be going to work in a nice ride, and doubtless, "Artie" will be going to A Voce for dinner, and that is a good thing. Artie takes a cab back to the city, and we decide to go to Coney Island for a while. I know it sounds cliché, but there you go. The crowds are terrible, and the price of everything is ridiculous, but it's Coney Island, and I have waited nearly a century to see it. Wow! Has it been that long?

After the Coney

A couple of hours of Coney is all we need, then we do a little more shopping for the ladies (this time on my dime), and then Meredith drops us back at the Peninsula Hotel. She has to go home to nap a bit before another regular night of work. On her way home, she figures out how to use the phone built in to her car. She calls us in our suite.

Ethyl answers, "Mister Danz' suite." She pauses, "Yes Meredith. Sure," hands me the phone and goes into the bedroom.

"Joshua," she asks when I get on the phone, "is this deal that you and Artie cooking up going to REALLY be worth something?"

"Yes, it promises to be worth a great deal over the next several years. Why do you ask?"

"I want in. I trust you, and I think I love Artie, but I would rather DO business than work for the people that do business, if you know what I mean."

"I really do understand what you mean. How much do you want?"

Ethyl comes out wearing a cute little shorts suit. It has a jacket that comes down to the back of her thighs, and the shorts are almost as long as the coattails, both in vanilla with a bright white silk blouse, with a modest ruffle down the front and an Amish collar, tails untucked but barely reaching past the waistband of the shorts. Bright white snakeskin shoes with four inch heels! Shiny!

"How much will 400,000 get me?" Meredith asks.

"That's a lot of money for someone that doesn't have any yet. Are you sure you want to go all in like that?" I have to ask because if it all goes bust, she is out almost everything but the car and, I think to myself, her school payment.

"Well," she says, "for starters, I would still have twenty eight grand in cash, but even more than that, I would own a piece of something. What can I get?"

"Well, let me see; 500,000 would and should buy one percent of my end, but we can let you have one percent of mine for four . . . if you are absolutely certain." I pause. "Also, this is business between you and me, not you and Artie, just so that we are perfectly clear. This is business."

"I understand Mr. Danz, and business is what I need to do. Otherwise, whether I am a waitress or an assistant to a VP, I am still just an employee, and that is what I look to change."

"Then we are on the same page, Miss McGill, and it will be done. Thanks for calling."

"What was that all about?" asks Ethyl.

"Please remind me to put Meredith down as a two percent share in my end of the enterprise."

"But, you just told her one percent," Ethyl corrects me.

"I know, but she has a vision for the future, and I want to encourage that. And . . . she's a sweet kid, don'tcha think?" Again, she grins at the "don'tcha think." "Besides, it's all just a dream at this point and could fall through completely. Why? Did you want a point or two as well?"

"I don't even know the deal."

"Doesn't matter," I say, "I'm in. That should be good enough for you. In or out? Dum dee dum dum, dum dee dum . . ." I am humming something that used to be called a *Jeopardy* tune from some ancient TV game show.

"You're kidding, right?" she asks. I shake my head, still humming that tune. I put my arms around her. "You're serious?" I nod. "Do I need money? Cause I really don't have much." I shake my head again, still humming. She waivers, "Well, okay then, I'm in. I'll take two." She snaps her feet together and stands straight up with a brief and flippant salute, palms up, like that silly British comedian in the late night reruns.

"So, since we are not talking about money, what is it that you are bringing to the table today?" We were face to face until . . .

The next morning I awake, like before, with that beautiful woman, but this time she is still in my bed. With her head on my chest, Ethyl says, "You said yesterday that you wanted to spend some time on the Maine coast. Is that still a good idea for us?"

"I think a couple of days would be great." I reply, "What do you have in mind?"

"Well, it's not really what I have in mind that matters, but what I have arranged. There is a little town called Bar Harbor, with a very nice old mansion turned B&B. Almost everything in the place is from a century ago and more. I've arranged for us to have a townhouse there, if you're still of a mind to go." She speaks with the first hint of trepidation I have ever heard from her.

"Sounds great to me. Can you fish there?" I ask.

"There are boats and piers there if fishing is what you want to do." She lifts her head to look at me for the first time and sees that I am at least half kidding. She smacks my chest, "You!" She pulls herself out of bed, throwing all the covers onto me, walks toward the shower slaps her left butt cheek, and says, "Well, you can kiss this good morning then." And she disappears into the shower. Watching her walk away naked is a wonder to behold. Suddenly I remember thinking the same thing about someone else from long ago – someone that was somewhat older and softer . . . shorter too . . . grey hair. Hmm. One day I will have that all figured out, or maybe not, but I hope so. I realize that I loved someone once before. I may be falling in love again.

We rent a new convertible Jaguar, and it is a five hour drive on the Coastal with the Autobahn-Toll lanes, but we take the scenic route with six or eight leg stretching, sight-seeing stops along the way – just to see the view, buy gas, check out the chotchkies – and it takes us about ten hours, but they are a beautiful ten hours engaged in conversation without business, a little sightseeing, and a little nuzzling, and petting along the way, on a journey to a wonderful destination. Sometimes the drive alone is worth the drive, though, this crate doesn't begin to handle like the XKE I drove back in the seventies. I suppose it's the sensations that make me think of that even though I can only barely remember it.

It is nine at night when we arrive at the Bayview in Bar Harbor. We check in and are shown to our house. We've rented one of the Townhomes for a week, because that is the minimum rental this time of year, though they have vacancies. We called ahead and let them know what time we would arrive, and there is a nice dinner delivered to the place about five minutes after we get there. We take it upstairs on a private porch. A whole chicken, roasted, split with dill and garlic butter, baby potatoes, and French-cut green beans, with cherry cobbler. Long drive, great meal, gorgeous company, and a beautiful balcony view of the Atlantic makes for a perfect end of day. It is a large deck with a two person hammock. We talk, we dream, snuggle, curl up, and make love under the stars. Life just continues getting better.

That was Wednesday, and we stay 'til Sonday. It seems like an idyllic lifetime of sand, scenery, and sumptuous meals with sassy pants Ethyl. She is so relaxed and carefree – for the moment – showing off her inner little girl, that it is difficult to believe she is the same woman that ram-rods my every command at home. In those few days, I don't even think about the office. In the back of my head, I know that everything needful in the world is just fine, and will stay that way if I never give it another thought. I don't think about the cost of the trip, the car, or the cost of the room. I don't even think about the gator boy, the sugar business, or the plane. All that matters to me for those few days is Ethyl, and the days we have. It is as if the word "vacation" means that we are vacating our minds and that our other lives had been left behind at our desks. It doesn't really occur to either of us, but if it would, we might try to cash out completely and just go somewhere, anywhere. Neither of us really has any driving call to remain on the job. I have enough resources that I could leave the entire Enterprise in the capable hands of Gerhardt and disappear. Ethyl is quickly becoming the siren that calls a man to veer from his course, and that's okay, as long as there is another course of some sort for him to follow. It really is the best time of my life, and if I die this Sonday morning, it will be as a very happy, satisfied, and rested man. My vision, at the moment, is small, but this is subject to change.

It is Sonday, late morning, and we are dining at a lovely little place called Galyn's, a seventy-five-ish year old place, third or fourth generation, you know. Ethyl has a steak, and I have local fish, both with fresh veggies on the side. It is a very pleasant passing of time, looking on the harbor from the table, Ethyl has taken leave to the ladies' room after the meal and before the dessert is ordered. I sit enjoying the view of the park and the boats chasing the wind to and fro, listening to everything about me. There is a young family across the restaurant, who is up for the week, but whose visit is not working out.

"Honey, I really didn't know that the cards were no good." The husband says, "How was I to know that they would be cancelled?" They are all the way across the diner, and we are all alone. If I had my old ears, over that distance, and with their whispered tones, they would never have registered on my scope.

"They fired you, Jim! Of course they cut off the cards."

"They didn't fire me; the New York offices of the bank were closed. Besides, these aren't the company cards, Babe. These are our cards; the cards we've had since college."

"Well, now you know what it means in the credit app, where it says that they will be checking up on your creditworthiness from time to time. If it weren't for the bank account, we wouldn't even be able to pay the gas and meals."

"Babe, there's still the savings, and I should be getting another job very soon. Really!"

"We've got to get back to the city," says Ethyl. "Something has come up, and you are needed. I guess that I could stay though." She says flippantly, "After all, I'm not needed."

"May I have your townhome key card, please?" I say to Ethyl, and she surrenders it. I step over to the table with the distressed family and extend it to the dad.

"My friend and I have suddenly been called back to New York and have to leave. There is still some time on our townhouse at the Bayview that I would like to leave to you."

"We really can't accept your charity," the father says.

"The place is non-refundable and paid up. It's three bedrooms and two baths with balcony views of the harbor for no money. Can you beat that deal today?" I say, "Show them my card to verify that you are the right people for the place." I hand him my business card. "We need about an hour to pack and go, if you can wait."

The wife is almost in tears, and the children by the window have stopped fussing with one another as if something very important is happening. "Thank you," she says, "how can we ever repay you?"

"I neither want nor need repayment," I tell her, "but if you like, you can send your resumes to my office in a week or two: Attention Ethyl Anders."

"We can send them today if you like," the father says.

"No, I want you to take this time to recharge and unwind with the family and be free for a little while. When your vacation is over . . . when the time runs out on the townhouse . . . then send the resumes to my e-fax, attention Ethyl. Understand? Oh, and with a three bedroom, you get meals, so there's that."

They nod and smile, there are tears and pleasantries, and we leave, but not without paying our check and picking up the tab for the family, with a generous tip. They should be well pleased.

"Why do we need to return?" I ask Ethyl.

"Something has happened to Gerhardt," she says. "He has been attacked and is in a hospital in Manhattan. The plane will arrive for us in half an hour or less. And, you don't get meals with the place."

We make our way back to the inn and pack up to go. "Could you arrange for that family to have a couple of weeks longer and paid meals for their stay?" She nods. "You know, this really has been the very best week I can remember?" I tell her.

"Me, too," she says, kissing me, "but we have to get back to reality now." She scratches gently with her thumbnail, removing some lipstick from my face, and a low whooshing noise in the distance gets closer and increases as a small VTOL jet approaches and hovers above the water right outside our townhouse. It lifts up and flies over the house and lands in a green space near the tennis courts. A knock soon comes at the door. Two men are waiting to take the luggage and do. Ethyl tips them each a hundred dollars, and they take the bags all the way to the plane and load them right into the cargo hold.

.

Return to NY

We get inside the cabin – one far smaller than the plane that Gerhardt and I took to New York – and we strap in as the engines whir up again. There is the whooshing sound, intensifying and then, almost like a bullet from a gun, we begin climbing. I think it is going to be like an elevator, but I am driven into the bottom of my seat, then the force switches to the back of my chair, and then disappears altogether. In about a minute, maybe two, we are doing over 800 miles an hour, about a thousand feet above the shore. We arrive in New York in thirty minutes and slow to city speed of about eighty miles an hour, then less, then none again as we lower onto the roof of the hospital. This descent is not as joyous as before, but queasy with dread as we touch down. I hate hospitals. I can't help think I have spent enough time in one. I think somewhere deep inside that I may not get out of the next one, but that passes before we get to Gerhardt. We are coming down from the roof of the hospital as we had at Artie's office a week or so before, but this is different. There is no sense of adventure, only the anxiety of finding Gerhardt in whatever condition he may be.

The elevator is fast as it descends from the 120th floor stop on the roof. At floor eighty-five a young man gets on and stands next to Ethyl as the car continues down. Suddenly, in a smooth motion, his left foot steps toward the buttons, and he spins on his heel to pull a gun from under his jacket. His hand rises as the barrel passes my face and continues 'til it points at the ceiling of the elevator, where the gun is discharged once, and I realize that his arm has been pushed up by Ethyl's hand, and it cannot come down. Ethyl steps forward facing him, in a single movement, to put her foot next to his and WHAM! She slams her knee up like a hammer into his groin. As he winces and bends forward, she rotates, locks her right arm behind his and forces a shoulder dislocation. The gun is released into her left hand where she revolves again hammering it into his head, twice, and as he sits there unconscious, she shoots him in the center of his left thigh. Left Handed!

The bell rings, "bing," announcing our arrival on thirty-five, and Ethyl presses the button marked "E" as she takes my hand and walks me, like a child shuffling in baby steps, to the nurses' station. She sets the gun down on the counter and says, "The man who belongs to this gun is in the elevator on his way to the ER. Please see that security meets him there and that he is available when we are done." The nurse that is there looks as though she may be on her first day at work, or maybe she is new to New York, because she looks thoroughly stunned.

A slightly older and wiser looking nurse steps into view from behind her. She takes the gun and sets it on the lower counter saying, "Man in elevator, got it. Gun – security – hold him. Got it! Should I call the police?"

"Not until we have a chance to speak with him, if you don't mind." The nurse smiles a knowing smile and shakes her head as if to say that she did not mind. She snaps our picture as she picks up the phone and calls security. "Where is Mr. Gerhardt?" asks Ethyl, still holding my hand like a five year old school boy, the nurse points down the hall and to the left, so we walk up almost to Gerhardt's room. We stop before we get there, and she checks me out. She pretends to be adjusting my collar and hair as she says to me, "Don't let Mr. Gerhardt see you looking scared, okay? Big boy pants!" I bobble my head in agreement.

"But, what's with the Bruce Lee shit?"

She gently slaps my face. No red mark. "I got all kinds of skills and moves. Don't you know?"

I gather my thoughts just before I walk into Gerhardt's room with Ethyl following close behind. "Thank God, you are okay," says Gerhardt. He is bruised a bit and has his right leg in traction and left arm in a sling. "I was worried. You have to be very careful right now."

"Wait a minute," I say to him, "you are the one in the hospital. Don't worry for me. What happened to you?" I step closer, and Ethyl goes to the other side of the bed and removes her sunglasses. I can't help thinking, "Pretty eyes."

"Ethyl, get my suit jacket from the closet, please." She does, and he reaches into the left inside pocket where I would keep my wallet, where he clicks a nearly silent button. A recording begins playing back the sounds of a car crash and then the scuffle that includes the beating of Gerhardt and the sound of several men taking turns at kicking him and saying something in a foreign language that Gerhardt and I do not understand.

"Well, that explains the elevator," says Ethyl. "These men are speaking Kongo, and they are reassuring you, Mr. Gerhardt, that you should not worry. You won't be dying today. You are just the lamb, but I think they mean bait."

"What elevator?" Gerhardt asks.

"We had an interesting ride from the roof, Mr. Gerhardt," Ethyl says, "but the man is in custody and should be getting treated in the Emergency Room."

"How badly did you hurt him, Ethyl?"

"Well, he won't be doing any sprints for a while, and the shot-put is out of the question, but he should be fine . . . ish." She waggles her hand at the "ish." She picks up the chart tablet at the foot of Gerhardt's bed and reads as she is speaking. "I managed to keep Mr. Danz alive, and really, wasn't that our primary concern? The other guy will heal . . . eventually. Mostly! Probably?" She is standing there, poking and stroking the tablet, opening new pages, and reading just about everything it seems. "But first, this chart says that you are in pretty good shape and can travel if we can get you signed out."

"How do you know that? Are you a nurse?"

"Yes, Mister Danz. I am a military medic, licensed EMT, as well as a Registered Nurse. But, it is time to get ready to go." She seems teleported from the room.

"If these people are willing to do this to me just to get to you, what else are they willing to do?"

"I don't know, Gerhardt . . . ?"

"Exactly," he says back, "I don't know either."

"No," I say, "I don't know what you have gotten me into, but it won't let me die of boredom. That's for certain."

"No," says Gerhardt, "we don't do a lot of boredom."

Ethyl comes back with a doctor, who picks up Gerhardt's chart and says, "Well, Miss . . ." he waits for a name she does not give, "he will need proper transportation, like an ambulance rack, and ample medical help when he gets where he is going. Can you guarantee these things?"

"There is a man with a fresh GSW to his left thigh in your ER. Have him patched together – cauterized if you must – and have him on the roof right away, waiting for us. Have his bills and an ambulance gurney charged to this room, swipe this Tex-Ex card for everything" she hands him her card, "and have all of it meet us at the elevator to the roof in fifteen minutes. And include the cost of this chart tab. There should be a fax in your hospital's administration office saying that all of this man's medical records are military contractor secured data, protected, and cannot remain when we leave. Have all information, including food cart info, forwarded to this pad and then purged from your records."

"It will take a little time to make certain of all this," he says back to her.

"And that is why we are not meeting at the elevator in three minutes. Please hurry." She is so on point and in charge. She knows exactly what to say and do, what is needed, and what has to happen to get it all done. I am amazed, thoroughly in awe, and more than a little turned on again. Wow, she is a dynamo. She steps to the door as if to stand guard, still looking soft and gentle. She's on the phone.

"How much of what goes on around you is recorded?" I ask Gerhardt.

"Everything, of course," He says in a matter of fact way. "As I go through my day I may have anywhere from five to fifty meetings of little consequence or of major corporate or international importance. I don't take notes, I never have. But I have all the information in the world at my fingertips when I need it and never drop a fact or an appointment because of my staff."

"I just thought you were the smartest man in the world," I say in a slightly flippant tone. "I didn't even know you had an assistant, but now that I think about it, you not having one would be foolish." I look sternly at him with something of a scowl, "But what about all that recording?"

"Whenever I get in the office or at home, my recorder automatically uploads, and everything gets securely transferred to my servers, unless I need something quicker. In that case I do a manual upload. I have a staff of seven people . . . ish, who review all of the recordings, and archive the less interesting things based on the projects that are involved, and keep the other, more interesting and exigent matters, closer at hand and research them. They look for everything that can be known about everyone I deal with and feed it to my tablet, phone, or headset, on the fly, as needed. And, I have two assistants, like Ethyl, but male and not so pretty. My wife can be the jealous type."

"I have learned that when talking to you, I should listen to every syllable, and you said, 'seven people . . . ish' which means that they are seven-ish; or they are people-ish? Which?" I ask.

"Well," he says almost sheepishly, "five of them are people, but two of them are different. They are manufactured people from selected or designed DNA with a predetermined history, and then they are trained and educated for their particular offices and operations by mem-loading. We borrowed the idea from Philip K Dick in his story 'We Can Remember It for You Wholesale,' which was made into a couple of movies and a TV series . . . 'Total Recall,' remember? No one else does, it was so long ago."

I do remember the movies. The first one was a bit cheesy, but the story was engaging, so I read it . . . way back when.

"Anyway, we learned how to put memories into people's heads, and when we have the right physical candidate, we put the memories of thousands of hours of training into them, and suddenly, they are the perfect employee. They are designer employees, made to exacting specifications. We call them Symms; Synthetic Emulations."

"How many of these are there?"

"In the world?" he asks, "Or do you mean just in our company?"

"Worldwide."

"Same as in our company; we own them all." He says.

"So why did you ask?"

"That look of childish frustration on your face tells me that you are relaxing a little bit about all of this threatening and hostility." He smiles, "We have forty, but only six are currently deployed."

"Should I be worried?"

"No," he continues, "their primary command function is to protect you first, then Ethyl, then me." He sees my curiosity, "Ethyl is the last person on Earth between you and dangers of the world. As you have seen, she will protect you. Don't make it hard on her, okay?" He sees me nod, "Good! Do whatever she says. Medic isn't the only thing about her that is military grade."

"Close patch." Ethyl closes her phone and turns to us, "The gurney is here. I guess they got in a hurry." She waves them into the room, and a nurse helps disconnect Gerhardt from the traction, and a couple of orderlies help move him from the bed to the gurney. The room is full of people murmuring a bunch of med-speak and scurrying about. The ambulance attendants get Gerhardt strapped down with his foot elevated by the handle of the gurney and his arm Velcro'ed to his chest with a cushion beneath. With handles up and Gerhardt following like a wagon behind the man steering the front of his ride, we make our way toward the elevator, and that is when everything is FUBAR.

Suddenly I realize that I am being pushed to the left, into the circle of the nurses' station and Ethyl's hand grabs the gun that has not yet been picked up by hospital security, and gunfire ensues. She fires the first round into the back of the head of the trailing orderly, splattering a red collage of blood and debris onto the man in the front and the wall beyond. The other orderly already has his gun in hand and is preparing to shoot. Ethyl's hammer draws back, but not fast enough, because at the same moment, the leading orderly fires at her. As the elevator door opens up, there are two more armed men with that man's blood on their faces and clothes. Ethyl shoots one in the face and the other in the chest as she is falling. The gurney handle blocks the door, so it keeps dinging and closing and opening and dinging. There are alarms going off all over the place. Every patient monitor is showing stress, failure, or panic in every single room, and more than a couple of the patient's code. Several patients roll out of their beds to be more hidden from the gunfire. Blue lights ignite, like flashing police car lights, above doorways all over the floor. The shooting has stopped, for now, but the emergencies have just begun here. I go to Ethyl and see on her chest there is a small hole, barely the size of a dime. But as I hold her in my arms, I can feel that there is a piece missing from her back the size of a softball. She reaches up to touch my face, "Get you and Gerhardt out of here, now!" she whispers out in anger. "Get in that elevator, go." Her gun goes off again, and another man falls who had been hiding in the elevator. "I'll see you soon." I lean close to hold her one last time. She whispers, shutters, and in a brief moment I turn to leave, but I look back.

"We'll take care of her," the nurse says from behind me, but I know Ethyl is gone. I feel like a sobbing mess, but I am still moving the dead men out of the way, dragging them and kicking them, and pushing the gurney into the elevator. I press the button marked "Pad," and up we go. I realize without surprise that I have pressed the elevator button with the barrel of the gun that Ethyl had used. I squat down to grab another gun from one of the dead men in the elevator, and I have to sit on the edge of the gurney for a moment, sobbing. Gerhardt is talking about something; I can't make it out through my own thoughts and tears. I stand back up at the head of the gurney, and time is up. Ding!

We arrive at the top of the ride, and the doors open to the breezeway where I pull Gerhardt toward the plane with one hand until the gurney blocks the elevator door so it cannot close. A man shows up from each side of the breezeway, and I shoot the one on the left with the pistol in my right hand, firing blindly at the one on the right with the gun in my left. I hit the man to the left in the lower chest and he falls like a rag doll to the floor. At that moment a string of shots, a half second long and loud as a cannon, ring out from the plane and the man to the right is no longer standing. As I had fired he shied back, out of my targeting range, but the shots from the plane all hit his right cheek painting the wall behind him with his every thought. I bet this isn't the retirement plan he expected when he took this job . . . but it is exactly what he deserves. As he falls the smear of blood follows 'til it is draining in copious flows and globules on the roof.

The shooter from the plane is the co-pilot, who is coming now to help with the gurney. There is also a large handgun sticking through the pilot's window of the cockpit as we run, carrying Gerhardt's gurney. We race the gurney with Gerhardt up the stairs, into an aisle, then, as soon as we are though the doors, they close with a slam-whoosh, and we set the gurney down snugly between the rows of seats, wedged firmly in place. "GO!!!" shouts the co-pilot, and before we can sit, the plane is lifting off. Ten feet up, then it sweeps right, throwing both of us into seats by the left windows, and the plane drops like a rock for over a hundred feet and then up at a steep angle above the street to about 30,000 feet and 700 miles an hour in what seems but a consideration of a moment.

We level off above the clouds, and Gerhardt gets a message on the phone in the pocket of his blood soaked jacket. He rummages through the mess to find his comm. He sighs visibly and audibly. He is almost sobbing, as he learns some distressing news. "Are you okay?" I ask, to which he quietly harrumphs and nods in resolution and gestures, with an old telephone sign and a finger point, that we should call the cockpit. I do as he asks, calling the cockpit, saying, "Gerhardt wants to talk to you," and I pass the phone.

"Who's there?" he pauses. "Okay. Tell the pilot that five is now two. This begins tomorrow morning." He pauses again. "Yes. Five is two. Thank you," he says gently, not as an order or a request, but more as a matter of fact, as if he were saying, "Tomorrow is Monday."

Sonday Night

The plane lands and it is only about seven in the evening. We step from the plane at Dancing Stag Tower, and we are greeted by our own security personnel, just to be sure we are left alone. They carry MP5's and stand on either side of the walkway from the plane door to the elevator entrance. The young lawyer that had the briefcase on my first day here meets us at the door. He seems a little bit softer around the edges. Gerhardt tells him from the stretcher, "Five is now two; take security and tend to it and have her confirm with me when you are done."

He says, "Should I arrange for your transport to a hospital, or would you rather I get you a doctor, sir?"

"Please, just see if there is a good GP that lives in the tower." Gerhardt says, "If we can keep all of this 'off book,' we are all the better off for it."

"Yes, sir, I will look into the matter. Also, sir! Mister Schroyer assures me that we have already recovered and confirmed the wipe of all onsite video data of the hospital events. We have the only remaining copies, and there are no digital fingerprints." And into the elevator we go, me, Gerhardt, the lawyer, and two security guards. The rest of the contingent heads toward the plane for some reason. I guess they're leaving. We take the general access elevator to Gerhardt's apartment and wheel him into his bedroom. The security guys sling their weapons on their backs and help Mister Gerhardt into the bathroom.

Mrs. Gerhardt is not totally surprised that her husband was in a gurney; she has been notified about our arrival and warned about his injuries. She has not been told about the activities at the hospital, so the presence of all the security is an attention grabber. "Holy cats, Hugo, into what have you gotten?" she continues to make worried wife noises all the way to the bathroom. "Vill he be alright, Mister Danze?" She holds my arm waiting for a reply.

"Ja, Helge, Hugo es-um-uh-a bin ein bearleener." I say in my worst broken Deutsch, with a New England accent, Kennedy impersonation. I know I have called him a jelly doughnut, and she knows I know, so it puts her at ease a little. "Some toughs put him through a ringer to get to me, and for that, I owe you a really great vacation, very soon."

"Na, Hugo never takes the vacations." She says, "He thinks that working is as much fun as any time off, and since I don't have a job . . ." She is about sixty, maybe sixty-five, and reminds me of Colonel Klink's secretary, Helga. Coincidence? She is, none the less, still quite a beautiful woman.

"When the security guys get done making him ready for bed and the doctor is gone, you should shed this heavy housecoat and show him how much you miss him when he is away, then tomorrow, maybe, we can talk about that vacation, eh?" She smiles and nods slyly. She has missed him, and with him being injured and her being worried, Hugo is in for a treat. Lucky guy!

The door to the suite opens and in walks briefcase boy and a man that looks like a doctor carrying a doctor's bag. The bag looks to be a century old and reminds me of one of those from black and white TV shows from when doctors still made house calls. For the past fifty plus years though, most doctors just keep a bag like this nearby, at home or in the car, just in case someone has a medical emergency they cannot avoid. It is not like they are expecting to work outside the office or hospital. It just happens, like a mechanic may find someone stranded on the roadside. He's not looking for work, it just finds him.

The doctor is fifties, graying, taller than me, and rather lean. He looks a little out of place as Bernard, the young lawyer, leads him over to me. He extends his hand, "Mr. Danz! Wow! I had heard that you lived here but never expected to meet you." He shakes my hand with considerable, even too much, enthusiasm. "We have lived here for over a year, down on fifty-one, and, wow, er, wait 'til I tell the wife I met you."

Bernard interrupts gently, "Mr. Danz, this is Doctor Daniel Thomkins."

"Dr. Thomkins, I appreciate your enthusiasm, and I will gladly meet your wife, in a more friendly and personal setting, sometime in the near future, but this meeting must never have taken place." He looks at me a little dazed. "For reasons too complicated to explain, this must be entirely 'off book.' No records at all beyond this group of people, a company nursing staff, and this records tablet. We will gladly pay far more than your usual consultation fees, but they must be paid in cash. Can you accept that?"

"Well, it rather depends on the severity and nature of the injuries that Mr. Gerhardt has suffered. Can I take a look?"

"He will be ready for you in just a few minutes. He is getting cleaned up from the trip. His injuries are not that serious, but we need to make certain that everything is functional and track his healing. You understand. We were in New York, and he was mugged." I extend my hand toward Bernard, gesturing for the pad. "The Americans cleaned him up, stitched what was needed, and set his breaks. His charts from the hospital are all here on this pad, and I understand any X-Ray or MRI info is there as well." I pass it to the doctor. "Feel free to peruse this in the meantime."

He takes it from my hand and begins flipping through the pages, pinching and zooming when needed, with an occasional "Hmm" and "ha," but little more for a minute or so, until he notices blood on the case of the device . . . and then on his hands. He realizes that my black cargo pants and dark shirt simply aren't revealing that I have considerable blood on me as well. "What the hell?" He looks at me like I might be a killer and he might be next. "Look Danz, I don't know what's going on here, but this is not the blood of a mugging victim that has already been tended in a hospital. This looks like something altogether more severe than that." He tries to hand me back the tablet, but I am not taking it. "For all I know, there is a gunfight in all this and all manner of crime and evil." He looks around the room for understanding. "I don't know if I am the man you need, or if I should be calling the police right now."

"You could call the cops, Doc, in fact, when you are done seeing Mr. Gerhardt, you are more than welcome to," I say quietly as I step slowly toward him holding out my left hand with the blood embedded under the nails, "but see him first." He looks at the blood and realizes that it is quite dry. "There was a gunfight. It happened a few hours ago, in a hospital, in New York where we were attacked as we were trying to leave. They lost about a half a dozen guys, and I lost someone very dear to me. The police in New York are aware; the police in the FNT don't yet care. I am incredibly angry about what happened, and confused and worried about who did it and what has to be done about it, but for here and for now, there is a beaten man that needs a care regimen established and a professional to look in on him from time to time. Can you be that professional?" I feel my forehead bunching up, and my eyebrows feel as though they are almost touching each other when I stare into his eyes.

"I can do that," he says, "as long as the rest of this mess is not related to his injuries, and I don't get involved in any intrigue. I am a doctor, not a spy."

"Don't worry, Doc, unless he caught a bullet in the escape and I didn't notice it," and I lowered my voice in humor, "and somehow he didn't complain about it for eighteen hundred miles, that should be a non-concern."

"He's ready," Helge calls from the open door of the bedroom. The doctor goes in, tablet in one hand, bag in the other. As he enters, Helge closes the door behind her. "Did I hear right? You lost someone?"

"Yes," my mood darkens; I am sure she can see it on me, "It was Ethyl. I can't begin to explain . . ."

She reaches to touch my face, "Ach du liebe! I am so sorry. I can see, she was more than an employee, ja?" All I can do is nod and quietly restrain the sobs a little. "I guess this is the story that was on the news an hour ago . . . all that blood! How could it happen to you?" She is honestly bewildered. "Was that why my Hugo was hurt?"

"No," I mutter, "it was part of a trap set for me. As Ethyl and I arrived, we were attacked, and again when we were preparing to leave. They were well armed and from Africa, near as we can tell. I will find out more very soon." Suddenly I am more determined than sad, and more angry than tired. "Bernard!"

Clamorously, a slightly out of shape legal eagle bounds to his feet and crosses the room, "Sir."

"What do you currently do here?"

"I am Mr. Gerhardt's legal liaison to the rest of the corporation and adviser in personal legal matters." He seems confident in saying this, "Essentially, sir, I work for him in whatever capacity he asks . . . sir." Then he doesn't look quite as confident when he says, "What did you have in mind, sir?"

"Nothing, Barney, I just need to get in touch with certain types of people, and if Gerhardt trusts you, I will trust you, that's all."

"Yes, sir. But, Bernard is my last name, not my first." He says with some bravado.

"Barney, if we are going to get along, there has to be some give and take, okay?"

"Sure, Josh."

"That's Mister Danz, but if we are drinking you may call me Joshua. But, since I am not a joke, a jape, or a jest, no one calls me Josh."

"Yes, sir."

"I need to know who I speak to about getting detailed investigating done, who does sneaky and possibly dangerous jobs, and who makes impossible things happen in physical and financial arenas."

"For the investigating we have a man named John Schroyer who is sometimes called . . . that is, if it is seriously hush-hush. Otherwise, we have contacts at the FBI, the FSB and the CIA. For the sneaky things, we have a guy that learned his trade from his grandparents on both sides, a 3rd or 4th generation sneak. For the dangerous and the physically impossible things, we have a guy that is fourth generation Special Forces, though he broke from the Green Beret pattern of the family and went MARSOC and then to help train Mossad. His name is David Rathke. For finances . . . well that depends on what you want done." He has a wry look in his eye. "Should I forward a list of these people to you in an e-mail?"

"No," I say, "I would appreciate it if you could be in my office tomorrow at seven. Can you do that?"

"As long as Mr. Gerhardt doesn't need me, that should be no problem," he says.

"Mr. Gerhardt is on vacation until further notice." I raise a finger to him saying, "Hold that thought, but get someone working on research right away."

The doctor comes from the room, and Helge goes to see him. The doctor speaks to her and glances occasionally at me. "He really is healing nicely. All the contusions are closed, and scrapes are sealed, and dry, the X-rays from before and after the bones were set show that the setting was done well, and should be fine if he didn't re-break anything exiting the hospital." He looks at me now, "He shouldn't be back at work for at least a week, and his leg needs to remain elevated, so that means bed rest for at least five days. This will allow for everything to get locked into place for the rest of the healing. Five days! Understand?" He looks at me sternly.

"Hey, doc, I have thousands of people working somewhere around here that will gladly take up the slack while Hugo rests. Right, Barney?"

"Yes sir! No doubt," the fluffy suit interjects as if commanded.

"And you, Mrs. Gerhardt, please, be gentle on him. Some women . . ." he pauses.

"Doc," I say, "Helge will take excellent care of Hugo . . . in every possible way."

"That's part of what I am afraid of," the doctor replies. "I will be back at lunch time tomorrow and again in the evening. If there is any kind of problem, call my cell phone and leave a message; I never answer." He writes his personal cell number on the back of his card, handing it to Bernard.

"If there is a problem, Doc, the message will just say that Hugo needs to see you. Nothing more," I say.

We all say our goodnights, leaving Hugo and Helge alone. We also leave two armed security personnel at the doors of the elevator and another two outside the door of the apartment. I ask if Helge wants one or two on the balcony, but she really wants to be left alone, and Bernard assures me that the electro-glass wall of the balcony is quite secure, and he activated an additional security shield so that, as he says, "You would need an aircraft to punch through the balcony door. That thing will also keep out mosquitoes." He may be right, but, there are three more men on the roof, five in the lobby and grounds, and tonight the lawn lights are on high, just in case. And to answer the question I am asking myself . . . yes, I am worried.

I go to my apartment and shower up. I take my clothes and put them in a paper disposal bag and drop them down the composter chute. In hours, they will be worm food; in a couple of days, they will be beetle excrement on its way to being compost . . . with buttons and a zipper. In a month or two, they will be providing nutrients to the lawn. The chute leads to a bin full of grass clippings, bark, some topsoil, and bazillions of beetles and worms that would eat and digest almost anything, except plastics and metals, and make it all usable for fertilizer. I don't begin to understand the details of it all, but it is supposed to be amazing. It is intended to be used to dispose of food stuffs from the hundreds of apartments and offices in the tower, and clipping and cuttings from the yard care, but regarding my needs at the moment, in short order there will be no forensics of our trip to the Big Apple anywhere to be found. Our composter provides its output directly into the sub-surface water and feeding system for the lawns and gardens surrounding our building. We have beautiful lawns.

That night is a toss-fest, and although I lay down for sleep several times, in bed, on a couch, and in a recliner, the only time I doze off at all is during long commercial breaks between newscasts about the hospital attacks. I have found a proper use for all those infomercials . . . two to five minutes of sleep. Between the naps, there is news of the men whose bodies were all over the hospital. Several litter the floor where Ethyl was shot, and in a few images, I can see parts of her body lying there, lifeless. There are dead men on the elevator and more on the roof. The most astonishing of all was the one in the ER; the first attacker, whom Ethyl had left alive and sent to the Emergency Room.

When he was conscious, he attacked one of the security personnel and, instead of trying to flee, he took the man's pen from his pocket and used it to rip open his own jugular vein. Before he gouged his own neck open, he stabbed a doctor in a femoral artery, which caused all the medical people in the room to try to attend that doctor first, assuring his own demise. He bled out in less than a minute, all the while fighting to make certain no one could subdue him. He really didn't want to stand interrogation. I don't care what he wanted; information will still be had.

Of the seven men, none had identification on them, and five had no fingerprint records that could be reached by the police, but two are registered as "Support Attaches" to dignitaries from what used to be the DRC. The Democratic Republic of Congo had long been a socialist nation that had expanded in the thirties by having taken over what had been Zambia, Zimbabwe, Mozambique on the southeast and Congo and Gabon on the west. They had changed their name to that of their language, Kongo.

They now have their eyes on everything northeast of them and want to shut down anything that is growing "Western" in Africa. That means the others which are growing more Capitalist. For Kongo it means, more than anything else, everything outsiders have been doing in Uganda, Kenya, Somalia, Ethiopia and parts of Tanzania. We have tech, glass, and plastics coming out of Somalia and Ethiopia, and we have almost fully "capitalized" Djibouti and Eritrea with manufacturing and shipping. We have crop concerns in everything else in eastern Africa and have made a good bit of that part of the world into first world, or at least strong second world places. There are resorts and trade centers all over the coasts of Tanzania, and the island nation of Zanzibar has become one of the jewels of culture and entertainment for the world. The resorts there are amazing and we have an interest, as do hundreds, if not thousands of others in the region.

There is even a Branson, Zanzibar – a small city built around most of Chwaka Bay, for the purpose of being a resort and entertainment town, thanks to the third generation of Virgin Enterprises.

In one century, Kenya has gone from being colonial, to post-colonial, to anti-colonial, to communist, to destitute, to Jamestown, and then almost to Eden. During the destitute days, the population devolved into tribal feuds with better weapons than they had used in centuries past. The twenty or so major cities, or what passes for cities, become virtual monarchies being headed by what had been a local police chief or mayor or whoever had banded enough men to their cause with enough power and promises. All one had to do was kill a few dozen people and have a few friends kill a few dozen people and in most of these towns and cities, it only took about a month of this multi-level marketing of murder and mayhem to setup a pretty successful monarchy. It was like the Joseph Kony days only in smaller examples, but many, many more times and places.

Of course, these little monarchies were setup "for the good of the people," which were too foolish to really know what their own "good" was. After all, each of the new monarchs argued, someone had to protect the people, especially from the other monarchs, which they painted as the evil jackals around them. But this time protection was, as it often is, just another word for tyranny. We westerners would usually liken it to the protection rackets of the mob families of the US, in the Twentieth and early Twenty First Centuries, but it is part of the condition of man and almost always has been. The Yakuza, Triads, and Tong have been doing it in Asia for nearly 3000 years, and there were similar operations dating back as far as ancient Babylon. There will always be men, or women, who will take advantage of others by any means possible. There needs to always be men and women who will do something about it.

So a coterie of capitalists brought that crap to an end, or at least they seriously marginalized it. They dropped hundreds of crates with thousands of chain saws, plows, and rototillers, along with thousands of guns, tons of ammo, and instructions on what liberty and garden farming could to for their families, in dozens of regional languages, sitting on the top of boxes of food stuffs and seed for crops. Someone even paid to have "The 5000 Year Leap" audio books on mp3 players dropped into the place . . . over thirty thousand of them. These helped explain the principles of the birth of America and became a huge part of the birth of their new nation. Millions upon millions were spent, and the crates were dropped outside the bigger cities, often in raw jungle. The locals figured out how to use most of the stuff pretty easily and shared their knowledge with their neighbors, and more boxes came with more guns and more seeds, more food, and with machinery to drill water wells, along with "advisers" – many of whom were engineers, construction foremen, farmers, and ex-special forces – to help facilitate all needed activity. Several hundred millionaires had put up about $20 Billion dollars into their "Food, Farm, and Freedom Fund." And in the long term, it paid off well. Some of the would-be farmer/rebels setup their own monarchies and quickly got dethroned, and some of those were replaced by others who would then be dethroned, etc. After about two and a half years, Kenya came to the same conclusions that Jamestown had learned nearly 400 years earlier . . . everyone succeeds better when each of us is allowed to do all we can to help ourselves and our families succeed by the fruit of our own labors. When free men are free to do what free men can to provide, they provide better or worse by their own hand. And (to paraphrase the words of that great political scientist, Saul Paulus of Tarsus) if you "will not work" you "shall not eat." And once that notion gets thoroughly spread through a populace, they go to work. They begin entertaining ideas of import and export and within ten years had become one of the world's best examples of capitalism done correctly. It looked like America of the 1920's without Prohibition, without Progressives, without racism, without unions or the ACLU, and without the last 3,000,000 pages or more of federal regulations. People worked hard, and they achieved a lot. It is a joy to behold.

But that only makes the die-hard Communists in Kongo even angrier. The fact that Kenya rose so quickly and so high was just salt in the wounds of the regime that was devout to the ideas of centralizing everything, and this is why the US was supporting Kongo, and why the FNT was supporting the East Coast. In reality though, even with the US behind them, that didn't bring the boost for which they had hoped. Fifty years earlier, the US had real money, or at least the illusion of real money, but since the Texas secession, their purse was pretty thin and their biggest exports had become technology designs, like phones, cars, etc. and University degrees. The cost of going to college had skyrocketed to nearly $75,000 a year at a state school, and three times that in what were laughingly called the "real schools." The only ones that could afford to get a degree were, for the most part, people that came from nations that produced something or the families of despots. The US has only been producing the ideas of things for some time. There is still the auto industry, but most of what is there has become mechanized because union workmanship has become so shoddy that no self-respecting Japanese, Chinese, Polish, or African businessman could allow his components to be made by them. Then it turned out that unionized mechanization wasn't much better.

But the men who tried to kill me were not of the self-respecting variety; they were the worst kind of soldiers, the worst kind of mercenaries . . . ones with government employment records. They were all from Kongo, and all had served in their army at one time or another, and in fact, some were apparently on duty that night in the hospital. Those with fingerprints on file turned out to be "embassy personnel" that reported to their version of Secret Service, which hired their personnel from any department or division they could, for whatever they needed.

Monday

Before he went to bed, Mr. Bernard had made a half a dozen phone calls or so, and in the morning had received a couple of dozen e-mails, and has in hand everything I will need to begin my day, and my corporate or personal war.

"That is from Mr. Schroyer," he says. "It shows that, after accessing their computer systems in Kongo, fingerprints of all the men could be had. Something else he found, with a little digging, was the name of the contractor of the attack, a Mister Michael Nkosi, one of the vice presidents of the Kongo. We are not certain which department of the government he heads up, but his department name doesn't much matter; it's like *1984* over there. Not the year; the book. In the book, *1984* by George Orwell, the 'Ministry of Truth' was the department of propaganda . . . same thing with all the jobs in Kongo government. It's all like an Obama Administration health bill. Anyway, it appears as though he decided that if he can get rid of the ten or twenty biggest billionaires vested in the region, then he can create the turmoil and the power vacuum needed to overthrow the governments around them, and become the savior of Kongo and maybe he can make himself president; maybe even king."

"The squad that tried to kill you," he continues, "was a ten man team with two more in the lobby and one in a van outside. Those three escaped because no one was looking for anyone on the ground since the action was so high up. Schroyer said in his after action account, that they boarded a cigarette boat docked off Caven Point Road near Black Tom." He tells me this while pointing to their route on a map. "They took it out to sea and then down the shore to a couple of miles north of Asbury Park where they pointed the boat to sea and locked the throttle on full, only to swim ashore. It probably would have disappeared for days except it ran into a freighter about three miles out. Satellite records show them swimming ashore where they disappeared into Ocean Township."

"So, we lost them?"

"Well, sir," he smirks, "lost is a bit of an overstatement." He hands me what looks like phone records . . . about a dozen pages of phone records. Each one has calls to numbers in area code 212, New York, but also calls to numbers with country code 242, Kongo, "Sir, Mister Rathke has triangulated those phones in a house on Ridge Avenue, near Bradley Park. There is a helicopter inbound for Neptune Township helipad from a cargo ship, fifteen miles out, that is headed for the west coast of Africa. To top it all off, he and a team of ten are onsite awaiting orders."

"Can they take the chopper or knock it down?"

"Could be tricky, sir."

"Don't let that bird be used to go anywhere and get all the ground crew we can into custody."

"That could have certain 'legal' ramifications, sir. I am a lawyer, I know a thing or two about these matters," he says sternly. "We could run a 'black badge' operation to buy time, sir."

"Give him a go and make certain we learn all we can."

He pulls his cell phone out, presses a single number, and says, "We'd like to order some pizzas" He pauses, "Um hmm. We'd like three large pepperoni and no extras. Please be careful not to spill." He hangs up and then to me he says, "He will do his best, sir. Spooks use the strangest language."

It seems like the longest ten minutes of my life, waiting to see if I had "pizza" or not. I would learn later that "pizza" was a reference to "Italian Style" attack, which means, to them, pain and capture for future use. "No extras" meant . . . well, you'll figure that out as we go. Finally, the phone rings again. "Yes?" he says, "good to hear," he pauses again, "I'll tell mom."

"Yes sir, they got all three of the ground crew and destroyed the helicopter. He said that he was uploading video for your approval. Would you like me to play it, sir?"

I consent, and he takes his tablet over to my TV in the office. He connects the wireless monitor function and shows it in hi-def six feet wide. The video shows six angles of view, one of which is watching the chopper come in over the town; while five others are watching the three men arrive in a stolen car. They leave the car as they see the chopper arrive and set down. The camera angles are looking down on them from five sides. They pass between some of the trees along Ridge Avenue, and as they get just past the trees, a rocket flies from the other side of the clearing to detonate the chopper. They turn to run and seven guns open fire on them using rubber bullets, spraying them into writhing heaps of sobbing pain. The troops drop out of the trees, hit them with Tasers, and drag them into a cargo van that drives into the park to pick them up and drive away slowly. The police and fire vehicles pass them seemingly unnoticed. It is nine thirty in the morning; still, no one cares.

By noon, Rathke has these men on a ship being water boarded in a very special way and has determined that the team was sent for me because I have been suddenly exposed with my new adventure into civilization and going into public venues like the night club and the restaurants. They figured that since I was going to be an "easy target," they could proceed to get more targets later on that same run. I had been at the top of their hit list for years, but until a while ago, I was pretty much an urban legend, an imaginary target. Still, I was at the top of the list and suddenly I seem tangible and targetable. The success of my killing was to be the hurrah that launched the other attacks, but it didn't work out that well for them. As Rathke puts it, "They underestimated his secretary, and she kicked their collective ass." She is much more than a secretary to me, and she has brought them some severe hurt. We would be certain to do the rest.

We find that Nkosi is only slightly less accessible than the average first world billionaire, and like all the other vice-presidents of his nation; he keeps a very low profile, especially since his attack on me has failed. No one else apparently knows of the attack, since he was planning to reveal his victory after there had been a success. While we were fighting for our lives, he was at a state dinner in their capital, with their president, and his fellow vice-presidents, but this morning he has been escorted out of the Presidential Palace in a motorcade at his request. There is his driver, in his car, along with his personal attaché, a car ahead and a car behind, each with four armed men as they speed away. He gives some excuse about having to go into dangerous territory for an emergency meeting with someone, from somewhere, but that is all bogus. The motorcade disappears into a parking garage and stays there. For a man whose name means lion – Nkosi – he sure can run and hide. This is the report from Rathke. Now what?

Schroyer says, "We have access to their money, if you would like to play a little shell game." We talk it over and I agree.

John Schroyer associates with a guy named Axelrod, when I video conference with the guy, he looks like a weasel to me. Barney says he is a world class sneak and over the past several generations, his family has cultivated connections to some of the most important and nefarious families, enterprises, and nations in the world. With this generation, he has given up the political aspirations that have so driven the family, always wanting to be the man – or woman – behind the throne. No, this one wants the money and the things that came with it. A real black sheep in his family, since they are all dedicated to death for the cause of what they like to call "Social Justice," which is code for Socialism or Communism, and everyone knows it by now. No, DJ Axelrod is all about the bucks and I am all about giving them to him; a big, fat, stinking pile of them.

Axelrod has been able to discover, and reveal to us, that the leadership of Kongo is as much a mob family as anything I have seen in my lifetime, which, as it turns out is considerable. The public politics shows a President with seven Vice Presidents, with cabinet heads, and so forth. What is really going on is more like Al Capone and his lieutenants, with an assistant boss, or under-boss, consigliere. The primary purpose of the organization is the feeding of the organization. Any other functions are secondary and must be subordinated to the first. If there is to be productivity in Kongo it has to be such as would contribute to the "government" somehow. That is seen first in taxes, and then in benefits that may include product discounts or freebies, depending upon what is being produced. Subsequently, there are no car makers in Kongo, or stereo and electronics manufacturers. Once we understand this, it gives insight into how the money works and then, the trap can be set. That is easily worth two million to me, no questions asked.

Schroyer employs, by contract, among others, about fifty top flight hackers and pirates in Thailand, where all copyrights cease to exist. He keeps an "information management service" in San Antonio as well. The Thailand guys usually work on unlocking operating systems and office suites or making movies and music available to the world. They aren't doing it because they don't believe in copyrights or licenses or profits, but because it helps them stay in practice for straight up covert Nerd-Ops. They also help software and entertainment corporations write security locks for their products.

Their projected scenario, which is about to go into play, is one which this group has been theorizing and working on for years, and it has a 96% expectation of success, from the modeling they have done. They have been looking for an appropriate target, reason, and of course, payday to warrant its launch. The results that follow and many other parts of my tale have been relayed to me by multiple sources that I consider very credible, or relayed in video form. So, if at any time it appears that I am telling you something I could not have seen . . . that may not be entirely true.

What they will do today is to hack the banking infrastructures of Kongo and the Kongo press. They will add a single sheet to the national, regional, and local papers that says that the government has a surplus of money and is going to share it to everyone in the nation because it is, after all, their money, and today the government feels it should give some of it back, in hopes of stimulating their economy. This is a line of crap because the government is certain that everything in the nation belongs to the government, which means it belongs to about one hundred people who own everything AS the government, even when it is, on paper, owned by someone else. But the message shows up in eight languages, on four pages of the paper, one half page ad each, moving the other stories around their added material, and by four in the afternoon the next day, everyone would know about it. CNN, MSNBC and FOX are informed about the "sharing" scheme an hour or two after the presses have finished rolling and the trucks have driven the product away. Schroyer's people will also infuse the television and radio channels with computer generated ads that say there is also a national reward, a gift from the President's own money. The computer generated character they will use is even made from images of the president. In some of the ads the "President" will even say that he has all this money because he has been "screwing you over for so many years of raping and pillaging your people and land." They'll take all of the money of the President, and all of the Vice Presidents, and cabinet members, and more, and move about a fifth of it into every private bank account of every citizen they can find and move the rest of the money into a couple of dozen accounts in Kuala Lumpur. Then, the pirates will go on what they call an eBay binge, and they order everything useful that they can imagine, and have it all shipped to individual people directly. They will use the federal citizens' registry database to get all the names and addresses, as well as employment situations they need. The federal treasury will be completely depleted after three hours, and even the military will not work on spec. They'll quit working entirely in just under two days because there is no hope of the money ever coming back. The process will be a complete success because they move the money out of the country so quickly and send the goods immediately. The people are going to be so ecstatic about getting so many useful things that they won't even consider what they need as opposed to what they got. The military will soon hunt down and kill the previous leadership, mostly because they are furious, and because they have hated them all the time they've been in power, and because they can. But afterward, they'll do it because they know that they cannot really pull off a coup in the newly established, bizarre economic environment, so they will retire. Most people will spend the next few weeks trading what they have for what they want or need, and in a couple of months it will be a fairly capitalized country, in real time. And although I would not see it, I will hear about it afterward and be glad.

Back in the Present

By now it is 2:10 in the afternoon, and the course is decided. In four hours, it will be four in the morning Kongo time, and the papers will already be in route to the readers. The banks will begin bleeding money to the tune of several billion dollars a minute but will not discover it for half a day or more when their accounts will be almost entirely empty. The hack will even cause all their internal indicators to show there is no movement of money until after noon. I have transferred the payment to Schroyer from my personal money, a literal box of cash that doesn't have a name on it. All of this is in place, ready, running, and unstoppable; then it happens.

My head gets hot, my vision blurs, the room begins to vibrate and go black. Spinning! Bang! "Hi, Honey, I'm home." What? "Ethyl!?!" Who said that?

My eyes open as the fog clears, and there is the doctor's face above me and a nurse holding my wrist, staring at her watch . . . the wall and ceiling in view behind them is mine. There are a few others in the room, including Bernard, who steps forward and says, "Is he okay, doc?"

"All indications are that he will be fine soon. He seems to have had a serious shock that resulted in what looks almost like a small stroke. Everything just misfired for a bit like a computer trying to run too many processes at once or having a sudden memory overload. In the old days, nerds would call this a 'stack overflow' error. It must have been her."

"Doctor," says the nurse, "he's stirring. All the vitals are good. All the tech reports are accurate." She hands him the tablet.

The doctor says, "Mr. Danz, you gave us quite a start. You had something of a minor ischaemia a couple of hours ago." He sees the baffled look on my face. "It's a small stroke! You had a shock, and then all of a sudden, you were on the floor twitching, and in a bit, you stopped. It was probably a combination of lack of sleep and the events of the day."

"Ethyl?" I ask. Had I seen her? Was she real or did I hallucinate?

"Yes," a voice comes from in the corner of the room. She steps forward and I can see her . . . Ethyl. "Are you okay, Mister Danz?"

It is her, but how? Right now, I really don't care how and don't even think "how?" Right now, all I really care about is that it is her and that I am not dead or dreaming or in a coma – though even that would not be so bad – as long as it is her. The doctor steps back as she comes to my side and takes my hand. Like the soup and the bed of the baby bear, her hand feels just right. "Is he okay, doc?" She says over her shoulder, "Does everything work alright?"

"Yes, Ms Ethyl, everything seems to be working fine," the doc replies. "I guess we could leave you in charge for now, if that's okay with you, Mr. Danz?"

"Thank you, Doc." I say, "How's Gerhardt doing?" I ask Bernard.

"He's worried about you, but otherwise, he is pretty good. I am on my way to see him now."

And they clear out, leaving me with Ethyl, who, once the door closes, rips open my pajama shirt, launching buttons across the room. It seems to be her thing. The door opens briefly, and Bernard says, "Oh, I'm sorry! I didn't mean . . . I'm sorry!" and he slams the door. Ethyl, barely slowed by his entry and exit, continues, and we are where I want to be, beginning again, and she knows it. The sun goes down, and she goes to the kitchen for a sandwich, which we share, but after that and a little digestive rest, we are back at it again, as if the only thing we need more than food is each other. The food and drink are but a necessary afterthought. We are like ferrets in springtime, and in the morning, there are covers to be found, but none to be had as they are almost all on the floor. Somehow, one of the pillowcases ended up on a blade of the ceiling fan. Not sure about how that happened. Ethyl says that in a moment of intense delight, she "accidentally" pulled it from the pillow, and having discovered it in her hand, she just threw it. Well, there you go!

The sun is coming up, and the glare is beginning to invade the bedroom as my eyes begin to clear. There she is, perfect and smooth, laying on my right side, her right leg over mine, and resting in my arms. I scratch gently behind her ear with my left hand, and her head lifts to face me, and I kiss her, "Good morning." She gives a low hum of a response. "Shower?" She shakes her head. I head for the shower, and in a few minutes, I am dressed and ready for the day. I find her in the kitchen, standing at the end of the counter, naked, eating some sort of sugar puffed cereal that is only legal and available in Tejas anymore. That is when I see it.

She is, for lack of a better word, perfect to the eye. She doesn't have a mark on her . . . not a scratch or a cut, no entry wound, and certainly not a chunk of flesh missing at the exit wound from the other night. "How could that be?" I think to myself. "That's impossible!" I say.

"What's impossible?" she asks.

"It's not possible that you not be . . . I saw you shot. I held you in my arms and felt the hole in your back." I have been too busy being too happy to really see her or think about it, and I was enjoying what we were doing so much . . . maybe it's a dream, that I have entirely failed to ask the reasonable question of "How?" But I am asking it now.

"Oh, wow!" she says, putting down her spoon and turning toward me, "I thought you knew." She looks at me as a mom looks at her child who has just learned that his puppy has died or that there is no Santa. Her eyes have that same empathetic pity and wish to console me. "I'm so sorry. If I had known you didn't know we would have had a much different reunion." She slowly approaches and places her hands on my face, "I am Five." She pauses for a moment and says, "She was Two." She pulls my face into the crook of her neck and shoulder and holds me for a moment that seems like eternity. I don't cry openly, and it isn't because I am being strong or manly, but because I am in an absolute state of shock, is my assistant and girlfriend – are we calling her my girlfriend – a . . .

"Are you a Symm?" I ask, not knowing if it was the politically correct thing to call her or if it would be taken as some sort of slur.

"Yes, Joshua, I am a Symm." She says it with clarity and without hesitation. "Last week, I was your pilot and can be again if needed."

"I don't understand. How do you know . . . did she . . . do you?" I can't formulate a question. It is like I have a hundred of them – questions – and they are running around like sugar laced children inside the bouncy house that is my head, and they will not stand in line and take their turns, no matter what I say to them or how loudly I shout at them inside my head. "Aaaahh!!!" I scream like a woman, and grabbing some keys, I bolt from the apartment. I take the elevator to the basement garage, and the questions keep stirring and swimming in my head like people jumping from the Titanic into churning waters full of more people. My brain seems to be drowning. DING! The elevator stops, and I run out, not knowing where to go. I look at the keys in my hand, and there is a remote. I press the "unlock" button on the blipper, and I hear a couple of honks and chirps behind me. I spin around to do it again, and with the honks and chirps, I can see flashing lights that showing my way to freedom. I get in the car that looks like a new Mercedes, and vroom, it starts like a race car. I put it in gear and speed out the garage so fast I think I snap off the plastic arm that keeps people from unauthorized exiting. Stupid arm isn't actually much good anyway.

My next conscious thought is pulling into a town in Mexico at least a hundred miles in country. I don't know its name. I have apparently stopped and gotten some cash somewhere because that is what I am using to pay for gas, thirty-five gallons of gas . . . nearly $300. Damn! I have lunch in Tampico and stop for dinner and another fill up in Veracruz and a bed for the night. The next day I drive to Merida, where the real disappearing begins.

Once in Merida, I get a room at a luxury hotel and let the concierge know that I am interested in selling my car. I am not amazed when he tells me that he knows a guy. The most important words when I was in Philadelphia were, "I know a guy." Same here. The "guy" in this equation is a mid-level family man, a runner who transports goods and individuals for a small cartel. They have a few hundred workers at various levels, but this guy wears nice clothes, not tatters, well pressed. We agree on $85,000 Texican, in cash, with a .357 Baby Eagle in the case with three clips and two boxes of ammo, for personal use, of course. I give him the registration, signed over, write out a bill of sale, just in case, take the money and the gun, and leave him with the bill for lunch. He doesn't mind. The car is worth over 175 grand, and he knows I want to disappear. The money will allow that pretty well because, even with a legal transfer of the car, which this is, it will take at least a month before the paper trail throws up any red flags back home.

I take $200 from the case and go into a thrift shop of sorts and buy half a dozen shirts, two of which are Hawaiian looking, three pairs of pants, three shorts, some deck shoes that do not need socks to be comfortable, and an old leather suitcase with a shoulder strap that looks like it has a million miles on it. Sixty bucks for all of it! That is a good deal, all things considered. I buy some disinfectant foot powder for the shoes and fill them up when I stop at my new digs in the barrios near Kanasin. It is twenty dollars a night for a room with a toilet and sink. That's all I need right now. I pay for five nights. I bring a pair of six packs back to the room, giving a cold beer to the guy at the desk, and take a day to review my options, and my life as I know it.

I am confused, angry, and unhappy with what I now know about a lot of stuff. I was confused by the enormity of it all, and the new "Ethyl," and the details of what she knows, and doesn't. I am angry that Ethyl is gone and more confused that she isn't, and I am unhappy that I had lost her, found her, and left her, and the confusion begins again. The following midnight, having had eleven beers for breakfast, lunch, and dinner, I dump out the disinfectant from my new used shoes, take a taxi to Tekoh, and in the morning, a trambilla to Dangringa. I sleep most of the trip, all of the way in the back left corner of the bus so I can rest against my bag, with it lashed to my body.

From the sea on the east to the western suburbs, Dangringa is about two miles wide and about the same size from north to south, and as it turns out, I am not the first gringo to disappear down here. I also figure that I will not be the last. It is a nice place and, for the most part, pretty friendly to yanks with a little money. "Yanks" is apparently what they call anyone gringo that was from the north. I could have been born and raised in Mexico City and I would have been a yank to most of these folks. That's okay, as long as the beers are cool, tequila fast, and the women warm and friendly, I don't care what they call me. Most of the bartenders and barmaids call me Danny. I like Danny! It is a warm and friendly name that is definitely "yank" but doesn't come off as rich or pretentious. It is a name that, when shared with a smile and a tip, gets me all the attention I want and none that I don't want. I'm not living high on the hog, but I don't lack for anything either. I have been there for six or eight months, I have dated or been with about three dozen women, I have consumed a hundred gallons of beer and a third as much tequila. I bought a small boat, learned to sail, crashed my boat, sunk my boat, and I still haven't gone through a third of the money. I have been fairly smart about one thing though, and that is that I don't build up too much of a presence. I will stay in one flop house for a week or two and use a single bar for that same amount of time, then I will move to another bar, another part of town, then to Belize City for a month, followed by Ladyville for a few weeks, and if someone sees me having known me from a few weeks ago, I would not be important enough to them for me to be truly noticed. I grow a beard, shave it, grow it, and trim it scruffy. But even this can't last forever.

Back in Dangringa, I am spending my third night with a woman named Leticia, and more than I can hope, she delivers. Leticia is about five foot three and a bit on the gordita side for some guys, but she is extra soft in all the right places, and she can dance, which for some reason is important to me. I have learned that I enjoy dancing and that I can; so we dance and drink and eat everything we wish. Then we dance some more, and after the dancing, she is even more fun than I can remember. No, really . . . I can't remember. If her sexual history were to be specified by my memory, she could still be a virgin from all I recall, but I doubt it. We are dining and drinking one night when we meet another yank, named Mike, who is keeping company for only the second time with a tiny little woman named Teresa. It is a rather charged and entertaining night until a friend of Leticia comes into the cantina where we're imbibing in libations and tells her that her "Sancho" has returned, a couple of days early, he is looking for her, and since Sancho has brothers on the local police force, he isn't looking alone. "They have been to the gringo's room and found a gun. They can't be far behind me."

Suddenly, the saloon style doors swing open so hard that one of them falls off the wall. "Sancho, no," is all I hear from Leticia as Mike reaches across the table and grabs my sleeve, dragging me out the back door and into his jeep. There is a chase by some cops that follow us through most of north town and out Melinda Road; we circle north into the neighborhoods and east again, then south like a bolt of lightning down Pen

Road and across the bridge where it turns into Ecumenical Drive, then another mile or so to an open field near Hummingbird Highway where there is a helicopter.

What I don't know is that Teresa had seen me the night before, when she was out with Mike, and had recognized me. Tonight she is "spotting" me so that I can be retrieved by Gerhardt's friends and returned to my previous life, already in progress. Apparently, the world had been informed that I had re-adopted my hermit ways. She thinks she has lost her reward when she hears Mike's chopper start up just a few hundred yards from the bar. The call comes in asking where to find me, and she has an answer, "He is in the big nosed helicopter leaving Ecumenical and Hummingbird Highway right now." As they enter Belize, there are reports of gunfire toward the chopper, which flies, smoking and limping, about three miles out Hummingbird, turns almost due west from the edge of town, and in about ten miles, it drops into the jungle on the verge of some farmland just southwest of Sarawina. They stay at about 3000 feet following the satellite reports of the copter into the night. When it goes down, they are on the scent, and in the pale morning light, they land in the crops just to the north. What looks like a S.W.A.T. unit discharged out of the rear cargo door of the eighty-five foot long Caribou 3, VTOL by Neo De Havilland. They come to the crash site where Mike and I are having breakfast, or what passes for breakfast at this moment. They make certain we are okay, gather all of Mike's personal possessions, rush us out of the jungle and into the plane. Two of the guys stay behind and meet us in the plane after about two or three minutes. We go up sixty or so feet, then south just past our wreckage, which immediately flashes into a Thermite detonation as we fly by, west about ten miles and then north at nearly a thousand miles an hour, still just above the ground. In a half hour or so, we turn north by northwest; I can see Polaris in my window. In an hour more, we are landing on my rooftop and I hope I have a new pilot and friend. Teresa has a $10,000 finder's fee; the police of Dangringa have a bag full of cash and a new gun for their chief. Leticia has her Sancho back, but Sancho decides that he wants Teresa instead, since she has all the party money. Leticia decides to keep her Sancho and Teresa, at least until the money runs out, and this makes Sancho a very happy man. So, happy endings all around, sort of.

We are met on the rooftop by Gerhardt and Ethyl . . . ish. Mike and I exit the plane and walk to the rooftop airlock. The Caribou flies off as the door to the airlock closes, and Mike says, "I liked that chopper. She took everything I had, but she was mine."

"We'll make it right," I say, fixing my gaze on Gerhardt.

"I could have fixed it, ya know. I had fixed worse on it," he continues. "Hell, just a little reframe and skin the tail and some new pots and rotors, and all would have been good as new. Not that much really." The more he rants, the more he sounds like Mr. Scott.

"Excuse me, sir. My name is Mr. Gerhardt, may I ask whom am I addressing?" He extends his hand for Mike to shake.

"I'm Mike Rollins, the pilot whose helicopter was just burned to a crisp by your jack-booted storm troopers."

"Mister Rathke's men do not wear jack boots, sir," he blurts out. "That would show very poor fashion sense." This comment slows Mike's roll, just a little. Mike looks at him, flummoxed at the reply. "Mr. Rollins, we appreciate your predicament, but . . ."

"My 'predicament' you say," Mike starts up again, "it is always the 'predicament' of the little guy when the big man rolls over his car or takes his job or . . . and then there is that 'but' which always means it is too bad for a guy like me." Gerhardt interrupts him again – loudly this time.

"Mr. Rollins, it is the 'but' that should have caught your undivided attention, BUT in a different way. I was going to say, we are grateful for your having taken care of Mr. Danz and would gladly buy you a brand new helicopter exactly like that one."

"Friend . . . that was a Sikorsky UH-34 D! The original 'Ugly Angel' and they don't make those anymore. You can't just go down to the chopper store and get one off the shelf. Oh, yeah," he gets silly with his head bobbing from side to side, "I'll take mine in yellow, if ye don't mind." Mike is about to blow a gasket.

Gerhardt places his hand flat on Mike's chest and says, "If you want another just like it, we will find it and buy it, or we could have one made from parts. Or," then there is the pause and this time Mike is on point, "would you prefer an upgrade of some sort." Mike's face turns into a singular question mark.

"We are very grateful . . . and very, very wealthy," I say, as if continuing Gerhardt's thoughts to their natural conclusion.

"Well," Mike says slowly, and half as a joke, "I did have my eye on one of those new Chinook's." He smiles, "I used to fly one of the old ones, and a jungle cargo friend of mine says the new ones handle like a dream."

"And they are made right here in San Antonio," says Gerhardt, "at Brooks City Boeing."

"Holy shit! We're in San Antonio?" I nod. "TEXAS?" he shouts.

Gerhardt chimes in, "Yes."

"I did not see that coming." He looks beyond the roof for the first time since we landed. I ease him into the stairway, and we walk down to my apartment. We talk a little about his flying experience as we go.

"Can you get me a resume tomorrow or the next day?" I ask as we get to my kitchen.

"Sure," he says, "but why?"

"Yes, Mr. Danz," asks Gerhardt, "Why?"

"I would like Mike to be my new flight guy, but I need some sort of skills sheet to know what I can put him in charge of. After all, if he is just a chopper jock, I wouldn't want to toss him behind the yoke of a hypersonic VTOL jet plane. Right?"

"Mr. Danz, you barely know this man." Looking to Mike, Gerhardt says, "No offense, but you just met."

"I understand," says Mike, "I may not even want a job with you guys," which tweaks Gerhardt just a little, and I like that.

"What do you mean, may not even," Gerhardt is off beam.

"Chill, dude," says Mike.

"Yeah, Gerhardt, chill," I say, "how about Mike stays with me tonight, and we discuss this and more in the morning. Hungry?" I look around, Gerhardt's hands gesture no and Mike is raising his hand while heading for the fridge.

85

Shaking her head to the offer of food, Ethyl says, "Would you like me to stay, Mr. Danz?" She pauses briefly then, "I could help catch you up on matters since you began your vacation, sir."

"No thank you, Ethyl," I say, a little bit angry still, "I will see you in the office." Then I realize that I don't even know what day it is. "Wait a minute. What's today?"

"Thursday, Boss," says Ethyl.

"See you Monday then. Mike and I need to decompress."

"Sir," injects Gerhardt, "I will see to it that you get updates on your desk about sweeteners, batteries and Kongo by first light." He is looking sternly at me like a chastising uncle that has been left in charge of the kids and has not had a good experience of it.

"Shall I see you on Monday too, or should I just expect your call?" asks Ethyl.

"Yeah, sorry. Look, I'm sorry you two. I will probably see you tomorrow sometime, but I really don't want to get back to the grind until Monday. Okay?" They both give me a bit of a smile and wave, "See you then, then, THEN." They turn to go but still look a bit concerned. "Really, guys, I will be okay." They leave unceremoniously through the front door.

"What's to eat here?" says Mike, still poking about in the fridge.

"I really don't know." I say, "I haven't been here in months." He looks at me like I just said something ridiculous. "Seriously! The last time I was here, it was January."

"She said you were on vacation. What kind of job lets a guy take a vacation for eight months?"

"I own the place." His eyes open and his jaw drops open a bit. "This tower is just one of over 150,000 enterprises that I either own, or own a piece of, in forty or fifty countries. So, in this particular case, what Ethyl calls a vacation is really more like me running away from home. But this time, there is no joining the circus. I guess instead, I kind of became the circus. It really has been a very strange several months."

"I wish I could have been there," he says.

"Yeah, I wish I could have been there too," I reply. "I don't remember all of it . . . or even most of it, most of the time. But, Leticia was a bucket of fun."

"Hey, if you're so rich, why am I digging around in a near empty fridge? Can't we go out for dinner or order a pizza or something?"

"I think if I head for a door again, the world may come completely unglued. But we can surely order something in." I look at him assuredly, "Is pizza what you want?"

"Yeah, that sounds great. How about pepperoni, mushrooms, and extra cheese?"

"How about beef sausage, mushrooms, black olives, and extra cheese?" I reply.

"How about adding some onions to that and we got a deal?"

I go to the desk and get my tablet and begin to place the order, and a security check pops up saying, "We haven't heard from you in a while. For verification of identification, please enter your pin." I enter the pin, place the order, specify delivery to arrive at the "rear access," and in thirty minutes it has arrived. Actually it is only about twenty five minutes because the store is just three or four blocks away. I also order a couple of six packs of Shiner for another fifty, and the night is planned. The pizza drone arrives, having stopped at the ice house first and picked up the beers, while the pizzas were cooking. Once the pies are ready, they are loaded into the delivery drone, which carries them to the "rear access," which for me, is on the balcony beside my pool, 138 floors above the lobby. You gotta love that "Super Pizza Executive Express Delivery!" It's a little pricey, but if you gotta have it delivered right away, it is the price that must be paid. Advantageously, the drone doesn't have any traffic to encumber delivery, either. The pizzas are $18.50 each, times two, plus $10 SPEED per pie, plus the beer, and a tip for the cook, comes to a hundred fifty bucks. But it's well worth it tonight.

While we wait for the beer and pizza to arrive, I show him around the apartment. I lead him to a suite with a private bath/shower and large closet. Also, I let him know that if there is anything in the fridge or cupboards he wants, that he is to make himself at home. When the pizza arrives, we get a couple of plates and stack three pieces of pie on each and a bottle of beer in our hands, putting the rest in the ice box; we check the video library and put on an old Schwarzenegger movie, from just after his political days. It is a thing called "*The Last Stand*" that shows just how tough an Austrian octogenarian redneck can be. Pretty cool! I love that part where Arnold bursts through the door and lands on the floor. The old counter clerk asks, "How ya' doin' Sheriff?" and Arnold answers, "Old." Fun movie! After that, we put in "*Unbreakable*" and both doze off in about ten minute's time. I don't know why I am drawn to the Pre-Secession movies. Hmm. We wake up in the living room, each in a Lay-z-boy recliner, about as rested as one can legally be these days.

When we get up, finally, I realize that Mike only has the clothes that are still on his back. I let him borrow some sweats and sneaks, and we go out to get some duds. I call to the office and ask Ethyl to have a car available for us, which she does. We each shower, dress, and go down to the car. In thirty minutes or so, we are in the North Star Complex shopping. Between the trendy teen and 'tween stores, Goth shops, slut-puppy stores, and the snooty clothes places, we manage to find a Penney's, a Macy's, and a Dillard's so we get him outfitted in some jeans and cargo pants, a collection of shirts that match his style, a new bomber jacket to replace one left at a Mexican table, and a couple of suits, just in case. We also get him outfitted with some new tech: phone, watch, and wallet. All in all, a small price to pay for saving my ass in Belize. This is, however, just the beginning.

We have seen a hundred people, tried on or handled a thousand bits of gear and walked a few miles; all inside the recently renovated six story mall. We have lunch in the food court at a gyro shop where we enjoy some lamb and couscous with a black lager beer. We talk about sports, though I know little to nothing, having been out of the loop for a while. We shop some more and get all the things a guy needs to have a life these days . . . razor, trimmer, body scrubber. All the while, every time I try on something, I come out and find him tinkering with his phone, like a corporate executive keeping in touch with his empire. After all of that we go to Casa Rio on the river for a mid-day meal and a bit of a business chat. It really is a wonderful place, with a wall of glass panel doors facing the river, carved Mexican architectural enhancements all around, bright fiesta colours everywhere, and some of the best enchiladas north of the Rio Grande.

"Can you give me your number?" he asks.

"Sure" I say, handing him my card. He shoots the card with the camera in the phone, and the NuGle Contax adds all the info to his contacts. He then opens an e-mail and sends me a note with an attachment. The attachment is a resume with all of the training and experience he has known as a pilot and trainer, ending with a rescue flight that crashed into the jungles of Belize. It turns out, he can fly, and teach about flying, almost everything from small props to fighter jets, from helicopters to passenger planes. He had apparently flown with American Airlines at one time, back when there still was an American Airlines – before they sold to Mexicana. "Is all of this true?"

"Yes," he says, "you can verify every line of it with an FAA background check, as well as my Texas registration and instructors history, which are all readily available." I mail him back an offer.

It says only, "Apartment in my building, two bedroom or three as requested, all bills paid, full health and dental, no co-pays or deductibles, $300,000 a year, and as a signing bonus, a brand new, turbo/electric drive system Chinook, right off the line. We will be replacing your Sikorsky UH-34D as a courtesy, fully restored and updated, as a repayment for the one lost saving my ass; yes, Ethyl found one. You will be my personal pilot and aircraft manager."

I then tell him, "Of course this means that most of the time you may be doing a lot of nothing. At other times, you would be unavailable for days on end."

"Is that Chinook for real? Free and clear!?!" he asks.

"Free and clear," I say, "and if you insist, we can even add your annual registry expenses to the contract."

"Joshua, do you realize that this is an $80 million dollar aircraft?"

"Then I guess we better make that a forty year contract, eh?"

"Fine by me! You gotta be the weirdest billionaire on Earth."

We shake hands and have a deal.

"I'll have Gerhardt draw up the contracts, and we can do the autograph part later on. But now, what? It's Friday, and I have no plans and no ideas for plans." I send a copy of my offer and Mike's resume to Gerhardt and suggest that he write up a forty year contract for the terms listed, and I suggest that he build in an adjustment for inflation that is triple whatever the economy does. I want Mike getting a raise each year, especially if he is going to be saving my ass again someday.

Rehumanizing

We're going out without a plan, to have too much fun. We start the weekend off with a trip to a bar that, unknowingly, was homage to Gilley's from back in the previous 70's and 80's. No one remembers the movie *Urban Cowboy* and only think of John Travolta as that kid from late night classic TV, always scamming to get over Mister Kotter. It never really worked out for them. Kotter was Ricky and all the kids were Lucy. Wow! Shows how old I may be.

Before we leave, I remember Gerhardt meeting us in the basement/garage and asking for my keys.

"Mr. Danz, it would be irresponsible for me to allow it, and unwise for you to be out and about, considering the events in Belize and the hospital in New York, without security and with your own hands on the wheel."

"Come on, Gerhardt. I can drive." I say glibly, "I got skills."

"That may be true, sir, but we have a considerable investment in you and the company that provides your insurance wants you protected." A man that resembles Terry Crews steps forward – large, black, six four or more, massive in the chest, narrow hips, and tight everywhere else, with a chiseled face of determination – he has an uncommonly affable smile. "This is Benson. Whenever you leave the tower, especially for entertainment purposes, Benson will be with you."

"Is he human?" I ask with a grin.

"Yes, Mr. Danz, he is quite human. He has a few associates that he will introduce you to so that you know who is on your side. They are paid by retainer, monthly installments, and a big bonus for every six months, one year, and five years that they keep you alive." He is quite stern when he says, "It is a considerable motivator. Is it not, Mr. Benson?"

"It certainly is," he says in a booming whisper of a voice. A stretched Bentley pulls into the garage, and it is amazing. It is a classic 2022 New Continental GT Speed Convertible with leather on Kevlar for the roof and Kevlar over ceramic and mesh body panels. It has been stretched to allow a rear facing seat behind the driver/navigator pod and a new polymer glazing that can withstand a .60 Teflon tracer round from thirty feet, up to fifty times per pane, Benson later explains. "Right this way, gentlemen." He directs us to the car. A man almost as formidable as Benson steps out of the right side of the car, where the steering wheel happens to be. It also happens to be pushed right up against the dash so the driver can exit the car in a hurry. I discover later that it extends by nearly seven inches for driving. The driver opens the door for Mike and me, and Benson introduces him. "This is Stephen. He is ex Navy Seals, proficient in urban, desert, and jungle warfare and survival, as well as expert in almost all small arms, foreign and domestic. He worked with Houston S.W.A.T. for four years in team building and non-lethal tactical options, as well as a stint as a sniper in the third and final Afghan war. He helped lead the final assaults that made any future wars in Afghanistan unnecessary." He is blonde, 6'3" and 245 and wears form-fitted body armor under his shirt. It is about a fifth as thick as those old police vests. Very nice tech!

In what may have been mock humility, he shakes my hand and says, "Nice to meet you, sir. We will do our very best to keep you safe."

I just now realize that my life has become a history of Travolta movies. Somewhere in the past I was Vinnie Barbarino, trying to get by everything and everyone. I did *Face/Off* at the hospital, while simultaneously playing as the *Boy in the Plastic Bubble*. Every once in a while I get to play *Michael* and help someone out for no apparent reason and now, in part thanks to this weekend, but in reality, because of my entire life, I am about to become more like Chili Palmer in *Get Shorty* and *Be Cool*, manipulating others into success and Gabriel in *Swordfish*, determined to plan for and overcome all obstacles for a greater good that includes my own personal success, but let's all hope I don't become Charlie Wax.

"If it is okay with you sir," Stephen says, "We would like to begin training you on Monday."

"What do you mean, training me?" I ask.

Gerhardt butts in, "We have listened to Mr. Benson's explanation of how to best protect you and part of that is teaching you to help protect yourself. On Monday, you will have your first self-defense class."

"Actually, Mr. Gerhardt, it is Defense, Resistance, Protection, and Evasion. And it is not just Mr. Danz, but you and Mike as well, if you wish." Benson explains, "It is a package deal, and trust me guys, it will be fun," he says with a grin, "except for the parts you hate," he concludes with a severe frown.

"In the meantime, we are still gonna have fun tonight, right?" Mike asks.

"Yes, sir." says Stephen. "The only thing you need to know before we go is that there is a red button-panel on the door next to your seat, Mr. Danz. If you slap that panel, no one can get into the car but one of our people. It will keep out almost anyone and anything. It is your defense cocoon. Not only do you have the locking system to keep people out and the bullet resistant glass and body panels, but the whole car becomes charged so that it cannot be touched." He clicks a remote on the keys, and we can all hear a sudden, single crackle, and a voice comes from under the car repeating, in English and Spanish, "Do not attempt to touch this vehicle, it will hurt you." He pushes another button and blip blop bloop, it stops. Stephen says, "The lawyers told us that the recording would keep us from being sued by any 'Good Sams' that may try to get you out."

Benson reaches for the door, and as his hand touches the handle, "Arrgh! Arrgh! Make it stop!" He writhes and jerks about like he is suffering terribly. "Just kidding! It would be far worse than that appeared for anyone that touches the car when armed. And we can arm it by remote from over a quarter mile away or by phone."

We do have too much fun this weekend. We go to that cowboy bar and dine at a Taco Cabana. There's still nothing like a chicken fajita taco with cheese and guacamole to fill the night. We go to an afterhours bar – legal, but open only from 1 AM to 10 AM – special license. We meet a couple of young ladies there – or maybe not – one gringa, Dawn-Lee from somewhere in Montana, and a one half Kickapoo maiden, who insists we just call her Feather. We dance a couple hours, get some tacos to go and then we all drink and sleep, sleep and drink in the back of the car as we drive to a casino in Eagle Pass . . .

Feather with me. Apparently the guys drive slowly because when we get there, the sun is well up. We pull into an underground or covered parking structure I think – I don't really remember – and we enter from behind. Those of us in the back of the car are a little toasted, so we don't see as much as we may have thought we did.

Feather is a rare and amazing beauty, being half Kick with a father of Japanese and Welsh heritage. The multinational combination is startling. I could stare at her for hours, and so I do, as I recall. It is nearly nine in the morning when we walk into the Casino. This place is old school in so many ways but also very modern in its décor, recently redone. As we walk in, we find the cages and swipe my Tex-Ex card for $10,000. They give me a cute little one pint plastic bowl of chips, one hundred chips, and a pair of key cards to a couple of suites above. I give Stephen and Benson each 500 in chips and Stephen says to Benson, "You got first watch." I don't remember much after that, but we must have had fun. I recall flashes of gambling, dancing, some sort of show with showgirls and magic, lots and lots of drinking . . . and I don't know what else.

I wake up next to Feather, and my phone says it is Sunday. The glare through the curtains says it is well after dawn, whatever time that is. The sun glares brightly through the window, even with the blinds drawn, and highlights the contours of her body. Most of the bedding is on the floor. She is lying on her stomach in the middle of the bed and, as I watch, she rolls over on her back. She is a vision of Sophia Loren and Raquel Welch with an unbelievably beautiful face. She stretches her arms and back and yawns; she curls her toes and pulls a bed sheet up enough to cover her hips and thighs and says, "Good morning." All I can do is to crawl across the bed and kiss her. Wow!

"Holy crap!" she shouts, bounding to her feet, pulling the sheet around her. "Is this the casino hotel? No! No! No! No! No!" She loses the sheet and takes her clothes and shoes into the bathroom, slamming the door. "If my grandfather finds out . . ."

"What?" I shout back, hopelessly expecting some sort of reasonable reply.

There is clumping and clamor from the bathroom and a little more banging about, "Where are my bra and panties?" she shouts, leaping from the door.

"I don't see them. What's wrong?" I ask.

"My grandfather runs this hotel, and all of his employees know me, and – oh, no, no, no – this is not good." She's scouring the room trying to find her panties. "I must have been really drunk or I never would have come here. Of all the places in the world we could have gone . . . HERE!?!" She looks in the drawers of the dresser and the nightstands, but there is nothing to be found but a Gideon.

"Look," she says, "you're a great guy, and I had a terrific time, but my grandfather is a really old fashioned guy. He almost killed my father for marrying my mom and contaminating the family line." She is crawling around looking under the bed and furnishings – found the bra. "If he knew I was with a white man . . . HERE . . . WHOA!!! . . . Something terrible could happen. He is not always a rational man."

"How bad can it be?" I ask. "It's not like you're some sort of royalty!"

She gives me a twisted ironic look that tells me that I have hit the nail exactly on the head. "Holy crap," is right.

"Fuck it," she says, "If you find my panties, burn them. This never happened." And with her bra mostly in her purse, with high heels in hand, she slams the door and disappears. Being naked, I am in no position or condition to pursue her.

I shower and dress and walk to a restaurant just down the road for breakfast. Their sign says something about pancakes, or waffles, I don't recall. Since it is a sunny and breezy morning, I walk, and it is nice. I order coffee and orange juice, three eggs over medium, and an English muffin. "Did you want bacon or sausage with that?" asks a waitress.

"No thanks. I don't eat pork." I say it, and then I wonder why. And I didn't say it mean, just . . . matter of fact. At that moment, a distinguished gentleman in his sixties walks in wearing a sport coat that looks as if it were made out of chamois, with a contrasting leather vest made of what could have been Moroccan leather, cordovan in colour. It is fresh. There is nothing American about his appearance. There isn't a tattered seam anywhere to be found. He has a bolo tie, ostrich skin cowboy boots, a solid men's cotton shirt with button down collar, and the best looking blue jeans I can recall, topped off with a sterling silver belt buckle which, as he gets closer I can see it says, "All Around Champion" over the top and "Calvary 2027" across the bottom. My limo pulls into the parking lot as he sits down at my table. I know who he is, and so does Stephen as he enters the room. I hold my finger up to stop Stephen, wag it a couple of times, as if to say "no," and point him toward the counter, which is where he goes. He orders a cup of coffee. Mine comes to the table, so I fix it with my usual five sugars and a fair amount of cream.

The gentleman at my table is Feather's grandfather, who introduces himself, but I honestly cannot remember his name. Still, his name is not what is important. What is important is his story. He tells me about Feather – who she is and what is expected of her and her importance to her people. She is a princess of some lesser degree, only because her mom had married sort of white. Mom was the eldest daughter of eight children – all daughters. Three died fairly young, and two had long since left the rez, found husbands and lives of their own, in New York and LA. Only the youngest (19 and 26) remain, but they are far more interested in trying to become pop stars, doing a bunch of weed and a little blow, and living more like modern Americans in a reality show, than anything primitive or tribal, which in this place isn't really very primitive at all. Whoever married Feather's mom could have been chief, but that was not going to happen for a white man, especially a mixed white man. She is still the hope of her grandfather, and he has already picked out a tribally acceptable groom for her. She is, from his point of view, engaged. He explains all of this, and then he asks me, "Do you love her?"

"Seriously, sir, I just met her a few days ago, and she may be the most beautiful woman I have ever seen," I tell him. "And there were several times in the past few days that I have thought 'I could look at this woman for the rest of my life.' But love? I think that Love, the kind of love I think you are speaking of sir, takes time. I met someone once, seems a hundred years ago, and I was struck like a coin between hammer and anvil. But even that, even then, it took years to mature into the kind of love we all think of when we say 'love' the way you just did." I bow my head a moment, then I look him in the eye, and say, "No, sir. I don't think its love."

"Then your weekend in our little nation never happened. Understand?" He looks me in the eye and sets a stack of cash on the table. "This is a refund from when you checked in. I don't want you and me to owe each other anything. Do you?"

I can say only, "No, sir." And he gets up and walks out the door. He stops for a moment to look at me and wave his right hand in front of him, palm down, not rigid, left to right. The waitress brings my OJ and refills my coffee.

"Your breakfast is about ready sir." And she scurries away. Stephen, Benson, Mike, and Dawn-Lee join me as my breakfast arrives. The waitress brought three more coffee cups, and Stephen brought his from the counter.

"Tip the counter girl, Stephen," I say, and he leaves her a five. I appreciate that. Lots of guys would have left a buck, but in my opinion, a classy guy never cheaps on a tip.

They all order, and I add a family size bowl of grits to the meal. I heard they do them right. I am not disappointed when they arrive. All they need is a touch of butter at the table and all is good. We all had a great weekend. Feather got out of her cage for a while . . . though I don't know how long she had been out when I met her or if she would escape again. Her grandfather got to hold on to some of his dignity, though I don't think anyone could actually take any of that away from him. Mike learned to eat grits and like 'em; Dawn Lee tried them, but didn't like 'em. Stephen and Benson are home boys from the True South, as well as being trained snake-eaters, who make it a policy to be grateful for any food that will stay down and nourish the body. But grits, like manna from heaven, nourish the body and the soul. Why do I know that? I think someone's momma used to say it. No matter, we'll be home a few hours after breakfast. My treat! School in the morning!

I leave the check sitting on the stack of cash with my coffee cup on top. The waitress comes running out to kiss me when she realizes what I left behind. I deserve to be without it, and in that moment, I can't think of anyone else that deserves it more. She must've put up with thousands of lousy tips, from unnamed and unnumbered customers, who would be ungrateful, and take it out on her, just because it was hot outside, the wife was grumpy, or they just did poorly at the tables. Besides, I need to do something good for someone today.

Live Fire

The room explodes as I awake to a face in my face shouting, "Get up!" All I can see is black eyes and there's the smell of bacon spanking my face as he yells at me, "Get up! Time to get you out of here. GO! GO! GO!" It is Benson. I don't dress or grab shoes. I sit up quickly, get my feet on the floor, and we are out the door. "This is Sean," he yells, as we pass by a shorter red-headed man who follows close behind with an early Glock – circa 2010. Sean is taller than me, shorter than Benson, more stocky in build, but quick in motion. We go through the apartment in what seems to be about four seconds, past the front door, and straight into the elevator. Benson puts a hand on a lighted pad and suddenly, whoosh!!! It seems to take an eternity in seconds to reach our destination. Sean keeps his hand over my mouth all the way down, and all the while, he seems to be listening. We come running out of the elevator into a place I have never seen before, and we stop right after Benson clicks a stopwatch. "That'll do for a start." I notice that Mike is already here, barefoot, in boxers, in a place that I have never seen. Also there is Stephen and a couple of others, but they are fully dressed.

"Alright men, this is Terry, Sean, and Bubba," says Benson in a commandingly clear voice.

"This was a drill?" I say, still half out of breath from the excitement, looking around trying to understand where we are.

"Yes, Mr. Danz," says Stephen, "we had to get a baseline of how well you would respond to our directions in an emergency situation." He looks at Benson's watch. "One minute, twenty-nine seconds from bed to bunker! You did quite well, actually."

"Are you out of your damn mind? What the hell time is it anyway?" I shout.

"Five-forty-one, sir," says Sean, "sorry we're late."

A light bulb comes on in my head; "late" he says. I suddenly realize that time of day is a relative thing for these guys, that emergencies and attacks can happen 24/7. I am thinking about being in a hospital in New York, going in and going out, and realizing that they are just trying to prepare us for any eventuality that we had not thought about 'til recently. I am pissed that we don't have any coffee yet, and that it is quarter to six, but I understand. "Okay, the emergency evasion phase is done for now, right? So, can we get some coffee?"

"Mr. Danz, in this bunker is also a small apartment, about 2900 feet, with clothes and shoes to fit you already and supplies to meet your every need . . . even coffee and fresh dairy products, thanks to Ethyl. There are even a few other things that we wouldn't want left alone for long, but not many."

"Sean," Benson says, "could you please go with Mike to his apartment and get him some pants and a shirt on him." Mike makes a bit of a glaring face. "Some socks and shoes would be okay too." He pauses. "Just kidding! Let him wear whatever he wants. Also, Mike," he redirects, "you may want to pick out a few sets of clothes and shoes, etc. to bring down to be stored here in the bunker . . . just in case."

Mike and Sean take off, and Benson directs me, Stephen, and Bubba to the "armory" which opened by a hand print scan. Bubba put his palm on a screen, "Stand aside," he says with a distinct accent, and it opens a steel – a very heavy steel – panel in the wall. It doesn't swing open like a door, but rather slides outward on four chrome-moly rods, each about three inches in diameter. It looks to weigh several hundred pounds but slides open by nearly three feet in less than half a second and comes to a cushioned stop with a swoosh. There must be rollers on the bottom. We all enter the door, and on the other side, Bubba says, "Once you are on the inside, if you are in danger, press this button," he points out a plain red button about three inches in diameter and one inch tall, "or shout 'close' anywhere in the front room, and this door will close." He presses it with his pinky and WHOOM! In far less time than it took to open, it is closed. Louisiana – that's the accent; Bubba is bayou people.

"Beep-beep-beep" a light lit up as a tone sounded on each of what looked like a car alarm fob on each of my new protectors. "The elevator that Mike just took is attached to you, Mister Danz. This remote is bonded to my ID by a thumb-print scanner on one side and a series of buttons on the other." Bubba says, "This being lit up means someone asking for your elevator to leave you and come to them. I press this button, and it goes." And he does. "Each of your protectors has one."

Benson interjects, "Actually, only the principle security agents have one. At least one of the five of us will be with you at all times. We are your team. If anyone claims to be with our company and one of the five of us did not introduce you to them, get to a safe place. This is a safe place." He turns up the lights to a reasonable level and I look around only to find we are in an armory. "That is a safe place." He points to the rear of the room, away from our entry where the wall has another heavy metal door with a scanner. I put my palm on the scanner and the door slides open like the other, but on the other side of this door there is an apartment that looks like it came out of a *Jetson's* episode or a *Matt Helm* movie, back in the Dean Martin days, or maybe a scene from *Mad Men*.

There is a large room, about thirty by thirty-five feet, that has a kitchen in one corner with a large island for prep and serving. To the fore of there we find a dining area with a table that looks to be expandable to seat twelve. Then there is the "living area," so to speak, with a projecting TV and stereo. I look to the right rear and see a pool table, and against the right wall, an American Shuffleboard table (I love that game), followed by a conversation pit, and in the corner, to my immediate right, is the computer center, almost exactly like my computer setup upstairs. Between the kitchen and pool table, there is a hallway that goes to the bathroom and bedrooms. Terry comes to the table with supplies on a tray. He goes to the kitchen and makes himself at home.

"Ethyl brought the fresh items, but they had Terry get the stores for this place since he's the cook." Bubba says, snickering.

"I know that Benson and Stephen are with us," I say, "but why not have you and Sean help out?"

"Well, Sean is Irish, and I mean like REALLY Irish, and no one wants haggis in their icebox, and me bein' coon ass, they figure we would introduce you to me jes a bit more gentle like."

Just then Mike comes through the door carrying several articles of clothing on hangers and a handful of socks and boxers; Sean has two pair of sneakers and an unpleasant look about carrying another man's shoes. "Dude!" Mike says, "Did you see that armory? And I put my hand on the wall, and it opened up and . . ." he looks about in awe, almost dropping his clothes, "Wow! This place looks like the lair of a Bond villain. You gotta be the richest guy I never heard of."

"Down the hallway. First room on the right is yours," says Benson to Mike. "Each of the four bedrooms has a nice closet and a bathroom."

Mike takes his stuff to the bedroom, and I get a coffee. Heck, everybody gets a cup of coffee, even Mike who has just laid his clothes on the bed. "Double cream and triple sugar for me, thanks!"

"Let's do the tour," says Bubba. We walk down the hallway, coffee in hand, past Mike's emergency bedroom, which is about thirteen by thirteen with a walk-in closet about seven by six and a bathroom about the same size. The next bedroom on the right is the same, but facing the other direction, so its bathroom is back to back with Mikes. The third bedroom is on the left, after the guest bath, which has a typical toilet, sink, and tub, with a linen closet – about five by fifteen altogether. The third bedroom is about fifteen by fifteen and has a larger bath with an additional shower and more space in the floor. "Dis would be good for de mom-in-law."

"I don't really need a mom-in-law. Do I?" I respond.

"Now," says Bubba, "dis be de' master suite." He swings open the double doors at the end of the hall. He could have opened only one, but what fun would that have been? "As you can see, it is sumptuous in every detail." It has a king size bed with Amish oak nightstands on each side. There are two dressers, a high and low, on each side of the room, which is about fifteen by twenty. There is a sitting area with a small table and two chairs and another two chairs hanging on the wall above each of the low dressers. To the left is the hallway back to the closets and bath, each of which has an empty space of about six by six in their middle. One closet is empty and the other has one row of clothes, including pants, shirts, t-shirts (I hang mine) and one suit, with shoes below – two pair of sneakers, two pair of dress shoes, one pair of simple corduroy house slippers, and two hand guns of my future choice. "We are one hundred sixty feet below the surface, and it still looks like a better home than I have ever had."

"But there are windows!" I say to him, only to be corrected.

"What you see are not windows, but screens. They are displaying images from whatever part of the world you want to be living in, at the current time of day for that location." He goes to one of the "windows" and finds a small button on the right side of the screen's frame and presses it as he leans in to speak. "Antarctica" is what he says, and in a couple of seconds, the image changes to what looks like ice-flows and snow drifts with a view of a small bay with some penguins frolicking. I look at the windows of this room, and they are all looking at different views of the same place. If I get close enough to one I can see a wider view of the surrounds that are portrayed. It turns out that we subscribe to a service that allows a direct feed from over 300 hidden viewing boxes – called a "hide" – run by nature studies departments, from several universities. I think it is gnarly. We go down the hallway, back toward the main room, and I notice as I look into each room, that they also have an Antarctic view. Kewl.

"There are three places you can get on the elevator that comes here; any floor of your home, your office, and the garage. On all other floors – even the lobby – there is no access to it, and without you or an override, no one else can use this elevator. It is attached to you." He looks at Mike and me, and says, "Let's have some breakfast and then we'll go kill something."

He leads us back to the kitchen where we sit down for some frozen toaster waffles, juice, coffee, and berry jam. We all talk about whatever comes to mind. How 'bout them Spurs? Can't believe the Missions lost their best pitcher to the show. Didn't we used to have a symphony? More about women than I care to discuss. And in a while, Ms Ethyl is a topic of conversation, but only for a brief moment, before Mike and I put the kybosh to that. After breakfast we go out of the apartment, through the armory, and on our way Benson grabs two matching handguns and Sean brings four boxes of bullets – two hundred rounds. At the entrance we turn slightly left and discover a rifle and pistol ranges, and at the end of the shooters area, there is a weapons maintenance area with reloading equipment and all the tools of a gunsmith. I have no idea what to do with almost all of it, but I am still impressed that it is here.

"These are your class work for the day, boys," says Benson. "Bubba is our arms expert, only slightly better than the rest, so we will defer to him."

Bubba points for us to stand where the shooters stand in the pistol range, and then he walks to the front of the shooter's table. He takes the two guns from Benson and sets one in front of me and one before Mike. "What you see here is a Sig Sauer, .45 ACP handgun in the 1911 in the 'Traditional Tacops' configuration. This weapon has many available accessories, and clips are easy to come by, and it uses a nearly universal bullet. There are almost always some of these bullets lying around. The Sig is an incredibly reliable weapon, and it is a top ten choice for all law enforcement, peace keeping, military, para-military, and personal purposes. It is not a girly gun, and if you hit your target anywhere in center mass, he will go down. Even in body armor, you can take a man out of the fight with the sheer pain of the impact."

"Do we have to shoot center mass?" I ask, immediately recalling the answer.

"Only pull a gun if you feel a distinct need to shoot a gun, and only shoot a gun to kill someone. Shooting to wound someone usually takes too much time and skill, and most people are not that steady in a fight. If you want to live, just point it at the middle of the guy and squeeze." In a fell and swift motion, he turns around, draws his weapon from his holster, and puts four rounds through the chest area of a target about twenty feet away. "Almost anybody can do that." He holsters his gun. "All they need is a little training and a little practice. Each week we will be training you on a new weapon and each day you will practice with that weapon. On Friday's you get to play with all the weapons you have already been trained on."

"There will be thirty minutes on guns and thirty minutes on environment," says Benson, putting on his ear protectors, gesturing that we do the same. "We will get to that soon enough, but today, it is all about THAT gun." He picks up a full magazine, slides it into the handle, shows us as he releases the slide to engage the round, then he hands it to me. "Shoot 'til it's empty."

I take it in hand, point it at the target, and squeeze off eight rounds; five hit somewhere on the silhouette while three hit the surrounding black paper. "Wow! That seems familiar. Lemme try again." I eject the mag and load another, release the slide, and take a half breath as I think about the target, not the gun. I remember this from somewhere, then BAM!!! All eight rounds are gone, and the new holes in the other target are four in the chest, two in the neck, and two in the face. "I know this."

"Some people are just a natural with shooting." Bubba continues, "Some people say it has something to do with being able to make a mental connection between points A and B without seeing the line. Others say your eye sees the line, and your hand joins the conversation. I knew some rangers who had great success teaching people to shoot moving targets by mentally pushing the weapon at the target. I have seen these guys shoot a tin can in the air five or six times before it hits the ground . . . depending on the can, to be sure."

Mike loads his weapon and releases the slide. He adjusts his right ear muff a little, and with a thumbs forward grip, like he remembers from school, he fires eight rounds downrange. Six hit somewhere in the chest area and two in the black paper. He ejects his mag and loads another; releasing the slide as the gun moves forward, he leans into it and puts all eight in center mass. He reloads and another eight in center mass, only a little tighter with each magazine. "Practice," he says, sliding his clip out onto the table, "That's all I need." He is smiling as he lays down his weapon. "I was military once too. Remember?" he says with a bit of a smirk. "Even us flyboys gotta shoot sometime."

"Then practice is all that is needed this week," says Bubba, "not instruction. But next week, we move up."

"Tomorrow you will learn to breakdown, clean and oil that unit, but now, it is time for environmental training." Benson turns his gaze to Terry, "Terry, take them upstairs to change their clothes into whatever it is they wish to wear today and take them on their first tour of the building."

"I really do know my building, Benson." I say with some assurance.

"Really?" He asks, "Do you know about the maintenance areas and 'dumbwaiter' elevator? How about where security is and what they can or cannot see? Before this morning, did you know about this room?"

"Well," I say, somewhat sheepishly, "No, but . . ."

"Did you know that there is a 14,000 square foot, configurable, live fire, combat range right upstairs from here?" He can see my surprise when he says this. "I didn't think so."

"Shall we start with the service areas, sir?" says Terry. Benson nods with some hostility.

As we walk toward the elevator, I can hear him say, "Either these two are going to be among the best we've ever worked with, or the biggest pain ever in my shiny, black ass." Terry sniggers a little because he knows that we heard it. Over the next few months, we do enough training that Mike and I are beginning to feel like SWAT team members.

Home Again

"Back to the Penthouse, guys," says Terry as we arrive. "Get showered and in your duds for the day, so we can get started." He plops himself down in the living room with the TV. It still hasn't been "Texas" configured, so there are still channels down the left. I don't trust the "Big Brother" cam, so I keep a box of Curad Dots on the table so I can chat if I want and keep it covered when I don't want.

Since Mike had gotten dressed earlier, he only took off to his place for long enough to get his pocket stuff for the day; his wallet, keys, folding money, and he likes to keep a little change on him. By the time I am dressed Terry is letting Mike in the door. He has *Fox and Friends* playing on the box and has been listening to it while taking in the view, curtain back. "A couple of things I want you to see about your place, and really wherever you are in the Tower, wherever you are supposed to be, come put your hand on the window; palm first, then tap all your fingers once."

I put my palm on the glass and tap all my fingers once, and the glass goes dark. It becomes so dark that I cannot see the sunrise but as a faint glare in the distance. "Tap your fingers twice," he says next, and when I do the glass is clear. "At night the default position is dark and cold. At night, even with an infrared scope, you can see nothing inside this apartment unless you raise the shield. Benson had me cue it to your hand, Mike's, Gerhardt's, and Ethyl's." He looks at Mike and says, "Your apartment is the same way because Mr. Danz is expected to spend some time there, and we don't want him to be a target just because he went to visit you. It can also be activated by either of you whispering the word 'midnight' almost anywhere." I test that out and, like he says, it activates right away.

He crosses the floor to the door waving us to follow and shows us to the scan sensor pad by the door, just like the ones in the armory and bunker. "Each sensor pad has another level of security that lets you override everything including us entirely. If someone has duplicated or stolen our biometrics, and is trying to get to you, either of you, just put your hand on this pad, or any pad like it, turn your hand a quarter turn toward the thumb, and it will lock you in so tight that even Benson can't get in until you say so. It takes your permission or it takes three of us with both palm and retina ID. These pads only appear in totally securable rooms, and their arrangements are being finalized as we tour."

"I gotta ask," I say to him, "how could someone 'duplicate or steal' your biometrics?"

"Well," he stares directly into my eyes, "they could chop off my hand and pluck out my eye."

I look at Mike, who is suddenly feeling something in his wrist and blinking a bit.

"Shall we move on?" Terry asks. We take the stairs from the apartment to the office below, and I notice that there is a pad on each end of the stairs and on each landing, meaning that I can lock myself into the stairs with a flip of the wrist. Another one has been embedded under the top of my desk, above my knees, and under the top of my desk, on the left side, is a holster that has a gun, just like this morning's gun. "There are literally a dozen weapons hidden for you to get to on a moment's notice. Since there is no physical door between your and Ethyl's desks, there is a proton barrier in the walkway, in front of the wall, and the former partition has been replaced with three and a half inch titanium spun polycarbonate wall with automated opacity and reflectivity, and at the doorway, on the inside, a descending titanium-polycarb barrier. When the barrier is active, you can't punch through it with less than 200 rounds in the same square foot of glass, or a LAW rocket." He gestures for Ethyl to come in the office, and she does. "Once Ethyl is in the office, you and she are totally safe. Pull the gun." I do, and the doorway is suddenly sealed, and less than a quarter second later, the proton barrier snaps and crackles out loud as it comes on. "Watch this." He takes out his gun, same as mine, and fires four rounds at Ethyl's desk, BAM! BAM! BAM! BAM! But each bullet is disintegrated in the proton shield, and alarms go off. "Nothing is getting through that if you don't allow." He puts his gun away then puts his hand on the touch sensor by the window, behind a curtain. "Demonstration − Terry − 05," he says, and the alarms stop. "Ethyl, can you show the boss around the rest of the office?"

"Yes, Terry, I would be glad to assist," she says, but as she says it, a message scrolls across my vision; "Can we talk? Please? I will gladly show you the security?" She does too. She demonstrates for me how to control my own communications via my new phone − I can block out everyone from contacting me but my security team. She shows me how, with a touch of an app on my phone, I can find the nearest secure zone and activate it, in silence. Then she shows me how if I press the power button thrice in a row, Security would locate me and come a running.

We continue to look at the toys about the office, and Terry shows me that Ethyl's desk is armed, just like mine, but hers has a pair of .40 Baby Eagles for her lady-like grip. Actually, I know firsthand that she can have the kung-fu grip of a ninja warrior when needed, or at least her predecessor did.

When we are done with the tour and Terry has gone, I call Ethyl into the office for a brief, private confab. She brings her tablet, as usual. I don't really know what to say or how to say it, but we have to talk.

"I have a problem," I begin. "You are Ethyl, and you're not." She looks at me with understandable bewilderment.

"I understand what you are saying, and from a certain point of view, it makes perfect sense, but then again, deep inside of me, it is also completely wrong," she says back. "You do realize that I am not actually a machine, don't you?"

"Yes," I stammer, "but in some ways, I can't help think of myself as a pervert playing with a blow up doll in his mother's basement." I can see that these words make her a bit angry, to say the least. "I need to know; was having an affair with me part of Ethyl's programming or part of the job?"

"No! The 'programming' is not that proactive. Come here!" she says, wheeling her chair around to the end of the desk. "Come, sit right in front of me," she demands. I roll my chair to face her, up close. She says, "Can a blow up doll do this?" Then she leans in and slaps me. SMACK! "Not only could it not do that, but it has no reason to." I rub my face and lean back a little . . . to a safer distance from her. "I am a real person inside here! I am a real and living, flesh and blood, human being. I have some technological enhancements, but so do many of the women in Manhattan or Dallas, even right out there. That doesn't make them non humans, does it?" She reaches her hand out to touch my leg, and I flinch just a little. "Don't you understand, the problem is in the death, not the life? You saw Ethyl die, and I haven't. I don't want to. What I have seen, and remember, is the week before Gerhardt got hurt and right up to our visit in his hospital room." She gets a little teary eyed saying, "Whether you realize it or not, that was the very best week of my life, even if it doesn't seem to you to have been my life." She sits back as if to ponder and judge my expressions as she speaks. "My entire past is in my memory, medic, pilot, soldier, trainer, security expert, chef's assistant, nanny, and for about a week, your lover. It's all there. Sometimes it seems like different stories, but mostly it is all the same bit of film." She leans forward again, with puppy-dog-eyes, "Can't you understand this?"

"Amazingly," I say, taking her hand, "yes, I can. It is what I see in my own memory every day of my life." She is puzzled with my answer, and at the same time, she understands. "Sometimes, I have no idea who I am."

"Look, even before my position was elevated, seeing you come and go in the plane, watching you deal with Gerhardt, there was a bit of a crush. Watching you . . . mmm! After my change in position, well . . . you are suddenly available and I am your assistant . . . and more." She gazes at me like a lady bull dog eyeing a rib eye. "Even when I realize that I am looking at her memories, I am still looking at the man in my life. How she felt about you is, believe it or not, it's exactly the same way I would have felt about you, even without her memories. It is as if you are exactly the man that I never knew that I have always been looking for. That morning, after New York, when you woke up, I climbed into the bed of my lover, not someone else's that had been handed to me." She gets a quizzical look on her face like she almost doesn't understand what she just said. "Understand?" Her head tilts the other way. "Does that make sense? I realize that there are some difficult elements in our relationship, Boss, but can we get something of a 'start over' going here?" she asks.

"What did you have in mind?" I ask, feebly hoping that she isn't going to suggest something right here and now, partly hoping she will.

"How about dinner? How about I cook?" She says with those "come hither" eyes breaking me down.

"What did you plan to cook?" I ask, a little coy, a little curious.

"How about shrimp etoufee?" She glares at me. "I take Cajun to a new level."

"But I don't eat shrimp." I say.

"Why not?" she asks.

I think for a moment. I'm sure she can see my eyes moving around in circles as I look for an answer, and then, "I'm uncertain, but I think I am rather resolved in this."

"That's okay! I make lamb." She says, "Should I cook at your place or mine?"

"I think yours would be better this time." Then I think, "Wait! Where do you live?"

"2907."

"Is that an address?" I ask.

"It is my apartment number, silly. I live in this building. Where else would I live?"

"Is that her apartment?" I ask.

"Well, yes. I suppose, that is, er, it used to be." She replies.

"How about we go out tonight instead?" I ask. "I don't think I can go there and look at you and think that anything is where it should be."

"But, you'd never been there with her."

"Doesn't matter . . . please."

She sees my trepidation and says, "I get it. If it would help, my middle name is Marjorie. Each of us has a different middle name. Would you like to call me that?" I shake my head.

"When we left New York, Gerhardt was saying, 'Five is now Two.' Was he talking about you?"

"Yes," she bows her head a little. "The Ethyl that died was Ethyl Two, your assistant and protector; I was in support position five, as your pilot and backup guardian. When that Ethyl died and I was reassigned, I was uploaded with all of her memories up 'til that point of her last update from the hospital, so that now, I am Two. It is rather like a moment from that old movie, *The Matrix*, where Trinity gets helicopter lessons uploaded, but different, because, first; obviously, it takes all day, and second; I get her entire life added to mine, and finally; in practical terms, I have to go to the data, it can't come to me. Because we are clones to start with, and because we were originally imprinted with the same frameworks, we each have the core memories of your step-mom, Ethyl Anders, uploaded upon our activation, and then added to that is our technical expertise and specialized training extracted from the best professionals in their fields. Try as they may, some of those personalities slip through as well, but not much."

Things begin making sense to me, so I ask, "So, who did you get all these skills from?"

"Well, some of the donors were outstanding in fields that never got any attention, while others were world famous. We all got our nursing, medic, EMT training from the twenty finalists in a national 'Best Medic' contest that paid three million dollars to the winner. To compete, each had to undergo a complete brain scan which was later edited, redacted, distilled down to include only their training and experience, not their personal lives. We also have training from drivers, soldiers, Mossad agents, and trainers," she pauses, looking me up and down, "even from a couple of porn stars, and an instructor of courtesans, so that, when needed, we would be skilled." I can vouch for that. "Then we are equipped with certain 'field specific' trainings for our vocations." I relax a bit.

"Ethyl Two was trained in international money management and finance manipulation, as well as all of the skills of a lawyer, legal secretary, and executive assistant. When you wanted your accounts used to buy a car and have it delivered, there was access to get that done before you even left the club that night. There was acquired a list of nearby Mercedes dealers from a map program, and then access to their inventories from their online websites, found the model wanted for Meredith, purchased the car with your Tex-Ex card – stored in memory – placed an order on the DMV website, paid the additional $2000US 'New York immediate process fee' to get the papers delivered to the car right away, and arranged the delivery of the car in the morning as soon as I knew the hotel and suite number." She smiles, "And with the exception of the hotel and suite number, all of this was done while you had your hand on the back of my head and you were thinking about my mouth."

"Hey! Stop that!"

"I'm sorry, but, from my point of view, IT IS ME." She says, "What can I do to fix this?"

"Well," I pause for a moment, "you can start by not talking about that week until I tell you that I am ready to assimilate it into our relationship, if that is what this is, and if that ever happens." I think a bit longer, "And, I really don't care for Marjorie as a name, but I like Five for some reason. Maybe it takes me back to 'Johnny Five is alive' or something. Still, 'Five' sounds like a team member's uniform number."

"Tu habla Español?" she asks.

"Si, poquito."

"Como se . . . Cinco?" she says.

"Cinco? Hmm! Cinco! I think Cinco would do just fine, if it's okay with you."

"You could call me Bambi or Bozo if it would encourage you to give me another chance." I think deep down, she really is her – or who she is supposed to be. Still confusing.

"I have to change the subject." I say.

"What do you need, Boss?"

"Do you know Flo? The waitress?" I ask.

"I remember Flo from that diner in Passaic. Is that the one?" she asks.

"I want you to find, buy, or build her a Dinermite diner, kind of like the one where I met her – preferably one of their largest models – in Savannah, Columbia, Charleston, or Myrtle Beach areas, so she can be near family. Make certain that it is truly profitable and overpay for it enough that the owner will stay on, make a job offer to Flo, and then, after a year or two, leave it to her. We want to put together a healthcare package for her and her son, with full dental, no deductibles, and no co-pays, and I want to offer the same to any of the other full time employees there. Can we do that?"

"Boss, with the kind of money that you allow me to dedicate to these projects, I could find a swamp, lay a ten acre foundation and put up an amusement park all around, if that were what it would take. We can do this easily in a city like any one of those. By the way, the couple you met in Maine sent in their resumes, and we got them positions in Savannah – jobs matching their histories, good pay, bennies for the kids, private school. They're all doing quite well."

"Good, thank you," I respond. Then back on track, "Flo's gonna need a single story house, fair sized with fixtures to suit a family with a special needs kid like hers. Set it up on a lease to own, discount the cost."

"Why do you do these things, Boss?"

"Cinco? Dinner! Tonight! La Fonda!"

"You know, after a while, all this Mexican food could go straight to my ass, Boss." She says with a bit of a laugh.

"Then we just won't do it every night, eh?"

And that really is the beginning of a beautiful relationship. From that day on, Cinco and I get together between three and five times a week. Sometimes we go out, and sometimes we end up at her place or mine for the night. Sometimes we just meet for a nooner or an after-work quickie or a late night snack – so to speak. But we begin to accept each other as we are and get to know and enjoy who that is. I haven't felt like this in a lifetime . . . literally.

Cinco will be moving, right away, into an apartment on 131, then four months later, after the renovation can be done, she will move into the Vice Presidential suite, next to my office. There is a separate office, 700 square feet, with a connected apartment of 5200 feet, which has never been occupied. Gerhardt had it set aside in the event we – that is him, me, and the board – would select someone to take partial control. I would rather have Cinco there; and she will become my right hand in all things. It takes some convincing, but eventually, Gerhardt agrees that – if nothing else – it would save endless wrangling with me to just let me win this one; though "let" may be too strong a word.

Part Three – Opening My Mind

Keith T Jenkins

.

Construction Project?

It is four o'clock on a Thursday when Ethyl comes on the box and says, "Mr. Danz, there's a Doctor Marquez here to see you. She says it's about your transplant of some sort?"

"Send her in, please."

"Call if you need me," scrolls across my field of vision.

Dr. Marquez is a very well presenting woman, with a look of personal confidence. She is about five foot seven or eight, wearing very expensive, very high heels, and what she will tell me later is the latest revision of the 2000 D&G collection, broad shouldered, double breasted, big lapels, and a tapered skirt. Her head is slightly lowered, looking knowingly up at me from beneath her eyebrows and the brim of her broad hat with a solid smile slightly to the left side of her mouth – and she looks like she knows a secret. It may be that she knows my secret. Let's hope.

"Dr. Marquez, what is it that I am to do for you today?"

"You have it in reverse, Mr. Danz; I am here to be doing something for you." She shakes my hand firmly and takes a seat in my desk chair. She opens a small brief case that she has placed on my desk and pulls out a tablet. "I want to tell you a story . . . a medical story, of parts, pieces, and about an assembly that you will find quite fascinating." She turns on her tablet and opens an image comparison program that has four images on the screen. "Take a look at these four images. They are four different DNA samples. They each look completely different from the rest, other than being human. The second one was taken from your brain when I did my surgery. I want you to bear that in mind, as we go through this story. Okay?"

"Sure. You have my attention."

She pulls a device from her briefcase that looks like two vertebrae of a spinal column. "This is my invention," she says, "and now I am told that it belongs to your company due to some sort of paperwork that was signed at the surgery when I installed one in you." She pushes a small hidden lever in between the two vertebrae, and the joint comes apart into two pieces. "The surgery I performed on you was, for lack of a more gracious way to say it, a head transplant – plus a little. What I had been given to work with was a corpse, fresh-frozen, with no head to speak of, being kept 'alive,' not having a better word, with lots of life support gear that could be found in almost any trauma center, but this was all built onto a travelling cart. I was also given a frozen head . . . or at least most of a head. I had a skull with its contents intact and the skin burned almost completely off and no face. My surgical teams worked for weeks on each part. Then we attached this upper unit to the head, collecting the nerves into nearly two hundred clusters and then connecting the clusters to the connector systems inside this spun titanium alloy vertebra. On the body, as you can imagine, we did the exact opposite on the other vertebra, so that when the two were connected, the processors in the middle could convey all of the instructions to the rest of the body. The processing system would 'learn' the signals from the brain, interpret them, and pass them on to the connections that feed data and electrical impulses to the body. It was originally powered only by a small plutonium cell, but it's designed to charge the power systems from the body. This is the device that makes it possible for you to live." Her tone changes from very matter-of-fact to much more one of both worry and treachery. "Now they tell me that I can never use this technology for anyone else because they hold the patents."

"Who holds the patents?"

"You! Them! Danzig!" she says, with no small degree of panic.

"They must have had some reason . . ."

"They told me that since they funded my research that they hold the patents and have absolute control of the products and intellectual properties. But I did all the work, and I knew that you would change their minds, once you got to understand the DNA testing results I brought today."

"This is beginning to sound like extortion, Doctor, and that is not something I cotton to at all." Then it hits me again, after all, what kind of city slicker, business man says "cotton to" – or for that matter, who the hell says "city slicker"? This keeps happening.

"No, there's no threat, I just wanted you to know – personally – and I was hoping that you would help." She pauses a moment, takes a breath, and turns her tablet around. "This is your DNA, it's the DNA from your brain," she says pointing to the second sample. She shows me the third sample and says, "A complete disconnect is what we expected between those two. And the fourth one is from the face, which is, again, completely different than the rest. This is to be expected since he was a stranger." She taps the first DNA sample on the screen and says, "This is the interesting one. This is the one that should have your undivided attention. This one was taken from your blood test the day before the accident. It SHOULD match the DNA of your brain, but it doesn't. The brain that this entire scheme was built around belonged to Russell Anders. But, that's not the brain that is inside your head . . . is it?"

"You're asking me? I woke up, and all this had begun, and to a certain degree I was a blank slate. Gerhardt told me almost everything, and the memories came on like little lights and connected the dots to a reality, which, for the most part, I recall quite well. What you are saying is a total surprise to me."

"I can help you with part of that, but not all of it, and I want you to seriously consider helping me with my problem." She looks at me in a non-threatening way, seeking approval. "Can we talk now? Or am I about to disappear?"

"No, Doctor, we talk. To have the life of a sultan is a wonderful thing, but I really do want to know why I have this fortune and power. I have to know how I got here, and what I have to do. For some reason . . . please understand, Gerhardt has been great about trying to give it to me in usable bites and keep my patience, but . . . I have to know it all."

"Good," she says, "cause I have to know a few things too, and I am going to need some assurances as we go."

"What assurances do you need, Doc?"

"For starters, there are some very powerful forces, agencies, nations, and companies, as well as some people with interests in taking it all away or in just knowing what I am about to tell you. There are a few details about things that people would kill to have or stop, including my work on you, so I would like to know that I am not going to disappear. Some of these people may also want to take everything from you." She looks a little scared. I think quickly, but deeply, as I realize how dangerous this could all be to me. What if the story I have been a part of and have been told is not completely true, even as it unfolded before my eyes, and what if suddenly I am not who I am? I remember what Gerhardt said about that.

"Look," I say, "I don't know how all of this is going to play out. I just discovered all of this in what you've just told me, and I am going to have to chew on it all for a while. Also, I suspect that what you have to say could be big. Huge! Not to mention that if it all gets out, it could be me who will disappear. I have no idea what all of this is going to mean, big picture, and how it is likely to change my life, or yours. But I can make you this promise, right now. If you help me learn the truth, in every possible detail, then I will do everything I can to keep you safe and make you prosperous." Then I think, "Who uses the word 'prosperous' anymore."

She sticks out her hand, and I give her mine. We shake hands, and she says, "Deal!" She suddenly looks much more safe, strong, and secure, like she knows she's sat in a good chair, in a warm and friendly place.

"Two days before the 'accident,' you went to San Antonio for a download." She actually does air-quotes at "accident" when she says it. "The process was done with a device that put thirty-two probes on your scalp which communicated with nearly 300 points of interest inside your brain and fed that data to a giant computer that downloaded your memories, in ten to twenty million byte files – billions of them – into a bank of servers housing two arrays of over 300 hard disks, each ten terabytes in striped RAID array, and those servers and banks were on-the-fly mirrored in a half dozen little server farms around the world, so that in the event of electrical calamities, or even nuclear devastation, your 'image' would remain secure. Some of the servers are in major cities and a few in more obscure locations.

"Your body was collected and preserved, as Gerhardt told you. It was discovered that you had suffered severe injuries in the crash, which is what killed you, so near-complete reconstruction would be needed if you were to return. The technology you directed before you died ended up, thirty years later, providing a means of transplanting every organ in the body, or to do a complete body transplant. We felt the rejection and failure possibilities were far less this way. We found a man who had died in a motorcycle accident and had simply struck his head on a pole. The rest of him was the right size, condition, desired maturity, blood type, and multiple tissue matches. Outside of a few scrapes and bruises, his body was absolutely perfect. We couldn't have asked for better.

"Although there had been numerous failures and a string of hit and miss, your cryogenics business had defrosted over forty people in a row without failure before we decided to plan for your restoration. When we pulled you out of storage, we saw the damage that had been done to the face. No one had physically looked at the body in a couple of decades; knew that we had to find a face, scalp, and neck. And, as you know, we did.

"I want you to be endlessly aware that the people whose parts you are using died of natural causes. As far as I know, no one in this enterprise has ever killed anyone. Not on purpose anyway. It may not matter to some people, but it matters to me.

"I performed the surgeries, with my teams, that connected your head to your body, stripped your skull, then shaved it down here, and built it up there, to match the skull of the face donor, as well as we could. I can assure you that none of our measurements on the skull were off by more than a tenth of a micron. For my team, a tenth of a micron is huge. Remember, we deal in nerves and spinal connections. It took over six months to create the upper connector joint to fit your neck perfectly. We also built thirty-five different lower connector joint collars, each connecting to the lower connector joint, but each one slightly different in size and shape to best fit the spine we were to use. The variance in size from largest to smallest was less than a millimeter and a half, front to back, and two millimeters side to side.

"Your computer technology made this possible. The reduction in the size and increase in the speed of the processors has opened doors never before contemplated. In your connecting joint are two sets of four processors, each operating four cores, each running at six gigahertz. Surrounding those systems and housing the transfer of information modules, from upper to lower and back, is a housing made from spun titanium. The titanium alloy is extruded in strands that are one and a half microns thick and twisted upon extrusion and then woven into a fabric pattern several layers thick, which is then heated and pressed into the shape we wanted . . . in this case the shape of a vertebrae – and then non-abrasively polished to a surface that is smoother than glass. Even though no part of the joint is over a quarter inch thick, you can shoot one with a Desert Eagle and not even dent it." I am a bit turned on when she speaks so plainly about powerful guns, and I notice, not for the first time, that she has very nice legs. "The top and bottom edges of the appliance fit into prepared slots, like puzzle pieces in the bone of the next vertebrae, and an agent comprised mostly of stem cells and progenitor cells, from your own body, were injected into the area and stimulated growth around the device, locking it in place for life. Then, we get to the hard part."

"Do you need me – should I go?" scrolls by from Ethyl. I reply that I should be fine, we'll talk later. I would see her in the morning.

She sees my momentary distraction. "We get to the hard part," says the Doctor again.

"That sounded like the hard part to me." I say.

"No, I really wish that were true. After your 'parts' were assembled, we waited about two months for them to fully bind to one another, hoping that the stress of what was about to happen would not pull them all apart. We took the completed 'Frankenstein' into the Technical Surgery Suite, and because the delta waves we were getting from the brain were so dissimilar from those of the previous scan in 2015, we did an 'Overlay Upload' of the entire collection of memories from the stored data, which we hoped would act as a stabilizing re-installation of an operating system on an old computer.

"Until we did this to the brain, everything else could have failed, and we could just start over with a different collection of parts and retain the brain for another attempt at this. This was a pass/fail event which, if it failed, could permanently damage your brain in every conceivable way.

"They connected the latest version of the thirty-two probes and re-accessed the hundreds of points in the brain and uploaded all of the memories of Russell Anders, just like they should have, but what should not have happened, and did, is that those memories simply recorded a lifetime over, or more accurately, right next to, a previously existing lifetime of memories. It was a good thing we had waited for the physical healing because there was some screaming and twisting and writhing in patches over the next several days. There was a fever that went to over 103 for nearly two days. Then, the fever broke, dropped down to 99.5 and has stayed there ever since. It may be a family thing to run a little hot. Not uncommon.

"About two weeks later, you woke up and you know the rest. What you don't know is what brought about my suspicions and led to this meeting."

"What did you know? What did you see, Doc?" I ask.

"This was never intended to be my insurance policy, but here we are. When we began the process, I measured the body. After all, we needed to be absolutely certain that all the parts were going to fit precisely. The corpse in the drawer, labeled as Russell Anders was only five feet seven inches tall, but the medical records said that Mr. Anders should have been five feet ten. I rechecked the measurements to be certain. Realize that, from an experimental and scientific point of view, I wanted to perform my process, not solve a decade's old matter that may well have been nothing more than a clerical error. It really was none of my business, and if I brought it up, I could have been out of business. Also, for a person of that height, you had a slightly large head, so I liked my odds that no one would be the wiser. Best case scenario: my processes worked, and you turn out to be the wrong person inside, or you couldn't remember anything of your old life and start fresh. No offense. Either way, I still become the new 'Christiaan Barnard' of brain transplants. Worst case scenario: I fail, you die, and this secret experiment never happened. I am terribly sorry that I risked your life in this way, and I am very glad it turned out well for you, but please understand, I had over fifteen years of my life tied up in this, and besides, I didn't know you from Adam."

Strange phrase 'I didn't know you from Adam' – but I know what it means. It is a reference that is rarely used anymore. Obscure! Obtuse! "What do you mean, 'fifteen years' tied up in it?"

"I began the dreaming of this process, designing and redesigning the parts and procedures, when I was a fourteen and in college for my bachelor's degree."

"Wow! Fourteen!" I am overly impressed. "Okay, Doc, here's the deal, you help me figure out exactly what happened, and I will help you in any way I possibly can, including a rather substantial 'thank you' present for saving my life. I will also do everything I can to assure your personal safety and security. So, let's go to dinner."

"Mr. Danz, I came here on business, not for personal reasons."

"First off, call me Joshua – you've got my brain in your hands. Second, I have an idea or two that I want to work out with you. And, third, while I understand that whole business-personal thing, Doc, it's nearly six PM, and I'm feeling a bit peckish, and there are some assurances for someone I wish to begin taking care of. So, how do you feel about Italian?"

"Italian is okay, and I do love a good chicken marinara." She says, "How about Luciano Ristorante Italiano? There's one in the mall at the North Star Complex."

"Perfect! I remember them from back then. Also, I can stop by an ATM on the way, and everything will be great."

We pack away her stuff, the whole show and tell. "You can leave that behind the desk if you like. It'll be safe here." We take the elevator down to the garage where Benson is waiting with my car. He opens the door, and I remember the ATM, so I go back to the machine in the garage take out $4000 from a personal cash account, and shove it into my coat pocket, minus a couple of hundred that I let Benson see me put into my pants pocket after counting. "We'd like to go to the North Star Complex, Benson," and so we do. In twenty minutes, we are in the underground security garage of the complex, getting out of the car and into an elevator to go up to the galleria level, right below where the restaurant is. I know that Benson has to keep an eye on me, but I ask him to give us a little space. He realizes that she is attractive – who doesn't – and figures I'm on the make, so he allows a little breathing room. It's a guy thing, to be sure.

Before going to the restaurant, we stop in at a few stores. We talk about a lot of nothing. I tell her about playing baseball when I was a boy, and she tells me that these are not the memories of Anders, but mine. She tells me of her childhood in Tampico, growing up by the beach and how Operation Holographic was her favorite game of all time and how she still loves the new 3.0 virtual versions. She tells me of the politics that she didn't understand at the time, but which virtually forced her family to sneak into Tejas when she was ten. Later, her family came in legally and became citizens. She had excellent grades, graduated from the Texas Instruments University of Science and Technology, with a major in neurosciences, then went to the Johns Hopkins University/Baylor School of Medicine at Waco, and did her post-doctoral fellowship in Dallas and San Antonio Transplant/Research Hospitals. She doesn't look old enough to know that much, but she is considerably smarter than me. She graduated from High School at thirteen, Bachelor's at sixteen, Masters at eighteen, Wow!!! And she is beautiful. She also tells me that, although she may look like a fashion genius, it is all due to her personal shopper. I tell her, "I know a guy." This is my way of expressing the same reality that I don't pick out my own clothes either, except to wear them. I have, however, begun, or just started to get my hair cut more the way I want it, instead of the way it was given to me. Well, sort of. There are still a few changes I would like to make.

We talk about the dogs we've had and some of the people we've dated; depending upon which memories I am accessing, these are either more personal in nature, or more financially and politically motivated. Hard to say which women are which all the time, but I am certain that the part about raising a stray Shar-Pei pup is not part of the rich guy's life. As we talk, we pass through shops that sell sunglasses, scarves, women's clothes, shoes, and technology; all under the watchful eye, but not within earshot, of Benson. We look at and touch almost everything as we wander about before we get to the restaurant and order. It is a very pleasant meal with all political and business agendas out of the way for the day. We both have the chicken marinara and water to drink. I thoroughly enjoy the garlic toast that had been off my diet in recovery. It is wonderful. Our waiter's name is Justin.

"Justin. How would you like to make a very large tip?" I ask.

"I would like that very much, sir," he says with a smile. "What can I get you, sir?"

"Come closer, Justin, and shake my hand."

As he reaches out, I shake his hand and leave $2000 in his grasp and tell him, "There's a little tech store just three doors down on the left that has the latest NuGleDroid smart phones on a pay as you go basis. Have you seen them?" He nods his head and grunts, "I want you to go there and buy two of them with a year of service with this money, and whatever is left over is yours, along with another really big tip later, to forget this ever happened. When you package our leftovers you will put them in a bag that already contains the phones. Okay?"

Justin stands up strait and clenches his fist tightly and asks, "Would you like any dessert?" and we decide the tiramisu would be an excellent idea. The dessert comes back in five minutes, and Justin asks, "Would you like the leftovers to go, sir?" I nod.

He disappears with our plates and comes back in fifteen minutes with a bag from the restaurant that contains the leftover dinners and two cell phones that cost him eighteen hundred dollars. I give him another five hundred dollars, just because. I shake his hand again in passing the new and improved tip and say, "Justin, you and I should be friends for life, and I hope that's a long while."

To this he says, "Me too, sir." I would return to this restaurant more than a few times, and Justin is usually there to take good care of my guests and myself. I think his tips from me would pay for most of his tuition at San Antonio College.

I pay for dinner with my Tex-Ex card and purchase an additional gift card worth three hundred dollars for Benson. After all, he has been very patient in waiting for us to come out any minute, and it has been nearly two hours. "Back to the house, Benson! I will see the Doctor to her car."

"Yes, sir," says Benson and we return amid pleasant conversation, just as we had before, with the privacy panel open. When we arrive at Dancing Stag Tower – my home – my office – I give Benson the gift certificate and the rest of the night and the next day off. I tell him, "Thank you, Benson. I will be staying in, so enjoy your weekend. See you Monday at eight sharp." He thanks me and drives off, I don't know where, but we go upstairs again to visit. When we get to the office, we remove her stuff from behind the desk and take it upstairs to my apartment, where I put on a pot of tea, open the bag, and for the first time, the Doctor sees what I had arranged with Justin.

"These two phones, Doc, have no traceable connection to you or me. They were bought with cash by a waiter. They will be our means by which to communicate. We won't use these to talk to anyone but us, until we know it is a safe idea. Understood?" She nods. I program the numbers from each of the phones into the other without using names. Hers is only set to dial a person known as 'him,' and mine is only programmed to dial 'her.' Then I set the volume on each to vibrate only.

"In my office earlier," I explained to her, "I realized something very common, but very important. We had been to the restaurant and we had water to drink, because after the take-over's, all of the soda makers were brought to ruination by the total crapification of their product, by government management. Even Dr Pepper, which was publicly held, suffered FRIA, became unionized, and federalized, had gotten so bad it was O-merged with Crush/Coca-Cola which had all become absolute rubbish, just like Big-Red, A&W, and all the rest that were now a part of AmeriPop, the only soda company in existence. And even the best of it didn't taste as good as an old diet soda. I had predicted some of this in my If/Then, and even acted on it to a modest degree. Out of the American national ego, they had also all been renamed. In the process of the unification, federalization, and unionization of it all, they had made some ubiquitous changes that made it all just plain bad. It's not so much that they were all bad, but the fact is that I had tried them all in recent days, and there is just no fun left in them at all. And it didn't get bad all at once, but the minor changes, which had been made in increments, had made it all 'not as good' each step of the way. They experimented with a collection of sweeteners to replace the corn syrup which had previously replaced sugar. Each of them met a new 'federally suggested' guideline, and each was just a little different in flavor than the others, and none of it was better. The change in the propellants used and even the fizzy water were the final straw. When I awoke and healed a bit and could have some fun in my diet, I asked for some sodas and found that all the fun was missing. That was when Gerhardt told me the story of the demise of the soda. If only someone had preserved some of the recipes from the good old days."

I go to my personal desk and bring out a box of random "personal effects" and open it. I separate a set of keys, must have been thirty or more of them, on six or seven different rings, all strung together. I release a set of three keys and take them to the Doctor. "I got something for you to do, Doc. Something very important. Could be world changing. Really, Doc!"

"You do realize that I have a name, don't you?"

"Really? What is it?"

"Ilyssa! Doctor Ilyssa Margarita Sanchez Marquez."

I'm not really attached to 'Ilyssa' right away, so . . . "Okay, Doc, that's great. Check this out." I open NuGle Maps on her phone and look up a hunter's deer and meat storage locker. I find it and tell her, "Take these keys and tell them you want locker 1101. It should still be mine since I paid as a customer for a couple of centuries in advance, as well as owning the place in a shell company. It was marked on corporate manifests as "Never Sell." The brass key will open the door. The locker I keep there is only about twelve by twelve feet. Once you are inside the locker, close and lock the door behind you and take no one inside. There is a key slot on a post by the wall next to the door. Insert the round key and turn it counter-clockwise. Don't scream. The whole room will begin to descend. It is an elevator that will lower about sixty feet, and while it is down, the door above cannot be opened. I want four things from there. When you get to the bottom, you will find an electric wagon with a manila envelope and a pile of canvas packing bags. The red key runs the wagon. Put two of each type of canister in each of the bags and put those sealed bags on a wagon with two boxes that should be marked something like 'mix station one' and then turn the key clockwise to rise back up. So, I want chrome canisters, maroon canisters, mix stations, and the manila envelope. Text me when you are clear of that location, and I will text you to say where we should meet. I promise you are going to be glad you made this trip."

"You do realize that I am a brilliant surgical doctor, the one that saved your life, and not some sort of errand girl, don't you?"

"I think I also realize that you are a bothered and bewildered, currently out of work brilliant surgical doctor who saved my life, whose patents are in danger and who might be looking for a job." She harrumphs at me. "So, how about this? You tell me the best income year of your life, and I double it for you to sign on as my personal physician, surgeon, and part-time errand girl? Besides, I really want you safe, and no one would dream of looking for you on your way to Waco."

"Waco! What the hell is in Waco?"

"Well, among other things, I had the Branch Davidian Complex rebuilt and opened to the public as a Modern Museum of Stupidity, but right now, there's a storage locker. Please? There's a spare suite down that hall and a closet full of clothes that I have never seen. Gerhardt said that it should be able to outfit almost any woman who is not obese or anorexic. Please. It is amazingly important, and I cannot go."

"Okay. But no funny business! We are on the clock here," she says. "I'm gonna be the most expensive gopher you have ever heard of."

"Not even close."

A New Day

The alarm goes off at seven, and I let it snooze once before getting up. Usually I let it snooze twice, but I remember that I have company, so I get up one snooze early. Mrs. Dennis is already hard at work and breakfast is on its way to the table as I arrive. As is her way, she has made more than enough for me, which works out perfectly today. From the other end of the apartment comes Ilyssa in some ivory silk pajamas that seem to fit her pretty well. She has a nice little body under all that finery she was wearing yesterday; some very pleasant looking curves.

She says, "Good morning."

Mrs. Dennis says, startled, "I wasn't aware there'd be company, sir. Should I put on . . .?"

"Nonsense Mrs. D., I am certain that there will be plenty. You always go too far in taking care of me, you know," and I kiss her forehead. "Doc, was there anything special you would like for breakfast? Mrs. Dennis is a marvelous cook, among other things." I give a wry glance and a playful growl as I bob my eyebrows, and Mrs. Dennis blushes.

Mrs. Dennis is about five foot three, built like a fire plug, sixty-five years old, and a live-in during the week, but stays with either her daughter or one of her sons on most weekends, each of which lives within a couple of hundred miles. Usually, one of the kids or grandkids will pick her up, or she sometimes takes the bus. Sometimes, if it is a special occasion, or if other transportation options are lacking, I have her flown out by plane or helicopter. She has all manner of complaints about riding in "dat whirly gig" but, I can tell, she enjoys the trips. Besides, dat whirly gig is an almost new Super Black Hawk that goes nearly 250 miles an hour, flies smooth as silk, and with the sound dampening turned on, it is so quiet you can talk inside without headsets. I love that bird. Today though, the Doc and I have other needs. So, I get on the phone.

"Mike? Yeah, this is JD. I want you to do me a huge favor."

"Is this a favor for favor kind of thing, Boss?"

"Yeah. Do this and you should be done for the day by noon and off until next Wednesday, at least, with a full tank on any bird we got, but only if it remains an absolute secret. Understand?"

"You mean to say, 'only if Gerhardt never knows' don't you?"

"Yeah, that's the gist of it," I say with a chuckle.

"That's a deal! Do I want to know anything more than what I have to know?"

"Not at this time. I want you to fuel up the Bandit and load her into Big Bird One. Leave the keys in it. Fly to Waco where you will take a watch of your choosing to the president of Baylor University. Put the watch on the company fuel Tex-Ex card. I have a passenger coming along. Just call her, Doc. And believe me, that's all you ever need to know, except that she is going to borrow the Bandit."

"Well," says Doc, "that was cryptic enough, eh?"

"I'm going shopping now," says Mrs. Dennis. "Whenever he starts talking in secret code, I don't care what he's talking about, I just figure I don't need to hear it. And besides, there's always shopping to do. Anything special you would like, sir? Should I plan on the ma'am being here later?"

"Yes! I think I would like a couple of Galapagos Penguins for dinner, or how about salmon, Brussels sprouts, and some kind of potatoes. Hey, Doc, what's your favorite pie? Mine's pumpkin."

Doc seems a bit perturbed and says, "Hey, focus here 'ADD boy' I have work to do and no idea what it is." Mrs. Dennis scurries out the door, and I think I get a new nick name. "What is my plan for the day?"

"You are to take your purse, your new phone, and your car to the airport. Go to the west side where the old post office used to be – the sign is still up – and you will see a large blue and gold gate that says 'Danzig Air.' You go through that gate and ask for Mike. He will take care of everything from there. Mike's a good guy. Okay?"

"Sure. So, when is payday, and what kind of benefits do I get?"

"I will try to have that taken care of before you get to the airport. If it is not agreeable, just sign on, and I will cover the difference in cash later, if you trust me."

She takes her last sip of coffee and heads down the hallway to prepare for the day. Even without the high-heels, she has a real nice walk on her. Kind of reminds me of a sixties movie siren kind of walk. Even in her seventies, Sophia Loren still had that kind of walk. Wow! Hey, ADD Boy, back to work already.

I call Gerhardt and tell him that I want to put Doctor Ilyssa Marquez on staff as my personal physician and surgeon and that she will only answer to me. I tell him the salary I want her to have, and he makes some noises that sound like he thinks that I am being wasteful, so I raise the amount by 25%, and he quickly shuts up. "She gets full medical and dental with no co-pay or deductibles and a company credit/debit card with the same limits as mine."

"Yours has no limits," he says with some amazement.

"Then make the limit fifty thousand, and that should be easy to handle, right? And I need that all transmitted to me immediately."

"I'll have to get to my office to get all that done. It should be in your hands by noon. Will that do, Mr. Danz?"

"Yes, sir. That will do if it must." I call Mike and let him know that his passenger's papers will not be ready as soon as I had hoped and to have him get some appeasements to act as 'assurances' for her, and he does.

When Ilyssa arrives, she parks her car in my slot, and Mike tells the guard that it's okay. He also gives her the appeasements I had requested of him. He has gone to the Travel and Trade office at the airport and gotten her several cards; one is a fuel card from his office, which was formerly used by Mike's assistant, who was fired. Mike had the presence of mind to take it before he left and not to cancel it. With this, she can buy fuel and sundries from anywhere but a Shell station or a CITGO, as we do not do business with either of them. He also gives her, at my request, a Tex-Ex gift card with a balance of $20,000. This can be used almost anywhere that used to take Visa and Master Card because the Tex-Ex people bought the others out. He also gives her a Wal-Mart gift card with $1000 on it, just in case she needs some basic supplies, and who doesn't?

"The boss also wanted to apologize about your salary that had to be changed when Mr. Gerhardt made some noise about it."

"He caved on my salary?" She is suddenly livid.

"No ma'am, he increased it. In my mind, I can just see the vein bulging on Gerhardt's neck. That is one of the greatest joys of working with JD. He asked if you could send him a text before we take off." Almost as suddenly she is relaxed and happy for my sense of humor with Gerhardt.

She sends me a text – "Ready 2 go."

I call her back. "If you need to call and I don't answer, it may not be convenient or wise, so leave a message with no names or locations, and I will get back to you somehow. If need be, we can always text. Okay?"

She snaps back, "Got you, Boss."

"I thought I told you to call me Joshua. Didn't I?"

"Yes, Joshua. I will try to remember that, Joshua," she says with a smile I can hear over the phone. "I still can't believe I'm doing this, Joshua. And I actually don't even know what it is I'm doing."

"I promise that making this trip could be one of the highlights of life so far. I would go with you but my day is jammed up and I don't want this idea to go to waste if someone else thinks it up. Besides, it could open up doors for the other things you want, things we have already discussed. Are you ready?"

"Sure. How hard could it be?"

"It's not the difficulty that matters, but the doing. Can I talk to Mike, please?" She passes the phone to Mike. "Don't forget your job is to take a watch to the president of Baylor because that is exactly what I am going to tell Gerhardt you are doing, got it? And make it a nice watch, okay? None of that pawn shop crap – spend some of my money on something decent. Something shiny!"

"Okay, JD, I've got something in mind and I know where to get it. But we gotta go if I'm gonna be done by noon."

Mike takes her to Big Bird One, his Chinook helicopter, painted yellow with a blue belly, and just for fun, pictures of Ernie and Bert under the pilot and co-pilot windows. As they enter through the side door of the cargo area, she sees a black 1977 Pontiac Firebird Trans-Am. This is what I had called "Bandit," for obvious reasons, but because Doc is so young, Mike will have to explain it to her. Still, even without the old movie reference, she thinks Bandit is a pretty awesome vehicle. Like most antique things on the road, she has been modified to accept liquid propane gas. There's a switch on the dash and a tank in the back for that, but whenever she is hungry at an airport, she gets a little helicopter fuel, and that's what she was born to burn.

The trip for them is pretty uneventful, a little small talk about where I met the Doc and how Mike and I got our lives tangled up. He had been a pilot instructor for the Air National Guard 'til he was RIF'ed, then he served in the Tejas National Air Force for another ten years or so before disappearing into Mexico for a while. Shortly after my restoration, I had gone to Belize for a while, seeing sights and senoritas when I met Mike in a bar, and both of us got pretty toasted. We were about to get arrested because of a fight that I may have started with some woman's boyfriend she called a 'Sancho,' but Mike dragged me out the back door, into a jeep, out to the air strip, and into an Ugly

Angel helicopter. This thing really lived up to its name. It was all nose when I looked at it, but Mike threw me into a cargo net in the rear and told me to hang on. The locals came on the field as we got off the ground and swept away before I passed out. I woke up, and we were 'resting' in a jungle a million miles away from town, and strangely, some of the rotors were missing, and the tail was bent. I was impressed beyond measure.

My head hurt when I fell out of the craft onto my face in the sand, but when I got up, there was Mike with a can of rations from what could have been a couple of wars ago and I would not have cared. I was starving, and he had food he was willing to share. This was the very definition of a friend.

"I have never seen anyone fly that well as drunk as I think you were last night. Have you?"

So, Mike said, "I have to say that last night I saw someone fly drunk better than anyone I know but me."

"Look," I told him, "if you can fly like that and you can stay sober, then I will give you a job and something to fly, provided we ever get out of here."

"Oh, we'll get out of here alright, but what makes me think you can give me a job?" He might have still been a little drunk. I know I was. "After all, you needed me to save your ass in the cantina, from that Sancho and the cops and now this. And look what you did to my angel."

I didn't think I had done anything to the helicopter because I woke up in the cargo net where Mike had thrown me before. Still, I didn't have enough recall of facts to dispute what Mike said, not that he did either, but what the heck, he had saved my skin. Anyway, that's how Mike tells the story.

When they set down in Waco, Doc takes the car, Mike unloads his Bonneville, and drives off to do some shopping at a jeweler for a watch . . . then to Baylor after. He gets the president a Rolex Oyster Perpetual and for good measure, he also gets a matching Ladies Oyster Perpetual for the wife. Mike can show a lot of class when he is wielding the right credit card. He has them boxed and wrapped with some sort of card expressing best wishes for the 'coming season' whatever that means. Personally, I couldn't care less about sports.

Before driving off, Doc texts me, "In Waco now. Leaving airstrip." I text back "Look in the console." She looks in the console and finds twenty brand new one-hundred-dollar bills and a .380 colt. My next message reads, "Just in case some palms need grease, we keep the cash in the car at all times. Safe trip. Go have lunch first. About 10 miles east on 84 there's an Outback Steakhouse. It's on the way. Victoria's Filet is off the hook."

She figures that there are apparently reasons for most of what I say and do. She has an early lunch, relaxes with a cup of Joe, and plugs the next address into the GPS. Within ten minutes or so she is driving into the parking lot out front. She goes into the office and meets with lovely young Bobbie, the operator. Bobbie is twenty-something, 5'5", buxom but tight in the middle, round in the rear, blonde to the eye, but the soul of a red-head. She is a bit gritty, and their conversation is almost pleasant, but in the end, the key matches the lock, and that is one of two things that Bobbie finds useful. The other is that Doc offers to buy fifty dollars' worth of lunch, so Bobbie disappears.

Doc enters the room, which is as small as it had been described, and the door has a deadbolt latch which she engages. She puts the key in and turns as instructed and almost screams when the floor begins going down at an alarming rate. Surprise! But she remembers the warning. As the elevator drops down, the lights below begin to come on, and she can see what is so secret. This room is about the same size as the entire building above, with ten foot ceilings and temperature control that keeps the place cool, about fifty five degrees. There are two fields of canisters, nearly a half an acre each, silver/chrome to the left and maroon to the right, no labels on any of them. She looks around and finds the electric wagon I had mentioned, and confirming the presence of the manila envelope, she unplugs it from the wall, starts the motor and drives it to the aisle between the fields of canisters. There are canvas bags in the wagon already, and each bag is just large enough to hold two canisters, plus a little if needed, but that is not needed. To Doc, the canisters are pretty heavy though – about thirty-five pounds each. She decides to just put one per bag and use four bags. There are plenty. She gets the canisters bagged – two chrome and two maroon – and sees the boxes straight in front of her by about fifty feet marked, "Mixing Station Assembly: ct. 1." They weigh about thirty pounds each, and she manages to get them into the wagon as well. She drives the wagon to the elevator and up she goes. She maneuvers the wagon out the room, down the hall, through the office, and out onto the parking area behind the car. That's when she sees that little blonde again as Bobbie gets out of the Bandit.

"Nobody has ever been here for that locker. I know because my daddy ran this place, and I grew up here. Then you show up and have a secret. Well, I want to know about that secret." She has a friend standing about five cars away. "This is my brother, Joey, named after my dad who sat here seven days a week 'til he died last year, and he wants to know the secret too." Joey is about the same height as Bobbie, but skinnier and ruddier, and a snappy dresser in those bib overalls with no shirt, but he doesn't speak a word in all the time that Doc is there. Joey just stands there, looking as tough as he can for a skinny runt, holding a stick in one hand and beating it into the other in a threatening manner. Bobbie has a gun. It isn't much of a gun, just a .38 long derringer, but it is enough to have Doc's undivided attention. It could, in truth, be enough to kill a fairly large man if needed. "Let's take a look," she demands quietly, and then, WHUMP! That is the noise that they all hear just as Joey falls to the ground. "Joey, no!" Standing there instead is Mike, and he has a gun. He has a Desert Eagle .44 pointed at Bobbie's face. Bobbie wants to run to her brother, but she dare not when confronted with Mike's pistol. She stretches her neck trying to see Joey a little better.

This is not a typical day for the Doc. Mike says, "He'll be fine little girl; but he will have a headache. Now, how about you lower that pea shooter into the car, and I won't shoot you right through your flapping gums," From that distance, Mike could have hit her square, dead in the mouth, but more importantly, Bobbie believes it, so she drops the pistol on the seat inside the Trans-Am. "Come on, let's go inside." He grabs the overalls on Joey and carries him along dragging his knuckles, knees and feet.

Doc gets the canisters and boxes into the trunk of the car while Mike watches over the Dalton Gang. He finds a fairly safe locker that is not locked and puts Joey in there. Mike suggests that they would be leaving soon . . . two minutes, ten minutes, doesn't matter . . . soon. He also suggests that if they wait long enough to come out, then this never happened, and no one needs to get shot, and no law enforcement needs to get involved. "We won't even lock it if you'll promise to stay put for a while." Doc gives Bobbie another five hundred bucks. Bobbie agrees that this all seems very reasonable, so after returning the wagon to the locker and locking it up, they leave. They meet back up at the air strip where Mike loads the car and the bike.

"This was supposed to be a secret mission. How did you know where I was?" Doc asks.

"If it was supposed to be so totally secret, Joshua would have had me load your car into the chopper, not my car with a locator on it. I always know where my car is and JD knows that. So I figured he would appreciate me checking in on you, and I did. Are you okay?"

"Sure," she says, with some resignation. "I'm just going to get some instructions from the boss and see where he wants me to go."

"Wow. Really got this thing going full on cloak-and-dagger, eh? Well, if there's a ton of money in it or if it looks like a bit more danger is coming, I'm in. That is, if you want me in."

She sent the text. "Loaded and back on the bird with Mike. What's next?"

"Amway corporate headquarters, Temple, Texas – Land in the west-most parking lot. Pick up Dr. Thomas Stark and come home," I send back. "Sending GPS coordinates now." Realizing that this is, for whatever reason, very hush-hush, Mike disables the tracker on his car and drops the power cell into the chopper's toolbox.

Back in 2030, the US had so decimated the economy with its government intervention that Amway had packed up and moved its headquarters to Temple, Texas. And while the distributors in what would later be known as the "left-behind states" were still allowed to operate, according to Amway, their profit structure had been all but destroyed by taxes. And because of the tax increases and the redefinition of capital gains to include residual incomes, there are Diamond Direct Distributors whose incomes, after taxes, are $85,000 a year. In Tejas it comes to nearly eighteen times that on average. Taxes are a bitch in the US. Dr. Stark is a chemist who works for Amway in deciphering how products are made so that they can be re-engineered into something better. But I find myself actively hoping his career path is about to change. I send Doc another text about twenty minutes later.

"Tell Mike he has an interesting way of taking the weekend off. Also, tell him I said 5% of your end, if that's okay, and to throw his phone away – NOW! Oh, and he has a new job. Until further notice, he's your protector."

Doc tells Mike that he can have 5% of her end of whatever they are into and that he has a new job if he wants it and to throw out his phone right away. That phone plummets onto IH 35 outside of Lorena from over a thousand feet up and shatters into pieces so small that no one even notices it. Thank God traffic is light and it doesn't hit any cars.

In a half an hour after that, they are landing in the farthest edge of the western parking lot, and two minutes later, they are leaving with one more passenger.

Dr. Stark has seen them descending, grabs his phone and jacket, and hits the door at a near run. It is about two hundred yards to the helicopter. He doesn't have a briefcase or anything when he enters the door that swings open on the co-pilot side of the beast. He leaps in and fastens himself into the 'troop commander's' seat in the walkway behind the pilot. No one says a word. Once he is secure within, and Doc closes the door, the giant craft leans a little bit to the front, and in moments, it is above and away from the complex. Noon has come and gone. Stark has left a note on his personal letterhead that reads, "I am resigned to take another opportunity. Please send my pension checks where my paychecks have been going."

Back with the Lollipop Guild

At 9:30, I walk into my office, right downstairs from my apartment, and everything is exactly as it usually is.

"Good morning, Boss."

"Good morning, Cinco. Anything special on my agenda today?"

As it turns, out there is a reason why the Ethyl model seemed familiar. She was modeled after my step-mother, Ethyl. And not even really my step-mother, or Joshua's but rather the step-mother of Russell Anders, and his extreme crush on her had been imbedded in my memory. She has a real "Donna Reed" sort of appeal, calm even tempered, well-mannered, and gentle beyond understanding. She is also rather curvaceous, which is a bit disturbing when pretending she reminds me of my step-mom. She was one of the last personal projects on the Anders plate. I am having near total recall of everything that Anders did or thought, just as if I had watched it happen in a forty-year-long movie, with the director's commentary from Anders' mind on every scene as we go. Still, Cinco, or any other Ethyl, is a major babe, and everyone that enters my office seems to notice, except for Gerhardt, who sees her as a droid. Well, almost a droid.

"No, Mr. Danz, nothing special, except work. You have a review of assets and actions with the Somali team, some cash status reports to review from the Cayman's and Switzerland, and the automotive division this afternoon to review the new power cell options for the SHV-17 models due out next year, sugar, chocolate, spices, tech . . . the usual. May I get you some coffee?"

"Yes, please, Cinco, I would appreciate that very much. Have we heard from Mr. Gerhardt this morning?"

"He put a pencil in your calendar for 10AM here, in your office. Would you like me to confirm?"

"Yes, please."

She replies, "Done."

Gerhardt had accessed my daily schedule from my UpLook account on the company EnChange server – both are new enterprise products from MS-Gates. As a member of the Executive Team he has access to my personal schedule during business hours, for company related meetings, and he can see what blocks of time are available, so he has "penciled" in the appointment for ten o'clock. It will become an actual appointment when I confirm it, via Ethyl, and then he will receive a notice of confirmation. Ethyl accesses it from her own internal office management and communication systems to lock it in. This happens between the time I say "please" and she says "done" – in nearly a half a second.

She hands me the reports on the power cell choices and configurations for the SHV-17, the seventeenth series of iterations of the Super Hybrid Vehicle which I had begun to develop back in 2012. The fundamentals of the vehicle are an onboard power generation, small uniform energy cells stashed throughout the body and a high-efficiency drive system that comes in three forms: single engine with a transmission, two-engine-two-wheel drive (front or rear depending upon the model) and all-wheel full drive systems, with an engine on each axle. The "SHV-17 C" is our new Carryall model that resembles the Suburbans of old, the ultimate SUV, but this one gets about eighty-five miles per gallon of gas or sixty-nine miles per gallon of liquid propane. And fully loaded, regardless of which fuel you use, it will go from zero to sixty in about five and a half seconds. This is what is available even though we are now only getting to use about 30% of the energy in the fuel. Thanks to a new invention that allows for us to get up to 50% out of the fuel – combined with the new batteries – we could bump that up to 130 miles to the gallon or more. Here's hoping, eh?

The US has become an Associate Member of the European Economic Community since shortly after the Tejas termination, and has reopened the deceased electric car companies of Tesla and Fisker, which had both fallen into receivership and then government hands. But their governments needed capital, so the US gave them promises – since the US was sadly lacking any real money. But, promises was what they really had to offer in recent days and years. To try to make good on their promises the US decided to go after Chevron. Why Chevron? Because they held the patents on some of the best batteries – energy cells – in the world. Still, being an oil company, they were averse to using their batteries to power cars. When the federal government turns their eyes on Chevron, Danzig offers them a deal; $25 Billion, cash, for all rights, production plants, research, and patents for all energy cells in their production and/or development. They want Danzig to sweeten the deal with a 2% interest in Danzig, but instead, the final price is 31.5 Billion, and the batteries are ours. The US, however, unaware of the details of the deal, buys into Chevron, and then – over a three year period of time – takes over, only to discover that they have no batteries. I do. We do, that is, and we we're not willing to share. Not with them. Before the US takeover of the corporation, each of the board members receives a quarter billion dollar bonus for the profitability of their business with Danzig. Some of them will almost immediately retire to Tejas.

We have been using the Chevron-owned battery makers since 2022, but now we own them. This is important because we are able to avoid sharing the technology with anyone while we are making improvements to the batteries. I found a young man who, by studying alligators, discovered a biological technology for accelerated muscle speed in these bulky beasts and he has applied it to amperage distribution, which, when successfully implemented, means that the battery can send power at a slightly faster rate, but more importantly, it can recharge nearly three times faster than before on the same flow of electricity previously used for each charge. This makes it nearly three times more efficient in the application of any electricity that is made available to it for powering other items. Charging systems can be smaller. The amount of energy provided to the battery can be smaller. Generators for that energy can be smaller. Engines can be much bigger. And that is what has put us at the top of the market, and should keep us there for a good long time. Mr. Gerhardt enters my office and brings with him the contracts for my personal doctor. She really will like the package we put together for her.

We discuss the final details for about ten minutes, just to make certain that what I asked for is included, and then he asks, "Why do you need a personal physician anyway? Having been fully functional and running the company for nearly three years now, you have shown no signs of failure, physical or mental." It is a fair question that deserves a fair answer, but what I say will have to suffice for now.

"She was head of the reassembly team and pioneered the technology that makes all of this possible, and she expressed some concerns that, although they may not be problematic, I would like to have it all watched by someone that already knows everything about it . . . not only the events, but also the technology. And we don't want more people in on our secrets than needed, do we?"

"No," he says, "the fewer people that know the better for all involved. There's no doubt about that. But, a full-time, personal doctor, Joshua?" His face sours a bit. "Is that something that you want to show up on a company ledger, board agenda, or tabloid?"

"Look, Hugo, they call me an eccentric multi-gazillionaire, and everyone knows that all of us eccentric multi-gazillionaires like to have things that no one else can have. So, make mine a doctor. Besides, when it comes time to review the status of my health, for the insurance package that all of you boardroom types want me to have, she will be on record saying what a terrific specimen of health I am, and getting you lower premiums and bigger payouts if I kick off. And I know that you boardroom types like that. His face still looks a little sour, but his head is nodding up and down. He is coming to my side of the discussion. "The next scheduled insurance physical is in about seven months, and you may or may not want to explain this billion dollar piece of titanium in my neck to some other doctor."

His lips curl a wry smile as he nods, not that he needs me to die to leave him a payoff; he is already scheduled for a substantial compensation in the event of my death, his retirement, or whatever else may bring his working days to an end. If he lives, he is filthy rich. If he dies, he would leave it all behind like we all do sooner or later. "Also, I would like the 'Ethyl' nurse that worked on me in my rehabilitation sent here as well. And, Doctor Marquez will need a half million dollar signing bonus. After all, I am an eccentric multi-gazillionaire."

One thing I know is that if I am figuring out the hidden or unknown truths of my background, then Gerhardt may not be far behind. It isn't that I think he may be out to get me, quite the contrary. I think that he is watching out for me and my company, to protect us all from anything, like he always has, even if it means that he has to protect us all from me. Another thing I know is that I have to have a very limited circle of trust on this. If Gerhardt knows what I know already, it could be, well, it could be rather problematic.

More Real Business for the Day

I meet with the car people and work out the details about the battery and car plans. We agree that we will finish building and open up the plant in Mexico this year to use whatever labor we can from the prisons there, which makes good sense because we own all the prisons in question.

Nearly forty years ago, the United States discovered that they were paying over $130 a day for the keeping of the average federal prisoner in the US. They began negotiating with Mexico to put a boat load of them in Mexican prisons, where they only spent about $5 a day on them. The US began paying Mexico about $18 a day per prisoner, which included an increase in medical care for the prisoners and slightly better food, but most importantly, it reduced the cost and got them out of the country. Ten years later, Danzig Services International took over about half of the US prisons in Mexico, at the Mexican government's request, and then renegotiated a $25 deal with the US. There was built fifteen new prisons, from the ground up, with much more tech, serviceability, and humanity. As part of the deal, Danzig also invested in job training and literacy for the convicts, as well as some programs that the federal government did not want to know about, because they were of a spiritual nature. As part of their training, prisoners were encouraged to work in making mining and drilling equipment. This could provide them with upgrades in their quarters and rations, as well as to pay them as much as fifty dollars a day, in the bank, so that when they got out, they could have a nest egg. Danzig never failed to pay on a prisoner's nest egg and even paid the taxes on the income and interest so that it would all be theirs when they were free.

The nest egg program is only open to prisoners with a release date. Lifers and death-row inmates are allowed to participate, but cannot save up the money for themselves for more than six months at a time. What would be the point? We do have things that they can do to make their stay a bit more pleasant, and any income that they generate, above the comforts they receive, can be sent to their families on the outside, to pay a lawyer, or a charity – and that is watched over very carefully. They are not allowed to work with dangerous tools and large equipment though. Support roles, so to speak, only. The prisoners that work in the plants get to stay in better facilities with better comforts and supplies provided. The married ones who do well can even plan multi-day visits with wives or family every once in a while in rentable suites. The suites look a lot like hotel suites, with wooden paneling, curtained windows, and the like. But the walls are still make of steel under the paneling, and the windows are illusionary screens, not real windows. Still, it is a comfortable, friendly environment, where a family can have a break from the harsh realities of their worlds. This really makes a difference in reduction of violence and discontentment as well as an increase in productivity and peacefulness. We wield a mean stick, but we hang out some sweet carrots too.

This year we are on track to open the auto making plants to be manned by trustees from five prisons being moved into a new facility that is 30% prison and 50% plant with another 20% in housing for half way house transition to another plant entirely on the outside. This new prison/plant is called Springfield, and it is the first of its kind. It can house nearly nine thousand prisoners and two thousand trustees or halfway workers. It will provide jobs for every one of those prisoners and halfway workers, at seventy dollars a day for the prisoners, plus their better room and board, and nearly a hundred dollars a day for the halfway guys. But, the halfway workers will also be able to spend part of their income on luxuries and service, like cable TV, (controlled) internet services, computers of their own, and restaurants in the halfway village we are building as part of the experience. I am going down next week to peek in.

Now it is a little before noon, and I still have some more Doctor related things to do. I need a chemist and a laboratory. I also need an unidentifiable stream of money that doesn't have to be big money, just a few hundred thousand from time to time. And it doesn't even have to flow on a regular basis. It has to buy parts and supplies. "Cinco, are there any empty floors in this building?"

"Well, sir," she starts, "it looks like out of the 130 rentable floors of the tower there are seven floors that are completely empty, two of those are under contract and being renovated, and there are 86 suites on floors that are partially leased or under company use. Those are between 2000 and 12,000 square feet. Would you like basic floor plans and spec printouts on those, Boss?"

"Yes, please, but only the plans of the vacant and available commercial floors, and some three bedroom apartments and bigger. And can you locate Mike's car for me?"

"Well, either he is driving 130 miles an hour through some farm land, or he is flying into Waco right now."

"Well, anything is possible, huh?"

Five minutes later I get a text, "In Waco now. Leaving airstrip." I send some texts in reply.

"Cinco, can you upload a list of chemists to my system?"

"What sort of chemists do you need, Boss?"

"I want someone that can reverse engineer a liquid product and replicate it for mass production. It has to be micronometrically precise. Does that help?"

"Well the list just went from 300,000 on the planet to a preferred five – possible twenty nine. I have put them on your system, Boss."

I activate my desk to review this information. Looking at the five premier resumes, I see that one is working for the US government in what used to be the Patent Office, now the Department of National Intellectual Properties. Another is currently showing as "disappeared" with a notation that the CIA may have had something to do with it, but it is also rumored to have been a "John Galt" abduction. There are continued rumors. Two more already work for us, so they are off the list, unless no one else was available. I don't want to use Danzig employees for an outside venture. That would draw too much attention, and maybe even compromise the schedule of ownership. The last name is Stark at Amway. It looks as if he is already doing what I want done but for someone else. And it looks like he is, arguably, the best in the field, or he would have been working for some other company already. He has been with them since they were in Michigan and is well into retirement age, or so he had hoped. They would probably like to keep him around another twenty, and they are already paying him a considerable sum for his skills. But I have something very special in mind, and if we pull it off, it could be worth a ton of cash, so I send him a text from my corporate phone.

The message has my picture on it, and underneath the image it reads, "This is personal, call me and receive $50,000 right now. J Danz." It takes the better part of thirty seconds for him to decide to make that call, or maybe it took less time to decide but longer to figure out how to dial. Chemists are not all tech nerds, after all. Either way, my phone rings, and with a single press of the button, we are speaking face to face.

"Dr. Stark, do you know who I am?" He nods quietly. "I have a liquid puzzle to solve, and if you will work to solve it, I will give you a $200,000 signing bonus, $300,000 per quarter for all the time you work on it. I will need a decision within an hour, doctor. And it goes without saying, but I am still saying, that it is also a matter of the utmost secrecy, so I appreciate your discretion on this. Text me with the place you want the fifty thousand for having this conversation."

"How long do I have to get my affairs in order before I have to be at work?"

"You would begin working on it, sampling it today."

There is a rather long pause on the line, and then he says, "Mr. Danz, I am sure that you can appreciate that I would also be burning my career at Amway, and my resume would be absolutely worthless if I left this job with no notice at all. And if we do something that is worth this kind of up-front investment from you, I imagine that there is plenty on the back end to go around. What kind of piece of the pie can I get, and how big do you think that pie will be?"

"The pie is likely to be ten to twelve figures, and you can be in for two percent, if you come today."

"How about five?"

"How about we make it three percent, and I buy you a house as an upgrade to your current home, a two million dollar solution bonus, and we call it a deal?"

Again with the pause, "Deal, Mr. Danz. Where should I go, and when should I be there?"

"I will text back the arrangements from another number. This conversation is absolutely confidential or the entire deal is off. Understand?"

"I understand, sir. I will be waiting to hear from you." I look up the Amway complex online and see a picture of the property taken from above. The date and time of the picture is a recent Tuesday morning about eleven. So my ducks are in a row.

I get a text about twenty minutes later, "Loaded and back on the bird with Mike. What's next?"

I send a text to Stark from the new phone that says, "West most parking lot in about half an hour. You will know it is for you. Don't tarry."

I get a text on that phone that says, "I will take the phone call money in cash when we meet, if that's okay with you."

I text back, "Sure." Now I gotta get something from the bank.

The Corporate Shell Game

Since Microsoft had seen the government coming for a takeover, thanks to an insider in the Department of National Investments, the Gates Family had done what many would later call the Midnight Miracle, or a high stakes game of Three Card Monte. They called the family money man, and the corporate comptroller, and had a meeting on Friday at midnight with about two dozen suits. The meeting lasted nearly seven hours, and what they accomplished was to move $80 Billion of the family's personal wealth, nearly a third of it, into personal accounts created for each of the employees of the company, at the destination for the corporation. Also, in their company e-mails were "vacation" plane tickets to Tahiti. There were 300,000 plane tickets, or so; for every member, of every family, of every employee. They had booked hotels on nearby islands for everyone, and nearly 13,000 quarantine layovers for dogs and cats on the way. Those that arrived at work on Monday were met with a banner sign draped over the Microsoft campus sign that said just, "Take the day off. Go home. Check your e-mail NOW." Over the next three days all of those e-mails were read and then deleted, the servers were wiped, then magnetized, and the entire campus was cleaned with an EMP. The tickets had already been printed and used, and on Friday, when the federal boys arrived to inform Microsoft of the "investment" they had made, all they found was a single, first-year attorney, with a note. The note read as follows:

Microsoft has dissolved, and the bulk value of the company has been disbursed among the previous employees. All employees have been made offers to work for a new software company called MS-Gates, based in another country, and many have accepted. The share-holders can have all the property, equipment, contracts, and the existing software and support in India. Have a nice day.

Two months later, Apple does the same thing, but having most of their operations in China already, they have less to share and move. And instead of a tropical island, Apple chooses Hondo, Texas for their headquarters, in an effort to re-nationalize some of their money and labor. They begin training and employing some of the Hondo prisoners to make many of their circuit boards. Some of their processors are now made at the Dominguez, Cagnon Road prison in San Antonio. Prisoners are taught to read and write, do math and to do a good paying job, and if they are excellent employees, when they get out, if they get out, they can transfer into one of the Apple operations already in motion. And when they go to apply for their new jobs, they come with references from Apple operations, skills for Apple operations, and history with Apple operations. It is a great opportunity for the employee and employer because they know for a fact the skills that each employee has before they have a job on the outside, and while they are on the inside, they can be on a never ending probationary status. Their retention rate – after release – is nearly 70%.

These kinds of business stories were becoming the norm. Toyota, Volvo, and Kia/Hyundai all moved to more friendly environments. Disney, having seen the government coming, followed in the footsteps of the Gates example, but put their California film and video production headquarters in Houston and Beaumont with a new monster theme park southeast of Austin on the Colorado River; "A thousand acres of adventure, discovery and water fun" is their catch phrase, and the original Disneyland . . . well, it is now the property of the city of Anaheim, but the name had to be changed. Disney World in Florida remains in operation as it was.

We are about to do something new, under the radar and almost worthy of James Bond and I have made it through the day without leaking a thought of it.

They stopped for refueling at Bergstrom in Austin, flew into the San Antonio airport, and arrive at Dancing Stag Tower about six, in Ilyssa's car and Mike's Trans-Am. They use my private elevator and come straight up from the garage to the apartment where I am waiting. Stephen called the elevator for them at my prior request. Mike is carrying two bags of canisters and Dr. Stark has two bags and Ilyssa is carrying a mix station – the other remains in Mike's trunk.

"So, Mike," I ask, "how is everyone?"

"I gotta tell you JD, I don't think they are any the worse for wear, but everyone is as curious as hell. You've got three people who never met before this morning, traveling hundreds of miles on a mission so secret that even though we're done, we still don't have any idea what it is we're doing."

"Dr. Stark! Nice to meet you. I read your resume, and of course, I ran a history and background check on you. Pretty impressive for a science nerd, no offense."

"Nice to meet you too, Mr. Danz," he replies, "and I take no offense at being called a nerd. After all, the world's greatest movers and shakers wouldn't have much to move and shake without nerds to think it all up."

"But" says Ilyssa, "I am still very uncertain where I fit into all this cloak and dagger, and how this stuff is supposed to benefit me. Isn't that what you said is our purpose?"

"Sorry to keep you in the dark, Doc." Taking the mix station, I shake her hand too, "But I am used to trusting Mike with some pretty next-level shit, and I am just starting to get used to you. Besides, I just realized yesterday that I know what I know, and how it can be used to take care of your monetary, and potential security concerns. If you would please just pay me a hundred dollars and sign here, I will gladly explain."

"What is this?" she asks. Reading it she finds it to be a very brief contract that has all the needful legal language to make the canvas bags, their contents and compounds, and any recipes resulting from them the property of Doctor Ilyssa Margarita Sanchez Marquez for the price of $100 Tex. She figures, "What the heck, if nothing else it has been an adventure." Besides, she has already made a small wad of cash for the day. Over $20,000! She signs and hands me a c-note. I sign, and the others scribble as witness of it. I have everyone follow me into the kitchen.

There is an electrical plug to plug in, and a little hose connecting to do, between the canisters and the mix station, but when it is done, there stands something that has not been seen in a decade, maybe much more. After venting the hoses into an empty glass, which I pour out into the sink several times to confirm the balance of the mix. I make each of them a glass, half full with ice, and I fill each of them from the fountain on the counter.

I raise my glass in a toast, "To our new adventure and whatever Doc decides to call it." We all drink, and the unanimous faces express happiness in having drunk; none more than mine.

"What is it?" asks Ilyssa.

"Well, it used to be called 'Dr Pepper,' but you can call it whatever you like when you are done with it. After all, you just bought the rights to the greatest soft drink ever made." She looks puzzled. She likes the drink, but she still looks puzzled. How is this going to solve her problems?

"Don't get me wrong, Joshua," she says, "I have heard of Dr Pepper. But I always thought it was an urban legend like Sears and Kentucky Fried Chicken. After all, who fries food? But what am I supposed to do with it?"

Mike knows. His eyes are alight. "Five percent you said, right? Five percent?" He turns to Doc and says, "In the beginning of the century, before the Michelle-ism of the food industries, people ate and drank, pretty much, whatever they wanted. And one of the things they drank a lot of was Dr Pepper. And before the government got involved, it was worth about six or seven billion dollars per year in sales, about one and three quarters to two billion in profits. That means that I would get . . . one fifth of an eighty . . . no . . . divide by two and then by ten . . . oh, hell . . . I guess it would be a ton of money. Is this even legal?"

"Yes, Mike," I assure him, "it is legal. When I saw the end coming, I warned the people at Dr Pepper about what I saw in their future, with the government working on every level to get control of everything, and I made an offer of five million US dollars cash for the rights to the Original Recipe, in the event of corporate ruination due to government involvement. They said I was crazy and that it could never happen. But after some conversation and drinks, laughter and general good humor, we decided to sit down with the board, and I upped my offer to ten million in personal payouts to the board members, and made it into a personal bet between us. We had someone in 'legal' over there write it up and put it in that manila envelope. Since I was unavailable during the collapse and they have not been able to give me the recipe, you've got goods, and you've got Stark, and there ya go."

"Are you sure about this?" asks Mike. "Five percent for me?"

"I promised you five percent, but I am kind of relying upon the Doc to agree to that. Same as the three percent I promised Dr. Stark. Is that okay with you Doc?" She smiles and nods, but she is still uncertain about how this is all going to work.

"If you had told me it was Dr Pepper we were to be replicating I would have had less trepidation in coming," says Dr. Stark.

"Dr. Stark? I have made some arrangements for you as well. I hope you don't mind. Since you said you would like the 'phone call' money in cash when we meet, I thought you would be agreeable with the idea of getting the signing bonus that way, too." He nods in stunned amazement and approval. "So, with that in mind, I had Cinco communicate with Ethyl when she was on her way over here. She stopped by my bank and picked up the $300,000 I had waiting for her to bring here. I hope it is okay in hundred dollar bills in a canvas shopping bag. I thought it would be less conspicuous for a modest woman carrying something that doesn't scream, 'Look at all the money! Please rob me!' If you know what I mean." He takes up the bag and looks inside dumbfounded. "Also, Cinco found that we had a few empty apartments below. I noticed that it is just you and your wife at home now – your bio said that two kids are grown and gone, and there are three kids at college – so I selected a nice five bedroom unit with gym access. That way, you can have a backup office in the apartment and still have plenty of room for guests, kids, grandkids, whatever. I hope that's okay."

"But you said '300,000' what's the other fifty for? I need to call my wife." Looking around, he says, "What should I tell her?" I think our doctor is an ADD kid like me.

"Tell her you took a new job and she should plan to move as soon as possible." I look at Dr. Marquez and ask, "Do you plan to do the work in San Antonio, or was there somewhere else you had in mind? Don't forget you have a day job with me. And the extra fifty thousand, Doctor Stark, is for you to buy into three percent of Doc's beverage enterprise. Or, you could just keep the money, I guess, and have a job."

"What do you mean, what do I have in mind?" says Ilyssa. "I have no idea what anyone has in mind with all the 'what and where and who.' Maybe we can discuss this like grownups tomorrow. I just want to go shower and sleep . . . but I also want to eat something. Anyone else hungry? I still have over a thousand dollars cash on me. Who wants Mexican food?" My hand and Mike's are up. "And a margarita?" All hands go up.

"Doc, now you know how I felt when you hit me with that bit of info yesterday, eh?"

We five, Doc, Mike, Stark, Cinco, and I, go across downtown in the Bentley; Stephen drives to a place called Mi Tierra for what has been called "the best Mexican food in San Antonio" for so long it stands out in both my memory sets from before. We talk about everything we can think of, politics, weather and helicopter rides. We discuss what kind of investigative chemistry Dr. Stark has done and learn that he began his career because his dad was a chemist in a crime lab in LA.

He got the bug for digging in the chemical ooze and dirt from the age of six when his dad took him to work, and he got to see all the magical tubes and beakers, and he saw his father put together the evidence that helped find a child's killer in a hit and run. Nothing could be cooler work than that. But then they had their third child and soon after were expecting the fourth, he knew that the crime lab was not going to pay enough for all those bills. Then one of the children got ill, and the bills piled up on them. If he hadn't been doing private chemistry, he would never have been able to afford the insurance to keep his son in the hospital, much less to save his life. I don't remember what the child had, but I am glad Stark had become so good at what he did that I could find him. I can't help hope that it will all pay off as I expect.

A couple of times when he is speaking about his children or his wife, I realize that I have set my left hand down on the hand of Dr. Marquez. I also notice that she often doesn't move it right away. Every time there is a "heart string" moment in the conversation we notice that our pinky fingers touch, or maybe our knees. We can talk and look each other in the eye without glancing away. I like the chemistry . . . and I like the chemistry. My right hand is usually on the arm of the chair next to me, frequently under the hand of Cinco, when I'm not reaching for a fork, a bite, or a glass.

We eat, we enjoy, and we make our way back home to the tower. On the way, I ask if Doc wants to be dropped off at her place, or if she wants to take her car home, and she says, "I don't live here. I live in Dallas. But, I guess that has to change too, doesn't it?"

"Let's all just sleep on it tonight," I say, "and we can discuss it over lunch tomorrow. Sound good?"

We get back to the apartment, and Mike comes up to help Dr. Stark with his bag – the bag of cash – and takes him back to his place. Dr. Stark wisely takes fifty thousand dollars out of the bag and sets it on a table for Ilyssa. Stark will stay tonight with Mike. Mike has an apartment on floor twenty, and Dr. Stark will soon be setting up on twenty two, both of them on the west side of the building. Beautiful sunsets and a view of downtown are theirs. Mike has a two bedroom, and on twenty, there are eight of them, and ten three bedrooms, while Dr. Stark's place is an eighth of the floor, forty eight hundred square feet . . . very spacious. It has a kitchen to rival any Westside restaurant and a balcony that can comfortably hold twenty people, seated. Not a bad spread for a chem nerd, eh? He can go shopping for some furniture tomorrow if he wants. He has money.

Decisions, Decisions

Bubba has the morning shift and checks in by phone at eight o'clock. It is Saturday and I am planning to sleep in, but this is not to be. "Were you planning to train this morning, sir?"

"Not today, Bubba. We had too much fun last night and will be in the building all day. If that should change I will let you know."

"Thank you, sir," he says with a bit of a laugh in his voice, and he hangs up.

The secret cell phone rings. "Hmm?" I say as I answer.

"Hey! There's a lot to talk about, and I have no one to talk to. Mrs. Dennis has made Belgian Waffles with chopped strawberries on top. Get out here," It is Ilyssa, and she hangs up. Don't people say goodbye anymore?

I guess I am getting up. I quickly jump into the shower with a bit of conditioner in my hair, and a quick scrub of the bod, I jump into the DYSON-T ("Dry YourSelf Off Non-Towel") for an all over body blow dry in about twenty seconds. It's really quite wonderful, and with a little rubbing, bending, and turning, one can dry EVERYTHING. I brush my teeth and hair, put on a decent t-shirt and some sleep pants – my mom used to call them clown pants – and I head out. Which mom was that?

"Good morning, ladies!" I say as I enter the kitchen.

"Mister Danz?" I turn to look at Mrs. Dennis, "I found what you wanted for dinner, but you had other plans, so I had them put in the pool," she says with a smile, "I hope that is okay."

A bit puzzled, Ilyssa and I get up and head to the pool which is one floor up and at the other end of the apartment. We open the door, and there in the pool area, one in the water and the other walking around the patio by the eight foot tall PlastiGlas wall and railing, are two Galapagos Penguins. The one in the water seems to swim full speed across the bottom of the water and POP up onto the sidewalk, only to waddle with haste over to his girl. He raises his beak, and she raises hers, and they nuzzle each other raising and lowering their beaks and gazes. They chatter and clack and waddle to the pool to start doing some laps together. He pops up, and she follows; they dive in again, then she pops up and he follows. It is continuous and graceful as they are sporting with one another.

"Aww," says Doc. "Look how he loves her." I am thinking the same thing, but it would not make me look very manly to notice such things. I could be wrong. Smiling, we watch for a few minutes, then we return to the kitchen.

"Mrs. D? Why are you here on a Saturday? And where did you get the penguins?" I ask her.

"The penguins are rented, so they go back on Monday; I guess I should call the pool guy to clean up after, eh? My kiddos all had something going on this weekend, so I thought I would look in on you two and check the fridge, shelves, and stores for needs," she says, looking a little lonely. "Also, I wanted to get some of the penguins lined up for E-1 coming to work here."

"Do you mean ducks in a row?" I jibe.

"Whatever it is you young people say these days."

"Yeah, what is it with you and ducks?" asks Doc.

"You know, Mrs. D, Bubba woke me wanting to do something, and I had other plans, but, how about I arrange for the two of you to take in a movie or something before the shopping?" I ask, and she shrugs with a smile of agreement that this is a good idea, so I send a text. He sends one back that says he would love to pick her up in half an hour. I tell her this, and she goes into the pantry to do inventory and make menus. Bubba says in his text that if he is taking Mrs. D to the movies and shopping, that I had better stay in the tower. I relent, and it is agreed.

I pick up my utensils and with a fork in my left fist and my knife in my right, both fists resting on the edge of the table on either side of my plate, I apparently bow my head and quietly say, "Thank you Lord for this food." I begin cutting my waffle in quarters and apply a few spoons of chopped strawberries and then some blueberry-maple syrup.

"I didn't know you said Grace. I would have waited for you," says Ilyssa.

"What do you mean, 'Grace?'" I ask.

"You know, that moment when you bowed your head and said 'Thank you Lord for this food' before eating?"

"Did I do that?" I don't recall doing it. I shrug. Is it common for me to do that and I just haven't noticed it, or is this something new? Hmm.

"What are we doing today?" she asks.

"Well, I thought you were going to do some thinking about where you wanted your corporate headquarters and labs." I reply. "But that doesn't have to be today. It is your enterprise and your schedule." I wave my hand dismissively, as if disinterested. "Do what you want, as you see fit. I am strictly here in an advisory capacity."

"Are you certain you are not going to want some sort of partnership or something? Maybe some stock? You deserve it, and you will doubtless earn it."

"Nope. No shares for me, but I may expect a lifetime supply of product. How much Dr Pepper would that be for me anyway?"

"Well, let's see. How old are you now?" she asks, almost as a joke.

"I was born All Saints Day, 1956."

"Russell Anders was born on 9 January of 1969." She glares at me a bit. "You mustn't let something like that slip again." Then she thought, "Still, it is a clue. What else do you remember?"

"I think I was born in South Carolina – Fort Jackson." She begins taking notes on her phone. "That's all I can recall right now," I say. "Can we have breakfast by the pool?"

"I suppose that won't be too bad if the penguins stay downwind." I am not at all sure if that actually means something, or if she is pulling my chain, so we will stay put . . . in the kitchen. I let her know that I have some spaces available for labs, here in the tower and several apartments available as well. She asks if we could look at them later and we set it up with Cinco. We look at about a half dozen places, and in the end, she chooses a three bedroom place with three baths and an open living/dining/kitchen area. She says it would give her a bedroom, a home office, and a guest room, just in case. It is on eighty-seven and an eighth of the floor; 2800 feet facing east. She is sometimes a sunrise person, and sometimes that is when she goes to bed. It will be a few days before she can have the furniture and tech delivered from her old apartment in Dallas, so she will be staying on as my guest, at least 'til all the details can be worked out.

We have a nice day looking at the properties available for her research department; we look at several partial floors and a couple of full floors and even consider connecting a few units on multiple floors, but decide that the stair and elevator situations would be less time and energy efficient. So we concentrate on the single floor opportunities.

She selects a floor that has space to serve as her doctor's office, to take care of my medical needs, and has plenty of room for several labs to be built, secured, separated, and supplied with a semi-private elevator possibility. During traditional work hours – eight to five – one of the elevators could be dedicated to her use if she wanted. At first she chooses not to, but decides about six months later to change her mind, but in reverse; she would prefer it be private during odd hours. It turns out that both she and Stark are, by nature, night owls, and they do an awful lot of experimentation and collaboration late in the evenings and sometimes in the early mornings. The elevator connects the labs to their apartment floors, my office, the garage, and the lobby level, by means of a thumbprint scanner.

The original rent agreements have to be drawn up with the leasing office to avoid any sideways glances from Gerhardt and the other owners or renters. It may be easy to hide an apartment like a pied-à-terre for a mistress, but to rent out a floor, over 10,000 square feet would draw some attention, and we would rather it all be as above board as possible, for myriad reasons.

Part of the space is dedicated to her doctor's office for my health concerns – about 900 square feet – another thousand feet for medical lab, tech, and x-ray stuff – but the rest of the floor is leased by her as a research facility, which is paid for from her own pockets, mostly her signing bonus, as far as anyone else can see. Of course, since she is an employee, she does get a substantial price break on everything, and we manage to work a lot of the other expenses into her employment agreement under "relocation, cost of living, and cost of doing business adjustments." On Sunday afternoon, we sit down with the building manager, and she signs papers on everything, paying cash for deposits and the first six months' rent, which encourages Mrs. Dunleavy to expedite the construction options on the property for the lab. Mrs. Dunleavy is an accommodating woman that has come in for a couple hours, after church with her family, but part of the reason is doubtless that I have promised her a significant bonus for the time spent on this matter. As much as she is a kindly Christian woman, Mrs. Dunleavy can surely have a hard business side to her, and that combination, along with an A&M born MBA specializing in property management, makes her an excellent building manager, so, I gift her a "time share" that I won in a bet a few weeks earlier. I liked the way one team sounded over the other and went with it. The time share can be used at over a hundred destinations, up to three weeks at a time, twice a year, so it is a real good deal for her. A much better deal than it would have been for me. I already own places to stay in most parts of the world that I am interested in, or I have connections to them. Mrs. Dunleavy will leave on vacation for three weeks, exactly three months after I give it to her. She, the hubby, and the four teen aged children will have a great revigoration, all thanks to a west

Texas oil man who chose the wrong team on a Monday night. Please understand that I have no formulas, systems, or even a good understanding of the inner workings of football, but some things are just too much fun.

Ilyssa will have her apartment furnishings arrive in a day or so, and business is going great toward her getting started. The labs are getting built with all the needful partitions and protections and water sources put into place, with all the needed filters and cleaners, fire safety, and ventilation – it is "ducks in a row" and she has them.

It is actually Wednesday, and I awake again, only this time, being happier than I have been for a while, I don't even press the snooze button but hop right into the shower for a quick rinse and don't even brush my hair after the DYSON-T, all the while singing *Oh What a Beautiful Morning*. As I go into the kitchen, content as can be, earlier than usual, toes wiggled into slippers and tying up my robe, I am singing "what good is sitting alone in your room" and there is Doc, making eggs and turkey bacon wearing a satin bathrobe that reminds me of Greta Garbo. She is startlingly beautiful and I am excited to see her, trying hard to conceal it.

"Gay, huh?" she says, almost as an aside. "I guess the show tunes are the last give away, but then I suppose I could have guessed." Her hips gently sway as she works the spatula turning the bacon, splashing the grease on the eggs. The satin flows like dreams on a breeze, gently, gracefully sweeping over her hips, thighs, and calves. The image would have been perfect if her glance came back with a cigarette in her lips, but her smile and knowing eyes did the trick pretty well on their own.

"Not gay." I reply, half in jest, not with anger, but as a simple matter of fact. "My folks watched a lot of musicals. It was different back then." She flashes a wry smile, like she knows something I don't, which is common with her. She often knows something I don't. I look her in the eye as she smiles and I say, "If you could see under my robe, you would know I'm not gay." She flips the bacon, one more time, and then the eggs, and then she turns off the fires under each of them, slowly, deliberately. I am seated with my coffee by now, and she crosses the kitchen to sit down as well, in the chair facing me; just watching her walk is intensely stimulating.

She replies, "What about if you could see under mine?" Her robe falls open outside her thighs and her legs open to where what she wants to show me is plainly visible. She is bent on discovering a way to prove I'm not gay. She kisses me sternly, putting her hand on my head she drags me to where my knees are on the floor, still locked in her kiss. She becomes certain of my sexuality in the most determinately validating way I can think of. At this point though, I am really not doing much thinking, but, thinking is not what she is expecting from me. She grabs my head by handfuls of hair, and takes my attention for what seems like a day and then some, all I can actually think is, "Hey, it's a Charlie Chaplin." I am on my knees, her one foot is on what had been my chair, her other is on the table. When she is done with me . . . when she is satisfied for the moment, she lifts my face to kiss me deeply again, and using one of the table napkins, she wipes my face and then hers. "Breakfast is ready, if you are."

She pours us a couple of glasses of orange juice and serves the eggs and bacon, and we eat our breakfast; I eat in silence. "I gave Mrs. Dennis the day off last night," she says at one point. Another few minutes pass by and she says, "I had something in mind that she didn't need to see." I can testify that this is certainly true. Several additional minutes pass as we finish our meal. "I checked your calendar, and you aren't due in the office for another hour or so." She dabs her lips with her napkin, then mine, and she climbs onto my lap, and kisses me again, grabbing a handful of hair again.

"I kind of have a girlfriend," I say, caught in her clutches, unable to hide my excitement any longer.

"Yes, and this morning, she's gonna be me," comes her reply, and she kisses me again, not slowed in the least. "Got a minute?" she keeps two hands full of hair, leans in close and licks the back of my upper teeth, "Or a little more?" I stand up, carrying her by her hips, with her legs tightly cabled about my waist, her arms around my neck and her mouth glommed onto my lips, all the way to the bed. I am about twenty minutes late getting to the office; my hair still looks a mess.

I can't help thinking, "I gotta love a sexually determined woman."

The Cinco Hypotenuse Conundrum

"Maybe I should have stopped by this morning," says Cinco, as I come in late, hair everywhere. "Maybe I should have been stopping by all along." She is a bit miffed, to put it mildly.

"Do you want something exclusive?" I ask, and the phone rings; she answers – I am rescued, but for a moment.

"Joshua Danz' office." Then there is a pause as the person on the other end is talking and as they speak, she raises her finger to me like a mother telling her school age child to wait, the adults are talking.

"No, the new specs on the prison contract have not arrived as yet. When they do, Mr. Danz will have me contact you." She listens, "Mmm Hmm. No problem, sir. Have a nice day." She hangs up the phone with some force. "I don't know if that's what I want. What I know is that I want you."

"And I want you too," I say, "but I am as personally and emotionally confused as anyone has a right to be." She is a bit confounded by that statement, so I tell her this, "Because you are the most crucial point of my life, in work and out, I need to have you get together with me this evening, or sometime soon, so that you can learn about me what I just learned about me." She backs up slightly. "Please!" I step forward, she slaps me in the shoulder for encroaching, but I find myself looking in her eyes and taking her hand as she wriggles as if feigning attempts toward freedom. "This is terribly important to me, and you are amazingly important to me as well." She softens a little. "Please?"

"Okay," she says, with a tearful voice, "Tonight! Do it right before dinner! Then, if we are still seeing each other, we can go out. You and me . . . someplace nice, right?"

"I guarantee it." She strokes my desktop screen twice and leaves my itinerary open on the desktop computer and heads for the door. "You pick the place; anyplace you want. In fact, if you want to make the reservations and even pick out the menu, we can do dinner at eight. You and me . . . someplace nice, right?"

"That I can do," she says with a bit of a smile, "but this had better be good."

"I promise you, it is," I shoot back, "and so are you." She smiles. "Thanks," I say, with hands folded in gratitude, bowing as she leaves.

All day long it is contracts, arrangements, agreements, and disagreements, settling issues with batteries, prisons, wardens wanting raises, prisoners needing "specialized health care" – whatever the hell that means – banks in the islands, chocolatiers in Europe having to work without sugar – I got that covered – international monetary funds, anti-terror training, and more, but at the top of my thought processes for the whole day are these two women and what they each know about me, and/or what they expect of me. Somewhere in the middle of it all, I phone Doc and arrange for her to do show and tell with Cinco at six thirty or seven, I really don't recall when. It is an interminably long day and what seems like a long commute home, up twenty-three carpeted stairs to the main floor of my apartment.

I arrive at about 5:45 and get jumped by Doc, with a lip lock, legs around my backside, her hands in my hair, and my hands on her behind, with a smile on each of our faces. She is wearing jeans and a cotton blouse – much harder to remove than the robe from this morning – or I could find myself in some serious danger from Cinco very soon. She climbs off of me and says, "My furniture has arrived early. It is being setup in my apartment right now. Wanna come see?"

"Not tonight," I say, sensing and almost smelling her disappointment. "We have to meet with Cinco in just a little while, remember, and I really need you to take her seriously as we tell her everything you know about me."

"Everything?" she asks.

"Everything!" I say, "She is the one person in the whole wide world that I have learned to trust with everything."

She looks a bit put out by that statement. "What about me?"

"Please understand," I begin, "you knew all of this before I did. I have to trust that your information is correct and true. I didn't have a chance to grow into trusting you." She is not happy with me right now. "I took you at face value, and you have proven to be exactly what and who you say you are, and that is great. Ethyl, that is, Cinco, has been with me for several years, watching over me and keeping my secrets from everyone since the very first day, and that should not and cannot be dismissed." She slaps my face and sits down. "You are a rational and reasonable woman," I insist. "And you are one who – by career choice and training – weighs evidence and information as it comes to you every day in all kinds of situations." I take her by the shoulders and stand her up, right in front of me, "I am asking that you do that with Cinco and this situation. She is, for all intents and purposes, the long edge in every triangle of my life." She rubs my face where she had slapped me, then kisses the same spot. "And, she deserves to be included and respected, whatever that means in this confusion that is my life."

"I'm sorry," she says with reduced intensity, "it's a woman thing, and it shouldn't be. You don't belong to me. I will be back for show and tell in a little while." She disappears through the front door, and I disappear toward the shower.

I stand there in the shower for what seems like hours, letting the water wash over me from three shower heads; and one of them is even dispensing a soapy lotion in the water. As there I stand, my hands against one wall, soapy lotion and lots of water wafting the troubles of the day away, or so you would think, suddenly, as if in a dream, I feel hands on my back, massaging, pinching, even clawing a little; then, I realize it is not a dream, this is Cinco. I turn around to face her; she pushes me against the shower wall. She kisses me; almost violently, as she sits me down in the corner seat and switches off the soapy lotion dispenser, leaving all three shower heads running torrents of warm, clean water. She sits down on my legs face to face, straddling my lap and says, "I want you to know, beyond a shadow of a doubt, that I really like being your woman, and I want to be your woman, no matter what, regardless of the context, and I don't want that to change." She kisses me, kindly, lovingly, deeply, and passionately for what seems like forever. I could have expired in that kiss and died a happy man. "I gotta get ready for tonight." She stands, turning to go, and then, ebulliently, "I have a date." She gives a brief scratch to my chest, and after a quick rinse, steps through the blower with a towel on her head, wraps herself in another towel, and disappears. Remember? A sexually determined woman! Wow!

Before I can move, she has left the bathroom, and by the time I am thinking of getting out, she is long gone from the apartment. I shave, rinse, dry off, brush my hair, get dressed and wait for what seems to me as if to be days – actually just about ten minutes – for someone to arrive. The first one there is Doc. She looks around as if to see if we are alone. We are. Her briefcase is in one hand, and with the other, she strokes my face and kisses my cheek. No lipstick; she checks. She takes her stuff to the living room area, and in a minute or so, she has her tablet connected to the TV and is ready to tell Cinco everything that she has told me.

Cinco arrives about five minutes later wearing a Mexican Wedding dress – not for the bride, but for a guest – and a tasseled shawl or scarf with coins along the edges, tied around her waist covering about half of the skirt. She wears no stockings, open toed flat shoes, suitable for a long stroll, and still mostly wet hair. She makes no comment about getting ready in a hurry, and she lets herself in like the lady of the house, gives me a brief kiss hello, takes my hand, sits down on the couch, pulling me along after her, and says, "Okay, show me what you got." It starts off feeling very much like a vacuum cleaner demonstration, with Doc selling an idea and Cinco trying to keep it at a distance. But as the program progresses and the facts become apparent, her resistance falls, and her possessive grasp on my hand becomes more of a scared or worried clinging than anything else. She sees the danger in what has been put in front of her, and as the information is winding down, she moves closer and closer, right up against me, with one hand in mine and the other grasping the inside of my thigh, as for security, I suppose. We talk only briefly afterwards, and hurriedly at that. After all, we have a date.

Doc is still moving in, and when 7:40 comes around, she lets herself out and goes to her place to help the movers get the last of the boxes into the right locations. She will spend the night washing dishes and putting them away, rinsing towels and drying them to be put where they belong, and finalizing where the furniture should sit in the dining and living area. Tomorrow she will move it so that the area rugs can find their natural locations. Tonight though, it will all seem like busy work as she muddles through, constantly concerned with how things are going with Cinco and me.

On that front, we talk just a little more about our situation – my situation – on the way to the restaurant, an old Lebanese place on Fredericksburg Road. In the limo, I take a moment to tell her, "I want to be your man, no matter what else, regardless of the context or complexities, and I don't want that to change. Do you understand?" She nods to me like a school girl who has just been asked to the prom and is excited to say yes, but finds herself speechless. She will spend the next five miles or so cuddling up under my arm as if for warmth and safety.

She has made arrangements for us to have a private alcove, out of view from everyone else. She has paid in advance for everything: music, belly dancer, wine, couscous, and lamb with a few other details that I do not now recall. The subject comes to her mind again, so we talk a little more about the dangers and agree that, at the office at least, we will have to be on a top secret basis and that no one, not even Gerhardt, can know what we know . . . not if we can help it. We are about done with dinner, and a belly dancer is performing beside me, as Cinco, to my left, reaches her right hand around to my jaw and pushes my face her direction for a kiss, as if to remind me that I am with her, and she digs the claws of her left hand into my leg again to drive her point home. Trust me, I have no doubts as to who is my date. I mean, really, the belly dancer is pretty and jiggles in lots of wonderfully accessible places, but I know for a fact that my date can do things to me that I have not yet fully begun to imagine, though I am willing to discover. I am happy to reach my hand to her face and reciprocate when; BANG!

"What the hell was that?" flies through my mind, so I look at the curtain, and so does Cinco. Benson had caught a man trying to come into the alcove, dressed as a waiter, but not our waiter, with a gun under his tray. Benson grabbed him by the collar as he was entering what would have been our view, had we been looking at all, and with a slight but forceful spin and kneel technique, he has thrown him down on the floor, landing him on the back of his head and neck. He proceeds to punch him in the side of the head one time, and the assailant is now quite unconscious. Benson is a formidable man, and I am glad he is on my side. Benson cuffs the man's elbows to each other with a zip tie and his wrists to his belt and sits him in a corner chair. The police show up and take statements and remove the attacker as we finish our meal. The attacker has apparently acted alone; and since the restaurant has only a front and back entrances – and only one way into our alcove – Benson decides that we can safely finish the evening's plans. The officers ask for an autograph and a picture with them before they take our intruder away, and I relent – they are nice guys, here to protect and serve.

By the time we leave, it's a little after 10:30. We make our mind up to take in a masquerade cabaret on the loop. For about a hundred bucks, they rent you a costume and open the bar. It is like a scene from *Eyes Wide Shut* as we enter separately. Men dress to the left, women to the right, then they exit the dressing chambers in different directions. Part of the fun is to find your partner, and no one is allowed to remove their masks. I am dressed as the Phantom of the Opera – the Lon Chaney one, not the musical – and she is dressed in a rather traditional Cleopatra – Liz Taylor, not Claudette Colbert. I recognize her by her walk, and I lay hands on her from behind, but she does not recognize my grip on her behind and almost takes my arm off, before seeing my eyes. She is a formidable woman. I like it! Before the night is over, we purchase the costumes – as many people do – and return to the car where Benson drives us around the west half of the loop, with the partition up, privacy at a maximum, during which time I will make a trip or two up the Nile and Cleopatra will collaborate with the Phantom so that we will make some beautiful music together.

As they used to say in the old days, it is a magical night. We must have totally exhausted ourselves because, it is about four in the morning when I wake up and find a half naked Cleopatra, still wearing her mask, sleeping across my lap and on my shoulder. This is going to leave me sore, I am certain. "Hey, Babe, we're home." She stirs with a slight growl and looks around 'til she sees my face – no mask to be found any more – she closes her eyes again. "C'mon, Babe!" I chide, "You can't show up at work looking like that." She looks down and sees her skirt is missing, but her shoes are still there. "You know what a pain in the ass the boss can be." She looks good in every way I can imagine, and if I weren't so sore and stiff from being in that position for so long, we could go again. But in reality, mine is the wrong kind of stiffness. We do eventually find our way out of the car. I slip her skirt up, and I carry her from the car to the lobby stair. Benson sits in the driver's seat watching as I get her out, not helping a bit. Still, he keeps us safe, and that is his real job. My neck hurts.

I keep her in my arms all the way to her apartment, resting quietly on my shoulder, and I carry her into the bed. As I lay her down and pull the covers over her, still dressed in what is her costume, she looks like a real Cleopatra to me. As I pull an extra pillow from under her head, she puts her arms around my neck and kisses me again, saying something that sounds like a drunk and/or sleepy version of "I love you." I lay down next to her; "I love you" scrolls across my closed eyelids quickly, with me on top of the covers and her under them, for the rest of the morning – in this case that was about an hour and a half.

Her alarm goes off, really loud, from the other side of the room at six o'clock, screaming some ancient rock ultra-classic that only I recall, blaring, "Hey, hey, momma, said the way you move." Holy crap that's loud I think, possibly out loud – she stirs slightly. "Gonna make you sweat, gonna make you groove." By then I am standing in front of the clock and have just about figured out how to end it. "Ooh child," click went the button. When I turn around she is sitting up, covers half down. Cleopatra's gilded outfit almost glaring at me, and she says, "Coffee?"

"Are you asking for some?" I say. "Or, are you offering?"

"Take your pick," she says, throwing back the covers. "I gotta pee."

I'll lay back down again, but just for a moment. "Time to get up," she says standing over me. She has apparently showered and dressed while I blinked my eyes. "Breakfast is ready," she chortles. I murmur something that could resemble gratitude, but may also be a request for my own demise. I have a hangover as big as the bathroom, which is what I need to see right now. I take the liberty of emptying my stomach contents, orally, into the toilet, and she brings me a cool, damp washrag, which is kind. When she is convinced I am done, she gives me a pill to help settle my stomach, and that is great. She gives me a mouthwash to get rid of that taste, and that is definitely good. She gives me a towel and points to the shower, and that is excellent. When I get done, I come out wearing her bathrobe, and she feeds me a small cup of espresso with a half shot of vodka in it, four ibuprofen caplets, three eggs, soft, dry, fluffy, scrambled in the slightest hint of oils, and a dry piece of toast, and while every minute of that seemed hideous and excruciating, it did the trick. In about a half an hour, I am ready to take on the world. Well, in an hour or so, I am at least ready to go back to work and muddle through another day.

We settle into a routine in which I have these two "girlfriends," if we are to call them girlfriends, but I would take someone out for the evening and sometimes stay over after. Sometimes I will go home alone after, and sometimes, someone will go with me, but I am not shackled like those married people I know and I'm not lonely or on the prowl like the others. I'm sure I could have had a better life, but I would have been very hard pressed to figure out how. The security team members are the only ones that know I am seeing these women on a regular basis, and we are never photographed out in the world. We only go to places that offer extensive privacy, like that Lebanese place, with private alcoves or rooms, so as to avoid starting rumors about any of it. We don't want to get curiosity going about Ilyssa's doings, and Cinco doesn't need any more scrutiny from Gerhardt than may already be there, just because she is my "right hand man" – so to speak – and overall confidant, and that used to be his position. As time goes by though, I begin to see Cinco more, perhaps out of greater familiarity, but partly because of the simple fact that Doc has become one of the busiest women in the world. Between research and staff management, finding properties for creation and distribution, lining up potential shippers and distributors, all for a product that neither exists yet, nor can she adequately explain, her plate is full and getting fuller.

I suppose when it is all factored together, over the next several months, Ethyl, that is Cinco, has become the first real love of my new life, even though Ilyssa is always heavy on my heart and mind. This will be molded, tested, and remodeled as we go.

Part Four — Opening Politics

Keith T Jenkins

.

November

It is springtime in Texas, and things are beginning to green up nicely. I look out my windows to the north and east and can see some of the farm lands in the distance. I can't make out what is growing, if it is just pastures or cash crops, but it is green, and that means that life is going on. It is the first Saturday morning that I do not have big plans on the books in . . . well, forever. Gerhardt said that this would be a weekend off and that I should try to "have one," but I am uncertain what that means. It seems like I have been "working" for months straight, if not years, not that it's hard work, and there is little or no sweat involved, because most of the work is mental, a test of wills and in some ways even highly entertaining, but it is still work. Though there are people that would testify it never happened, I can remember working with my hands and my back, when I was younger, and in some ways it was easier. For one thing, at Miller Time the work is done and it's left behind. But what the heck is Miller Time?

I have left the TV on and am listening to the news while I am taking coffee on the balcony. The sliding glass doors are open, and the TV is pretty loud when I hear some talking head say that the election season is heating up nicely and that the Republican candidate has a substantial lead, but that these things tend to get a bit closer as Election Day approaches.

I zip a text off to Gerhardt asking, "Am I registered to vote?" It takes a few minutes for him to get back to me; after all, he is with his wife at Natural Bridge Complex. The reply comes as a phone call.

"Sorry, we didn't think about that one. Would you rather go to them, or we can have them come to you?"

"I don't understand. I thought I would just fill out a card and mail it in."

"Not any more. Your palm prints have to be taken and they have to be associated with your driver's license. If you are poor or immobile, they come to you for free, but you are neither, so the service is an extra $500, or you can go by the DMV, and it could take as much as fifteen to thirty minutes, depending upon the lines."

"I think I would like to go to the DMV. When can we do that?"

"I'll get you an appointment and get back to you."

He calls me back in about twenty minutes and says, "I got on the web and booked an appointment at a Quarry outlet for Tuesday at 2 PM."

"Excellent! Thanks again and sorry to disturb your outing."

Where had I been? Had I missed the primaries altogether, and, why am I just now learning that there is an election going on? What is the chief office that was being sought? Who are the candidates? What do they stand for? All of these questions are going through my mind in the time it takes to cross the deck and close the doors. I sit down to learn something. Actually, I sit down to learn everything. I don't even know what the significant issues of the day are, how they would impact people, my business, international relations, and more. So, I go to my "table" in front of the TV. This is the single coolest device ever. It is kind of like something I had seen on some *NCIS* program from forever ago, but this one is even cooler because this one is mine.

It is in front of my couch, and it looks like it has a top made of knurled walnut unless I put my fingers on the top and my thumbs on the edge in front of me. Then the walnut image disappears and reveals a twenty-two by forty-eight inch computer touch screen. It is, in fact a giant tablet that interacts with the TV, and it even has an interactive screen to the left, if I need more space. The wall on the left side of the room is another screen that has to be activated from the table. Until it is activated, it displays whatever super-high-resolution image of art I prefer. Under normal circumstances, it looks like Venus Rising by Botticelli. To activate the wall, I just pinch the left edge of the table while it is active, and the wall reveals the operational desktop. The wall panel is five feet tall and hung a foot or two above the floor, and it is eight feet long with a resolution that comes out to about 300 dots per inch. And it is – here's the cool part – a touch screen computer in its own right, still connected to the table.

The TV is a marvel of the age, and I haven't even had my unit "Texas Configured" but used it right out of the box, so to speak. But I am getting tired of the thing running the "US Standard" and have scheduled someone to come fix it soon. The US standard has the screen displaying several channels down the left side of the screen, like picture in picture, and one main display that plays along with the sound of what you are watching. You could either touch any one of the smaller channel panels and bring it to the front and listen or just move the sound over to that one, and it can be controlled by either a remote or from touch on the table. A triple-tap to any blank space on the table will bring up the remote panel for the TV, and it is amazing.

The left edge is topped by a small screen of MSNBC, "The National News of Today" and that screen never moves unless it is called up as primary. It is locked in by the government. Below that is a scrollable list of over twenty more news channels that can be pushed up to where your news choice is on the left screen, then it could become the primary screen. The list would reset each time you would start the TV. At the top of the list are CNNNBC, CBSBC, PBSNBC and CNBC when you turn it on. These news channels are moderated by the US Department of Transmittive Liberty, a descendant of the old FCC, whose motto is "To Affirm the Truth." It is directly affiliated with MSNBC because of their undying loyalty to the federal agendas of Social Justice, Redistributive Fairness, and the welfare of all. Below that is Al Jazeera and AJ2 (formerly Current TV) etc. 'til you get down to Pravda, right before FOX at the very bottom. They can't actually get rid of FOX, and Pravda has begun to speak truth to power in a truly embarrassing way, so they were put on the bottom with FOX. But Pravda and FOX still have better ratings than all of the others, even being in the most inconvenient channel locations.

Also a part of the US standard is that the chat cam is online all the time, even when the user has not authorized it, and it is being mechanically watched and listened to and recorded by the feds for future review. Few of us actually know this, but government computers are listening to almost every conversation in every room within range of a TV, personal computer, digital entertainment system, and they're listening for nearly two hundred general key words like "jihad" and "explosives" and keeping track, as well as another four or five hundred words that are trending at any given time. If there is any sign of suspicious word use frequency, then recordings can be pulled and reviewed for audio, then if it seems warranted, video can be scanned and examined in various levels of detail. Mine is not hooked up yet, and if or when I get it hooked up, I want a physical connection I can terminate. Maybe I will just leave the Band-Aid on it.

Tuesday comes, and at 1:30, Bubba drives, and Cinco goes with me from the office to the Quarry Shopping Village, and leads me straight to the Department of Motor Vehicles Contract Substation. Bubba follows close behind, scanning the shoppers as we go, standing guard at the entrance as long as we are inside the facility. It is far different from the DMV that I had experienced in 2010. Back then you could come in the door at 9AM and not leave by noon. Sometimes the lines were out the door and even around the little state run building. But this is more like a customer service department at a Wal-Mart or Penney's, only about three or four times as big and much faster, without the carts full of products to return. There are twenty agents at service counter desks, and even though there is a steady supply of customers coming in, it takes less than ten minutes to get from the back of the line to the counter.

"Hello, sir, welcome to the Quarry DMV Substation, my name is Angie. What can I do for you today?"

"Angie, I need to register to vote. How do we do that?" I ask.

"Wow! Where have you been? Under a rock?" She asks.

"Well, sort of a long story, but, yeah. Just tell me what to do and we shall do it."

"First, do you have a driver's license?"

I say, "Yes," and produce it for her.

She holds it up so that it faces her monitor, which captures an image of the card completely. Then she swipes it through a groove in the edge of the desk. "Place both hands, palm down, on the screen." I do as asked, and a pale green light passes below my hands. She swipes the card again, has me step back for a photograph, and says, "There you are. That will be $34 and we're done." I pass her my Tex-Ex card, and she swipes it through the same slot she used to swipe my license, hands me a receipt, and that is it. "Your new license with Voter ID will arrive, by standard carrier, in a couple of weeks. You have a wonderful day," she says, and I believe she really wants that wonderful day for me.

I ask Cinco about the DMV, and she tells me the story of how it was suggested by some "redneck" that two things could change the DMV for the better, for everyone. She does not mean the word redneck in any derogatory way; she had once told me that in her vocabulary it means "a hard working soul that toils in the outdoors." She goes on saying, "He had suggested that if the workers at the counters could receive an additional compensation as small as a quarter or half dollar for each transaction they completed properly, that their demeanor and productivity would increase exponentially, and he was right. The state increased the cost of the tags or stickers or licenses by sixty cents so the commission could be paid and it went into effect. For most of the employees, it didn't make much difference in their attitude . . . the first month. After all, they had only been promised some vague number added to their income. Most of them, having been drones and state employees for so long, had no idea how 'piece work' could pay off, so they reluctantly went through their days and duties, that is, until pay day came around. They were paid twice a month, and the average counter worker processed about 700 units a week, times two for two weeks' work, paid an additional fifty cents per unit, and BAM! There was an extra 700 bucks in the check. Suddenly they weren't so miserable to be around. Well, some were still miserable, but they got weeded out in a few months and replaced. As for the rest of them, they began to smile at customers and treat them like the friends and neighbors that they had always been. It was a wonder to behold. 'Why hadn't anyone thought of this before?' was the number one question of the day for a long time."

"You said there were two things. What was the other?" I ask.

"You just experienced it," she says. "It is the notion of contract servicing instead of having to go just to the DMV. The office that we were just in is able to handle any kind of renewal or application that requires the acceptance of money, notary activity, etc. for any license or plate, so long as a test, other than vision, does not need to be administered. If you need to take a driving exam, or a written test, it still has to be done at the DMV, and there are still only about fifty within a hundred miles of here. Those are still run by state employees and cops, but since they are all getting a little more in their checks – all but the cops – they are also still a bit less miserable. Don't get me wrong; they are still state employees and still complain about the hours and the pay, but they also make more for their work than anyone else doing their kind of job. But it seems that complaining is, apparently, in their nature." She stops to think for a moment and says, "Maybe that really is one of the personality requirements to be a satisfactory state employee – being unhappy with whatever it is you receive. Hmm."

"Do you want to get dinner later?" I ask.

"I have to go with Gerhardt tonight. I'm sitting in for you at a fundraiser. Then I have the weekend away."

"What kind of fundraiser?"

"It's a dinner for Mikel Moore." She tilted a crooked smile. "You'd probably like him."

"And the weekend away?"

"We can talk about that later. I gotta go now." A little kiss goodbye and she is gone.

Election Fraud, How Could That Be?

Today, I want to know about the elections. I pop MSNBC to the front screen, just because it is at the top, and listen to the presenter talking about watching the Texican elections to see who would be the next president, as well as who is running for office in the US. The news man says, "But first, we look at Texas, or as they prefer to be called, the 'FreeNation of Tejas.' In that election, we see the incumbent, Mikel Moore, son of immigrants, military man, and one time VP of and successor to Ted Cruz, the third president of Tejas. Moore is a staunch conservative that is said to be even more conservative than Cruz, but that is opinion. What is not an opinion is that he is praised with perfect ratings by every Family Values organization and the NRA, which still operates openly in the fledgling nation, and he is marked as an enemy by Planned Parenthood, which does not operate in the FNT anymore because of their zero funding for abortions and abortifacients."

Perez Hilton once said of Moore, when he was running mate of Cruz, "This is a man that everyone at GLAAD wishes was dead. There's no more room in this world for god-damned Christians like him." About the Administration and Tejas, Perez had said, "Those people and the whole fucking state are so bigoted that I wouldn't be caught dead there." Ironically, the aged Mr. Hilton died six months later of a form of HIV for which a cure had been developed and was readily available in any San Antonio, Houston, El Paso, Waco, or Dallas Baptist hospital. The drug had not been approved by the US Food and Drug Administration, and Mr. Hilton refused to go to Texas under any circumstances.

"Mr. Moore's lead contender is Harold Wallace of the Americrat party," the talking head would say, "the great-grand-son of one time Governor of Alabama and US presidential candidate, George Wallace, and the great-great-grand-son of Coretta Scott and Martin Luther King, Jr. Wallace is running on what could be called 'Old School Democrat' ideas that have, for the most part been settled in Tejas. He promises to establish a greater 'safety net' for the poor, which looks a lot like President Obama's American Assistance Act of 2015, which increased the welfare numbers from twenty-five million to sixty million in his last year in office. Wallace also promises to remove the drug testing mandate for all those on any Texican assistance, saying that it is a violation of their medical privacy to have to be 'poked, prodded, or pee in a cup to get their daily bread' – which was the same argument that had lost ground when the law had been created by then Governor Rick Perry and friends. The counter argument is that 'these people don't have to share their status with us, but we are under no obligation to share our hard earned money with them either.' This became the supposed standard by which all assistance and welfare of any kind has been handled in Tejas ever since." Another thing that makes Wallace's argument hard to win with is, if you are a welfare recipient in Tejas, you are not allowed to vote.

The screen changes to clips of the debate from last night where we see Wallace saying, "These poor people have no other options than to rely upon the kindness of the people of the FreeNation, being unable to work on their own." But then the clip switches to Moore saying, "If people will not seek help in ending their addictions that keep them from being able to work, there are over a thousand shelters across the FreeNation that can give protection from the elements, sustenance for the body, and essential medical care. These things are provided by people who have chosen to willingly contribute to those causes. It is not fair for us to forcibly take the money from those that work and give it to those who won't work and won't change." And then back to the newsman, "This is a primary lever for Moore . . . the challenge of letting the working class keep more of their 'hard-earned' money. The other big issue is what used to be called 'women's rights.' But that means something else in Tejas than in America." I mute the TV and begin reviewing "old" news about the American presidency on the table and tube.

I found video of Wolf Blitzer in 2027 saying, "In the American elections, we see that President Castro has chosen the former US Congressman, once Secretary of [I can't remember what] in government, and his twin brother, Joaquin Castro to be his running mate in his re-election bid. Here is their announcement." The background zooms to the foreground, Julian Castro speaking, "I can think of no man or woman that more closely reflects my vision for America than my own twin brother, Congressman Joaquin Castro. He has served tirelessly in the San Antonio City Council, the US House of Representatives, and as my personal advisor for my entire life, and while we have had our disagreements about girls and cars and the usual things that twins argue about, we are of a single mind when it comes to the continuance of the vision begun by the founders, defined by that great President Barack Obama seated there," he said pointing to a seat in the audience, "and the late three-term Vice President, Joe Biden. And so, it is with great pleasure that I nominate my brother, Joaquin Castro as Vice President and announce him also as my running mate. I hope the Senate accepts this nomination and confirms him quickly, but either way we expect him to be sworn in come January." Fade back, newsman in front, "That was Wednesday, and in a surprise move the Senate had an Orange Juice Session and announced this morning that Joaquin Castro would be sworn in on the first of May on the floor of the Senate, marking the start of the first fully Hispanic Administration." I close that window. I scan the headlines – 2020 – Barbara Boxer wins election with running mate Julian Castro, making her the oldest elected to the presidency. Nov. 2027 – Boxer passes away, before launching her election campaign, leaving Castro to take her seat as the President Pro Temp. Castro selects Sheila Jackson Lee to be his VP. Candidate . . . Lee comes out as "Bi" locking down the gay vote. "Lee and Castro Win!" says the headline. Lee passed away from some cancer and is replaced by Joaquin Castro. 2036 – Joaquin Castro elected in longest single party White House victory string since the founding of the nation.

I'm done. This is too weird. Just the mathematics of it is astounding. Another thing that is astounding is that it is now six in the evening. I have been watching the past forty years of election video and reading news for eight hours, and I have come to realize two very important things: first, I really need to give Mrs. Dennis a raise for all the help with the day to day chores around here more than the bi-weekly house care I used to have, and second, the results of the elections in the US was statistically impossible. Not improbable, but impossible. There is a tipping point where the improbable becomes the impossible, and the first victory for Julian Castro had tipped that scale significantly – undeniably. But the subsequent election victories pushed that improbability to extremes never before imagined. Still, I soon discover that there may be relief on the horizon in the form of a business college research program being evaluated by the Supreme Court.

Apparently, the Metropolitan College of New York, a community college with a focus on business and a concentration in "Financial Services," has been performing a Probability Study on the American Elections as an exercise, and have found some anomalies that date back to 2008. There had been some before that, but none since 1960 have been as totally decisive as in 2008, and the anomalies grow exponentially with each election cycle following the 2010 mid-term.

At first it is a numbers game . . . what were the odds of . . . Later it turns into a quest that results in search warrants and equipment inventories and audits. And in the end (so far) there were nearly 380 arrests.

It got interesting when it was discovered that in the 2008 Presidential election there were over 140 precincts that had more people voting than were registered to vote. In all other elections, in all other precincts throughout history, there have been fewer votes than registrants because there are always people who simply will not go this time. But somehow, magically, they all turned out, and then some. There was blatant voter intimidation, caught on camera, that made the circuit on YouTube, and when given to the Justice Department, it was said to the press that convictions would be a "slam dunk" – but those charges were dropped outright by the incoming in-Justice puppet master, Eric Holder, for racial reasons. There were rumors of voting machine manipulation that arise, but that was never examined for one simple reason: no one wants to be the person, group, or agency that says the first African American President had cheated his way into office. After all, most of the media was already calling anyone that disagrees with Obama about anything a racist. It didn't matter if you disagreed with him on taxation, birth control, unions, the auto bailout, socialist healthcare, or the distance to the moon . . . you are a racist. No debate – You Racist!!!

The 2012 elections are worse. Fifty nine precincts of Philadelphia have zero votes for the Republican candidate. Nine precincts in Cleveland are the same, and a total of one hundred precincts in Cuyahoga County, Ohio have no votes for Romney, and in some others nearby, Obama got 99% of the votes. Even in the Reagan landslide of 1984, where he soundly won forty nine states, there were some percentages of opposition votes in every county and precinct in the nation. It is mathematically impossible to not have opposition votes. Even the most staunchly "Democrat" states will have some Republican voters . . . in every single precinct. Even a single precinct that is 100% on a candidate's side is a monstrous statistical anomaly. But dozens? Hundreds? This is impossible. "Let's look deeper," they say.

Headed by a young Professor named Rathbone, the students in the project take it from a class project for "Statistical Reality: A Study in Probability in Real Life Situations" to a real life investigation of elections for the past fifty years, and it has an impact.

After finding the mathematical anomalies, they began to research everything from the ACORN voter turn-out model to the property holdings of the who's-who of the Democratic party for almost a century, nationally, on the state level, and even the personal real estate of the leadership at the precinct level.

They also found an old, actually an antique YouTube video of a guy in Ohio on the 2008 Election Day, saying, "Yeah, I voted about 45 times, but they found nearly 30 of them so far, so what good did I do?"

The news person asked, "Would you like to tell us who you voted for?"

"Barack Obama, of course."

In Minnesota, a professional comedian who had forgotten how to be funny won a US Senate seat with more people voting in thirty-five counties than were registered to vote. In 2012 there was a "recall" election in Wisconsin that was launched by an alleged 2,000,000 people having signed a petition to get rid of the governor. When the election comes, the recallers lost soundly, but there were just barely 2,500,000 votes. How could that have been with so many allegedly honest signatures? And it continues to be the case. Too bad the original petitions were "lost." They had found their trends, Rathbone realized. Now the cause has to be discovered.

The dirty little secret of property was discovered in this part of the research. In New York, Ohio, and New Jersey there were, owned by the party, small warehouses, under 4000 square feet, in ten locations; each one is paid for from national committee funds. In six other states, there are smaller warehouses either funded by the state level apparatchiks of the party or owned outright by senior party members. Understanding this, with the bulk of the student population being die-hard liberals and Democrats, many of them began dismissing the properties as, "Well, they have to have places to store stuff. I'm sure that they have lots of stuff." But there were other trends in these properties as well. They only had utilities turned on for three or four months, every two years. The keepers of these units had discovered that they don't need to pay for lights and heat or cooling but once every couple of years. These places light up with a fervor, just prior to the elections, and then for a couple of weeks after, wrapping up. Rathbone is as much a die-hard lib as any, but he is also one of the rare honest academics of the ilk. He says to his key investigators at the time, "Many of you will end up working in actuarial fields, some in insurance, and others in shrinkage. The question that you have to ask yourself is, 'Are you willing to follow the evidence wherever it leads?' If not, do something else. The day may come when you have to investigate and even prosecute someone you know. Will you turn a blind eye or learn the truth?" Too bad he doesn't teach journalism, eh?

One of the students leading this investigation, Aubrey, was the daughter of a Hollywood dad who makes his money in the movie biz. While visiting home for Christmas break, or as they call it in California, "Pride Week" (twelve days of debauchery), she had dinner with dad and a friend who searches for projects for LucasFilms division of Disney. She told them some of what they had been researching, their methods, and what they have found, and within a week, they are well funded – but LF/Disney owns the rights for film. They have a twenty five million dollar investigation budget.

They use their new resources to expand their search and their investigation parameters. They get several private investigators in the mix and even a few ex-spooks and Special Forces operators. Two weeks later, at a project update meeting, it is shared that some of the warehouses they are watching are active again and that the lights have come on, which is to be expected. The gas is back on, the windows are glazed over, and there were small numbers of people coming and going. Late at night in the first week of activity, one of the ex-spooks breaks into one of the warehouses in New York, and another breaks into one in Cleveland, and guess what they find. Exactly what Rathbone expected to find . . . voting machines and computers! One of the spooks managed to clone a hard drive from one of the computers which had a voting machine connected to it, and could you guess what they discovered? That's right, the voting machines are being equipped with a virus that will change the count of the votes and then delete itself when finished. As soon as the count is concluded, at the end of a voting day, the numbers would be re-tallied, according to the desires of the programmer, and then the virus is instructed to clean itself from the system. The system will then report the "results" of the day and, viola, an election is settled. It was even slicker than the Harry Reid election of 2010, which was the initial testing ground for another, similar program.

In 2010, it was widely reported at the close of voting hours that there had been a "state-wide electrical anomaly" according to the cable news networks. And even though Sharron Angle had come from fifteen points behind in the polls, two weeks before the election, to a lead of ten points the day before the election; the election went almost exactly the opposite direction. What was the difference in all of this? It was because of a "state-wide electrical anomaly." Still, the tech was a success.

To test their theory in a practical setting, they commission ten voting machines be purchased from the various makers that are represented in the states of Ohio, Pennsylvania, Indiana, Illinois and Michigan. They have the makers set them up with actual election software that is going to be used in the school's student government elections in September, with the notable addition of a Disney character to each race. Once the machines are delivered, they take a single laptop, built from the cloned hard drive, and set up each of the machines for the desired result. They then take the machines and post them in some of the common areas where people are asked, "Please go into one of the booths and vote at random for anyone you wish. This is a practice run for the elections." Each booth has video monitoring and they learn that, in each case, there is a variance of votes, and most people vote for their candidate, while a small number actually think the process is silly enough that they vote for the cartoon people. There are exit polls and people told on themselves, and according to the video records, they told pretty reliably, especially those that took the Disney vote. In the end though, the Disney characters would each win with between fifty two and sixty percent of the vote. With a total of nearly 3500 voters, with video recorded voting that is counted manually, the wins are decisive, even though it was also totally false. In most of the races, there is an actual living winner, and sometimes by a very notable margin, sometimes it is close, and in a few races, it is low forties to high forties and a few percent going to the Disney characters. As an aside, there is also a race for Dean of Students, and even though the name did not even appear on the ballot, SpongeBob won with a 54% "write in" vote, with perfect spelling – but, according to the video record, no write in votes were cast.

Armed with this information, the academics take their documentation and research materials to the Federal Election Commission, and after a three hour run-around, they find themselves summarily dismissed. But unknown to the academics, the ex-professional field operators and ex-spooks – who have been in service to a nation without a political agenda, but for a belief in something bigger – well, they have a different plan in mind, and it is about to unfold in the boldest possible way. Remember that these men had sworn to "uphold, protect and defend the Constitution of the United States from all enemies, foreign and domestic." They are about to do exactly that.

They actually make over 400 posters that they apply to the tables at the operations in the warehouses, defining areas as "voting machine goes here," and "input candidate names here," and then, "insert vote fraud virus here," followed by, "verified fraudulent voting booth loading," and they get hundreds of their ex-spook and special forces friends to break in and post these posters in working warehouses across the nation. Then there is a mass calling of State, County, and Local police organizations with reports of "major drug deals" going down at these warehouses, calls report brothels and human trafficking, and these calls are followed by calls to local news agencies that are filming live when many of these raids take place.

Some of the warehouses are protected and don't make the evening news, or even the police blotter, but the result is still profound in more ways than one.

The next day, Professor Jerold Rathbone had apparently committed suicide, in his car, in a Jersey City park, with a gun that was registered to him, and is said to have been bought by him, along with the ammo, at a gun show in Tennessee. That is what the receipts say. This is particularly strange since he has never been to Tennessee, and because he had been part of numerous anti-gun rallies the past five years, before trying to drive legislation to force gun owners to surrender their weapons. It is then that the spooks realize how deep and high this might actually go.

I am looking forward to seeing how far this investigation will get when I get a call from Mike, and then it gets interesting in a whole new way.

"JD, I need a favor for a friend. He's ex-CIA, and he's got ledgers."

"Where are you now, Mike?"

"We're right outside of Indianapolis. This is hot, JD, and we gotta move." I can hear someone in the background.

"Tell him we got over thirty years of records, names, amounts, accounts, and more," the voice is saying.

"I got that, Mike." I think quickly, "Can you go south? Can you keep it all under wraps and go to Lexington?"

"I'd rather go to Frankfort, if you don't mind." The voice behind him says something I can't understand. "I got people in Frankfort."

"How quickly can you get there, and undercover?"

"Give me two hours, and I will call you back," he says.

"Switch off your phone 'til you get there and take out the battery," I tell him.

I disconnect from him and dial Schroyer, who is not happy to hear from me, because he is incredibly busy. It is, after all, election season, he has plenty of work to do, and money to make, so I have to make it well worth his while. "John, who are you backing in the upcoming elections?"

"In Tejas or the US?" he asks.

"Either one."

"The most conservative candidates I can find! You?"

"I'm backing my pilot, who says he has ledgers and names and pay-offs and dates for elections going back decades." There is a pause. "Can you guess what they have found?"

"No, but I want to see what they've found. And if they found what I pray was found, eventually had to be found, then I want to let the whole world see it – page for page, dollar for dollar, as far back as it goes. I'll come to you right now."

"It's not here, but I will be leaving to get to it in less than an hour . . . so. You wanna go?"

"Hell, yes! I'll be at your place in just a bit."

He comes, and we go as quickly as we're able. As he arrives in the parking lot my personal jet is landing on the roof. The pilot is relieved, soon to be reporting to the Executive Game Room, and Cinco takes the left seat as the company co-pilot also exits the plane. I meet Schroyer in my office, and we make our way up to the roof straight away. Benson is in tow as we board, and he seals the door. The plane lifts up, and Benson checks the back and then goes up front to sit with Cinco and he asks, "Where are we going?"

"They didn't say?" she asks, and he shakes his head. Her eyes are on the instruments, the tower, and the horizon, so she says, "If you nodded, or if you shook your head, I didn't hear you for some reason."

"No," he says, "they didn't say."

"Well," she says to him, "in an hour and a half, we should be in Frankfort, Kentucky."

She gets us out of San Antonio air space and drops to the deck – or close to the deck. We are going nearly 800 miles an hour at an altitude of about six or eight hundred feet. Let's see, it took Schroyer nearly half an hour to get to the office and a couple minutes to get to the plane, then another hour and a half of flight, and there is the call. *Little Deuce Coup* plays on my phone letting me know it is Mike. "We are in a barn at my uncle's farm. I have left my GPS on, so Cinco can get a fix on us. I will turn it off in one minute." He hangs up. Cinco has the fix locked in, and it is doubtful that anyone else can fix as quickly as she does. She has the advantage of having the number on ping from the jump, waiting for Mike to activate the phone again. We stay low as we approach, but we fly a recon loop around the area for about five miles around the farm, before we descend on Mike's location. We set the plane down about a hundred feet from the barn and exit the plane.

Schroyer, Benson, and I hurry into the barn while Cinco keeps the plane warm. As we enter the barn, we are met by Mike, his uncle Carl, and a guy who says, "Call me Bob," sitting on the door frame of one of our Hueys.

Bob is not his name, and Mike is not breaking his confidence to tell me what it actually is. I don't mind, this time. "What do you got, Bob?" I ask.

"What I have is a ledger, actually several ledgers, from the Chicago office of the Democrat party from as far back as Mayor Richard J. Daley, and it has pay-off records that go back to the Kennedy election in 1960. This thing ties the mobs and unions together with the Democrats so tightly that it got John and Bobby killed, or at least it shows the connections to those who paid to have them killed." He looks around as if checking to see if anyone else is looking in, and then he says, "There were a few lesser elections in the 45 years that followed, but in 2008, they started going bat-shit crazy with the corruption, graft, vote buying, manipulation, and more. There are media figures that had thrills up their legs, election officers, computer programmers, and voting machine makers on these payrolls, as well as unions – from teachers to teamsters and from auto workers to government employees and screen actor union members – as well as anarchists and even terrorists. They have been paying them all to manipulate the social calculus of modern political thought into making people actually believe that maybe, just maybe, Socialism is a good idea and that the Democrats have the best and maybe the only ideas out there. I tell you, this thing reads like a Redford movie script. There has to be an Academy Award in this somewhere, except it is on the wrong end of the political spectrum for them to ever consider." He looks around the barn again.

"We should get you, and that, out of here." Schroyer says, "We can put that information out into the world right now, if that is what you want. But, I think it would be better if we manage it."

"What do you mean, 'manage it.' I thought we would just dump it onto every news outlet in the world," Bob says, clutching his satchel to his chest.

"No offense, Bob," I say, "but if we dump it, then the news media will just begin picking you apart as a nut-bag and then start tearing apart the information, and then the government will do whatever they can to get the information back or destroy it, including us and those around us." Now I look around the barn. "No, we have to be careful who gets what and when." I turn to Mike for a minute and look back to Bob. "Do you trust Mike?"

"I put my life in Mike's hands before," he says, "and it has always worked out well for me."

"Then stay with Mike in my bunker, and we will all work out how this should be revealed to the world. Okay?"

Mike put his hand on Bob's shoulder and says, "Come on, buddy. You gotta trust someone, and no one else came all this way to get you." Bob nods in resignation, slowly with his head down, and then there is an intense rush and rumble from the wind of Cinco, turning up the power and setting the plane to hover, as she lifts the landing gear while the steps are still down. We know that means that we need to go.

"Mike," I say, "can you fly that bird out of this barn?"

"Piece of cake, Boss."

"Then we will lead them away and you wait a while and head south a little while, then get your ass home," I say, "Okay?"

"Sure thing, JD," he japes, giving a mock salute, "whatever you say."

Benson goes first, gun in hand, with Bob behind, followed by Schroyer, then me pulling up the rear, weapon drawn. We don't need any fire power, but I am glad we have some, just in case. We step lively as we ascend the stairs. As the cabin closes and Benson seals the door, we can see a couple of Black Hawks speeding over the trees from about five miles out. "Buckle up, everyone," says Cinco over the intercom. "This could get bumpy." The vertical jets on the plane kick into some sort of superdrive, tilting almost straight up as the rear thrusters power up, and the bird rises to four thousand feet in very short order, and then we head north by northeast at near minimal speed. We have to get those choppers to follow us a while to facilitate Mike's escape. They are following but fading from view. They turn around and head back to find the chopper they lost – Mike's – and with their speed advantage, they might find him. Cinco turns the bird around, seeing that they are in pursuit of Mike, and she buzzes past one of the choppers, about three feet off the blades, then she blasts the left bank of vertical thrusters, throwing us into a right roll, and tossing the Black Hawk into a roll that dumps it out into the tree tops. As our plane stabilizes from the roll, Cinco has to take evasive measures to avoid a missile fired from the other bird, and she accelerates to supersonic speed and altitude to bug out. Being unarmed, there is little more we can do for him now. The rocket follows as well as it can, but in the end, it will run out of fuel and drop into the Gulf. Up we go, faster and faster. At altitude, we cruise at far greater speed, and we are in my bunker in little over an hour and the staff pilot is taking the plane back to the airport. He is elated about his new high score on some game he'd played.

Benson takes me aside to confer a moment, and we decide that Bob, though a guest in the bunker, should not be entered into our security protocols because any access he could have to anything at all should be accompanied by Benson or me. I make some lame excuse, "I would have you entered into the system, but we would need another technician to set that up, and he can't come for a day or two," I say. "You have access to anything we have here, but it is all keyed to me and Mike." I nod my head as I say, "You understand." He nods his too. I don't know if he fully believes me, and in reality, I don't care as long as the information is good. Benson could have put his hand on one of the scanners and then pressed Bob's hand against it; with a voice command, Bob could be on the list of cleared persons, but this is my palace and I am not ready to trust Bob with the keys to my kingdom just yet. After all, he was a spook once, back in the day, and I don't even know his name.

Word came that Mike has been forced down near New Orleans by a Black Hawk which then fired on him as he ran for cover in a warehouse area of town down by the docks. Before hitting the pots on the rotor of the bird with a lucky shot and grounding it, he took an injury and crawled out of sight, only to be found by some dock workers after a few minutes. They called an ambulance that took him to a hospital where he was patched up and remains resting by the time we hear. I wish we had just left that Huey in Frankfort and taken Mike with us to the tower instead of worrying about the hardware.

It seems that a bullet from a Black Hawk missed him but struck a door frame that he was standing near, and a splinter, over a foot long, flew off and stuck through his flight suit from the lower left of his back, only to reveal itself to his front. He has lost a good bit of blood, and he is in a public hospital, so I do the only thing I can think to do – I send Ethyl and three quarts of my stored blood supply. I am O-negative – universal donor – and my blood has been cleaned and stored in our facilities, which means the best in the world has been done for it. After all, it is meant to be used for me.

She has been in the "shop" being upgraded at Gerhardt's request, to have her medical training elevated to those of an ER doctor with surgical skills as well. It is a brilliant idea having her get four years of med school, residency, rotations, and who knows what else, in a three day period of time. We should train all our doctors this way.

This could open up a whole new market for all kinds of information assimilation from cooking school to medical doctor and even just the training of a new skill or task for a fairly menial job. Imagine if your company usually uses a training program that requires sixty hours to educate a person in company procedures. What could it mean to have it transferred into an employee's head in an hour . . . straight into a person's brain? When I trained for telemarketing, we trained for two weeks to learn to do it their way – read the scripts, press the right keys. They trained thirty people per class, two classes at a time, all year round, and tripled that from mid August to early December. At just ten dollars an hour, how much did they spend? For Ethyl to get the full "Doctor" upgrade cost a little over $3 million, which is one and a half times the cost of a medical degree. But, it is also the whole program, not just the four years, and it is a prototype. It will be duplicable and reusable. The cost of the products could be far less. Gerhardt says we should be able to give full medical training to a "worthy candidate" for about $60,000, maybe less – and a worthy candidate would be someone with the right aptitudes, not the right cash reserves.

We spend the next two days pouring over those ledgers – one is a very large, old fashioned, handwritten book, another is on a dozen large floppy disks – we have to get a disk reader from some ancient storage – another is on a sixty four gigabyte jump drive – more antiques – and the last is on an asynchronous cloud transfer and storage reader. All of them are originals – no copies among them.

We sort through the documents from the cloud-X and post on the front pages of several news agencies the graft of the latest elections in their own towns. We post Chicago election and racketeering frauds on the front digital and physical pages of the Chicago "papers," and in New York, we post the election frauds of the last four years, which it turns out is most of the elections there. There are similar stories to be had for Philadelphia, Pittsburg, Los Angeles, San Francisco, St. Louis, Detroit, Milwaukee and a dozen or two other, smaller cities. In addition to sending it all directly to the front pages, we send copies with newly invented e-mail addresses and burner cell numbers to the "letters to the editors" and to the editors themselves, and to hedge our bets, we send additional copies to all of the FOX outlets and Pravda, as well as Al Jazeera and La Prensa online. Most of the city newspapers take the stories down in a couple of hours or less as their readers make them aware of the stories because they don't want that kind of info allowed into the world. But within a few hours, FOX and Pravda have been running the story, not only about the stories, but also about the news agencies removing the stories that they already had. It is amazing to behold. The tapestries begin to unravel, and the ivory towers begin to crumble and crack.

In Philadelphia, the physical papers are thrown from the news-stands into the streets as litter, many stands are lit on fire and there is a riot in the streets where the mayor is burned in effigy and leaves his office, via a back exit to the underground parking in city hall, before he is burned in reality instead. In Detroit, the racism of the elections is so thoroughly revealed by recordings and citations of the Mayor, that his office and his home are burned. He escaped from the home, but having run over a couple of people who are part of a mob attack on his house, he panics, losing control of his car, drives it into a stone wall right beside the gate even as the police have come to the outside of the gate. When the mob of angry citizens attack the car and tear him from behind the wheel, the police are not motivated to help him. They are, in fact, motivated to cheer the mob. It is like Mogadishu in October of 93. The Mayor's wife and children manage to take a servant's car to the docks and get on a boat that allegedly drops them off in Canada, but no one knows for certain. In New York, the police know all about the graft already. Hell, for the past twenty years most of them were in on it, and when the defecation strikes the rotary oscillator, they will protect their mayor and meal ticket. The same is true in DC, Pittsburg, Cleveland, Boston, and LA. There are a few more cities that have some serious shaking up, but besides old fashioned destruction of property – which some consider a very reasonable way for these crowds to vent such anger – there is not as much violence as there could have been. Hell, an Occupy Wall Street gathering made more of a mess, and the crime count was often higher, but no one even remembers them anymore, showing up only in obscure mentions in college history books. All in all, there are about a dozen city officials dead, and another couple dozen or so ousted, but the calculus doesn't change, just the names of the masters. And the higher puppet masters still pull the strings.

In the subsequent several issues of information over the seven few weeks, Schroyer begins to put out the information about the election frauds perpetrated on the populace regarding the selections of presidents, and there are serious doubts by large volumes of voters as to who actually won each of the last several elections, and then it happens. It is the big possible bomb of information, way beyond all the rest.

A bastard grandchild of someone in the Obama Administration, born way back in the twenty teens, publishes a book called, *The Pilfering of the Presidency: How the World's Greatest Republic was Brought to Socialism by an Illegal Alien*. It is the tale of the Obama election to office and how it was entirely fraudulent, that it never should have been allowed to happen, but that no one had verified that he could meet the legal qualifications for the job, or that in fact, he did not. Accompanying the book and a tour around the globe is the author and the only known copy – a certified, original, vault form – of Barack Hussein Obama, Junior's birth certificate from Kenya, dated June 3, 1961.

It was in the possession of Rahm Emanuel, Obama's first White House Chief of Staff. Emanuel had been sent to Kenya right after Barack was elected in 2008. Emanuel's mission was to destroy all copies, but apparently, he kept at least one. As a shrewd Chicago politician, Emanuel knew that it would be just the insurance he may need for his future political aspirations, and while it was useful for that – guaranteeing his office as Chicago Mayor – it was more useful later on to his grandson who was never recognized, and never given the family name, but who managed to steal the document and write the book, telling the tales his grandfather told around hushed tables, late at night. Rahm Emanuel had managed to secure the wellbeing of three generations of his own family, with only one political betrayal.

Suddenly, every piece of legislature that president signed into law is not law anymore, according to the Supreme Court. Still, the Congress will not act accordingly, and through a decision from a "committee of the whole," they come to consensus agreement that all laws will have to be reviewed on a case by case basis, in committee by departments, to determine if they would have carried their victories by enough votes to have passed without a presidential assent as if overriding a veto. Those laws will remain in effect, but those laws are very few and far between until about 2034, when the majority was so decidedly Democrat-Socialist that almost all decisions were by a "Super Majority."

Then again, in a year every Democrat Congressional seat will become in question and the doubt will be great enough that there will actually be people running as Republicans, winning seats left and right, even though, for the most part, these Republicans are not conservative enough to be recognized in the early Twenty-First

Century as being Republicans – even compared to John McCain. But we have to hope that it is a good start.

We help Bob to get all of the information digitized and stored on dozens of servers around the world, available to every search engine so that it would never be able to "go away" – ever – and we give him a new identity, which he is already working on anyway. We put together a "retirement plan" for him and send him on his merry way. Mike is in on the plan, and it all seems agreeable to him and to Bob, and the threads of the political nightmare tapestry called American government are being pulled at from every morally or politically curious computer in Tejas, America, and beyond.

There is almost nowhere that the revelation is not being discussed, mostly in open and honest ways, but also sometimes in shameful and covert, even nefarious ways. For the next five or ten years, there will be some politician that has been in the national or international spotlight that is retiring or resigning, every month or less, and that is a good thing. It doesn't matter that some are leaving due to sex scandals, and some from election fraud revelations, some due to graft allegations that just will not go away; it really doesn't matter why. The entire government needs a political enema, and, thanks to Bob's acquisitions, Schroyer has just the right cleansing solution. Still, the puppet masters remain, even though the number and power of their puppets has been seriously reduced, and the Sorosites have all but died off in the political world. Hell, NBC and its affiliates are down to a combined market share of only six percent for all their networks, which means that without significant government funding, they would have to close their doors. If the government takes the long deserved pendulum swing to the right that many expect, there could easily be thousands of far left enterprises that will lose their tax fed federal sponsorship.

For a period of nearly six weeks, Ethyl's primary job is Mike and his healing. He thinks that all the nurses are cute, and no offense to anyone, but Ethyl is hot, and skilled; talented with a med kit and a gun. At that moment, Mike confided to me later, Ethyl is his Florence Nightingale, Wonder Woman, Nikita, and Seven of Nine from that classic space program. Those last two sure looked good in spandex. Mike doesn't stand a chance and can't help himself. I might have seen it coming if I had thought about it for a minute more, but I didn't think about it. It could have been terrible if it had gone differently, but surprisingly, in little over a week, Ethyl is on the same track, which is just plain, wholesomely good to see.

Between the pain killers and Mike having to assimilate his new blood supply to make up for his loss, it would be well over a month before he is on flight status again, and that is okay, really, he needs a life that doesn't revolve around me. At least, that's what I tell myself. In the meantime, Cinco can fly me anywhere I need to go, eh? And when did I ever do telemarketing, much less sit still for so much training?

Part Five – Opening My Life

Keith T Jenkins

.

Feather and the Knife

I am browsing the web for some intel I can use in a pillow deal for a chain of hotels we have acquired. It includes a continuing supply of belly down from young chickens in Smiley, Texas. Smiley, as some may know, is just about the chicken capital of the world. In this case, there is a farmer that has found a way to get the chickens plucked quickly – which all farmers want to do – and he still has usable down at the end of the process. In fact, he has nearly twelve hundred pounds of down per month. To burn it seems a waste, and a stench would go up which none could bear. And being the bright young capitalist that he is, he decides to sell it . . . as stuffing for pillows, comforters, jackets . . . whatever he can. It seems to be working out great all around, but before I am willing to commit to it, I need to know more about feathers. I can sometimes get wrapped up in the details of a deal, above the big picture, occasionally to my detriment or the harm of the deal. But here I am, sweeping and gleaning knowledge for the deal, and then I see a headline. It is nearly three years old. "Feather Eagleheart Will Face No Charges." What the hell is that, so I click on it to find . . .

Feather had done her best to fulfill her obligation to the tribe, and about two weeks after we were in Eagle Pass, she had married the man that her grandfather had picked out. He was a prize choice . . . on paper. His mother and his father were descended from very significant families, which made him the Kickapoo equivalent of a Rockefeller or an Astor. He had the bloodline, but not the temperament. When his wife went into labor, he had her taken to the hospital in town, but didn't go with her. He had business . . . . Rockefeller and Astor, remember? When he heard that it was a boy he got absolutely stupid with excitement and decided to "whoop it up" as they used to say. After all, if he had a male child from Feather, then his son would someday be chief. His lifelong dreams were at hand, so he thought, "Why not celebrate a bit?" It was five days before he went home to see his son; still more than half in the bag when he came home, where his wife and son were already sleeping.

The web news said that it was half past midnight when he came into his house, and tripping himself closing the door, he fell across the entryway and stumbled into a stand of fireplace tools with a terrible racket. He would have been greeted by her personal body guard, Leon, but he was away fetching something for the baby – no one can remember what. He was shouting something roughly equivalent to "Hi, Honey! I'm home!" and when he got to the top of the stairs, he was met by a disgruntled wife who had been abandoned when she needed him. She was not going to allow him to disturb the baby in the middle of the night, but he was insistent, he was drunk, inconsiderate, and he was more than half again larger than her, maybe twice.

She tried to coddle him and entice him another direction, but he would not be deterred. She threw her arms around him and tried to kiss him, but he decided that she was trying to stall him, which she was, and he shoved her aside with a sweep of his arm. She flew across the upstairs landing and crumpled in a heap beside a small chaise, and without looking to see her condition, he entered the nursery.

She heard the click of the light switch, a small baby gurgle of being disturbed, followed by a brief whaa-wah of a baby not happy with being disturbed, followed by a blood curdling howl of full grown anger, accompanied by more screaming upset baby noises. The child continued to scream as the man turned from the crib, and stepping toward the hall, kicked the door from its frame and hinges. It fell with a slam to the floor bringing more screams of distress from the nursery. The baby cried and wailed, but no one came to comfort him.

Feather came running across the floor not knowing if she was going to try to hug her husband or tackle him, but none of that mattered because before she could get within range of touching him, he slapped her to the floor like a rag doll. He grabbed her by the hair and dragged her down the stairs and out into the lawn where he threw her into the pea gravel of their cactus garden. He pounced on her, squatting then sitting on her, and started punching her in the face with both of his mammoth hands.

He was pounding her with rage coursing through every cell of his body and sweat pouring from his hair as if he had been running all day, then he felt it, like a bolt of lightning in his belly. She had managed to pull his knife from its sheath at his belt – a bright and shiny Bowie knife with an elk horn handle and a blade that is almost three inches wide and a foot long. It had been a gift from her father on their wedding day to commemorate his entry into the royal family . . . so to speak . . . but tonight it is marking his exit from that same family. Tonight, it drives deep between two of his left ribs, through his spleen, then she latches on firmly with two hands and twists it clockwise, snapping the lower rib as she drives the handle down and the blade up, through his heart. "Asshole!" she yells as she drives the knife and divides his heart. He is almost cleaved in two.

The crying of the child could still be heard along with the gurgling of her husband trying to breathe, coughing blood onto her face and hair. She heard the crackle of gravel on the drive, the wailing of her son, the wheezing and gasping of the man bearing down on her, and he is growing heavier on her blade and neck as he is groping to choke her with his last breath. An explosion rips through the night, along with the distant cry of a screech owl. She was unaware that the body guard had driven up and, seeing her being beaten mercilessly, makes no attempt at reason, détente, or even a body block. He just unholsters his 1980 model Ruger Super Blackhawk .44 magnum, and a bullet swiftly ends the life of her husband, the body of whom falls suddenly on top of her with a final, painful thud.

The body guard, Leon, runs across the garden and, throwing the dead man aside, checks to be certain that Feather is going to live. She is beaten badly with cuts around her eyes, broken nose, a fractured cheek bone, and a dislocated left shoulder; "Get Dancer!" she cries. "Take care of Dancer! Get my son!" He runs upstairs to the child, returning with a gurgling baby boy in a blanket. With a few minutes of swaying and humming and stroking his face, the little guy dozes off again, and Leon lays the little bundle on the gravel to tend to his mother. He dials the phone for an ambulance, which comes with the police, but before they come, he brings her a drink of water, a washcloth, and a shot of whiskey, then he moves his car out of the way, only after he pauses long enough to take a deep breath with a short prayer to reset her shoulder and change out his gun. He keeps a spare in the glove box and knows that someone will want this one for evidence, so he leaves it on the seat of his car. It is all he has of his inheritance from his grandfather, and he will want it back.

As soon as the police arrive and asked the needed questions, the same ones they ask in all the TV shows, Leon takes the woman to her bedroom to shower and little Dancer to his crib. A girlfriend of Feather's, Sarah Marie, comes over to help her shower and redress. With a sling on one arm, Feather emerges, still beaten and bruised, but showered and bandaged, only seeing from one eye, in a bath robe wanting to hold her son. Sarah Marie brought Dancer to her, sitting in her rocker in the nursery and peeled back her robe, so the boy could feed from his mother's breast. Leon can't recall being able to see the details, but with her so badly beaten and broken, still wanting to provide the boy's sustenance, Leon does recall thinking that this was an almost perfect picture of ultimate motherhood. He thought of what kind of love and commitment it must take to put aside your own pain and grief and care for another. He thought of how that must be the love of every true mother. Then he takes out his cell phone, at nearly four in the morning, and calls his mom.

The following morning, Leon takes mother and child to a hospital where the cheek bone can be x-rayed and set properly, whatever that may mean. But she won't leave her home until her child is well at ease and that means feeding and rest. He is going to have no dad, so she will want him to at least have the security of knowing he has a mom that shows her love for him every day . . . starting now.

The grandfather and the tribal council convene in the morning, and given the testimony of the police and ambulance personnel, Leon the body guard, and Feather, it is ruled a justified, though unneeded, shooting. As it turned out, Leon didn't really need to shoot the husband because the coroner determined that there was likely less than a few seconds left to the man's life from the knife wound. No one can say for certain if he could have mustered enough strength to snap her neck in his last moment. However, the vantage point of the shooter did not allow him that knowledge. He couldn't even see the knife since he drove up from behind and to the right of her assailant.

This child, Dancer, was white. I don't mean he was a little pale from having a mom that is half Kick a quarter Asian and a quarter white. No, he was full on Anglo, gringo, honky, pale-face, cracker, WHITE! At least that was how he looked, and this had made "dad" very angry. He had dragged the child's mother and beat her almost to a point of destruction, all the while yelling about how "someone has been in his squaw," and how she was "no doe" to him, "nothing but a white loving, half-breed, cur bitch, she wolf in heat." And now he is dead, but the baby still has his mother.

I consider asking Gerhardt to check into the matter more fully but then decide to ask Benson instead. Since he and Stephen had been on the trip, I don't have to let anyone in on the events who doesn't already know most of it. Benson gets me all of the details that the UberWeb had failed to supply and more.

He learns that because Feather had given birth to a white baby and the husband would not keep her, she had to leave the tribe. She had shamed her family, especially being royalty, and had to be dismissed . . . shunned. Her grandfather still loved her quite profusely and managed to setup a secret trust fund for her. It allowed her to buy a medium small home in Quihi and pay her utilities and expenses. The trust had an additional account to allow her son to go to college later if he wished, or he could cash it in at thirty. Being a hundred twenty miles away was a blessing because people who were feeling angry or hateful toward her and her son could not stop by whenever they wanted to shame and abuse her. But once a year, at about Christmas time, "Gimpa" could make a flight to Hondo, and she would pick him up to spend a weekend with little Dancer.

Leon was so impressed with her that he came by about every other month, just to check in and make certain they didn't want for anything. He drove his own car over and took them to Dairy Queen in Castroville for lunch and an ice cream something. Each time he comes, there will be a trip to the Super S grocery to stock up. And later, after the groceries were put away, he would take them to Castroville again, for a first class meal at Sammy's . . . every time he comes. He told her once that coming to see her and Dancer helped him remember that night when he saw the most horrific example of unconditional love played out in a rocking chair. From time to time, he was able to bring Sarah Marie with him, but she never came alone. Every time he leaves alone, he calls his mother from the road once again.

I send a letter in the most old fashioned way; I write it in pen and have it carried to her by hand. There is no physical postal service to her home, and this is too personal to trust to a parcel company. I send Stephen. He takes his personal car, a 2055 Audi Cabriolet RS 10 – robin's egg blue – very nice, but anything will do for this trip . . . anything but a limo. He finds her house, as Benson had mapped it, knocks on the screen door and hands her the letter when she opens up, saying only, "I have a letter from Joshua Danz, ma'am." She takes it and breaks the seal, then sits down in the entry to read it, as Stephen waits on the porch looking on.

"Dearest Feather," she reads, "How is the most beautiful woman I have ever seen? I only just learned what happened to you after our weekend, and I need to know a couple of things. First, do you need anything – anything at all?" She reads on, "I know this comes out of the blue, but you came rushing back to mind when, last week, I discovered your husband's death and all the details I could since. It has taken me this long to find you and did not want to turn up on your step unannounced. Second, do I have a son?"

She looks at the bottom and sees, "Truly, Joshua – Ph: SAT 724-RA56.

There is no reply.

Africa

It is springtime in Burundi, and we are meeting to make a third annual review of our operations in the sweetener biz. This time I am going personally, with Cinco, to take a look at all there is to see. It is doing very well and has, in fact, taken an unexpected bump to the better in the past fifteen months, even more radical increases in the last half year. We have gone from having 15,000 acres of land growing cane to nearly 270,000 acres in this time. We haven't bought the land, and we aren't leasing it all, but we have gotten individual farmers and tribal villages to work together, large families and co-ops, for the single common goal of creating a sound economy, based on making a product available. Most of it is in Kongo. Actually, the "sound economy" thing is one of my goals; the rest of the farmers just want to make a living that pays better this year than last . . . and they will.

With the help of the onsite executive that Ardit has put in place, we have managed to create a continual stream of product that is being harvested during the day or processed 24/7, all year long. There are friends and neighbors working in teams, and those who had been enemies or strangers just a year or two before, are sweating elbow to elbow. And this isn't any kind of bizarre religious cult or a political movement; we just make it possible for people to work harder or smarter, and the benefit would be theirs. And from our profits, we have built water systems, clinics, and schools, and of course, roads to get from the product to the processing plants and shipping. We are looking at building a high-speed passenger/freight rail from docks in Mombasa to Bujumbura to the docks of Libreville in Gabon, and a spur is planned to reach into Rwanda. We want to get everywhere.

We are an hour late to the meeting because a street preacher has said something that shook me to my core. Cinco and I had to step aside and talk for a while. We talked and wept and called Doc. We gathered our wits and washed our faces and go to the meeting with Ardit Iselin and his Managing Executive of African Operations

Ardit is introducing us to the COO, and when he does, we are surprised. For starters, it is a woman, a white woman. She is very well coiffed yet still looking very strong and capable. She looks familiar somehow, and then I get it. She is Meredith – Artie's girlfriend from New York – but she looks so much more confident than she did then, and she also looks to be about seven months pregnant as well.

"Meredith," says Cinco, "you look absolutely amazing. I hope Artie isn't working you too hard in your condition."

"Not a chance," she replies, "but Artie will tell you that I work harder and happier than he ever did. Still, I must say, he dotes on me like a queen." She strokes Artie's face with her whole hand. "He's going to be a great dad, and he's really been a great benefit to me, learning the ropes of business and opening up doors."

Artie says, "Once we got this operation running and somewhat stable, she had some ideas that seemed good to me, especially with her powers of persuasion over me," he rolls his eyes like Groucho Marx, "so we tried out a few things. At first, I was a bit worried that I was going to let my girlfriend ruin my business – my shot at the big time, so to speak. But then, it seemed that almost everything she tried worked, and if it didn't work, we learned, adjusted, tuned, and tweaked it until we found success. She's brilliant!" he says, sounding very proud and still, somewhat surprised. "Thanks to her, we have nearly 300,000 acres of land that we either own, lease, or help manage, and from which we buy crops, and it could be five times that in the next year or so, and we have pledges and prospects to expand by that much again in another three to five years, depending on how well the farmers do what they are taught. Some do, some don't, and most fall somewhere in between."

Meredith takes over interjecting, "But even the ones that don't follow the first year will likely learn the error of their ways and begin to fall in line the second or third. These people are profoundly ready to work and make money. After your first visit to New York, there was a sort of political upheaval followed by an economic decimation in Kongo, and someone invested billions into seeding the people and territory with farm gear, food, seed, machinery, weapons and – not to put too fine a point on it – freedom." She continues, "Once that happened, the Kongs – what they call the old leadership that was so oppressive – were thrown out, and the Jesus people started coming here in droves." She pauses with a little bit of a smirk and says, "It really has been a lot of fun to watch . . . but even more fun to help facilitate."

"Jesus people, huh?" I say somewhat sarcastically, but also with genuine curiosity. "Does that make it more fun?"

"Oh, yes!" she says, like a teen listening to her favorite girl power band, live for the first time. She is a bit fired up and almost giddy as she continues, "Look, about six months ago, we went to a funeral for one of the foremen here, and the preacher said the strangest thing, but it made complete sense to me and changed my life. It changed Artie too!"

"What was it?" I ask – not wanting to sound too edge-of-my-seat, but really, I do want to know.

"He said, 'You are a good-for-nothing sinner, sitting on a mattress, blinders on your eyes, headset blaring in your ears, listening to the music of the age, not even aware that you are squatting on a railroad track, and the train is speeding your way.' He said that Jesus was reaching out to pull us from the track. All we had to do to be rescued was to accept that Jesus could set us free and safe on solid ground, out of danger. He went on to tell us that . . . that our life was about to change forever and that we needed to keep an eye out for it. He was speaking to the crowd, but Artie and I knew that he, or somebody, was also speaking directly at us." She pauses again a moment, rubbing her tummy gently and says, "The next day we learned about the baby. We went from the doctor's office straight back to the church, got saved, and then got married. And before you go wondering if it is good for business; our profit margins are up 348% from that day to this."

"I don't doubt it," I say to her, "and I am not looking to replace you, by any means. I have seen the reports of the productivity here. Besides, something similar happened to Cinco and me, just an hour ago. But that's a story for another time. Still, it occurs to me, after your negotiating in New York, then seeing what you have done here and how you have done it, that you, Meredith, might be the perfect person to use something I have been using for a long time. It is called my 'If/Then Manual for Business,' and I want to see what you can do with it. Start local, within this enterprise first, and then reach into the city and nearby countryside and update me in about ninety days as to what you have done with it and what you think. Okay?"

"I would be glad to do that, Mr. Danz," she says.

"I thought we were on a first name basis."

"Joshua," she begins again, "it would be my pleasure."

"If you do, I'll tell you exactly what happened in Kongo, or Ethyl, that is Cinco could tell it better."

"Cinco?" she asks.

"Oh, yes," Cinco says. "Call me Cinco. I will explain later and it will make sense."

So, I open my phone, chose the If/Then book from my Dropbox, download it to my device and then tap it on hers to transfer the file into her possession. She opens it in her .pdf reader and makes certain that she can view it. "You can read it when you get home. It's only about a hundred sixty pages and no complex formulas." She puts her phone away as I ask, "When are you due?"

"Two more months they say," she replies. "But he seems in a bit of a hurry, so maybe not. Take a feel."

I put my hand next to Cinco's on her belly, and the baby drags his foot or fist across her tummy, pressing outward from her right side to her left. No sooner do we both make "ooh" noises, than he does it again, in the other direction. It is pretty amazing. I notice that when Cinco pulls her hand away from the baby, it rests a moment on her own belly, and a wishful look comes over her face.

"Really?" I think to myself, "Is she ready for that? Can she be? Can she even have children?"

"By the way, Joshua," Meredith says, "thanks for the percentage bump you gave me on my buy-in. I really appreciate it. It will become someone's college fund, if he decides to go. If not . . . mama's going to retire to Cabo."

We take a couple of days to see the sights, and there are a few sights to see, some of them business and some of local or historical interest. We hop a fairly new Bell Super Ranger to visit some cane fields and processing. We watch as it begins with a harvest, then we follow a truck to the plant where it is pressed, shredded, pounded, and processed into granular sugar with some additional nutrients for US marketing as sweetener. We call it sweetener because it is not pure cane sugar, which is illegal in the US. It is technically a botanical extract. Still, as I expected, the rest of the world is beginning to fall off the bandwagon of banning sugar, and we are marketing it in different packages from a Kongo based subsidiary company as sugar. There are eleven different degrees of refinement from raw sugar that is beige, to powdered sugar for baking, and molasses blended brown sugar, as well as standard granulated table sugar, and more. It is a wonderful little enterprise, and it has bettered the lives of about 70,000 people who are personally involved with it from field workers to office personnel and salesmen. Cinco does a breakdown and discovers that there are over 300 secretaries and clerks in the process. She says that when you figure the size of the average family in each region of the operation, it comes to a total of over 490,000 people directly benefiting from our work there, not to mention all those people whose businesses benefit from their spending with them . . . and we went there to make a profit, and profit we did, and do. It is a great enterprise, by every definition.

Cinco and I return home confident that our operations in Africa are in the best hands and having made a request of Doc, though she is busy. We had asked from Africa if she could get some Bible software and create a mem-load for us to install. She finds that we have – the Enterprise that is – has a corporate interest in one of the best Bible Study packages in the world – thousands of volumes – and she acquires and reduces the source code down to become memory files that can be mem-loaded. It takes most of her spare time for the next three weeks to get it done, two and a half hours each to load it and suddenly, like never before, the If/Then makes all the sense in the world.

Still, there are some ne'er-do wells in Africa that want to try to force their collectivist ideals on us all. Even in Kongo, where so much progress has been made in so little time for so many, they still insist that they know something that we don't know. I can't help recall the words of Ronald Reagan saying, "It's not that our liberal friends don't know anything. It's that so much of what they know just isn't so."

From time to time, there are outbreaks of violence in the fields, but we find a solution to that. We begin to train and arm the workers. They have the option to go through a Texican handgun training course that provides the same training as a Concealed Carry Permit back home, in addition, they are provided much of the firearms training for body guards, from friends of Benson and Bubba. If they get fully trained and weapons qualified, they can pick up a side arm in the morning and return it in the evening. If they have a 95% work attendance record for a year, and no other reason not to allow it, the gun will be theirs, free and clear. Everyone gets a new Glock .45 ACP, and over 90% of them will get to keep their guns after the year is up. Some will continue borrowing our guns, some will decide to buy their own, and a few will decide to go without – but later most of those change their minds. Only two will be stolen, but we will recover both of those and someone loses a job for each, and someone goes to jail.

When the rebel commies show up trying to shoot up the place and scare off the workers, the workers shoot back at the rebels. And rebels, being not so well trained, and often not actually aiming at the people, tend to not hit people. But people shooting back tend to hit the rebels, some of whom die. A few dead rebels and the collectivist, commie movement tends to quiet down quickly, especially since the commies discover that they can find a far less dangerous line of work in the fields and plants . . . and it pays a lot better too.

After a little over three months, we are going back to Burundi to celebrate that Ardit and Meredith have had a son and named him Y'hoshua – which is Hebrew for Joshua. I am touched. Artie says, "We want you and Cinco to be his godparents, if that's okay with you." We agree and are profoundly honored, of course.

In a more personal conference, Meredith tells me that since she has begun using the information in the If/Then, she has given a raise to everyone that has been with the company for six months or more. She has expanded their medical coverage and established clinics in the more remote villages, and even though the clinics are rather rudimentary, the vaccines and basic medical care they provide have made a huge difference in the lives of those villages already. There is little in the world that changes the condition of a people more quickly and extremely, than the presence of medical care and clean water. "In addition, if there is anyone that is seriously injured or ill, needing transport to the hospital in the city, a company chopper goes out to get them. This is a real advantage that comes from having a clinic with trained personnel and satellite phones. The good will it has brought us, for the next few hundred miles, is so valuable that it could be worth it to purchase another chopper to do nothing but emergency medical runs and medical deliveries." Probably later, I think. "Further, the company shuts down an hour before sundown on Friday and opens up on Monday at dawn, in observance of Sabbath and Sonday, for church goers. Also, we have begun rotations in the southernmost, fully harvested, company fields with Cannabis Indica and Sativa – but not both in the same field – with a plan of growing it for two years in a location then plowing it under, replacing it with beans for a year, then corn for a year and plowing them under for cane for five years. We have a botanical engineer that has managed to get the THC levels up to a steady 35% in the plants he is using as seedlings in our fields. We are also exploring the possibility of a rotation of two years weed, two of beans, two of corn, and three to five of cane, to see what profit margins can be made and if the bean and corn markets in Africa can become staples to the region." She explains, "While the percentage of our profit margin may be smaller, the overall economy of our enterprise in Africa has enlarged by nearly 35%, so the dollars harvested are actually increased by more than 15%. Additionally, we have an employee base that is so happy to be with us that no union has had a single shop to give a foothold."

"I gotta say, 'I am very impressed.' You get it much better than most people that have seen it." She smiles, and I don't mean the smile of a child being told she is good, but of one who knows she is good and appreciates that you appreciate it. It is as though she is proud of me for seeing it in her.

"Something else I instituted is based on your Afghan War Victory Plan that was never used, and I gotta say, even though it is just starting up, it's working like you said it would," she says.

"Which part is that?" I ask.

"You had suggested that if the Americans had taken warriors, builders, and missionaries to Afghanistan, they could have won the war and the people. The US never did anything like that, but we are doing it now . . . as an enterprise." She is almost giggling when she tells me this. "Remember I told you that the Jesus people flocked here?" I nod. "Well, I began almost immediately funding them and supplying them with water well equipment, motor homes with medical supplies, generators, and sat-phones, as well as the occasional chopper hop, and in just a little over a month, there was fruit on that vine. There is a small army of people now, making a good living, armed and trained, many of whom are born again Christians, getting discipled in honest to goodness churches, and bringing others to a job and to Jesus – and the cycle continues." She smiles again, almost all the way across her face. "I love it," she says, with a tear in her eye. "It is the most fun, the most profit, the most reward I have ever seen, and more than anyone could ever have expected."

"So, now we're in the weed business, eh?" I ask.

"Actually," she responds, "we've been in the weed business for a long time. We've had our hands in medical marijuana on the US west coast since 2012. And we have been supplying glaucoma and cancer studies for nearly forty years. We are just now preparing to take it mainstream in some never before seen market-share-biting ways. Right now the weed market is run, primarily, by the former tobacco companies, but most of their thought processing has been around adapting their previous delivery machine to what they see as a slightly different demographic, using the same old management systems that had been in place since American colonial days. That barely works."

"Really? Weed? That's our next growth market?" I have to ask.

"Really!" she says, "We are not just redesigning the cigarette market, but we are approaching it from a collection of different angles. For starters, the land is not dedicated to that single crop. Second, we will deliver it in packages of smokes with four different densities of THC and four different price levels. Further, we can package it in droplet form for a much higher price, flavored and sugared for use in beverages, or as a tea in a bag at the end of the day as well as a gum based delivery system, and we already have a breath-strip company online to put it into those little dissolving strips that taste like cinnamon. In addition to which, THC has a much lower hazard per use level than alcohol, and users rarely become violent or want to drive stoned but are more inclined to bouts of laziness and lethargy." She makes a good point, and she could have been presenting a prospectus for the overall plan to the board, and at first glance, it looks good. "In addition to all that, the seeds are also used to make hempseed oil which can be used in cooking as well as in lamps, lacquers, and paints, but also for birdseed. You told me to run this place." Having concluded her report, I gotta say she is really making progress on every front, and her grasp of the If/Then is amazing. She asks about what had happened in Kongo, and I tell her. Well, I give her the highlights of what we had planned to do, and Cinco fills in all the details of what actually occurred and why.

"You toppled a government because someone killed your girlfriend?" She looks at Cinco, "No offense!"

"None taken!" she says in reply. "I was rather amazed at the intensity of his anger regarding the matter, after just a week or so, but also impressed at how he didn't just start up some sort of stalk and kill mission."

"Don't get me wrong," I say, swallowing slowly, "I wanted that son of a bitch dead, and he's dead, but I couldn't just murder him, and I couldn't destroy a people, or leave them without some sort of hope at the end of the tunnel. Besides, it wasn't just a week or so, but all the time before that . . . she was always my friend." It hurts just thinking about Ethyl's death and the rest, "I know that there were good people that got hurt, and I hope to make up for that somehow. But I can't help feel that the results, on every level, were worth the pain. Besides," I say, stroking Cinco's cheek, "you really are an amazing 'girlfriend,' Babe." I use air quotes at "girlfriend" at Cinco.

"Oh, yeah – girlfriend! In the meantime," says Cinco beyond my melancholy moment, "the reason we came today, besides wanting to see Y'hoshua and get an update, was to see, if you were up to it . . . would you and Artie . . . would stand up with us as we get married." Meredith is shocked. "Would you do that for us?"

"When . . . where?" she asks.

"Tomorrow at ten, we are dedicating a new wing on the Centre de Santé Humura Hospital. After that we will go to a little church down the road." Meredith smiles, and Cinco smiles back. They hug like sorority sisters who haven't seen each other in years, the both of them vibrating and gyrating in excitement. "We want to keep the ceremony a secret, but the Boss thinks of you as his adopted children thanks to business, and we really want you there . . . not as a part of the business, but as family. Will you come?"

"We wouldn't miss it." A tear falls from her face to her blouse, "I will tell Artie."

We are staying in the Ancient Presidential Palace. We meet about fifteen minutes south of our hotel, at the Centre de Santé Humura at about 9:30, Benson and boys in tow to secure the location. Benson watches over us in the car, Stephen clearing the stage area, and Bubba on the rooftop looking for snipers. They aren't alone; of course, they are in charge of their particular departments of coverage. The event only lasts for about twenty minutes, starting at ten – a couple of speeches, and instead of a golden shovel, I get to use a backhoe with a gold painted scoop to dig the first hole – that is fun. Someone says a prayer of benediction and we are done. We get into the Bentley and head to the church, a couple of miles south on RN3. It is a very quiet ceremony and very private. There are six of us in the front of the sanctuary, Meredith, Ardit and baby, Cinco, the pastor, and me, and the three security experts wandering around outside the church. They don't even bring support crew. They figure we are there to baptize little Yehoshua, so we'll do that, too. The pastor is so quiet during the wedding part; I didn't think that Ardit and Meredith could actually hear anything. Meredith asks Cinco later, "Did the Shepherd call Joshua 'Bill' in the vows? I couldn't hear very well, us kneeling at the rail and you three at the altar."

"Did he?" is her reply. "Hmm, it was pretty quiet, huh?" I overhear the exchange and realize it is unusually evasive for Cinco, but I refuse to turn my head and acknowledge that I am listening to a quiet conversation between women. Meredith opens her dress at the top to feed her son, and I can't help see the look on Cinco's face. She is totally enraptured with what she sees and does not have. It is begun. Well, we have been celibate for well over a month and looking at her face when she looks at that baby . . . "Well," I think to myself, "I've had her all to myself for over a year. I suppose we can do this; I guess we are at the end of needing birth control."

"You keep calling Joshua 'Boss.' Is that going to remain?" Meredith asks.

"I hadn't thought about it, really," says Cinco. "It's just what I have called him forever, and that hasn't changed. In the office, I still work for him, and in our private life, he really is in charge." Meredith looks a bit befuddled, so Cinco clarifies, saying, "Christian marriage isn't like servitude of any kind, but a wise and willing submission. He has to be the head of the house; it's God's way. And really, what kind of a woman wants to marry a man to whom she can't willingly submit anyway." I love this woman, in every way I can imagine.

We stay in the Ancient Presidential Palace – really the word Ancient is in the name. We take the "Presidential" suite, not wishing to arouse any marital suspicions from any press that may be snooping around, or even security. After we go to dinner Benson drops us off in the garage. Stephen walks us to the elevator in the lobby, figuring Cinco can protect me if needed.

When we get to the suite, and as Cinco begins to step through the door, I grab her sleeve and spin her around to face me. I hold her against the door frame for a moment, kissing her. Putting my back to the door, I take her up in my arms, like a newlywed, walking her through the door and push it closed with my foot. As I do, I see someone in the hallway looking on approvingly – an elderly couple probably remembering the night he carried her over the threshold. Not wanting to draw attention to ourselves, we are dressed in common business attire.

As we walk through the living area, almost in a normal fashion, Cinco stops me and pushes me into a large chair. I sit as she steps to the center of the room, right beside the coffee table. She looks at the room a minute and pushes the table aside, leaving room in the middle for her and her alone. She starts by removing her jacket and slowly, gracefully, unbuttoning her vest. Her hair is up on top of her head, but then it isn't, falling around her shoulders, expanding in every direction, a magenta shower – light from the window lighting it from behind like a halo. She slips her vest off and throws it at me. By now, I am beginning to breathe a bit heavier, starting to sweat a little. She peals open her shirt, popping off one button at a time, almost as they had from another shirt opened in New York, but much slower – buttons falling closer. Then goes the skirt – slowly with the zipper, she drops it to the floor, and then she steps out of it. She is so gloriously beautiful, standing before me in her open shirt, white stockings, and shoes, like an old world pin-up meant to arouse – succeeding in every way. Her beauty to me is unimaginable as she comes to my chair, holds out her hand for mine, which I willingly and eagerly give to her; she leads me to the master suite. But she is in charge of everything that night, so maybe, tonight it is a mistress suite instead.

As the night wraps up, morning arrives, and we prepare for the day. I follow her into the shower and we are lathered up, rinsed off and dried soon enough. While we are getting ready, I notice that her magenta shades go all the way to the roots of her hair, so I ask her how often she has it coloured. "It must take all day," I comment before she can reply. "You must do it on weekends, but I can't recall you . . ."

"It isn't died," she claims. She explains that it is a DNA alteration that was selected by the Enterprise for my primary protector. Along with the colour of her hair, this particular DNA shift also seems to have provided her freckles. The magenta mane makes it easy to spot her, and maybe me, in a crowd, and I can be protected. She won't have to do much protecting this trip, and that is never again going to be her primary function in life – first job now is wife.

Our honeymoon would be two nights in Central Africa, two nights in Thailand, three in Tahiti, two in Alaska, and two more in Mexico, each stop with at least one business meeting or a dedication of some sort on the first day. Altogether, there are probably ten or twelve hours of actual business to be done in those eleven days, and then it is Friday evening, and we are back at the Tower for the weekend. All in all, a pretty good honeymoon, and no one has to know.

After telling Meredith about the mem-loader and the Bible upgrades we both had, Cinco agrees to return in a while and do the upgrades for Meredith and Artie. It won't actually happen 'til our trip to the Holy Land, but it will happen. Smart people, these two, and Meredith will far outshine me in every way if she is given the opportunities.

Liberty Burgers & Sodas for All

It really doesn't take as long as I thought it might for Dr. Stark to get a recipe out of the products we gave him. We have fully dedicated a pair of floors, eleven and twelve, to the "Marquez Industries" offices and labs. There isn't much in the way of offices, at first, because there is little to manage, but the labs are busy, busy, busy, and Ilyssa has to learn to be a glorified lab assistant for a while, if only for secrecy sake.

Stark had gotten half a dozen actual lab assistants from UTSA to speed the processes along, but some of them believed that they should have a piece of the pie instead of wages. When Ilyssa declined their generous offers to partner up, they were caught attempting to leave the premises with data drives – which was and is a huge no-no. That was the impetus for increased security measures in the lab and office areas.

There was a data cleaner installed at the entrance to the labs, which is little more than an enclosed EMP that can zap anything that is carried inside it into complete uselessness, and everyone except Stark and Doc must pass through it coming in or going out. The staff is stripped down to Stark, Doc, and five techs. One of the best assistants of the bunch had to be released because he has a pace-maker, which, if he passes through an EMP, the pacemaker would be destroyed, killing him. Since we can't exempt him from the security, he is given a fifty thousand dollar severance package and excellent references that get him a job at Dow Chemical in Freeport, Texas. Doc also offers to pay his moving expenses, for which he is additionally grateful.

They have taken the twelfth floor and converted it into five separate labs, each of four performing a single process of reducing the syrup to its components. Instead of one lab working it out, Stark oversees each of the labs, working with different methodology to reach the same conclusion. The fifth lab works on just the carbonated portion, since that is fairly rough chemistry, or so Stark thinks. Three of the four processes yield the same result in thirteen to seventeen weeks each, and then those results are cross verified by repeating their processes in the other labs, run by the other techs. Having successfully produced the same results, three times, with three labs, and three different discovery processes, they are absolutely confident in the mix, so they produce it. Then they attach it to the mix station along with a new batch of the carbonated product, and it is not quite right. When tested, it tastes to me like the diet sodas from way back when, maybe worse. We try it again with a canister of the original carbonate, and it works great. It tastes like Dr Pepper is meant to taste. To the drawing boards we go.

Stark sets up the same experiment processes again to discover the other half of the equation, but only in three labs this time. The processes take nearly four more months to qualify all three results and have a successful trial of the end product with the new syrup and the new carbonated water mix. It is genuinely wonderful, but . . . what of the other two labs: are they left fallow? No, they are not. Dr. Stark takes gallons of the Dr Pepper and allows it to sit on one of those magnetic mixer things that spin until all of the carbonation has been released and begins reducing that compound down, on a molecular level, to find a recipe that will allow it to be transported in a more seriously reduced form, extra concentrated syrup, to be mixed with water and then carbonated at the fountain head instead. With the mixing station doing the work of converting the mixed concentrate and plain water into the product we all enjoy, we hope to have something that has never been done before. But then the question becomes, "How do we control the water quality?" And that turns out to be easier than we first think. It is a two step process, and we eventually market that, too. It all comes down to a distilling process that is followed by a mineral deposit and chemical cleaning carbon filter. Rather than build a new water purification business, we recommended the stills, built by a Kansas company, and we tell all the vendors that they should buy their carbon filter systems from Amway distributors. This way, we only have to re-invent half the wheel, so to speak.

Cinco points out that, because I have nearly three million dollars tied up in this project that I should look into it, and check on my investments. She wants to go too, so we arrange it. I make an official visit one day to get the whole tour. We don't have to pass through the EMP since it would either kill or seriously endanger Cinco and me . . . thanks to all the tech we each carry inside of us.

We walk around a corridor of PlastiGlas that surrounds the floor and separates the individual labs from one another. Each wall is made of two panes of three inch thick clear polycarbonate PlastiGlas, with a three inch thick panel of actual wire-meshed safety glass in between. A twenty-five foot wide corridor runs between each of the labs as storage space and a buffer, even though they only need about a quarter of that space for storage. It serves as an insurance barrier to make certain that one lab cannot detonate into the next, even though most of what is done there is very safe, until today.

As we round the corner to see Doc's lab, she lights up with excitement and waves, glad to see us both, then she hears something we don't, and she looks across the room. I look but don't see what she sees until it is too late. I look back at her, and she is ducking behind the counter as a huge fireball blasts across the room. Before the flame reaches our side, the doors slam locked because of the fire safety protocol to secure the room and protect the rest of the labs and building. Then, as the fireball collapses on itself, it is sucked out of the far side of the room, outdoors through the ventilation system for the lab. It takes nearly twenty-five seconds before the room is deemed safe by the computer systems that secured it, and for them to unlock the doors. CLACK! With the release of the door lock, I am already on the handle with Cinco pushing our way in and running to Ilyssa who lies panting on the floor. Thank God she is breathing! I reach toward her face which looks somewhat sunburned but I withhold my hand. Her hands look mildly burned as if protected somehow, but that appearance will change in a few minutes. All of her clothes are slightly singed and smoldering at the collar, shoulder seams, and hem, but otherwise, intact. The lint, commonly left in the seams after drying had ignited. Her hair is another story though, as we will soon learn. When the ambulance drivers arrive, they are met at the lobby by one of the security staff who lets them know that they will not be taking their gurney upstairs. The two EMT's go up to the lab where they find Ilyssa, already laying on one of our gurneys, being drawn to the elevator by Cinco, Ethyl, and me. Ethyl has already entered all the vitals into a tablet and has Ilyssa being monitored on it, so that she can hand over the gurney and the tablet with Doc, and after reviewing a little of the stats, off they go. Instead of down they go up to the roof, where one of our

"LifeBird" Black Hawks is arriving, with a full medical supply, unmanned except the pilot, since it is not officially in service yet. Ethyl goes with them as Ilyssa's doctor.

Benson meets me and Cinco in the garage from whence we head to the hospital. On the way, Cinco plays back on her tablet everything she saw at the labs, recalled from her memory banks, every visible detail. It shows that Doc had seen us coming, and she did smile and wave, just as I recall. She appears to hear something and turns to look, also as I recall. What I didn't see before is a safety strap that held a propane tank in place snaps, and the tank falls. That is what got her attention. As it falls, it strikes something out of sight on the floor that breaks it open, and the contents of the can blasts out in every direction, igniting on a Bunsen burner as it exhales across the room and back, ignited. The flames expand back toward their source of fuel, reach the high pressure zone at the can, detonate it and expand back across the room, blasting past the Bunsen burners to the wall. Soon the flames filled the room. Even Cinco's view of things becomes a bit obscured, partly by her own tears of concern. As Doc sees the can falling to be broken open, or heading in that direction, she has the presence of mind to try and cover her head with her hands, stop breathing, and duck behind the heavy furnishings. This probably saved her from greater injuries or even death. The flames quickly advance and recede, engulfing her rather thoroughly, but moving so quickly, they have little opportunity to do great, direct damage. When the flames blast across the room, however, they take with them the sum contents of the counter tops, and slam them with the force of a train into the walls of PlastiGlas. Had she been standing up, and not sought cover by crouching, she too would have been blasted against the next wall, and all of this could have been far worse. As it is, she will need some attention for little more than bad sunburns everywhere she had been exposed – her hands up to the forearms, the sides of her face, neck and upper chest, as well as a bald spot where the flames burned off her hair to the scalp in the rear center of her head. It is like a monk's spot, surrounded by scorched hair that had to be cut fairly short to find any that isn't frizzled. Fortunately, there is no severely burned flesh on her anywhere, so it will probably all heal fairly soon, and just as pretty as before. Though, it will take a good long time for her gorgeous hair to return.

When we bring her home from the hospital, we move Ilyssa into my place where she first stays, for a couple of weeks so that Ethyl, Cinco, and I can take complete care of her almost every waking minute. After her initial haircut, she has to leave her head uncovered for several days and then keeping the baldness from public view for a while seems a welcome idea. She looks a little "Joan-of-Arc" to me. In less than a week after her return, her burns are healed enough that she can wear a hat, so she puts on a cap of mine and goes out hat shopping with Cinco, more than a time or two. Every time I look at her, hiding, healing, I am near sobbing in my fear of having nearly lost her.

"You know," she says, "I feel a bit like the 'Shadow' lurking about in corners and hiding behind hats and coats in Texican springtime."

"You're still the ingénue to me," I tell her, "but soon you are going to have to get back to work."

"Wow! I haven't even thought about work since I got here. How are they doing?" she asks.

"Well, they seem to be muddling along without you okay, but doing without your lab has been a devastating loss," I say, half in jest. She punches my shoulder fairly hard. "Still, they have managed to find the answers that Stark was searching for, and I think, we are going to be 'surprised beyond all reason,' or so he says."

"This I gotta see." She starts to leave, checks the clock on the TV, and realizes that it's late. "How 'bout, tomorrow?"

I tell her that tomorrow would be just fine, and I text Stark that we will be there before noon. "Expect the boss while the sun is still rising." I show it to her.

"Cryptic much?" she asks.

"Hey," I reply, "he should be smart enough to figure that one out. If not, we have bet on the wrong horse."

We arrive at ten; all the principals are in place. There is Doc, of course, Stark, Ethyl, Mike and the ever watchful Ms. Cinco, who is in on everything.

Stark shows us the canister operations, and we all try the old formulas, then we try them again with the new mixtures standing right next to the old, so we can compare products head to head, and none of us can tell a difference. This is good. This provides a product line that is ready to roll out to be used in systems that are already pumping crap into restaurants and bars across the world. "So much for the standard delivery system," he says. "Now, let's try something completely different." He takes a two gallon bottle of product and screws a cap on it with a hose attached and switches on a pump. The pump delivers the new super-concentrated syrup to the mixer which uses water that comes from the tap – since the building is thoroughly filtered it should be close enough – and at the mixer, it is carbonated by air infusion in line, like one of those pump systems available in homes a half a century ago. From a new delivery spigot that he has designed, he pours the product into a glass with ice and hands it to Doc, who tastes it and is both pleased and amazed. I take mine room temperature, and it is just right. It is so close to the taste of the other, that neither she nor I, nor any of our entourage can tell the difference. We will later try it on over three hundred test subjects, and the only ones that can tell the difference are wine snobs who have amazingly discerning palates, but nearly all of whom say that, in their day to day lives, they would never drink anything so vulgar. I call this a win.

We decide that, er, I mean, Doc decides that we have it ready to go, and we make an offer to buy the old abandoned Coke plant just a few miles away. Since the US government couldn't control it and no one was getting paid to run it, the plant had lain dormant for decades. The US tries to wheedle a piece of the action by demanding the right to invest into the operation, which, after only a little discussion, Doc realizes it is their way of trying to FRIA her from day one. She says that she can get backing to build one from scratch anywhere in the world – and she has that option because I would back this project anywhere she likes. So, being desperate for the cash, the US settles on a direct sale and we are done. Two realtors split a $190,000 commission for a few phone calls. Not a bad day's work for either of them. I don't mind giving America the money this time. It will take nearly two months to get the place thoroughly cleaned and back online, producing something, then another three months before the systems are creating the mix consistently, even with just a ten man crew.

On the day we close on the purchase of the plant, we are on the verge of a giant breakthrough, and Cinco comes up with the best idea of the day for a product launch. "Remember Flo?" she says to me as we are headed back to the office.

"Yeah. Waitress. In Jersey, right?" I reply.

"Yep. In about six months, she's due to take over the restaurant in Myrtle Beach. If you want a stupendous launch, I think it could be particularly profound for you to do it there. What do you think?"

"I think we need to talk to Doc, but it sounds like an excellent idea, and it could be a lot of fun." I will make the necessary inquiries and we'll make even bigger arrangements with the "owner" to make the launch of the new soda there, and to put a diner into Flo's hands. The owner and I have a lot to talk about, plans change, goals must rearrange. Cinco makes purchases, expands everything to include a huge new project, kicks down doors, and works out the full and final details with the man, the city, and the city council. She has a knack.

Ten men work at the plant, then twenty more join them as we stockpile product that is never opened. There is nearly two acres of canisters, three levels deep, stacked up in the back yard of the plant. In South Carolina, there have been crews of nearly forty men assembling a new Dinermite diner with the new 300 seat configuration right across the street from the beach on a thirty-five acre piece of land, 190 yards from the other one, and no one knows it.

We are technically in North Myrtle Beach, where Main Street meets with North Ocean Boulevard. In an urban renewal project, all of the properties that were over fifty years of age, but not landmarked were determined to be in bad enough condition to need replacement – well, all but a few. Catalina Manor is still in pretty good shape, but everything between there and the diner on the corner of 2nd Avenue South, which is a Dinermite diner from long ago – large, shiny, chrome and steel construction – well, the rest was unworthy of restoration. This move to plough under all of the other structures was already in play long before we contacted the city with ideas of expansion. When the land was to be leveled we decide to take it up a notch.

Between the two sites, there is a huge common parking lot, and facing the coast, and around the parking lot, there is a strip center going in with dozens of shops for tourist retail less than a mile up beach from the downtown attractions. The diner project is being built behind a thirty foot wall of purple vinyl that keeps it from view unless you are inside the wall. That wall is twelve feet inside of an eight foot chain link fence with razor wire all around the top. All materials are lowered into the work zone by crane. Secrecy is paramount on this project. Everyone working on the project is guaranteed a bonus of three months pay if it gets through opening day without anyone spilling their guts about the job. That's a pretty good incentive. On the day of the grand unveiling, the outside fence has been removed, but still, no one realizes that they have been invited to see a new building; they are just expecting to try a new product that will "change how the world enjoys their day." At least that is the hype.

There are about ninety visitors from the press and a few dozen people who will wisely wish to invest in whatever is to be the "next big thing," no matter what that happens to be. They know if I am in, it has to be good. When they all sit down in front of the old diner, which has been spruced up and polished bright, they hear Ilyssa tell them about a new taste sensation that will soon be sweeping the globe, "That is," she says, "everywhere except the United States and its cultural sycophants. But for the rest of you, we present this location as the launching point of 'Doc Marquez,' the greatest soft drink available to man." A balloon on a tether is released from the distant structure, attached by about 200 yards of line, connected to the vinyl wall of the other project and another one attached to a vinyl cover to the sign right here. "That," pointing across the parking area, "is the first restaurant to carry it and introduce it to the world, and this is about to become the Official Home Bar and Grill of 'Doc Marquez,' where you can get your first sip with a nip. And thanks to Mr. Harold, whose original plan was to leave this as a restaurant to Flo, we have been able to launch our product here, open his bar, and build that restaurant across the lot so, as these are revealed, I introduce you to 'Bennies' a new tavern of toxins here and 'Flo's Homespun Heaven' over there."

At that moment a C130 flies overhead with a snag-n-drag rig that grabs the balloon tethers and strips away the sign cover at the bar and the vinyl walls of the other project to reveal the finished work, "Flo's," still surrounded by a PVC framework that just moments ago held up the vinyl walls. That framework is now ready to go. "So, without any further adieu, please, ladies and gentlemen," a dozen waitresses in snug fitting racing coveralls, large lapels, and zippers to mid-chest, pour out of the bar with trays and chilled double shot glasses full of Doc Marquez to distribute, "start your engines." Bennie's has the name emblazoned in red letters on black, white, and chrome with checkered flags at either end, fully lit from within. A bunch of guys begin disassembling the PVC frame around Flo's; there is no sign of them in ten minutes time.

It is a huge success, well beyond expectations. The product is amazing, and Flo's restaurant is absolutely as beautiful as could be. Bennies took its name as a tribute to Flo's dead hubby while also giving Mr. Harold, its owner, an opportunity to try something new and stay in his home town. The reporters make glowing reports of the day, for the most part, even though there are a few sourpusses, who would grouse if they got free money, and so they complain about the events of this day as well. Most of the reporters are gone by the time we sit down for lunch. Some stay to dine, and there are a few who won't leave until they are certain that there is no hope of any addition to their stories. Some have even found out about my involvement in the project, regarding the restaurant. Most keep that to themselves because it was not a story that they would like getting out; "Billionaire Helps Common Working Woman" doesn't fit their narrative and agenda. One of them is hoping to create an unpleasant scene and does leak it, out loud, to Flo, and she has something to say about it.

As we are all enjoying several fine meals in one of the corner booths, there is Mike, Cinco, Doc, Stark, Ethyl, the usual security, plus a few, and we even brought Mrs. Dennis along, as well as a dozen or so kids and grandkids, all of whom are sitting at nearby tables, Flo comes with a chair and sits down right across the table from me. I am a little worried, but I'll get over it.

"Whychew do all dis?" she asks.

"What do you mean?" I evade poorly.

"Whychew arrange ma job an da move an dis res'runt fo me 'n mine?" She is almost weeping; actually, almost is gone. "Whachew spec fo all dis?"

"Nothing, Flo. Absolutely nothing. A while ago I met an excellent woman that was doing the very best she could for her family, and I wanted to help. That's all." At that moment, a reporter comes by, looking a bit like Jimmy Olsen, and I point to him and say, "Back off!" Bubba steps up to escort the fellow closer to the door and keep him out of earshot.

"Hey, the press has rights, ya know?" he shouts out.

"What you have a right to today, Friend, is a free meal; anything on the menu on that side of the diner," Bubba said, pointing away from me. "If you have friends who want to eat with you, the next booth is all yours – on me."

"Flo," I say, "you were a victim once, and now you are a champion, and you are helping others have a good life through honest work, and that is everything I want from you for the rest of my life. I promise."

"But, whychew do it?"

"You know, Flo," says Cinco, from the end of the table, "I have been working with Mr. Danz for several years now, and every now and then, I get to help him do something like this, and no one ever knows about it. He likes it that way. I have asked him in the past why he does these things, and," she looks around briefly, "to tell you the truth, I don't think he knows. He just does them because they need doing. And he seems to have some sort of vision as to what some people can be and do, for themselves and others, when given a chance to do it on their own. Well, this is your own and your son is your own. Tend them both and help them both grow strong." She hands Flo her card with her office number, "And if you ever need any help or advice, about anything at all, you call. We ain't dead just 'cause we're gone, Honey. Okay?"

Flo takes the card, shoves it into her brassiere, hugs Cinco harder than she's been hugged in years, and says, "I r'member you bofe. Tree eggs, ova meedyum, English muffins. Thanx you fo evathin. I'll do ma bess." She composes herself, just a bit, dries her eyes, then stands, and looking to the waitress she says, "Dis table on da house."

After a superior meal for each of us, all home cooked country style with lots of butter, we get up to leave, and as we get to the door, that pesky reporter follows me down the stairs and cuts me off, then SPLAT! I feel a pain in my left arm as a mist spatters my face, and then CRACK echoes the report of a high powered rifle. Weapons drawn, Bubba and Benson are joined by Stephen and another five, as the rest of us hit the floor, some more by choice than others. The reporter falls on my feet, bleeding from the neck as I crouch down, waiting for instructions from my team. Ethyl is tending to the reporter whose neck is creased and is bleeding profusely on the decking in front of the diner. "Get me ice – lots of ice." She removes her scarf, a beautiful pastel silk over three feet long, and wraps it with an iced napkin, pressing into the wound to slow or stop the bleeding. Cinco, I discover, is tending a wound on my arm where the bullet passed through cleanly, but not, I realize, where it stopped. There, on the wooden slats that lead to Flo's, lays a waitress that was coming out to thank me for her tip. Hell of a thing, to be shot for trying to say "thank you," eh?

"Everyone goes with us," says Benson. The waitress is unconscious as Bubba snatches her up. We get a little help from some bystanders to carry the reporter onto the plane that is parked on the high side of the parking lot. Cinco runs full speed and fires it up before any of the rest of us can get there. The reporter and the waitress have to be carried, but I jog over under my own steam. Up the steps we go, into seats and the engines cry out their power as we rise.

In two minutes, Doc is tending the waitress, and Benson has the bleeding stopped on the reporter. In nine minutes, we have a location on a hospital and are descending toward the roof, but Cinco realizes that the weight limit of the pad on the roof is too light for this plane. The markings say 60, which means this roof is approved for crafts up to 60,000 pounds, but this bird weighs at least half more than that. She leaves the landing gear up and lowers the stair, hovering just beside the hospital; we all off load to the roof of the nine story building. EMT's and nurses are waiting on the roof with two gurneys and a wheel chair as requested. Between eight security folk, three wounded, and all the help that got us on and off the plane, there are about twenty-five people in all. We file across the roof in order of urgency, spectators last. The stairs retract, and the door closes on the plane, and Cinco finds a place to set her down in the farthest corner of the hospital parking lot. I will gladly pay any fines later. When she shuts down the plane, leaves the cockpit, and prepares to exit, she discovers that there is someone still onboard. "Why do you really think he does these things, Cinco?" asks Mike.

"I don't know, Mike." She would tell me later that she told him, "I don't think he really has a choice. I believe that he is driven to do something good with whatever comes his way. As near as I can tell, he has something deep inside of him that makes him want to give and help and invest in others for what only he can see. Maybe that's all part of why we love him. I know I do, and I think you do too. Isn't he pretty heavily invested in you?"

The reporter lost a lot of blood getting to the hospital and codes on the way to the ER. For nearly three minutes, they work on him to get his pulse started, and it seems they are about to quit when that familiar "beep" comes from the equipment. One doctor sews frantically to close the wound on the neck using a plastic shunt to replace part of an artery, and about forty stitches to lock it in place and close the tissues. While he works, another pair of nurses get a bag of whole blood connected on his left arm and a bag of plasma connected on his right. There are some other drugs being administered by a cadre of attendants. As Cinco would remind me later, more than once, much of the knowledge needed was, in this case, well beyond my pay grade.

The doctors have me cleaned up, stitched, shot for tetanus, antibiotics, and pain killers – done – within about an hour. I go to check in on the reporter, but there is no news for a while, so I wait.

He is third generation in America. His family had originally come from Germany to Texas, but his grandfather had moved to New York in the nineties. They still have some old world ways, and this carries down to the current generation as an odd cultural hold-over. The reporter's given name is Johann Heinrich Friedrich Christian Georg Wilke, but he writes under the name of Johnny Wilkes. He had worked as a stringer for the New York Times at first, part time – a story here, a story there – 'til the paper went under. Then he worked for the Post, and he had just gotten an actual Reporter position with them. After about ten weeks of small time local stories, I was his first big assignment in that job . . . well, me and the soda launch, of course. There had been some noise on the gossip rags that Doc and I are involved, but he didn't come for the gossip.

With each passing hour we are more hopeful of his recovery. When he comes to, I am in the cafeteria with Doc, Cinco, my security, and nearly half the people that had come with us. The rest of them had caught a ride with Mike back to the diner . . . and their cars. Just for fun, Mike gave a few rides up and down the coast for some of the families of restaurant and bar workers, after he had the blood removed from the floor of my plane.

A guy in scrubs walks in and says, "Mister Wilkes is conscious now and would like to see Mister Danz." I get up and head that way. Benson gestures with a finger that Stephen should go along, and he does.

We walk down two interminably long hallways, through what seems like some catacombs, and around a couple more corners before we slip into a room with a window on the far side, two beds, and all the needful, noisy, doctor toys connected to two men. The reporter, that is "Wilkes," is in the far bed. I ease over to his bedside and let him know how terribly sorry I am that he has been hurt from violence aimed at me. I tell him that I have never granted interviews, but when he is able to sit up and talk, take notes, record if he likes, I would be glad to sit down with him. He nods and squeezes my hand, and I know he means something like, "Thanks," or maybe it was more like, "well, that's the least you can do, Bozo." I suppose he can let me know later. I see to arranging for a private room when he gets out of ICU.

The waitress is another story. She is brought to the ER with a puncture wound through her abdomen – clean and true – about a half inch in diameter. There was no expansion of the bullet for the exit wound, which is particularly strange since it hit Wilkes first, then my arm and then passes straight through her. It takes a while to find it, because the bullet has passed right through her and into a post that had been part of a sort of decorative handrail for the steps to the diner. It is, in essence, a short phone pole – almost one foot thick – creosote infused pine, and the bullet has disappeared into it with only the slightest trace of its entry. The post is sliced below and above with a chainsaw to remove a disk about ten inches thick, just in case the bullet had traveled up or down a bit on impact, which it didn't. The post will be replaced in a few days by a small construction crew, but again, it is decorative, so it is not a priority. Some orange cones and yellow tape will do for a while. The slice of post is split open to remove the bullet in as clean a condition as it could be found, and it is clean. Nearly all of the blood and tissue had been scraped off in the six inches of wood through which it had passed.

The bullet itself is amazing, and unusual by any standard. By means of a scale it is found to be thrice as heavy as if it were lead and copper. According to a mass spectrometer, it is an odd variation of uranium hexafluoride with something added for even greater hardness. This bullet is a Teflon coated, fifty caliber round, that had been fired from at least a quarter mile away at an incredibly high velocity. It is determined that the force required to graze Wilkes' neck, pierce my arm, and the belly of the waitress, followed by about a half a foot of wood, is approximately three times the force provided to a .44 magnum round out of Dirty Harry's big ass gun. Sorry, classic movie reference again. When a search is concluded, it turns up the brass from the shot, nearly 800 meters up beach from the impact. It had been fired from a lifeguard tower on the beach just off the rear of the Ashworth resort, and when ejected, it had fallen through the floorboards into the sand. The shooter had probably disassembled his weapon and left with only a cursory look to see if the brass could be had, then, having not found the brass right away, and not wanting to be seen near the scene with a big gun, he fled. The investigation would continue.

By the way, it is not the police that found the shell casing, but a scavenger. Yeah! It is a guy with a metal detector looking for treasure that found it. He is doing his usual sweep and beep routine when he gets a chirp under the tower that he is hoping is a watch or a nice lighter or even a bit of jewelry, but when his spade turns over the sand and reveals a really large bullet casing, his disappointment sets in, only to be replaced with excitement. It isn't the kind of excitement that says, "Wow I bet I can get something for this." It is the kind that says, "Holy crap, it's gotta be about that shooting. I'm going to spend the rest of the day answering questions from cops." He has seen more than a few crime scene and coroner shows, and as soon as he dug it up he didn't touch it; he called the cops. I will send him a reward later. In the meantime, the investigation continues along; I need to call Schroyer. The hospital bills for all of us will go on my Tex-Ex card.

The waitress, Caroline, is having a better day than first glance would have offered. For starters, there was no damage to the bullet when it hit Wilkes and me. If there had been damage, the hole it left could have been hideous and huge, but it wasn't. It passed through her like a hot straight pin through a milk jug. Another blessing is that it hit her appendix, which the doctor discovers was already aggravated and may have needed removing in a few days anyway. Third, when she is hit, she is surrounded by professionals particularly suited for her needs. There are doctors and a nurse/medic and pilots and protectors. If you absolutely have to get shot outside of an Emergency Room, these are the circumstances under which to do it. The doctors do a simple appendectomy on her and patch the bullet path from front to back and take extra time to try to make the entry and exit wounds as non-ugly as possible. She will only need plastic surgery if she really wants it. The way the doctors closed the wounds, each would be little more than an elevated "X" on her belly and lower back. I tell her, "I've seen much worse." I tell her that, and I have. Sometimes, I am haunted by losing Ethyl in New York. I still hate that town. Caroline should make a full recovery though and be back on her feet in a few days, wearing a swim suit in a couple of months – maybe less. I arrange for her to take a few months off work to recover without losing her job. Flo agrees and is willing to pay her wages as well, but I insist in taking that responsibility, and she consents. We keep all of that between the two of us and even offer her a vacation in San Antone, if she wants to go for a visit, or a week or two almost anywhere for a little RR&R – rest, relaxation, and recovery. She stays in the hospital a few days more, at her home for about ten, and then takes a week in Puerto Rico, on us. Good for her. We have a small seaside villa she can use. A staff pilot flew as Cinco and I dropped her off on our way to Africa.

I begin to think to myself that attacks on my life are not how I want to spend my time, and I start to formulate a way out. I stay up nights talking to Cinco and Doc, one at a time or three of us together, about ways to step out of this life. When we get back from our journeys, I will book a lunch with Schroyer. For now, there is business to tend in the present, and an anniversary to enjoy with my wife of one year . . . this coming week. We make business related excuses to Gerhardt – expanding opportunities in Africa – build morale among the farmers – yada-yada – and for her anniversary, I give Cinco the trip she wants above all others.

We spend nearly a month with Meredith and Ardit looking at production technology and results, checking out the crops and seeing what they are doing, as well as the militant resistance in the area and how very successful armed farmers can be at keeping their personal enterprises safe. We spend a lot of time just hanging out with friends and watching Y'hoshua grow and go. We have brought the mem-loader and upgrades. Some things are more joyful than others, but all in all, it is a blessing to be there. For Cinco and me, it is rather like a pilgrim's journey. And that is exactly what we would be up to next. Well, almost next!

Yerushalayim

The only permanent ally of Texas, or I should say the FreeNation of Tejas, is Israel. We had decided that, since the US had become such a weak supporter and because it was the right thing to do, that Tejas would be an eternal partner with Israel from now on. It is our only fixed alliance regardless of world conditions. We, as a nation, had decided that God's promise of Blessing and Cursing people, and peoples, according to how they addressed Israel was real. Actually, it wasn't so much "decided" as "realized," since what was done was to research history for three thousand years and see what had become of every enemy of Israel and what benefit came to every friend.

Related to that, a Danzig Enterprises division – Danzig Tactical Instruction and Supply – has an arrangement with the IDF – Israeli Defense Forces – that provides them with facilities, instructors, weapons, and more, in remote locations all around the world, almost everywhere we do business. In some locations, we have combat shooting domes that are up to two hundred feet tall and over sixty meters deep – with up to fifteen levels of combat arena that allow a group of trainees to use live fire on targets in simulated situations with quickly re-configurable floors on each level. The only things we don't move are the stairs and elevators, but we are working on that. We call in a favor, Cinco and I.

We have been to visit our operations in Burundi again and to upgrade Meredith and Ardit, as well as to visit little Yoshi before we take off on our more important and personal mission. We fly into Botswana to drop in on a Mossad training camp that Danzig has created, literally, in the middle of nowhere. The communications tower is nearly two hundred feet tall, and from the perch on top of that, you can still see . . . almost nothing. For this reason alone, it would have been a great place to go, but there is more.

When we arrive, a Colonel Avram Dagan, third generation Mossad, has selected two operators that are approximate doubles for Cinco and me. We meet them inside the shooting and staging dome where we swap identities. They put on wigs, and I shave my head. Lucky girl, Cinco gets a light brown dye job, and her hair is braided down her back. They go on vacation to Bali as us, and we go into training for about a week before we can be relocated. They will have to suffer through some of the best room service and accommodations, while we do some close quarters physical combat training and weapons maintenance, improvised detonations and urban defense technologies, followed by – of all things – jump school. We are about to go out on our first jump when Dagan tells us that our intake trip is ready to go. We hop a C5 with twenty other operators – well, operators . . . even if not "other" – and several tons of cargo headed for Israel. We stop in Uganda for fuel and to pick up a few other things, then on to our destination. We land at Yerushalayim Airport, and from there, we take a transport directly from the plane to Qalandia Camp, where we stay for a few hours until the right shift change, which will allow us to exit the base – unrecorded. This gives us a chance to clean up and change into some civies and even prep some cheap luggage for the journey.

Schroyer has arranged our wallets including ID, credit cards, and our passports, which are all impeccable. Whenever we swipe a passport, a debit, or credit card, everything is better than the bank. When I swipe my Tex-Ex card as Yitzhak Cohen, it goes through faster than Gerhardt can pick up a check, twice as fast, and no one even asks me a question about my passport at a check point or an airport. There are no problems for Mrs. Cohen either.

The report comes back on the bullet fired at me in Myrtle Beach, and it tells a different story than expected. Because it was made from depleted uranium, it had been compared to military sniper bullets for recent decades and it's discovered that it is a match for a sniper that had served in the last Afghan War, who, further investigation reveals, is the boyfriend of Mister Johnny Wilkes' wife. She had thought of just divorcing Johnny, but when he got that job as a reporter . . . with all those wonderful benefits as a government subcontract employee, her plans changed. Now, his life insurance was worth nearly two million US, and if he died on the job – while covering a story – it would double. So, as soon as she heard that he was going to be covering me, she began to cogitate a plan, and her lover was willing to follow up. After all, he has killed before, almost likes it; and a four million dollar bonus with the girl of his dreams thrown into the happy meal, well, it is a temptation he cannot refuse. He is certain that he will get away with it, and if the bullet had gone anywhere but into a post, it might have been lost forever, and getting away with it could have happened. Then there is the cartridge found by the beach sweeper with a partial print. The partial was far too little information to run for a match on its own, but fit perfectly, once there is a suspect in hand. Combined with the match to the metallurgy of the bullet and then the ballistics match to his weapon, bullet residue in the barrel, and this case is a slam dunk. The shooter implicates his woman using all manner of anti-female invectives for ruining his life, but regardless of everything he says about her, it was still him who took the shot. No one forced him. Between them, they are scheduled to serve about 211 years. I will still grant Wilkes an interview. But, now, back to us!

We are ordinary, everyday, pilgrims, and it is great. We are among the people, amid the crowds, seeing the sights, the shrines, the churches, and trails without any attention being drawn to us because of who we are, and it is a continual stream of relief, like resting in a shaded string hammock, in a breeze, beside a brook. We haven't felt this rested and at peace since . . . well, we can't remember ever being this relaxed.

We walk the streets and roads of the Holy Land, and that adds colour and texture to the Bible materials we had uploaded into our brains some time ago. It activates our uploaded knowledge with experience, and we realize that we have made a serious mistake in having all of those commentaries loaded in too. We are experiencing a lot of contrasting opinions in our perceptions of the tours. I don't mean me seeing things differently from Cinco, but each of us seeing everything differently from everything, just like my memories; there are numerous perceptions of the Scriptures in the commentaries that are in conflict with one another. The commentaries may have been helpful as a starting point, but now maybe, it would be a mistake to rely on them given our expedited maturity. We contact Doc and ask that she have the data stripped down to the NIV, NASB, and ASV Bible texts, manuscripts, dictionaries, lexicons and language lessons only. We are planning to do an overlay of just those materials and no opinions or wisdom of man at all. Maybe that would help solidify our understanding. Cinco has gotten the plain data files from the previous installation and tells Doc where to find them on my personal server. She then creates the "memory files" to be installed again, just the way we had asked.

It is possibly the busiest month of Doc's life, and we have thrown her an additional task on top of running the fastest growing company on the planet. She will manage, because we have set everything in place for her to hire the help, to take the orders, to load and ship the product, and hire more help. By the end of the first week, she has orders to have all of the stock in the back yard shipped out. Starting the fourth day after the shooting, there are trucks loading up from the yard twenty-four hours a day, and that doesn't let up for about five weeks. She has to hire another sixty people to work at the plant to create product and ship, but that is easy enough because she already has nearly 300 applications, with over a hundred of those are pre-approved for hire and sorted in order of preferred employability. So, when she sees Ethyl a couple of days later, this happens.

"Hey, I got those memory upgrades that you and Joshua wanted," she says.

"What upgrades?" is Ethyl's reply.

"Oh," Doc tells her, "I'm sorry. I must have gotten the wrong Ethyl. I'm amazed this hasn't happened before."

"I can understand that, but, what upgrades?"

"Well, Cinco and Joshua called the other day and asked if I would create an upgraded version, or actually a stripped down version, of the Bible training package we had used a while ago." She looks at Ethyl, not really expecting understanding but getting it.

"Oh? I had heard something about it from Cinco's official and periodic updates, but didn't have any real details. We haven't spoken or even exchanged more than the work required information since . . . well, since she became, sort of, the boss' girl, ya know?"

"Yeah," Doc says, "I know. There's a lot of that going around."

"I would be interested in trying it out though," is the unexpected response from Ethyl. "It sounds like something that could be fun. Besides, I want to know if it is actually useful for absorbing anything I want, even unrelated to my previous training. Also, because my medical training went so well, I'm kind of eager to see what else I can do."

"When is your next free hour or two?" asks Doc.

"This is Tuesday? I have," her eyes rolled slightly left, "three hours on Thursday, starting at two. Will that do?"

Doc checks her desktop screen and taps the calendar app with her finger. Looking at the week, she sees that she has time on Thursday as well, but not as much. "I can start it, and when the load is finished, I can have someone else disconnect you and give you a check over. Would that be okay?"

"Sure! How about I bring Mike along to watch over me?"

"He is kinda cute, isn't he?" Doc says back to her.

"Hands off, Doc," comes a response, almost with a growl. "That one's mine."

I remember it as the Tower Life Building long ago, but it has a new name since, and I can't seem to lock it in. This is the thirty-third floor . . . where I had been rebuilt. They are holding hands as they come out of the elevator and into the "hospital" for the first time together. Ethyl has been here before, of course, but for Mike, it was a trip into the Starship Enterprise, or more accurately for today, the Starship of the Enterprise.

They stroll over to the receptionist's desk, and after a brief exchange, Ethyl hands the receptionist the disk for mem-loading, a small version of an old-school DVD, that holds two gigabytes of data that are the "memories" that are to be installed today. This is the disk that Cinco and I wanted made because it has no commentaries or analysis, just the texts of a few Bible translations, original language materials – Nestle 27, Masoretic Text – the Lexicons and Dictionaries, the Treasury of Scripture Knowledge cross references, and the language lessons. The goal is to get just to the Word, translated and in original languages, without any opinions of men, as well as possible. There will be some contamination due to translation, but we are all hoping that this can be minimized and mitigated.

They don't even have to wait; the staff and Doc are waiting for them. So in less than a minute, after only signing a couple of papers, Debbie, the receptionist gestures them into the next room.

Ethyl asks Doc, "Why did I need to sign those papers? I never had to sign anything before."

"You never had 'personhood' before either." Ethyl glares at these words. "Joshua had your personal profile recreated as a person, not a corporate property, over a year ago, when he realized your classification and status, and Cinco's."

"Hmm," was her only reply . . . for now!

The north and south walls of the room are covered with hard drives that can be replaced on the fly should one have a failure, as part of the giant RAID array, ten drives wide, thirty drives tall, on each wall, but today they remain silent and still. In the middle of the room is what looks like a dental chair, surrounded by technology. It does have the mandatory sink, with a collection of tools on a rack, including a suction hook, but this one has a moisture sensor on the end to measure when to suck. There is also a device hanging over the upper end of the chair like a chandelier. As she sits down in the chair, Ethyl unties her hair – normally kept up in a large swirl of a bun – and lets it fall to her shoulders and beyond.

"Wow," Mike thinks to himself, "I never get tired of her turning loose the hair." It is impressive.

She sits in the chair, as she has many times before, and the chandelier thing is lowered into position; its tendrils reach through her hair to engulf her head with small wires and sensors, which move around on her head 'til it finds the right places, is settled in and stops. When it stops, when each of the tendrils has found its destination, a tiny barb penetrates the scalp and latches into the skin to hold it still for the transfers. "Ow!" Ethyl cries out a bit, just like all the other times. Each of the barbs is a tenth of a millimeter in width, but it still hurts a bit as they puncture the skin, locking the sensors into place. There is a cream that can be applied to prevent the pain and reduce the bleeding, but Ethyl never cared for what it does to her hair, and subsequently to her disposition. She will gladly tell us all that having sticky, shabby, disheveled, or unhappy hair makes her grumpy. As it is, her hair is a beautiful mane of flowing golden brown, wafting in the gentle flow of the air conditioned breeze. She lays her hands on the arm rests which have another set of sensors under each wrist and hand, which keeps track of her vital signs, blood oxygen, skin statistics, and more. It takes a light anesthetic and ten minutes to get her into a state of reception, where data can be put into her brain directly then, amazingly, it will take only twenty-five minutes to install the upgrade. Every bit of data will be laid into nearly ten dozen locations on the brain because the brain stores data more like holographs than data files. Each memory is kept in several locations, and in most memories, the different locations store different aspects of a memory. No single location is responsible for keeping anything or everything, and that is the brain's way of creating a RAID array with, around, and inside the memories. With data memories, we store them whole, in numerous places, because we still don't understand how the brain decides to divide them, but also because that makes them more accessible.

In less than an hour after having entered the building, Ethyl's eyes open up, and the suction device is removed from her mouth – the chandelier is already off her head – and she looks at Mike and says, "Hmmm." It isn't a question or an exclamation, but rather an expression of a singular awareness, much like a scientist that puts two things into a test tube and finds some reaction that he wasn't expecting. "Hmmm." She says again and then, "Huh?" She looks up and to the left all of a sudden, accessing current information from her external interfaces. "We gotta go," is all she says as she grasps Mike's hand, and they head for the elevator.

"What's going on?" he asks, anxiously waiting for the door to open.

She puts her finger to her lips and pulls his hand as she enters the elevator car and pushes the lobby button. "There's news, but we have to confirm. It came in over a broadcast to me." The door closes and the car begins to descend. "There's a report on the wires about an attack on Joshua in Bali, but Bali is not where they are." The car reaches the ground level, the heavy brass doors by Tiffany open, and they hurry through the marble corridors to the garage, where her car is pulling down the ramp to meet them. Suddenly she says, "Whoa!" Ethyl stops and falls toward Mike, who catches her under both arms as her legs give way. He sits her down gently on the carpet at the garage entrance to the building and rests her back against the wall. "Whoa!" she says, "I had forgotten about the lag."

"What do you mean?" asks Mike.

"Whenever I get an upgrade there is a lag when I sit there, have some juice, and gather my thoughts, which is followed by a brief check up. This time though, there was the news post, and I got caught up in the moment." Her eyes cross a little as she refocuses on Mike. She shakes her head quickly, "We have to go."

"I think we should go back upstairs for that 'brief check up' you mentioned." Mike says.

"And I am sure that I will be fine in just a few minutes, but you should probably drive." She never lets anyone drive her car. "Get us back to the tower, and then we can get me checked out, but right now, we gotta go."

Mike picks her up and sets her in the passenger seat on the left side of her car. It is a 1947 MG TC Roadster, fully body-off restored, numbers matching except the carbs. She straps in, and Mike speeds around getting into the driver's side, on the right side, which is weird. The shifter is on the wrong side for him, and the pedals are backwards to him, but he manages to adjust. Besides, they only have to go about three miles, left out the garage to turn left again on Navarro, right on Market and through downtown to go left on Cherry and into the garage. They hit most of the lights as they turn red so that he has to start from a dead stop several times. But with each stop light and start, he gets a little better at it. He used to have an antique Italian Harley, so he is familiar with the idea of everything being in the wrong place and growing accustomed to it quickly.

Ethyl is a different piece of work altogether. As soon as she is fastened into her seat, she reaches into the glove box – physically stabilized – gets out her laptop, pops it open, and with a few clicks and passwords, even before they get to Market Street, she is linked directly to Schroyer in a high-speed conversation the likes of which Mike has never seen and shouldn't be watching if they are to arrive safely. She gets all the details of the incident and even video from security cams and forwards all that information to my office. Then she has Schroyer update that info as it develops.

It takes nearly ten minutes and when they arrive Ethyl already has the laptop put away and lets herself out of the car faster than Mike can – though, to be fair, he still has to put the shifter into first, locate and engage the parking brake, find the keys to shut her down, then slide his seat all the way back to exit. Ethyl uses her biometric access to open my elevator, and in another minute, they are in my office on the phone to Cinco.

We are in Basti Restaurant on the Via Dolorosa, having an orange juice with a bit of strawberry in it when the call comes. "Aloo," says Cinco in a slight French accent, "merci, un moment," she continues. "It's for you, Yitzhak," and she hands me the phone as our order arrives: the Special Basti Pizza.

"What is it?" I ask, feeling rather interrupted, I may have even been a little rude.

"There was an attack on you in Bali reported in the news. There are no bodies, but two Israelis, presumed to be your security detail, have been injured," there is a voice on the phone just like the one beside me, speaking to our waiter.

"How are they? What happened?" I ask.

"They were headed toward the plane, and the attackers may have assumed that, since your security was approaching the plane alone, that the principals must already have been on board. That's when it blew. BLAM!" she yells at the phone. "The crew was strapped in the cockpit, which is secured and armored, so they just got knocked around a bit when the nose of the plane dropped to the ground. The onboard assistant was in the restroom behind the galley, so while she was not in the blast directly, she was also not fastened in somewhere safely. She got a broken arm, collar bone, and rib, as well as a few minor shrapnel wounds. The Israelis got the worst of it because the blast threw the stairs off the side of the plane as they were climbing them. Between them, there are known to be three broken femurs, four fractured wrists, six cracked ribs, two concussions, and a vast collection of not so minor shrapnel wounds. They are deep into surgery, and I will keep you posted as best I can, but right now, you gotta go."

"What do you mean, we gotta go?" I ask.

"Your face is about ten minutes from being on every TV in the world as a dead or missing billionaire, depending on whose story is going to be believed. Either way, you cannot be exposed to a traffic cam or video surveillance connected to facial recognition, or you are going to be had. You are exposed. You and Cinco both. GO!"

Cinco is so much smarter than me in these matters. Our food has arrived again, this time to go, and we go to the southeast, into the bazaar. In five minutes, we have new hats, scarves, sunglasses, shirts, and we are on our way eating pizza as we wander westward. The phone rings in a few minutes, "Where are you now?" chides Ethyl's voice.

"We went south-ish and are headed west on Via Dolorosa, and it is about to become Saint Francis."

"Catch a cab at Beit HaBad and go north to the walkway that crosses to the Sultan Suleiman and turn left. Where it reaches the HaNevi'im – the Street of the Prophets – you will be met by some of our Mossad friends in a piece-of-crap-mobile. They will get you to the airport and onto a military craft headed to Port San Antonio."

In fifty yards or so, we get to Beit HaBad and catch a cab. It is slow slogging in the traffic with all the pedestrians. We eat a bit more pizza on the way. It is only a quarter mile or so, but we ride instead of putting our faces out there, just in case. We must have appeared a little strange, almost draped for winter, hats and glasses in sweatshirts, eating more pizza, but we remained undetected until we arrive at the Street of the Prophets and step into the most innocuous car in the world: a ten or fifteen year old Fiat mini-four-seater. It may have been a middle forties model of the "500," but that may be assigning luxury where none is due. The guys in the car get out, letting us into the back seat – it is a two door – and then we take off with the acceleration of a tuk-tuk at first, but it does get up to speed, and eventually we find ourselves headed back to the service side of Yerushalayim Airport at over ninety kilometers per hour. We get there safe and sound. The driver honks his horn as we drive up to the gate, and the guards open a lane to let us through and close it after we have gone. As we pass the gate one of the guards salutes the driver. "I hope he doesn't get in trouble for that," the driver says.

"What's wrong with that?" I ask.

"Well," says the driver, "we can't fully secure the nearby houses, woods, and hills, so the policy is that no one gets a salute at the gate. It can make them a target for a sniper."

"No one gets a salute?" I ask.

"If Moshe Dayan – may he be kept in Ha Shem – comes back from the dead and drives through that gate there should be no salute."

We approach the airport, and we're waved through another gate, which closes after us, and then the car drives right onto a plane. I can't tell what kind of plane from our entry point, but when the car stops, four men strap the wheels in place and let us out of the car, to get into some rear facing seats behind the cockpit. As soon as we are all buckled in, one of the crew shouts into his mic, "All good, sir!" and gets into his seat. At this time, the cargo gate closes, the engines roar up a bit, and the plane begins to move forward – backward to us – and to accelerate, then to tilt and lift. We can see only slightly through some windows that are rather small and nearly ten feet away at the nearest point, but we can tell that we get up to about two thousand feet or so and level out. I can see the city out the port windows, and then it is gone. We keep that approximate westward bearing and altitude for about an hour and a half, maybe two, when the cabin goes dark with a single claxon sound, and then a red light blinks, illuminating the cabin. Two of the crewmen stand up and fasten safety straps to themselves and to the cable running the length of the ceiling. They each stand at the two sides of the car, and crouching, they pull the release handles at the front of the car and the rear, releasing the straps that hold it in place, and toss the harnesses into boxes along the walls. The man on the port side releases the emergency brake, puts the gear shift into neutral, and the car rolls just a little, settling into place. They both return to the front of the car, and the cargo bay door opens as we fly along. The men make certain that their safety straps are nowhere near the car as they begin pushing from the front, and in just a few seconds, the car disappears from sight and the cargo ramp closes as if nothing ever happened.

The car is a disposable, that is, it is intended to be disposed. It belongs to an imaginary person in Syria who had bought it and insured it with half a dozen companies, in Syria, and had reported it stolen right after we took off. The car is worth a few thousand dollars, but it has served its purpose in this mission, and it will be fully refunded, several times over, to a non-existent Arab whose bank accounts funnel indirectly into the coffers of the IDF. In the meantime the money will come from companies that help fund terror organizations the world over. It is the ultimate win-win, especially for me and mine, because we get out of town safely.

The plane catches a refueler somewhere over the North Atlantic and flies non-stop to Port San Antonio where Mike waits with Ethyl and a company Black Hawk. When we get on board, Mike argues with Cinco about who is "driving" home. It's about fifteen hundred hours in SA when we board and with howdies all around; she gives him a break, letting him keep the stick. The tower is in sight almost as soon as we lift off, and I feel like I am home for the first time in a while. I can't wait for Cinco to get back to her usual hair colour. As we approach the Tower, someone is standing on the platform. We get closer, and I can see, it's Stephen.

We exit the craft and head to the elevator when Stephen approaches me and says, "Mr. Gerhardt wants to see you, sir," and he shakes my hand. "Welcome home, sir."

"Thank you, Stephen. Would you let Gerhardt know that I will be down in a little while? We need a clean up after that trip, unless you think this look would be more entertaining overall?" He smiles at that thought, so we are off to see the wizard. "Hey Cinco," I shout to her, "We're going to see Gerhardt first. Okay?"

"If you say so, Boss!" She is not happy with that, but at least we will have gotten it out of the way, then we can get on with life, or at least our version of it. I finger twitch at Mike, point at the ground beside me, and have him join us from the cockpit. The company pilot can take the chopper to the airport from here. Mike knows we are going to see Gerhardt, and he is not thrilled about it either.

Der Gerhardt Conflagration

When we arrive at Gerhardt's office, he is already raising his hand to point his finger at me, so I interrupt him before he can speak saying, "I quit!"

"What? Hey! Wait! You can't quit," he sputters, "you owe us. We own you! You can't do without the Enterprise. And we are not going to let go that easily. Do you know why you can't quit?" he ranted on, so I interrupt him again.

"Okay, I don't quit!" I raise my hand and my voice to a near shout. "But, do you know why I don't quit?" I ask, stamping my foot at him twice. I have his attention now.

"What?" he stammers again, "Huh? What? Why?" he says.

"Because, Gerhardt, I don't work for you!" Gerhardt suddenly has a dumbfounded glare. "You have forgotten that you work for me. It says so on all the letterhead and contracts. This is Danzig Enterprises and, for better or worse, I am Joshua Danz, so let's settle a few things." I point at his desk chair and nod, he sits. "I was never more than an hour out of reach for the past couple months. Within a half an hour of the events in Bali, my people had works in motion to secure me and the interests of this Enterprise. Did you get that? My People! Half an hour!"

"Where were you?" he clamors to the front of his chair. "With all you mean to this company, to the Enterprise as a whole, we have some right to know what you are up to. Don't we?"

"No," I say slapping my hand on the desk, "you don't." I stare into his eyes as if we are about to draw weapons and duel. "It is my name on the letterhead, and it is I who has a right to know what my Enterprise is up to, not the other way around. I am a free person, not a parolee, and I will not have my actions and adventures monitored, controlled, or dictated. Still, I will try to inform you where I have been, within limits of reason, but not where I am, or will be, unless I deem it is in my, or our, best interests." I glare even harder. "Remember, it was my If/Then that brought all this into being – admittedly with your wise application. And it was my car designs that funded it from the very start, with very little support from anyone outside. So, let's all realize who built this empire, and even in my absence, who and what kept an eye on it."

Gerhardt looks deflated, "We have interests, and we have concerns."

"I understand that," I reply, "and I will not fecklessly endanger myself on a whim, but I don't plan to cancel our plans to go skydiving either." I am way more than half kidding about the skydiving.

"Really, Boss?" says Mike. "You want to go skydiving? I can help with that."

At the same time Cinco says, "Really, Boss? I could get into that."

I am taken aback slightly by their responses to the idea. "Now, if you and Helge are up for it, we would apparently love to have you come along with us on a skydiving adventure; otherwise, I will let you know where I have been, not where I am about to go."

"Well," says Gerhardt, "I know that Helge has wanted to go skydiving for a long time, but I can't handle the heights." He sits back in his chair, "I will have her contact you about it, if you are serious."

"Hells yeah, we're serious!" says Cinco. "I'll check calendars and make calls to get equipment." She glances about, "Stephen! You are Jumpmaster qualified, right?"

"Sure," he replies unenthusiastically.

"Good," she continues in glee that rarely arises, "then you can set us up with all the training and gear! Right?"

"Sure," he says again, still not what anyone would mistake for excitement.

"But I want it understood that while I was in the hospital, and even when I am out of contact, the If/Then can run things just fine, as you have proven many times over. If we are done here, Cinco and I need a couple of showers each after a long and dirty military flight from Yerushalayim."

"Are you out of your damned mind? Jerusalem? How long were you there?" He is fuming, but he calms quickly. Almost as if asking through his teeth, he says, "You did say that you would tell me where you had been, within reason. I think I have reason."

"That is true." I look over at Cinco who gives me a "go ahead" tilt of the head and bat of her eyes, "Well, okay," I continue, "we were in a Mossad training camp in Africa for a week or so before we actually disappeared into Israel." I glance at Gerhardt, who has almost started percolating, "We did maneuvers and live fire exercises with Field Operators, as well as weapons training and tactical studies." Gerhardt's blood pressure seems to be elevating, so I look around to Stephen and Mike and say, like a kid at Christmas, "We had been to jump school and were just about to go on our first jump when our covert access to Israel became available." I look back at Cinco, "And you looked great in all that tactical gear, Babe. It is 'Babe,' isn't it?" We had watched *My Chauffeur* in the hotel in Israel, and we're planning to watch it again after showers.

Gerhardt is getting a bit on edge, and my calling Cinco, "Babe" only fueled the fire.

"Why the hell would you want to go to Israel?" is Gerhardt's response.

"Because, Hugo! Cinco and I wanted to see the Holy Land, from ground level, as a couple of nobodies." Gerhardt glares angrily. "Look," I assert, "if we go as Joshua Danz, plus one, we get the royal treatment, but we also cannot get into the crowds and mingle with the people, hear their insights, share thoughts, and touch the dirt. Everywhere we go, it is with an entourage that resembles an army that disrupts and interrupts the lives of everyone around us. Don't you get it?"

"Don't you get it?" he fires back. "That is what the entourage is for! You have to understand how important you are?"

"Yes," I say, "and you have to understand how important I am not. Do you?" At this point, I turn to leave.

"We are not done with this conversation," says Gerhardt.

"We are unless you want it to continue as you scrub my back in the shower." I stare directly into his eyes. "I have been several thousand miles without a wash, and several hours before that, so grab a body sponge or call it quits." He sits back down with a grunt of exasperation and flopping hands. "That's what I thought."

"I want to argue," says Cinco under her breath at me as I pass.

Stephen goes back on duty, so to speak, Mike goes with Ethyl on a date, and Cinco follows me into the shower, but she really doesn't need to argue to get there. Mike and Ethyl look so cute to Cinco and me. It is just a ton of fun watching a new relationship grow into something profound. We scrub each other from head to foot with hair conditioner and some cute little nylon scrubby puffs, and a foot brush, but use no shampoo or soaps at all. It is amazingly soothing, and with all that scrubbing we are as clean as we could have been without using a disinfectant – and who wants that? Not Cinco and me, and I hope, not you.

We talk briefly about those Mossad agents that were busted up pretending to be us, and at first we consider an invite for them to San Antonio to express our gratitude and to at least offer some sort of reward for their heroism toward our safety. Since Cinco is, in all reality, Mrs. Danzig Enterprises, she and I are doing a little day dreaming and brainstorming on what we would like to do for those brave people and their families. Families! Wow! Neither of us has thought of families until just now. What can we do for their families? "Well," she says, "first off, we could offer to send the families to Bali to help with their recovery and put them up in a really decent hotel with all expenses paid." It is Cinco's idea because, as she says, "The worst thing I could think of would be being unable to get to you when you are hurt or sick." Sometimes she can get a little mushy, and that's alright too. Then it was fun sharing the DYSON-T and getting blown dry on the way out of the shower. So, after the shower and blower, we get on the phone to Colonel Dagan. It is nearly midnight in Africa, but he's still up. We broach the possible plan, and he says that each has a spouse in the IDF and that Chayyim has three children as well. The Colonel makes the connections to the proper people who can make the needed decisions, and we work it all out.

At first we think we might just cover the cost to pay for military flights for the family. But, considering the immediacy of the needs and the miles of red tape involved in estimating the cost replacement idea, yada-yada, and the fact that we are trying to show gratitude, not hide it, they allow that it is permissible for me to send a company jet for them, and make arrangements in Bali. But they note that it would be preferred if I do not attend anything personally. My presence could also make targets of the families. I agree, and Cinco arranges for a pair of staff pilots to take a jet right away, and she arranges for an open stay, starting with a month at the W Retreat and Spa in Bali, with access to every amenity, all bills paid. They won't even have to pay for souvenirs, if they remember to take their Tex-Ex gift cards that each family has been given to cover any expenses outside the hotel.

It turns out that their stays have to be extended for nearly three months, and some of the family members have to return to their jobs or lose them. So, we have some of our staff from one of our Aussie hotels go and act as support for the families. Of those family members that had come, those that had to go home in about a month were a grandfather, a mother, a father, and one son of Chayyim, the captain that had, for a brief and dangerous moment, impersonated me.

Chayyim and Rivkah had put themselves in harm's way to protect us, and harm had come to them. While the Mossad will not allow for a direct reward such as cash or properties of any kind to be given as an expression of gratitude, there is a work-around that is considered to be acceptable. We setup scholarships to the Hillel University for every member of their families. It is the best idea that Cinco and I can think up, for honoring the service of these exceptional soldiers, and for honoring the Word of God within us. So, we create a fund that will pay for anyone directly related to either of them, from grandparent to great-grandchild, who would desire to attend. In fifty years, it will become a part of the general scholarship funds and be available to any needy military or ex-military Israeli. In fifty years, according to Schroyer, the Rivkah and Chayyim Scholarship will be worth nearly fifty million Texican dollars, even if half the current members of the families go to school.

When all this is settled, and survival passions have been expressed, we can sit back in bed and watch *My Chauffeur* again, and just as before, enjoy it immensely. "It is Babe, isn't it?"

Skydiving and a Thrill Ride

Stephen agrees to be our Jumpmaster for the training and even gets training equipment brought to the combat range above the bunker. We practice falling with a tuck and roll every few days for a month. First we fall off curbs, jump off short platforms onto mattresses, then higher platforms onto mattresses, 'til we are jumping from four or five feet up, but onto gym mats. We are geared up and primed to fly. On the flight roster is Helge, Cinco, Doc, Ethyl, Stephen, and Mike, and oh yeah, me. Our first jump is coming up, and it has to be a tandem jump, as will be our second.

Stephen arranges for three of us at a time to jump. Since the first couple jumps have to be tandem jumps, this means that someone has to be fastened to us and control the chute when we jump, so that means that the space on the plane is a bit more limited. First up will be Helge, Cinco, and Mike. With those three out of the way that leaves Doc, Ethyl, and me as first timers. Stephen helps out on each flight and straps to one of the ladies. He jumps with Helge and Ethyl on their first jumps and with Cinco and Doc on their second jumps. Someone from the jump school fastens to the rest of us on each flight. We all manage to survive and we all want to do that third jump.

The day is fast approaching and finally arrives, the red letter day . . . March twenty-eighth, 2059. A cool front has blown in last night, and this is a chilled Monday morning. Stephen stands on the lowered ramp of the cargo gate on Mike's Chinook as one of the staff pilots manages the stick. We are flying along at about 12,000 feet, into a forward wind of about thirty knots, and it is almost as if we are standing still in the sky. The wind is furious around us as we each step to the door, and one at a time, we step off the ramp and into the sky, with the static lines pulling the rip chords of our chutes for this first solo jump. Mike goes first in black, followed by Ethyl in white, then Helge, also in white, followed by Cinco in red. Cinco had asked me earlier if the bright red jumpsuit made her butt look big, and I told her that it made her butt look "perfect . . . like a bright, red, shiny apple." Following her, I step to the end of the ramp and drop off as the tether pulls the handle, a nylon strap speeds out of the sheath that guides it to the catch that releases the chute, and as it deploys, I jerk a bit and swing below the canopy. I am rotated around as I watch Doc in her blue jump suit leap from the deck like a bird. Look at her fly! Hey! She is not supposed to be flying! Before I realize this, Stephen is unhooked from the static line and jumping out, unleashed. He has his hands by his sides, and he is plummeting toward the earth like a rocket. They are out of sight in a moment, and I am looking around for the others in a panic. It is a long ride down, I want to know something. And by God, I want to know it, NOW! What was supposed to be the most fun in our lives so far has turned dangerous for her, and fearful for me. It seems to take hours to get to the ground, and when we do touch-down, we are nowhere near where Stephen, and hopefully Ilyssa must have landed, and we might have to wait for word or to be carried back to the jump school. Almost immediately a chase jeep arrives and in the back are Stephen and Doc, the latter of whom does not care to move for a good long while. I can find no blame in that as she lay across the back seat with her feet up. I just have to hold her for a moment to make certain that she is okay, that she is really here. Cinco puts one hand on my shoulder and another on Doc's back, squeezing us together. After a moment, we look around and take a count. We have Stephen and Doc in the jeep, Cinco and I holding on to Doc; Mike is on the other side of the jeep, walking up with Ethyl and . . . hey, wait a minute. We have all been so worried about what happened to Doc that we didn't even notice that we are missing Helge.

She had tried to steer her chute a little more than the rest of us and managed to get herself into a stand of trees, not too far from where the rest of us are gathered. We find her by the simplest possible means; she calls Cinco. "Is Ilyssa alright?" she asks.

"Yes, dear, she is fine," Cinco replies, "but, where are you?"

"I am hanging around in some trees, but I can't say where, Liebchen. I was hoping you could help me out with that," and so, Cinco does. She uses a GPS tracking app on Helge's phone, and in a minute, she has a fix on her location, and we have the jeep headed there as the rest of us, except for Doc, well, we all roll up our chutes. Sadly, when they get to Helge, it is discovered that she has broken a leg coming through the canopy of the trees and is going to have to wait for a cherry picker to come get her down. We have already called an ambulance for Doc, and when they get Helge down, they bring her to the ambulance, where they set the leg, splint it, and transport her to a Baptist hospital on the north side of town, about a half an hour away. They'll keep her overnight and fit her with a synthetic cast and a pair of crutches, as well as a motorized wheelchair for a while – courtesy of Hugo – and she seems quite happy about everything. That could be the drugs talking, but in the following days and weeks she will say that she wants to go again, and she has no drugs in her at the time.

As the ambulance takes Helge and Doc away, for a checkup after each of the ladies' ordeals; Cinco says to me, "What are you going to do about it?"

"What do you mean?" I ask back. "I'm no doctor."

She leads me away from everyone else, so we can be alone for a moment. "Not the medical stuff, you boob. I was talking about the way you were clinging to her, the fear that went through you when you thought she may be dead. I know that you are still in love with Doc." My eyes must be bugging out from under my brows. "And you know that Doc is still in love with you. She has been since a few weeks after she arrived, and regardless of how much of everything has been business, down deep, she is hopelessly bonded to you. The lab explosion told me all of that, but I was kind of expecting it might have lessened, or subsided with time."

"So," I say, "what do you expect me to do about it?" I am literally in pain, "You are my wife. I love you. That hasn't changed, and I would never want to hurt you. So, what do I do?"

"I hope that you'll do the most honorable thing you can do, given your circumstances, dumb ass, and marry her." The blood runs from my brain so quickly that I almost faint. We have never discussed this before, and I didn't want to bring it up because, well, some wives get pistol-packing mad at these thoughts. "Look, Babe," she says, "I came into this marriage after telling you that I wanted to be your woman, no matter what. Right?" I nod. "Well, this is exactly the 'what' I was talking about." I can feel the deer-in-the-headlights look on my face. "When we got married, you and I had been celibate for a while – the forty days before the wedding – but before that, neither of us thought you were exclusive to me, did we?" I shake my head, almost in shame. "Well, why does everyone think that has to change?"

"What about the church?" I ask.

"What about them? Are you concerned about the church" she held her fingers up about a half an inch apart, "or the Church?" she spread out her hands like describing a fish. "The greater Church has no problem with you having another wife if I don't mind . . . and I don't mind." I shrug. "In fact, since so much of the 'world' has accepted homosexual sin for marriage, most of the church has practically embraced polygyny. Why not you? We can be married by Brother Skaapwagter, who married us, or Brother Julian in India, if you prefer. Either of them would be glad to do it. Besides," she pauses for a moment, "my lady doctor said that if we are going to have kids, it would take a miracle." I almost cry and nearly crush her hand. I look up at her, questioningly, "She's sure," comes her reply to my eyes.

She takes my hand, and we begin going back toward the others. I say, "Okay, let's pray on it tonight and talk with Doc about it tomorrow." She agrees, and we will.

I talk with Stephen about what had happened, and he tells me that it wasn't anything nefarious, just that the tether snap broke. "It rarely happens," he says, "but when it does, it's a good idea to have an experienced Jumpmaster around. I caught up with her about half way down, pulled her chute and then mine, and we had plenty of time to recover. When I got to her though, she had fainted and was falling butt first towards the earth. It made it easier to reach her rip cord, but gave her an extra hard bit of a jolt when the chute caught the air. She is likely to be sore for a few days. The suit and the rigging should have absorbed a good deal of the shock." I can tell that he had been plenty exhilarated in the action, but his colour is returning quite nicely. "I just want to get into a shower and bed."

Just then, Benson drives up to get us. He has pulled right out into the open field with the Bentley and gets out opening the door like a chauffeur, which I guess he sometimes is. We remaining few pile in as the press arrives on the scene. As soon as the chopper lifted off, someone on the skydiving staff called the press and told them that I was there. He thought it would be some great free advertising. The news vans had begun to arrive about the same time we were bailing out. And then, there had been reports of a bad jump, and someone had a bad landing, and so they came scurrying like rats to the cheese. I really hate being the cheese. We get out for a couple of minutes to give a brief overview of what happened and to answer a few questions. Stephen explains the events that resulted in two of us leaving in an ambulance – the snap hook, the tree landing, and there are some murmurs about how he should be investigated for these injuries while he was the jumpmaster on the flight. Stephen allowed that he would welcome an honest investigation, but it would be by professional skydivers and jump masters of the Tejas government, not the inexperienced press. All in all, it probably took about ten to fifteen minutes, plus the time to get them to move their vans. In the final analysis, it is Benson directing everyone back into the car and closing the doors that convinces everyone that we are going to leave. Still, we have been live on the air, with our location disclosed in some detail for a couple of commercial breaks, and that always sets Benson and gang on edge a bit. It turns out, they have good cause today.

We are coming south on 281 toward downtown on the upper level, on that five lane part of the highway passing by the airport, then Basse Road, and then the zoo before the exits for Corpus, Laredo and Austin. It is as we are passing Loop 410 that we find ourselves boxed in by a flatbed tow truck in front and large trucks on each side of us. Benson tries to slow down and go around, only to discover that another large truck has pulled in behind us. We are going about sixty, and the truck in the rear hits our bumper – hard! Stephen reaches into the armrest of the door and removes a Sig 45, and Cinco does the same on her side. There we are, Mike, Cinco, Ethyl, Stephen, and me, in the rear as Benson drives. "Everyone? Strap in and buckle down!" says Benson, "This could get hairy." We are already in our belts, but we all do as he has instructed and tighten down. He slows against the pushing truck far from the one in front as it lowers the bed of his Jerr-Dan platform, the one behind starts pushing us closer, as the tow platform extends well behind the wheels, lowering almost to the pavement. Well behind the truck the bed contacts the highway, sparks flying into the grill of the Bentley, and Benson speeds up putting the front wheels on the truck bed a little, then slams on his brakes, driving the truck behind us into the trunk of the car, with a BANG and a CRUNCH like I have never heard before. He puts his foot into it so that, between the impact from behind and the acceleration of that awesome motor, we get to the truck in front going about ninety miles an hour, maybe more, drive right up the truck bed, crashing through the forward barrier, and through the cab, probably taking out everything above the dashboard, and I am certain it took off the head of the driver. We will find out later that it did. The car flies for what seems a half a minute, but it could only have been a couple of seconds, before crashing to the ground with a bone jarring jolt, slamming the forward barrier of the truck onto the cement and throwing it far to the left of the roadway as the shreds and shrapnel of the roof of the truck whips in the wind past the right and top of the cab of the car. We speed away at over 130 miles an hour, then slower, exiting to the lower level, then slower to exit at Commerce Street, and pretty soon, at the Tower.

The three trucks continue down the road, unnoticed by police until they look at the recordings of the events from the onboard surveillance systems of the Bentley. The license plates of all trucks can be plainly seen and even the drivers' faces are captured, as well as verifying that it is not Benson to blame for the highway mishaps when that tow truck came crashing off the bridge at Josephine Street and into a bar. Fortunately, it is shortly after opening and not quite lunchtime, so there are only a few people in the place, all seated by the bar, when the truck lands abruptly. Also, the bridge is high enough that the truck is going almost straight down when it hit, so an area of only about twenty by twenty feet is damaged in the front corner nearest to the highway. For those people in the bar, the biggest danger came from flying bits of glass from the truck and the chandelier that it took out. Minor cuts and bruises from the sudden panic and from diving behind the bar were had by all, but really, the diving was unneeded. The police will find the other three trucks covered with Thermite, burning on the south side of town, in the parking lot of an abandoned Centeno market the following morning. Two of the trucks had been stolen from the fleet service department of the Ford dealer out past Nakoma. The tow truck was taken from an auto repair in Hollywood Park, and the big one in the rear was a San Antonio garbage truck. The photos of the drivers never get a hit. I can't help wonder if someone is guiding the cops to that conclusion. I have to ask, but I don't get an answer.

Even the dead guy, the one who lost his head, hasn't turned up any identification so far. Though, to be fair, the corpse was crushed beneath the weight of a truck falling over a hundred feet, almost entirely onto him.

The head was found, having been separated from the body on the upper level, but it had struck the cement barrier and bounced into traffic, where it was hit by several vehicles, so facial recognition and dental records were of little use. Did they check DNA?

Cinco and I get to her apartment and stop to pray about the Ilyssa marriage issue. "You know we are going to have to tell her we are married?" I say.

"Don't you realize that she already knows?" she says in return.

"Really? How? What? Are you sure?"

"Yes, dummy," she says to me, "she expressed suspicions when we got back from the honeymoon trip, so I told her." I give her a "holy crap" look and she says, "Look! I have two real girl friends in the world; Ethyl, who knows EVERYTHING, or almost everything, and Ilyssa. They are the only two women I can truly confide in, although, sometimes I may get a little advice from Helge. But, she's not saved so she really is operating by the wrong play book in some of these things. And, by the way, I want to tell Ethyl." She is shouting at me as she is getting undressed.

"Well, that means that I am also going to have to tell Mike or it will become a wedge between them. I don't think we want that." I am probably a little loud with her as I entered the shower. She agrees, and we agree that we should tell them at dinner on an upcoming Friday night, if Ilyssa says yes. We pray a little more and come to more agreements regarding just about everything else, like that we would ask Doc in the morning when we pick her up from a night of observation, that we would rather be married by Brother Julian, because of his wonderful heart and presence of God, but also partly because I can't pronounce Skaapwagter, and that, if Doc is on board, she and I would take a few weeks of honeymoon to ease into the idea.

We ate a light meal of tilapia by my recipe with rice on the side and broccoli for greens by her recipes – I can't make rice for nothin' – followed by a small amount of lime sorbet and about an hour or so of extremely wild "glad we're both alive" sex. We have learned that a dangerous day, even one with a little danger, tends to fuel the more primal passions in us. It was all I could do to keep my hands off her in that Mossad training camp. I gotta say, it is a great reward for a harrowing experience. We doze off with her head on my chest and my arm around her back, in her bed. Someday . . . our bed . . . someday! Someday . . . ?

Glad You're Alive! Ya' Wanna?

It is about 7:30 in the morning when we arrive at the hospital with Cinco driving the Hummer. It is a classic H1, from Operation Iraqi Freedom, still equipped with the radios, converted for cell, satellite, and stereo function and still Level I up-armored, but now in a lighter, stronger version of Kevlar. It is terrible on fuel – eight or ten miles to the gallon – but fun to drive. You never have to worry about speed bumps or humps or those damnable "rubber turtle" bumps that everyone hates, because the wheels of this baby straddle them completely. She pulls the thing into the parking garage at the hospital. I'll stay in the car as Cinco goes in to get Doc, since we don't want my face on the news again and a repeat of yesterday's driving adventures.

I am glad that Benson is comfortable enough letting Cinco take me out, armed and armored, but without any of his troops. Besides, Cinco loves driving this beast. In about ten minutes, the ladies come out the door, and Cinco opens the back door of the Hummer, letting Doc in. I am already in the far side of the backseat, and Cinco smacks Ilyssa on the ass, saying, "Scoot over, bitch!" with a laugh, and she hops in as well. The thing is almost a full foot wider on the inside than the Bentley, so we have plenty of room to visit, and two of us are almost sitting completely sideways, facing Ilyssa. The vehicle stays running, locked and idle, while the air conditioner keeps us cool. After all, it is late March in South Texas, which is almost the same as summer most times.

"Doc," I begin, "Ilyssa," I correct, "when we saw you falling out of view, it scared the hell out of us . . . both of us . . . then we saw you were okay in the jeep, and, well, my heart was restored, and Cinco felt the same. And that was when Cinco asked me what I was going to do about it."

"Are you gonna tell the story or ask the question?" Cinco interrupts.

"Well," I say, "I thought I might do both."

"What question?" says Doc.

"Well, Doc," starts Cinco, "We know that you love Joshua . . ."

"Look, I don't want to be a problem for you two," she says.

"That's not it," says Cinco, "Joshua loves you too, and so do I. You are the sister I always wished I could have had . . . but that's another matter." She pauses a brief moment and says, "We want you to marry us."

"Will you?" I say, still fully bewildered in the moment myself.

"Wait a minute!" Doc says, almost blaring, "Do you have some sort of kinky threesome arrangement in mind?"

"No!" Cinco says, putting her hand on Doc's hand, "I don't think so. I'm really not into girls, and I don't think that would be quite right anyway. I think it should always be separate beds, always one wife at a time, maybe in separate residences? I don't know! We can work out the details as we go along, but, Doc," she looks into Ilyssa's eyes and says, "we want you to go along . . . with us. Almost like when Joshua was dating us both," Doc glazes over a bit, "and yes, I knew. But this time, it can be as an honest to God family."

"I don't know." She said, "This is quite a handful to take in all at once, but I must say that I have thought about something like this more than a few times, and I am intrigued. I was married, years ago, when I was at med school, but nothing about that was destined to work. Since then, and maybe even before, Joshua is the only man I have ever loved. And I do love you both, more than I otherwise should. So . . . if you are sure," she looks at both of us, each smiling and nodding, "If you are absolutely certain this is what you both want?" She looks again to be doubly sure. Finding no hesitation in our demeanor or expression, "Then 'yes' is my answer." A group hug ensues. "The answer is yes." There is weeping all around and more slightly nervous hugging and both of them have a hold of my hair.

Cinco decides she will drive and leave Doc in back to canoodle with me on the way home, and to discuss all we know about my past, all we know has been done to and for me as we hold hands, and talk. But talking and a little touching is all we do, even though I have been missing her amazing body for . . . well, for a while. Since Doc is Saved already, this is an important concern that we don't have to address – being bound to an outsider – it also means that when we discuss the idea of pre-marital celibacy, we all understand what we mean and why. We will set a date for the wedding that includes, as part of the pre-wedding plans, a forty day abstinence period, for all of us. We just thought it would be better for all of us, personally and spiritually. So, the making of the arrangements has begun.

We send out e-vites to Mike and Ethyl and decide that we should limit it to them, and then we reconsider. We will meet at La-Fonda, off Fred, and have arranged to have a room available to ourselves, which is much larger than we need, but for a price we can lock out everyone we do not want. Benson checks IDs, so to speak, as guests arrive. He knows Mike and Ethyl, and of course, since he drove Doc, Cinco, and me in the Bentley – it turns out the security company has four more similar to it remaining – he doesn't need to check IDs as much as keep the door. Special guests from Africa are Ardit and Meredith, with Y'hoshua in tow. Benson guards the main access, while Bubba covers the kitchen; his favorite room anyway.

The menu is whatever anyone wants from the restaurant menu, and they serve classic Tex-Mexican cuisine here, as good as anywhere in town. We all have some great food and friendly conversation, and after the dessert orders are placed, I raise my glass and attempting to ring it gently with a knife, I shatter it. I guess I am a bit nervous, but I have everyone's attention. Benson looks in, but, seeing everything safe and sound, returns to his post. One of the wait staff brings a broom and dustpan for my mess. I begin the announcement once he has left the room.

"Friends, we are gathered here on a very auspicious occasion," I begin. "As some of you already know, Cinco and I were married about a year and a half ago in Africa." Mike is almost apoplectic. "We have been staying at each other's apartments almost every night since then. We have tried to keep things in the office, and in the world, as 'business as usual' as much as we possibly can, and for the most part, I think we have succeeded."

"Our first goal," says Cinco "is to not let Gerhardt and the world in on it. It's none of their business."

"Artie and Meredith stood up for us when we got married," I continue, "and we wanted them here when it became public, private, er, um, personal, family knowledge, and I hope that everyone will join us . . ." and I look at my girls, "I would hope that Artie and Meredith are willing to stand up with us again, when we marry Ilyssa into the family, in a couple of months."

There is mixed applause with laughter and confused murmuring. Of course Cinco and Doc are on the train, and Artie and Meredith seem pretty easy in hitching their wagon, but Ethyl is a bit confused, and Mike has both hands flat on the table and his mouth open, slightly contorted . . . Elvis like. After a moment, he speaks. "Are you serious?" he says. "You tell us, for the first time, that you are married and then, in the same breath, that we are supposed to join in a bigamy?" He sits back and shakes his head for a moment, slowly. "I gotta think about that one for a while," he says. Then he gets up to walks out.

Ethyl says to Cinco, "I'm with ya, Babe . . . I think, but, I gotta go be with him. You understand." We do understand. He is her man and he needs her; even if she is a hundred percent supportive of our commitment, she still needs to be a hundred percent supporting of him right now. "Call me later," she says to Cinco as she heads for the door.

Benson comes in, "I just saw Mike leaving in a huff, Ethyl in tow. Is everything alright? Are you okay?" I can tell that he is concerned on a personal level, but I still can't tell him yet.

"Yeah, just a little good news that may have gone down the wrong way – like picante sauce on blue Jell-O, ya know?"

"I can dig it," is all he says as he returns to his doorway duty. I thank him as he heads out and ask him to order whatever he would like to take when we head back. He does. Bubba never visits a kitchen without enjoying a sample or two.

We eat and drink – within reason – and enjoy dessert immensely, and return to the Tower, all six in the Bentley, with a police cruiser following close behind as we go. When we get there, Doc goes to her place, and the rest of us go to my apartment, but this time, Artie, Meredith, and Y'hoshua go down one hall and Cinco and I go to my room. Tonight, for the first time in almost forever, someone knows that we are together in this place. It is almost like being freed from a terrible secret, though all we have done is to expand our circle of trust, so to speak. Still, it has a new sense of family. I just hope Mike can keep it all in perspective.

As I shower up after loving my wife a little, Cinco calls Ethyl, who confirms that, while Mike is upset, he is most upset about being left out of the loop for so long on something so big, and that this next decision has been made, completely without input from him, if only as a sounding board. Ethyl says she understands the reasons for the secrets, and that she thinks that by morning, or maybe lunch, Mike will come out of his funk. By dinner for sure, he will probably be fully accepting of our arrangement, but for now, he is gone to the range. My wife and I have enjoyed each other, known by others, for the first time since we were dropped off at the hotel for the honeymoon. I am so excited I can't sleep, so I think I will check in on Mike.

It is late at night, or early morning – about two – when I find him in the combat range of the basement, having already finished off a couple of boxes of ammo through his Glock – he'd come to favor the model 40. As I come through the maze and find him, he unloads four rounds into a bad guy – classic bandit mask, striped shirt – and the gun is done. He turns to me, holding the weapon where I can see the slide locked back, and says, "I thought we were buds." He releases the slide without replacing the mag in the handle. "It never occurred to me that you would, or even could, hide something that big from me for so long. How did that happen?"

"Wow!" I say, "Huge story. Somewhere along the way, I fell in love with two women, got saved, which changed all of that, got the Bible stuck in my noodle, and I married one of them. Now I'm gonna marry the other one," then, almost with glib reverie I say, "and it was all Cinco's idea, really."

"Okay," he says, "let's tear that all down to where I can understand it because I'm having a bit of trouble, as you can see." He starts off in the right place by asking, "What do you mean, you got saved." So I tell him about meeting a street preacher and receiving the prophecy and realizing my Salvation – that Jesus had paid my price, and I knew that I needed that price paid for my sins in order to live with God. "I'm not certain that I can buy into that . . . not all the way . . . not right now anyway."

"Well, that's okay." I assure him, "It's not a condition of our friendship, but it will be endlessly important to you one day."

"What do you mean you got the Bible stuck in your noodle?" So, I tell him about how we used our means of inserting knowledge, directly into the brain as if they are learned experiences, so that it can be retained better than going to classes and doing studies. I explain that this is how 'nurse' Ethyl had become 'doctor' Ethyl, and he had already been told about that. And as "sci-fi" as it may appear to others, he got it. But this is the first time he really understands that we had done it too. He had been with Ethyl when she got her Bible upgrade, but now he really understands that it can be done on anyone, probably with any kind of material, and he thinks he understands why I know everything I know and how. But that is a story I am not yet ready to tell. I trust him a lot, but based on the past few hours' events, I think the truth about my long-term past might literally blow his circuits. We talk a bit longer and shoot another hundred rounds or so, he with his Glock and me with my Sig. We enjoy a cup of coffee together at my apartment, decaf, and now being fully 3:45 in the morn, Ardit and Meredith are ready to start their day, still being on Africa time, whatever that is. Y'hoshua and Cinco are sleeping soundly on the couch. She had volunteered to read him to sleep when he awoke, probably just a little jet lagged. She looks so natural with a babe in her arms, even one that's about to be two.

"She found out the other day," I explain to Mike, "that she likely can't have children. You can see what that would mean to her. Sometimes I can barely imagine her being a mom, and other times I can't imagine her not being one."

"Is that part of the reason for another wife?" asks Mike.

"I don't know. It may be part of it, but she'd brought it up right after we knew that Ilyssa wasn't dead from the fall. We were alone with our thoughts, and that is what she brought up. She knew that Doc and I have loved each other for a long time, but neither of us would act on it, and long ago, I was dating them both, and Doc just became more and more busy. Cinco and I spent more and more time together, then in Africa I married Cinco, and that was the deal I chose. I'm not regretting it for a moment – never looked back." I look at her, there on the couch, "It may be that someone in the house having a baby will be all she needs in that arena. But, I believe that she encouraged this marriage because she loves me, and Doc loves me, and I love both of them, and together, we can't find a reason not to."

"What about your head full of Bible?"

"We have been over it from cover to cover, and in trying to understand what someone named Weatherhead called, in an ancient book, 'The Perfect and Acceptable Will of God,' we have come to understand that, in God's perfect will, there should be one man for each woman and vice versa; but several factors have spoiled that plan. For starters, the world is screwed up by sin, and there really are more women in the world than men. The ratio is actually about fifty two to forty eight percents. Also, most men, or at least a lot of them, are just no damn good, or I should say, they are nowhere near as good as someone deserves for a husband. Frankly, there are a lot more good women out there than there are good men to match with them. Being raised a Lutheran; I had to ask myself, 'What would Marty say?' So I checked. Though he said it in Latin, Luther said that 'marrying several wives does not contradict Scripture.' And, unless I want to be a First Century elder or bishop in the Mediterranean, there is no Biblical prohibition against having a second wife – or a fifth or tenth one for that matter, so long as she," I say, pointing at Cinco, "and later, they are in agreement."

"Well, you know a lot more about that Bible stuff than I ever will, but I'm not certain the rest of the world is going to agree with you," he says.

"I don't expect the world to agree, Mike; I just expect to find a way to get along in it."

"I gotta say," says Artie, joining in, "when I first heard the idea, I was taken aback for a moment, but it is somewhat common in Burundi, where we live and work. And Joshua does make a good case for their arrangement. Also, a study half a century ago showed that men with more than one wife seem to live 12% longer. Heck, America didn't even outlaw it, not in practice, 'til after the Civil War."

"And, it wasn't even my idea to start with." I point to the woman on the couch, "I have the best wife in the world, so far."

"Well," says Meredith, pouring coffee into several mugs, "Artie and I will stand up for you, even if no one else does, and we will wish you all the best, and we assume you will make that happen however you can."

"Thank you, Meredith, but right now, I want to take my woman to bed. So you enjoy that coffee and make yourselves at home; eat anything you want and feel free to wake us if you need something. Also, Mike has the keys to the kingdom." I go over to Cinco and jostle her arm a little, "Come on Babe, it's time for bed."

"But, I'm already be sleepin'," she murmurs.

"I'm haven't." I say, poking fun, and she climbs into my arms and I carry her to a long snuggle in bed – our bed.

We have a great visit over the weekend and even manage to escape our own lives for a little while. I have scruffed up this week and am sporting a half a beard. We let Mike buy a junky mini-van, and we all go to the zoo as tourists, with me and Cinco touring again as the Cohen's, with sunglasses, hats and sneakers, cargo shorts with knee-high purple socks; we fit right in. Benson joins in with one of his agents, Jacqi, going along as his "date" for cover. We have a wonderful day of sticky food, dusty air, and

Y'hoshua pointing at the animals and making noises like he wants them to sound. Cinco spends a lot of the time at the zoo volunteering to carry him on her shoulders. We buy burgers at the train station across the street and ride on the oldest remaining iron rail system in the nation. All the other big systems have long since replaced all their operations in favor of newer tech and newer rails made of polymers. The times, they are a changing.

Sunday night the African contingency has to return to their home, and we let them have a company jet for the journey. Well, actually, that's not so, they take my new personal jet; it has a better collection of kid videos onboard, because Cinco has been collecting them ever since we got married. They have a smooth trip, both personally and in terms of the plane passing through the sky. We lay our groundwork for the rest of the wedding plans.

It will be in two months, in Bujumbura, and we make arrangements for Brother Julian to perform the ceremony and arrange his family's lodging and from India. Ethyl requests that, in order to minimize the number of outside involvements – partly as her wedding present to us – she would like to have Cinco's pilot training and experiences mem-loaded into her, so she could serve as our pilot. We also prepare for the transport of Mike who, with Ethyl, it turns out, would be happy to stand up with us when the time comes. Most important is be the marriage partners, without whom the wedding can't really happen.

A Wedding and a Redemption Conflict

Hotel accommodations are made for everyone but Doc and me, who will be staying the first night at Artie's country house and leaving the next day; we are settled in everything. The gown was created, and in the final week, it is fitted to the bride. We have set aside our physical desires for the forty days prior to the wedding, and Doc and I never did anything more sexual than to kiss and cuddle, from the proposal until now.

We both want to start this off right; or I should say, "We all do." I think it may have been harder on Cinco, since Doc has been wrapped up in business and has not been getting any loving for a while anyway; she is somewhat more used to celibacy. But Cinco would continue to ride the celibacy train for another three weeks after the wedding as well. We figure that a Bridal Week is Biblically standard, but we want to dedicate three times that to the initiation of our union . . . three being the Biblical number of perfection and seven the number of completion . . . three times seven days is our goal.

The ceremony is a simple and magnificent thing. Artie is holding Y'hoshua, standing next to Mike, who stands next to me. To my right hand is Ilyssa, followed by Cinco, Ethyl – looking like a twin sister – and Meredith on the end. Brother Julian gives a brief sermon about how every one of us is a bride of Christ and how every one of us, regardless of number, is fully loved and fully intimate with our Lord, Master, and Husband. He says that this permanent, personal, loving relationship is a reflection of that relationship between Christ and the Church, but also, between Christ and the individual believer.

We step forward about three yards and kneel in front of Brother Julian by a baptismal font, and he stands before us, leaning in close, and quietly administers the vows, which take about a minute, and then he stands to bless us with water. He places a hand on each of us and prays for God's blessing on us in every way, especially for our marital success, lifelong happiness, a fruitful union, and a never ending stream of friends that love us.

After a brief dinner party, we each kiss Cinco goodbye and go by limo to Ardit and Meredith's home away from home, which is a small country house, about 1500 feet, with a large living room/kitchen/dining area all in one, which opens onto a master suite that is luxurious in its simplicity. The room has clean lines, contrasting dark wood and light, the bed has a down comforter that is pure, white cotton on the side we can see, and there is a striped gazelle skin in the middle of the floor.

I carry Doc over the threshold, and we kiss for a moment as she leads me into the bedroom. She lets go of my hand as we pass through the doorway and proceeds to stand on the gazelle skin, where she turns and says, "Don't you want to come unwrap your presents, my husband?"

I really do want my presents; there is no doubt about that. From an ordinary "guy" standpoint, I have been celibate for forty one days, and I really do want to get a little sumpin – sumpin, but more than anything, I want to drink her in like cold water after a long desert maneuver. She stands there in a gown designed by Cinco, plaited satin folds around her middle, micro sequins of pearlescent white across her bust, and several rows of French lace on the skirt, filled out by six layers of white lace crinolines.

As I approach, she lets me know that there are zippers on each side, starting right below the armpits, so I slide each zipper down to its bottom. Her bare skin beneath each zipper is smooth and dark, almost olive, and perfect, and I am soaking in the contrast between her flesh and the snowy white of the fabric. "Pay attention ADD Boy, your presents are waiting to be unwrapped too, you know?" There are also three buttons on each shoulder connected by three spaghetti strap loops and with each hand, I unbutton one at a time so that as each hand unbuttons the last button on each shoulder, the dress falls to the floor in a slow, flowing reveal of her presence.

She stands there, with strong, tanned legs in white stockings rising up from a pile of white fabric, from which she is stepping, and above the stockings about fifteen inches of smooth, bare, amazing thighs, topped with a shimmering white satin thong, and the rest is a perfectly coiffed, completely bare woman, with a white orchid corsage on her left wrist. It takes a moment for me to realize that she is walking toward me because she is so beautiful, and I want to just look at her. I put my finger up for her to wait, just a moment. I wish I had brought a camera – I envy Cinco and Ethyl their enhanced memories right now – but she waits, and I look 'til I can't look any longer. I step to her, reaching around to her backside, and she lifts her legs so that she presses up against me as I kiss her. With her legs and arms locked around me, I carry her to the top of that pure, white, cotton comforter and begin a love breakfast that will take all night to complete.

We have been left a large bowl of fruit on the dining table with a note on it that reads, "Don't worry about the mess, we expect it," and, in our breaks from lovemaking, we eat all but the papaya. Gone in the morning are a pair of bananas, four oranges, three apples, several plums, a couple of bunches of grapes, and we had both had to shower after the mango we shared, and I do mean shared. At noon, Ethyl and Mike are there to pick us up. We go by Ardit and Meredith's city home for lunch, a proper thank-you, and goodbyes. Then Mike drives us all to the airport, and off we go.

During the honeymoon time, Cinco takes charge of anything in the Enterprise that needs a handle on it. To satisfy the legal eagles, without letting them in on our lives too much, I leave a power of attorney in her name. She has absolute control over Danzig Enterprises in my absence, which probably pisses off Master Hugo Gerhardt more than a bit. We also leave the excuse that Doc and I need to scout out some remote factory locations for her soda. Since that is not Enterprise business, he is not happy with my continued involvement.

Doc does the same with her company, leaving Mike, the second biggest share-holder at five percent, in charge of logistics and Cinco in charge of contracts and fulfillment. Really, there is very little that needs their attention, though Cinco may want more business action, since there is no "personal" action in the home at the end of the day.

We have Ethyl as our personal pilot and security and tell only her where we are going. She stays in a different accommodation than we do and she only becomes visible when we call. She arranges all travel, rooms, and dining experiences as we want, unless we want room service. When we leave Bujumbura, we head to Rio where we have a suite booked for a week. We really want to see the remnants of the World's Fair and the giant

Jesus on the hill. Now, that is amazing. But the favelas around the city are totally depressing. Literally hundreds of square miles of poverty and ghetto, houses made of tar felt and tin, surrounding one of the most modern and beautiful cities in the world. It is such a stark contrast that we have difficulty enjoying it, so we do what any newlywed multi-billionaire couple would do, we go to Mexico. More specifically, we go to that part of Mexico in which Ilyssa was born.

We land in Tampico and spend a couple of nights taking in the town. Then she says we should check out the countryside. Ethyl gets us a new model Toyota Super Mega Cruiser, and we take off into the woodlands. We look like any other turistas in the area, checking out the local colour and culture, except that our driver looks like Laura Croft. As we tour around, we realize several things, part of which is that we really like the territory and the people, some of whom knew part of Ilyssa's family from way back when. We also realize that we can be useful here in many ways. We think of what we can do, and a list of dreams comes to mind, ranging from raising cattle to starting an amusement park, but all of the ideas we consider hinge on having land, and in that discussion, being a native is a God-send. Ilyssa is a native.

We buy, or at least begin the process of buying, what is almost a four mile square north west of Tampico by about four or five dozen miles with highway thirty-nine cutting through the middle and Laguna La Salada on the eastern edge. It had all been part of a government seized property from a decade ago or so. Apparently, some drug cartels had moved in and taken it from the locals, as an operations center, and when the cartel was "shut down" with the Texican assistance to the Federales, the land had no owners to whom it could revert. So, Doc buys it with the money that I had moved into her accounts as a wedding present . . . as part of her bride price. She owns the land, outright, or will when the papers clear. There is much to talk about with our other partner, but 'til we get home, it can wait. We are cruising around, looking about, on our own.

We decide to take the last days of our honeymoon and go camping on our own land, so we are going to need some gear. We will need to equip for a week or so, so we go back to Tampico and meet up with Ethyl, who has been met by Mike. He had taken a commercial flight down a couple days earlier – first class – when Ethyl called and said that we didn't need her, but that she needs him. Since the boss is nowhere to be found, Mike feels confident in shirking his duties. It is good to see them both, especially together. We have lunch and go shopping for camping gear, and Ethyl suggests that they tag along to see the place we have bought in such haste. "Why not," I think, so we go shopping to gear up to do camping for four.

Looking on the NuGle Maps for an outdoor goods store in Tampico is an adventure of its own. We discover that not all in Mexico is as the map has it defined. One place turns out to be a huge auto repair shop, another is a spa, still others are actually hotels, but because they are so "rustic," they listed their services under "camping," and the list goes on like that. We finally locate and identify a place called, Club de Regatas, Campamento Las Gaviotas – and I have no idea what that means so don't ask – but there we can actually buy camping equipment and supplies, on the Paso Dona Cecilia at the coast. It is down the road past an old white school bus that was left in the paso years ago to reduce bypassing traffic, and we shop our faces off. We buy tents and sleeping bags and more mosquito netting than I thought existed, but Ilyssa insists that it would be good

Keith T Jenkins

to drape our beds and our tents. We buy insect repellant in the economy size container, and at Ilyssa's insistence, we buy cots, to keep the bedding off the floors and semi-foam mattresses. We come out of the store with three carts of gear and see that our Mega Cruiser is being towed away. Mike goes running after it, but he isn't fast enough. He looks up where the car had been parked and sees a sign, almost entirely covered by the branches of some sort of mesquite tree – small leaves and big thorns – and it says something that he can't read, but when he peels the branch back, it has a picture of a tow truck and a phone number. He dials, and as they answer, what we can hear is Mike, about half shouting, "Ingles, Ingles, por favor." Someone does speak Ingles, and he does get directions, then he comes to give us the news. "It seems that they like the idea of not trimming the trees around the no parking signs. It helps them get more Yankee dollars. I have the location – it's just a few miles away – and we have to go with fifty thousand pesos to get it back."

"How much is that in Texican?" I ask.

"Between twelve and fifteen hundred dollars," says Doc.

"Fine," I say, handing Mike a wad of cash that looks to be about twice that, "This should be able to get you a cab and a drink and even a bribe or two, should it come to that."

"I'll stay with the lovebirds," Ethyl says to Mike, "if it's okay with you, Dear. We can get a snack at that Restaurant Bar El Pikio, and we can stay out of the sun."

"Sure thing, Shugga Pie," he says, in his best – really bad – fake Texican accent, being a bit tongue in cheek about her cheerfulness, and grabbing her ass as he kisses her. "I will be right back after I redeem that heisted buggy for my damsel in distress." He is tender as he strokes her face and kisses her cheek before he leaves, but he doesn't notice that she is stunned by what he has just said.

It is the word "redeem" that catches her attention, and it hits her like a hollow point round in the forehead as she watches him leave but can't say a word to him . . . she's been "redeemed." It had not come to her until that moment that her car is an example of what is meant to be redeemed – bought back from a dispossession of some sort – that she had been "possessed" by a world-driven life and choices, and that there is a cost. She is having an arduous, almost painfully focused, redemption conflict.

Though she is far from a selfish person, she is living for work and living for her own desires, and some of those agree with Mike's desires, no doubt, as well as mine and Doc's and all of us. But she is not God-driven. She had heard this message in the original Ethyl personality installation, but until now, it hadn't mattered to her. It is as though she suddenly realizes the precarious position she has been in all her life. There is a cliff right before her; if she does not make a certain step, she may go over. She starts crying and Ilyssa and I take immediate notice and come to her. Ilyssa puts her arms around her and straddles her as they sat down on a bench in front of the store and I go behind and put a hand on each of their shoulders.

"What is it, Mija?" Doc asks her, but she keeps crying, almost uncontrollably blubbering.

She sputters out a few words that don't connect together into anything that anyone would confuse with a sentence, and then she signs, "Just wait," and so we do. We just stay together, Doc holding Ethyl, and Ethyl holding her, and me looking on like a passerby that stopped to be in the picture. In a few minutes, Ethyl is able to say, "Redeemed!" She wipes her face, red with tears, "I've been redeemed."

"We know," says Ilyssa.

"But I didn't know. I didn't have any idea, 'til just now." She sniffles and cries and wipes her face some more and looking straight into her eyes, she asks Doc, "What do I do?"

"You pray, Mija," comes the reply, and she leads her in prayer, and Ethyl is saved. She is crying tears of happiness and jumping up and down, tears flowing, and she starts chattering about what she just realized regarding a dozen or so passages in the Bible download she had taken in San Antonio nearly half a year ago. It is a very real "Road to Emmaus" moment, to be sure. Suddenly, everything in that upgrade is coming online. The emergencies of Cinco and me in Yerushalayim, at the time when she got the upgrade, must have pushed the data to the back of her memories, waiting for something to trigger their rise to prominence. "Redeemed!"

When Mike returns with the car, we are practically dancing around our lunch like children in a playground. We are laughing and chattering away like a bunch of school kids talking about some movie we had just seen. It is good to share with Ethyl, and so cool to watch her assimilate the data, completely without the commentaries. She doesn't care what Karl Barth has said about anything that Luther had written, and she was un-altered by Matthew Henry; not that there is anything wrong with their input, but it had too strong an influence on Cinco and I when we upgraded, and the opinions of men are ever present. Ethyl doesn't have that problem, only the input of her life to get in the way. As Mike approaches, we all come to meet him and hug him with a big howdy.

We have ordered for all four of us, and the food has just arrived, nachos, chicken quesadillas, enchiladas pollo, rice, and beans for all, with a second round of Corona – since that is the one word that is painted on every wall of the place.

"I'm saved!" shouts Ethyl when the hug subsides. She is almost jittery with excitement as she says it, with a huge smile on her face and her hands so widely open, and again, reverberating so that they may have been mistaken for spirit fingers or jazz hands, as she hugs him again.

Mike doesn't have any idea what that really means, and in reality, it will take days for it to really begin taking over her life, but for now he simply says, "That's great!" and he hugs her back. After all, he does love her. Still, I am unconvinced of his happiness for her in this matter, and a little concerned, considering our conversation a few months ago. I want Mike to be saved, but I really don't see it in him. Maybe later?

We set up camp on an escarpment that overlooks the lake more than a mile away. We have two tents, each with an extra large cot and mattress, each with a mosquito net big enough to drape the entire tent and rest on the ground, staked on three sides. We set up a campfire and the Coleman stove. We have three lanterns and frozen fish for tomorrow in the ice chest, and fresh fish getting ready on the grill. We have four days in the outback, so to speak, and we do some hiking, individually, as a group, or as couples. We see all kinds of wildlife, from small pigs to large birds and a few snakes, many of which are harmless. Ethyl says she even saw a jaguarundi, or, as the locals call them, yaguarundi . . . a sort of medium sized cat, like a small jaguar. She is a little miffed when

Mike discounts her account, but she tells him that, "When we get back to civilization, I will print you a copy from my memory."

He says, "But how will I know it's from this trip?"

"Because," she replies slowly, "as I saw it, my hand was on a branch in front of me, and the bracelet you bought me the other day is on my wrist." He begins to feel corrected.

"Hmmm," I say, "a bracelet, huh?" I turn to Ilyssa and say, "That's almost like a ring, ya know?" Mike glares a dangerous glare at me. I am almost intimidated, but not really. "Glare all you like, Mike. You can even kick my ass if you want. I am on my honeymoon with the most wonderful doctor in the world, and no matter what you do, she can fix me. In fact," I glance at her for reassurance and get it with a smile and a nod, "she built me in the first place."

He laughs at first and then notices that I am not smiling as I say it, not even a little bit. "You're kidding, right?" He brings his beer far from his lips. "Right? What do you mean, she built you?"

We sit down as we eat, and Doc tells them both the whole story, including the DNA puzzle and what had happened in Africa and how my memories have come back and my true and complete history, as well as one can tell a story that large in a single sitting, without blowing everyone's mind, and possibly requiring medical or psychiatric care.

Mike is a little pissed with me for not sharing all of this with him from the jump, but, as we explain it to him, when we met, I didn't know about it all, and when I did know, it was too much for me to process, and it was too big to even fully believe. And by the time I had fully accepted the idea, I was months away from having answers, which God would give. And then, well, by then things were flying on God-control so fast and so strangely, that I couldn't imagine opening up for more scrutiny, and I had gotten used to compartmentalizing everything according to whom I could trust with what. It had just become the way I could effectively juggle everything in my life without dropping a ball. I let him know that only the four of us, and Cinco know everything. Everyone except Cinco, Ilyssa, and God have compartments of some sort. When Ethyl hears it all, she just says, "There's some seriously weird shit in your life. Huh?"

We had been in the woods for almost a week when, in the middle of the night, Ethyl is crying and Mike is heading out to the car, putting on his shirt. I am wondering what he has done that is so totally stupid that it leaves her crying and him walking, and what he has done is actually the same thing he has done most nights the past many months. He is expecting her to open up to him, sexually, and tonight she doesn't. In fact, she says she can't because it is a sin.

Mike doesn't understand how sex could have not been a sin last week, even yesterday, and suddenly it is a sin today, even though the particulars of the situation, for Mike, haven't changed. But Ethyl has now received and accepted the ability to see and understand sin. She is now sin aware, like a smoker who has quit can smell a cigarette across a street but never noticed the smell when he was smoking. This doesn't mean that she will not be sinning any more, or that she will ever be able to fully shut down sin in her life; none ever do. But it means that she wants to be a better person tomorrow than yesterday, and better in behavior, by God's definition, not the definitions of men, or of a single man.

There is nothing for Ilyssa or me to do or say at this point as Mike locks himself into the Cruiser and Ethyl zips closed the tent. I want to talk to one of them or both of them, for sure, but Doc says, "It's your honeymoon, Darling, and they will work this out on their own. Come to bed." And I can see through the mosquito netting, as the lantern is being dimmed, her gown sliding gracefully, gently, flowingly from her ample behind and floats to the floor as darkness falls. I don't want to talk to anybody anymore but her. Yes, men are just that simple.

When we get back to Tampico, I suggest that Mike take the plane back to San Antone, and the rest of us will follow another way. I have secretly made arrangements to surprise Ethyl on this trip. After seeing Mike off at the city airstrip, we drive to Altamira, where we come across a private airstrip, and after some brief flashing of the identifications, we are waved onto the tarmac, and with the folding in of the mirrors and laying down of the roof, we back up into the tail of a plane. We park the Cruiser, and its wheels are strapped down as if for shipping, because shipping is what we are doing. I let the ladies know that the "rented" Cruiser has been purchased, so they don't worry about stealing a car. We climb out over the hood of the cruiser and step off the cargo ramp to the tarmac behind the plane. It has a monstrous large tail fin and wings that seem almost as long from front to back as they are from side to side – though they aren't really. The cargo ramp/door whirs as it rises up and locks into place, and a Mr. Santiago comes from the office to meet me. I have made a purchase from the Costa Rican Air Surveillance Service.

"Your check has cleared Señor Danz, and our complete inspection of the craft has determined it to be worthy of our ninety day warrantee," and he holds out some keys. "Who gets these?" I point to Ethyl, and he tosses them to her.

"Can you fly this thing, Ethyl?" I ask, pretty much expecting the answer to be yes, but she stands there with her mouth open for a moment.

"Is this yours?" she asks, happily.

"No," I say with a pause, feigning sadness, and her countenance falls a bit. "It's yours." And she almost faints. Doc holds onto one arm as I get the other as she regains control.

"Joshua and I thought we should get you some sort of extravagant gift for all you've done for us on this trip and for all the years before as well. You really are a good friend, Joshua's oldest friend, and we really do appreciate you every day."

"She is fueled up, checked out, and she is ready to go, Señor," says Santiago, "but I imagine su pilota would like to go through the check list again; si?"

"Si," says Ethyl as she practically sprints to the plane. She jets around front to the far side, and before I know it, she is in the cockpit with her headgear in place, clipboard in hand, going over the list. It is a De Havilland Caribou – model DHC-4 – cargo plane. It can carry over 8000 pounds of freight and can go a little over 200 miles an hour for about seven hours at a time. It is slow and ugly for our times, but it is amazing all the same. It is a little over five hundred miles from Altamira to San Antonio, so that would be almost three hours at cruising speed, and Ethyl has no reason to hurry. In fact, she is practically whistling almost all the way, except for the moments she stops to talk about the plane and what it can do. It turns out that her father – the original Ethyl's father – had flown one of these in Viet Nam and bragged about it just about every time they got together, and she dreamed of getting her pilot's license, even as a little girl. He was terribly proud of his little pilot and usually remembered to tell her. He had passed away many years before this Ethyl was born, or I should say made. Her registered "birthday" is the same as Cinco's – September 5th, 2039, but they'd both only been in operation for a couple years or so when I got there. She is still upset about Mike and the whole sex thing, but for now, she is enjoying her day and her plane.

"You won't forget," I say, "that you can't land this thing on the building, right?"

"Maybe not, sir! But, if pressed, we can set it down in the back yard, behind the building." She lets me know, "There's about a thousand yard long strip of grass with small trees down the edge of Hackberry Street. I can set 'er down there if you like."

"No," I say, with some anxiety, "I think the airport would be a fine place to put 'er."

I tell Doc that we have a few hours of "happy pilot time" and suggest that we could make out in the Cruiser if she likes. The back seat is about as long as the one in the Hummer, and that makes for a lot of fun on the trip home.

We get home to the tower, parking the Mega Cruiser in one of my spaces, and Benson comes to meet us as we arrive. He says he will have some of the building porters unload all our gear and dump it in the elevator for us in a while. We go up to my apartment where Cinco is waiting with a huge kiss for me and hugs for the girls. In a couple of minutes, I excuse myself to the shower, saying, "You know, Ethyl, in the morning you should probably move your Cruiser out of my space." The ladies break out the decaf coffee and a small bucket of cookies-n-crème ice cream to commiserate Ethyl's lovelorn state. While I am still enjoying the soak that I had not had in several days, they finish their coffee, and Doc takes Ethyl to her apartment for a girl's night sleep-over, and to finish the ice cream. Cinco appears in the shower, as naked as the Lord made her, and she begins scrubbing my back with one of those loofah things. I lean against the wall on my outstretched hands, and she scrubs my neck and back and my behind, then my chest and legs, and in a very few moments, any thoughts of cleanliness have completely left my consideration. The same can be said for Cinco.

Over the next several months, Ethyl and Mike will break up and make up, and he will get frustrated, then she will give in. He will try to be the man she wants him to be, then he will want a little sumpin – sumpin, and then she will "find her virginity" again. It is especially hard for her because she loves him as much as anyone loves anybody, but she also wants to be the best woman she can for the God of her life. Further, it isn't as easy as some people might suggest, if only because Ethyl really does enjoy every single thing that Mike can do to her body to bring her pleasure, but he isn't actually hers yet, and that is a problem she is hoping to remedy someday. About five weeks after our return, Mike decides that he has to move out of the tower, because having both of their residences in such close proximity makes it too easy for Ethyl to fall into the trap that she is beginning to accuse Mike of setting for her.

He gets an apartment near the airport. It is nowhere near as nice as the tower, but what is? There is a pretty decent three bedroom near San Pedro and Sahara that is big enough, and it allows him a large master suite and an office, of sorts, with a spare bedroom if needed. It is rarely, if ever, needed as far as I know. Mike begins spending less time at the tower, and I only see him when I need him, or one of his aircraft, or a confidence kept and a gun carried on a trip. Then one day he tells me that he needs some time away, and I tell him that is fine, but to let me know if he needs anything. We have just come back from a trip to Dallas when we have this talk, and he goes from shaking my hand to starting up the Angel, and before Benson and I have my stuff loaded in the car, he is gone. I don't see him for a while after that. Cinco will check the location of his phone, the car, or the chopper's transponders, but most days he doesn't even call.

Keith T Jenkins

Part Six — Open Warfare

Keith T Jenkins

.

American Turmoil

In an effort to further their new agenda, while sounding more and more patriotic, the American political leadership takes a step backward, to the Great Depression, into an even more depressing reality, by re-inventing the National Recovery Administration (NRA) of FDR. The stated purposes of the NRA were to eliminate what they called "cut-throat competition" by bringing industry, labor, and government together to create codes of "fair practices" and set prices. And then, history repeats itself.

According to *Wikipedia*, the National Recovery Administration under FDR was explained, in practice, as having, "negotiated specific sets of codes with leaders of the nation's major industries; the most important provisions were anti-deflationary floors below which no company would lower prices or wages, and agreements on maintaining employment and production. In a remarkably short time, the NRA won agreements from almost every major industry in the nation. Six months after the NRA went into effect, industrial production had dropped by 25%."

In the new reality, it has reduced production by 31%, and production was abysmal already. But the tabloids that still pass for news agencies in the US are saying that production is up – up 3% in some, 10% in others – but none tell the truth about the losses. They tell about how production has gone up after three years by almost 17% – and every rag, blog, and news agency covers the hell out of that because that is the official government report, but none mention that it still leaves a net loss of over 14%. Worse yet, a huge portion of reduction in the "increased percentages" are adjusted due to the reduced population of the nation. When considered together with population loss and the cost in dollars to the government, well, it is almost a bigger a waste of time and money than Project Head Start had been.

Back in the 1930's, the head of the National Recovery Administration, Donald Richberg, had said, "There is no choice presented to American business between intelligently planned and uncontrolled industrial operations and a return to the gold-plated anarchy that masqueraded as 'rugged individualism' . . . Unless industry is sufficiently Socialized by its private owners and managers so that great essential industries are operated under public obligation appropriate to the public interest in them, the advance of political control over private industry is inevitable."

He was advocating some reigning in of business autonomy by progressive government controls. So they began to offer choices closer to "rugged individualism" and then farther and farther and still farther away from it until, by this time, they are attempting to outright nationalize all things that aren't theirs already. So the very laws and procedures that were originally, allegedly, intended to protect the people from monopolies are now being used to create monopolies that belong to the government, instead of individuals or corporations. The American Communications and Telephone Services (ACTS) is a prime example, along with AmeriNet web services that provide almost all American web hosting, e-mail and internet connectivity to everyone in America, even dial up, which still exists in more rural areas where the cable companies have been nationalized out of operation, and the government can't make them all work. There are American Water Works, National Gas, Electric and Power, USWaste, and FedMart, and all of them are managed by international concerns because the government can't manage to keep products on shelves or water and power in lines for their customers, but the Japanese can, and they manage a ton of it . . . from Japan. The Germans have their hands in lots of communications systems, and the Texicans handle almost all of the techno-security for anyone that asks. The Roosevelt dream of Progressivism – belonging to Teddy and Franklin – is just about complete, and it only took 123 years to get here. Mussolini would be overjoyed to see government running industry in such a way. It is the very soul of the Fascist Party of Italy a century and more ago. Interestingly, when Fascism fell out of fashion in Italy, due to its blatant failure, it was made illegal there, and then, for some unknown reason, Americans began attempting to reinvent it almost right away. Now, however, it is late 2061, and the only real commerce in America is done with or through the government somehow.

We have been doing business with them for quite some time; actually, we have never stopped doing business with them, but that business is getting to be more than a little bit strained, and when listening to the constant campaigning of the politicians and their anti-capitalism and anti-Texican grumblings, one can feel a storm brewing on the horizon. I do, and anyone operating on the If/Then has seen it as well. Meredith and Artie have called me numerous times with their concerns and are working to get the US off their customer lists.

Our first business with America was selling them vehicles to replace all those Suburbans, Explorers, and Expeditions that were in use by many government agencies. We had managed to create one that had an additional cubic foot of cargo space over the largest of them, and it got over forty miles to the gallon, with a heavier and sturdier frame and body; even after we added in the body armor and bulletproof windows on the executive models, they got over thirty mpg. Because of the new drive systems, they could go from zero to sixty in about four seconds . . . with five grown men inside and a full complement of extra weapons in the rear. We currently build the descendants of these near San Antonio and outside Yuma, in Mexico, Israel, and Kenya, seventy miles north of Mumbai, and 150 miles east of Perth, Australia. We also build a great replacement for the old Hummer, which is being made in Mexico and Kenya; Toyota is our only competition in that arena. We had determined a long time ago, to never put a production plant inside the United States, or any other Democrat Socialist or Communist nation, after the secession. It just doesn't seem to be in our best interests.

I mention all of this to tell you about the cathartic days that follow, and those which force an undeniable and refutable change in my world. It is a Tuesday afternoon, and four men in suits walk into Cinco's office, outside of mine, and one of them stands in front and demands, "We are here for Mr. Danz," and he extends a small pile of paper, stapled together, with a blue satin strip across the top, folded in thirds. It is an arrest warrant from Washington, D.C. She examines it closely, turning the pages quickly, only for a moment.

"You can't have him," is all she says – the intercom is on and the one way glass effect is engaged, so I can hear and see them, but they cannot see me. She scrolls to me, "Warrant from the US." She refolds their warrant and shoves it into a slot on her desk that whirrs very quickly for a little over two seconds, followed by a brief vacuum whoosh, like that tube thing in the drive through of a bank, and they realize that she has just shredded it. It has in fact been shredded into bits as small as a housefly and transported by vacuum to the composting system, like all dry waste paper and food garbage in the building.

The obvious alpha male in the group looks at the name plaque on her desk and then he says, "Ms. Anders, we have no intention of leaving without Joshua Danz."

"Are you armed?" I ask, as I enter the room. I scroll Cinco, "They will have their backs to you in a second." She affirms with a raised eyebrow and a "thanks" scrolls back.

"Yes!" comes his sullen reply.

"So am I," I tell him, showing them the pen knife with which I am cleaning my nails. Strolling slowly, not looking at any of them as they all turn to face me, I only glance up briefly as I continue, "And so is almost everyone that works for me in this building. A dozen security men will be in this office in a very few minutes and," I've walked around the opposite side of them from Cinco and stare the leader in the eyes, "and, Ms. Anders is ready to kill two of you right now." They all hear the subtle clicks of the safeties on her Baby Eagles being disengaged. They all look around and almost reach their side-arms under their jackets.

"I don't believe you should be thinkin' about that," she says. When each of them can now fully see her and they all realize that she has two guns. Their hands stop reaching. "Hands down now. Put 'em in your pants pockets, boys." They follow her instructions through her Edward G. Robinson impression. She's getting addicted to those old movies right along with me.

"Why can't they have me, Ms. Anders?" I ask.

"Well, Mr. Danz, for starters, the FreeNation doesn't have an extradition arrangement with the US, so their warrant is no good here. Besides which, I have absolutely no intentions of letting them take you out of this building, Boss. Is that sufficient, Boss? Or did you have something else in mind?"

"That'll do, thanks. Who sent them, Ms. Anders?" I ask.

"They were sent from the Justice Department, but the warrant was initiated by the State Department along with Homeland Security. It said that you were wanted for 'terroristic market practices and price manipulation' as regards vehicles sold and delivered in the US and for 'fraud' in the matter of sweeteners sold to the government though some African concerns." The leader, followed by the rest of the men, slowly turns to look at Cinco because she is able to recite all that information from the warrant after only glancing at it for about five seconds. "I would love to tell you more about it, Boss, but it is really quite boring, and I quit reading it almost as soon as I realized that it was useless."

The security contingent arrives, led by Stephen and Bubba – six guns in all, plus Cinco. "Now, agents, are you planning a stand-off or a shoot-out?"

They all stand there with their hands in their pockets and shake their heads as the leader steps forward and says, "We have orders to arrest you and return you to DC." His name is Robert Cragar, and I believe he was probably a pretty nice guy, and he is determined in his quest.

"Tell you what we can do." I say to him, "You call your boss, whoever signed that warrant, and tell him that we can meet at the Texican Embassy in DC in ten days if he wants to speak to me. Ask him if that will satisfy your mission." I hand him my personal phone.

He makes the call and asks the questions, and a look of relief comes to his face. "Okay, guys, we are on our way home." He shakes my hand on the way to the door. There is some grumbling from another of the guys as they head for the elevator. He says that he had told them that it would end like this. Another says that he had expected that they would all be dead. I let them know that I almost never kill guests in my house, and that if Robert wants a less dangerous job he should leave his number with Bubba. Robert slips Bubba a business card unseen as Stephen passes his card unnoticed to another of the men. Soon on the agenda, there is an appointment coming up, and arrangements to be made.

The Texican Embassy is a very important and prestigious location that has some history. Not only is it one of the largest embassies in the world, but also among the most accommodating. The FreeNation has purchased the individual parts to, and reassembled ownership of, the old Watergate complex. Even though it is now about a hundred years old, and refurbished several times, the last time was by Danzig Construction and DTSC – Danzig Technologies and Security Concepts – it will serve us well. It is a beauty of the age, and the age before.

We schedule an interrogation room in the security area of the Hotel-Office building that had housed a scandal some years before. This is a specially fitted room that is encased entirely in mirrors, backed up by cameras, ceilings laced with microphones. I sit, waiting with Cinco and Gerhardt, and an American suit arrives with two young lawyer-looking men who are a little lighter than when they arrived, having had to leave their weapons at the Welcome Center. They are FBI. The suit introduces himself as Davis Gherardi, Senior Assistant Secretary of Homeland Security. He has in his hand another warrant, just like the one that had been presented in San Antonio a few days before. Cinco takes it and looks at it, "It's the same as the other," she says as she passes it to Gerhardt, who examines it more closely, folds it back up, and hands it back to Gherardi.

Out of habit, Gherardi takes it back as Gerhardt says, "No, thank you."

"What do you mean, 'no, thank you'? I am not offering you anything. I am here to arrest you, Mr. Danz. That's the only thing on the table."

"I looked at your warrant and you have no viable charges, Mr. Gherardi, and you are on Texican sovereign soil," is Gerhardt's reply. "Do you plan to violate that?"

"Mr. Danz, by fixing the prices on the vehicles that you build for the US, and managing the line of credit, having fixed the rate of interest, having created a line of automobiles that no one can reproduce, you have created a monopoly in violation of our anti-trust laws. And because of the anti-trust nature of the matter, it is reasonable to assume that you are charging an excessive amount for the vehicles and the interest. After all, $185,000 per unit is a huge amount of money for a government vehicle. Three percent is steep interest. Then there is the sugar matter."

"What did you pay for your car, Mr. Gherardi?" Gerhardt asks.

"I don't think that has any bearing on the matter at hand," is his retort.

"Just humor me, Mr. Gherardi; how much?"

"My Town Car cost me about $125,000, fully loaded. What of it?"

"Depends on what you call fully loaded," I say. "This particular vehicle is bullet-proof and bomb resistant, the tires will never go flat, even if running over a hand-grenade, the thing carries up to eleven people and has a gun turret on top, can drive through five feet of water without stopping, comes with satellite telephone communications built in, with five years of sat-phone service provided, goes from zero to sixty miles per hour in five and a half seconds, but at less than twice the cost of your personal car, and you think this is too much money?" This is what I put into the mix. "What do you think it would cost to make your Town Car do the same?"

"What I think doesn't matter; the Department of Homeland Security, the Office of National Intellectual Properties, and the Department of Transportation say that you are a profiteer, that it is too much money, and that the monopoly you have created is allowing it to be charged beyond all reason."

"Reason is the only thing that makes it possible to make this amazing vehicle in the first place." I tell him, "It is reason that came up with the ideas for all the features in the car, and very fair and friendly reasoning that fixed the price where it is."

"So, you agree, the price is 'fixed' by you," he pokes his finger across the table at me in a determinate and accusatory way.

"I absolutely agree that it is 'fixed,' and in fact, I admit that I personally 'fixed' it." I use air-quotes to make my point. "I 'fixed' it so that you could afford it. I 'fixed' it so that it was only a hundred eighty five grand, because when we sell the same model to millionaires and billionaires, without the gun turret by the way, they pay $300,000, get custom paint, and say 'thank you for charging me a butt load of money,' and we pocket the difference. Would you like to buy one? The newest model gets about fifty-two miles to the gallon, which is nearly three times better than your POS Town Car." I can't help jibe him a little with that, "You should make up the price difference with just a few years of fuel savings."

"All that really doesn't matter." he continues, "When the government decides to get a better price from you, they are going to get it, regardless of what you want in the deal. They have their ways," he says, with quiet confidence.

"No, they don't." I tell him quietly, and confidently, as I scoot forward and then lean back in my chair. "There is nothing that has ever been signed by any of our people that says that we have to do business with you at all."

"But we are your biggest buyer. Do you want to lose that amount of business?" He is certain he has us over the barrel, so I look concerned briefly and whisper to Gerhardt and then Cinco and I listen to their whispered replies in my ear.

"Nope," I tell him, "I don't want to lose that business because we make nearly $100 per combat unit and between two and three hundred per other vehicle and keep several thousand people employed by those plants continuing to produce them." Mr. Gherardi looks pretty smug. "But," I continue, "I can sell every car we make for you at retail, for a price of 30 to 50% greater than you pay, and even if we produce less of them, everyone stays working, and we make even more money." And he realizes that the barrel is under his back when I say, "So, I don't care if the US never buys another piece of our equipment, and Ms. Anders here is ready to shut down all sales and order fulfillment to the US right now, before we leave this room." I pause to let that sink in.

He looks at my face then into the eyes of the others, he almost whispers to his suits before realizing that they were not really lawyers, just lawyer looking muscle. "I will have to get back to you on that."

"No, Mr. Gherardi, you won't. We don't want to take one more minute to treat the US badly, which is the claim that you have brought. We don't want to be the cause of any further national hardship as a result of anything considered by you and yours as a mistreatment of any kind. So, since you are here as their spokesman, their hired mouthpiece, you let me know." I glare into his eyes without flinching. It takes a few seconds before he has an answer, and that isn't really an answer because he asks if he can make a call. To this I say, "Do you see a phone?" He looks at his cell phone which has no bars, and the screen that says there is no service. "We are waiting, Mr. Gherardi."

"I can't make that decision," he says, almost exhaustedly. "I don't have that kind of authority."

"I do," I say, and his countenance falls like a stone to the floor as I say it to him. "I have that authority, and I am passing it to Ms. Anders." I hand her my Monte Blanc pen. "Ms. Anders is cancelling all purchase and delivery requests for the United States of America, and all of its subsidiaries, for all vehicles of any kind, from mail buggies to OTR trucks, and rail engines. We sell these products to thousands of companies and nations around the world, and they will all be happy to know that their orders will be expedited because you just stepped out of the line."

"No!" he shouts. "You can't do that. That's not what I said."

"You are correct," I tell him, "and what you said is not really what you mean either, because what you mean is that the US is demanding a lower price on the goods, right?"

"Yes, but . . ." he is stymied.

"Then, if that succeeded, your plan was to demand the price reduction on all the automotive products, right?"

"That's only fair! We are the largest buyer, and we need them the most." He says what makes the most sense to him, in his need-driven society, but then he realizes shortly thereafter, that he has said the exact wrong thing.

"Imagine a thief complaining to his victim about what is 'fair' or what he needs. When a man breaks into a house to steal some silver, money, or cars, he always tells someone along the way that he needed them. Then he goes to jail. WHY!?! Because, regardless of the circumstances and regardless of who does it to whom – whether he is robbing a commoner or a king – to take something from someone without just cause or due process is a sin, and in all circumstances, it either is or should be a crime. In this case you, and the American government, got caught before you got out the building with the goods."

"That's not it at all," he pleads.

"Yes, it is, Mr. Gherardi, that is exactly it," I insist. "You were trying to extort a $300,000 vehicle from me for less than half its value."

"That's not extortion," he demands.

"Really," I ask, "what would you call it?"

"We call it negotiation," he replies smugly, and he slides the warrant toward me again.

"Do you always negotiate using threats of criminal charges?" I ask, taking the warrant up in my hand, laying it down again as he shakes his head, with a smug look on his face. "Then let's agree, just for the time being, on the term 'negotiation,' and then let's agree that it is a failed negotiation . . . that all terms and conditions are unacceptable to the seller . . . and the deal is off." I push the warrant back at him saying, "Do you want to talk about sweetener now?"

"But we are not done with the vehicles," he sputters.

"Yes," I insist, "we are. I'm done with the vehicles! Are you done with vehicles, Mr. Gerhardt? Ms. Anders?" They both nod.

"This is not what's supposed to happen in this deal."

"There is no deal."

"But we have contracts in hand," he says, again in a demanding tone and this time banging a fist on the table.

"Then you want those contracts fulfilled?" Cinco asks.

"Damn straight!" he says, confidently, a bit like a petulant child.

"Ms. Anders," I ask, "how many vehicles do we have contracted to deliver to the US and all its subsidiaries?"

"By end of business today, including all of Government Sponsored Entities and those victims of FRIA, again, from mail trucks to tanks, their requests for vehicles should be down to about 375,000 vehicles, large and small."

"Then," I say to her, "if that is the case, and if all parties at this table can come to an agreement," I glare at him again, "then we will fulfill those contracts, with a 5% aggravation fee on each sale, paid in full, FOB, with the additional fees going to fund the ministries of Ms. Anders' choice, and when we are done with those contracts, when they are completely fulfilled," I look at him again, "Mr. Gherardi, you can get your Danzig products from retail vendors." I scroll Cinco, "Take over."

"Well, everyone at the table is not in agreement with that," he says.

"Then we shall simply cancel all contracts and deliveries and call it a day, as you prefer," Cinco replies. "I am waiting to notify our people of your decision on this matter, as we speak."

"You are acting as if you don't care, either way," he says, partly as a whine, partly in self-righteous indignation.

"You misunderstand, Mr. Gherardi," Cinco replies, "I care very deeply. I am dripping with care for the customers that are standing in line, waiting for products that you are trying to extort for less than they are willing to pay, in a fair market. I am fraught with concern for the men and women that work to produce products that you desperately want, but have so devalued that, you have devalued their work as you have discounted the price. I am deeply and profoundly distraught that you value each and every one of those people to be less important, and less useful or worthy, than you and your suit wearing bigots, and I would rather cancel all further dealings with you and yours, right this minute, and never have you darken our door again, and I am confident that Mr. Danz is in agreement." I smile and nod. She is on a roll and I wave my hand that she should continue. "Given a choice, I would give you a big sloppy kiss goodbye and let you explain to your bosses what you have achieved today. But we have an obligation to fulfill the orders that your people have placed with us in good faith, but then again . . . in all reality . . . 'good faith' is out the window because you, and the others, have attempted to extort us out of what comes to hundreds of millions of Texican dollars, and that is worth something." She takes a breath and lifts her finger at him, "No, Mr. Gherardi, thieves and blaggards like your bosses, and maybe even you, would improve the condition of all mankind by leaving them. But your time is running out, right now, right here," she extends her index finger and slowly points it down to the table 'til it touches her brightly painted red finger nail to the surface, "before we move on to that next subject – and you are not going to enjoy that discussion either – but right now . . . do we have a deal, with a five percent aggravation charge, paid in full, FOB, or are we done completely?" She stares at his vapid face, tapping her finger on the table, one single index finger, and then stops.

As she withdraws her hand from the table, he realizes that his time is completely gone, "Send the cars. We'll pay." He is totally bamboozled and has no option except to agree. "But you know that you are going to pay for this someday."

"Is that a threat, Mr. Gherardi?" Cinco asks. He doesn't say a word. "I'm going to suggest that you don't even begin to make a threat. Do not test my resolve in this." He just fumes a little. She asks him, "What is the complaint about the sweeteners?"

"It's not a sweetener," he responds.

"Don't be silly! Does it make things sweet?" I ask him.

"That's not the point," he says.

"No, that is exactly the point. If it makes things sweet, it is a sweetener," I confirm.

"It is not a sweetener because it is actually sugar," is his complaint.

"It does contain sugar, but how is that a problem?"

"Because," he says, "sugar is illegal in the United States."

"Then, why did you buy it if it is illegal?" I have to ask. "There's no reasoning with these people," I say to Gerhardt.

"We didn't contract for 'sugar' we contracted for 'sweetener,' and this is not that by any measure," he says, in all confidence.

"Did you happen to bring a copy of the sales contract?" He produces it, and I take it.

I look quickly through the entire document, and I inform him, "I don't see my name, or my company, or any of my holdings on this contract, so . . . I have to ask: Why am I hearing about this from you?" I hand it to Gerhardt.

"Look," he starts aggressively, "we all know that you own the sugar operations in Africa that provide the sugars in this product."

"I don't think that you can start off with 'we all know' anything of the sort, Mr. Gherardi," I say inserting air quotes as needed. "You have no paper trail, no smoking gun, and no signature of mine on your document. You are in business with a company that I do not own and complaining to me about it. Would it be okay for me to complain to you about the president's sister-in-law? No! I don't own these fine, exquisite enterprises, and champions of Liberty, but I am a friend of the owners, and a mentor of theirs in business. If you pursue them in this matter, you will find that they will have the resources available in this room on their side of the table." I sit back in my chair. "I own, or my holdings own, about 30,000 acres of sugar cane growing land in central Africa, and the crops are rotated with some other things, so at any given time, we have about 10,000 acres of sugar cane growing. Is that sufficient to do all you say? I don't think so. And, with whom did you make this contract? It wasn't made with me and my board. And, when you made this contract, did anyone read it?"

"What do you mean? Of course someone read it," he says.

Gerhardt asks, "Was it you that read it?" Gherardi has that deer in the headlights look now. "Have you read it since?" He looks even dumber for a moment. "Have you looked at the agreed upon contents of the products to be delivered?" Slowly and patiently, Gerhardt asks, "Did you even see page seven?"

He snatches the document from Gerhardt and starts fumbling through the pages 'til he gets to seven and looks at the agreed contents of, "botanically extracted natural sweeteners, enhanced with nutritional supplements and colour additives," as the basis for all future description of the product, "hereby to be known as sweetener," followed by myriad vague means by which it would be processed, packaged, and delivered. "Damn!" he shouts. "Shit!" he stomps a foot. "Damn! Crap! Hell!" He slams the contract down on the table and slaps it at Gerhardt.

"You see, Mr. Gherardi, there is no case. The product is exactly what the government ordered, regardless of what they told you they ordered, regardless of what they thought they ordered. And, as you can further see, mine is only a portion of the sugar providers to your product. But make no mistake, it is your product, according to a simple ten page contract. If you don't read it before you sign it – metaphorically speaking – then who is to blame if you don't know what's in it? Who is to blame if you don't get everything exactly as you wish, or in this case, if it comes exactly as you ordered? Didn't 2010 teach you anything?"

"You know," he is absolutely wroth, fit to be tied, as he spews, "law be damned. There will be a come-up-ance for all of this. You are not going to get away with treating us this way."

"What do you think you are going to do?" I ask, becoming quieter, more pleasant, and not giving into anger and alarm at his threatening tone, which only makes him angrier.

He leans in close and says, "You think you're safe, sitting in your tower?" His fists are virtually grinding into the table as he speaks. "You have all the wealth you may ever need, but that isn't enough, is it? You all have to have a little more. You always have to have more, don't you? Just because someone needs what you make, or wants what you provide, you think you have a right to make a profit on it, regardless of the needs of others. Don't you?" He is beginning to spit and sputter as he shouts. "But maybe that tower of yours won't be as safe as you think it is. Maybe someone can reach out and touch you, just like anyone else that tries to profit when doing business with America, bleeding us dry, putting your needs above the needs of the common good."

"No, you are absolutely right, Mr. Gherardi, I am as human and vulnerable as anyone else, but you are dead wrong when you say that in doing business with anyone – even America – I should not make a profit. Making a profit the most important reason to be in business! If you do business and don't intend to make a profit, that is called ministry. Now, I don't hold it against you that you lack the fundamental understanding that goods and services are traded as commodities and that money is simply how we manage the transactions. I realize that you don't have the background or capacity to realize that we provide something that you want and that you don't get it for free because you cannot see what went into the creation of a product or service that we provide. You have no way of realizing that when you drive a car, built by my company in San Antonio, that there have been a thousand people working on the building of that car, that thousands of man hours went into designing and developing that machine, that thousands of dollars of materials have been extracted, molded, bolted, sewn, and soldered to make that machine into something in which you would like to be seen. No, you stick in the key, and it goes, and you cannot see beyond that. And if you don't have the understanding to create something or provide a service that you can sell or market something made by others, then the only place for a man like you is either in government or academia, where reality is so far away that you might never have to experience it. And, by the way, I was doing business with America, and continued doing business with America, based on a memory of an America that used to be, where each and every man had an opportunity to make his way, by his own initiative and create a profit to provide for his family, not the America that lives to be a safety net for the greatest stage for the promotion of mediocrity in the history of man. But now I realize that the America that I used to know is dead and gone. In your world, they have lost track of the means of production. You have lost track of the fact that money is just a tool of exchange, the medium of transferring value from one item or service to another. You misunderstand that money is not an end, or even a means, but the intermediary product that is not even actually a product, but a record of values for which all things are traded, and the fact that we all trade in money to avoid, finally, trading in the lives of men. Yet that is the trade that you have approved, adopted, been bamboozled by. Yes, you remain a slave to a system that doesn't value you enough to pay me everything that every product is worth, and as a result, they have to own you outright. They have to own you, and you have to be owned by them, if only to find value in yourself. They own people like you, because they cannot own me and mine.

"No, the America that I fell in love with, so many years ago is dead and gone. It's been murdered by the likes of you and yours. Thanks for that, you festering fever tick among a nation of parasites."

"Know this, you son of a bitch," he rants, "I'm gonna out live you. I'd give you a very short life expectancy after this meeting." One of the men with him lays a hand on his arm, which he shakes off in a hurry. He is pissed; stuck for words, finger waving, barely breathing.

"That may be," I say, "but I will never be the kind of slave that you are now, Mr. Gherardi. I will never allow any of my people or loved ones to fall victim to your pitiful excuse of an existence." I feel empathy for him since I could have gone that way too, "I will do two things for you today, though, and I recommend you do the same. I will do a good day's work to earn my way, and I will pray that you get out of that bondage."

He pushes the table out of his way, toppling it a bit, and he storms out of the room, followed by the others.

We get back to our hotel room after that, and I say to Cinco, "You know . . . I remember one day sitting on my porch with my old dog, Baggins, and there was a stray mastiff wandering around in the street, picking through whatever garbage he could find in the trash cans that had been left open by the neighbors. He went from house to house, collecting his subsistence as it had been made available to him. He looked to me as if to be about six years old. He suddenly looked up and headed toward our house. I had not called him, and Baggins had not barked at him, we were just watching; Baggins watching and me petting. As he intently crossed the street, on his way to my house, where the lid of the trash was tightly fastened, he was hit by a dump truck and killed instantly. For some reason, after our meeting with Gherardi, that dog has been on my mind."

"Makes sense."

"Babe," I say, "could you make certain that the video recordings of today's meeting are uploaded to my personal server at home?"

"You bet, Boss."

"And cancel all of our life insurance." Then I tell her, "Damn, you were hot in that meeting today. I am rarely as turned on as today, when you told him how much you cared. You sexy thing, you." She says I'm pretty sexy too.

A Hard Fought Win!

It is Sonday morning, and like every Sonday morning – well, almost every Sonday – for the past fourteen months, we are where we belong . . . at our unassuming Bible Church on Huebner Road. In what I call Sonday School, what they like to call First Hour, we have been working our way through the book of Leviticus and covering chapter nineteen, what most Bibles have labeled as "Sundry Laws." When I was a kid I thought that said "Sunday Laws" and that didn't make sense to me, but I got it straightened out later when my dad took me into a store that sold sundries. He explained that it meant they sold more random items, or a wide variety of things. So, this is a variety of seemingly random laws, or so someone thought. It touches on lying, stealing, cheating, sex, haircuts, tattoos and more, but it is, the teacher would point out, about how we as Jews or Christians are not to be like the world, and in fact, we are to be visibly different. We are chewing on this and talking about what lunch plans we may make for after church. "Do you think Bob and Connie would like to go to Luby's? Should we see where the older or younger crowds are headed?"

I see a Hispanic fellow, 5'9" and 165, with a big moustache, in a black Mexican suit with a red shirt and bolo tie, carrying his hat, headed directly at me. His eyes are stern and focused; his face is creased with age and labor, time in the sun, walking like a man that has something difficult on his mind. I can almost see him grinding his teeth and I begin extending my hand. He is sharp looking, and that is not all. Just as he arrives, Stephen steps quickly between us and a look of pain shoots through his face. He is being stabbed from behind, almost in my arms. He falls against me, and I feel the man's fist, holding the knife, and I grab it with my left hand as my right hand happens upon Stephen's gun. Three shots rapidly ring out, like cannon fire striking the would-be assassin in the groin, the belly, and the chest, as the gun's trajectory is raised, twisting in the holster under the weight of my hand and the cover of Stephen's jacket. BANG! BANG! BANG! And the man lay nearly ten feet away, dead, blood oozing from under his back. A tire in the distance is now flat with a pop, and crowds of people are running and screaming, not knowing who shot what, where, why, and who is next . . . or if it is all over. I sit Stephen down on a planter by the sidewalk where it happened; all the while, Doc is right behind me.

Bubba speeds to us and stops the car with a squeal and takes a cursory look at Stephen. "It hurts, but he'll be fine." He grabs Stephen's phone and dials 911; when they answer, he says only, "Stabbing, shooting, one dead. This location! One of the victims will remain on the line." He hands it to Stephen, saying, "Stay awake! They're on their way," he says, deliberately. Cinco is just coming out of the far office door at the rear of the church. I glance at her and point at Stephen; she will stay with him when she gets there. "The ambulance is only three minutes away, but I gotta get the boss out of here." Stephen nods, and Bubba slams us into the car, and off we speed, down Huebner to IH-10 to 35 to 37 and exit Cesar Chavez, and go east to get to the Tower behind the

Alamodome, while it still stands. It's scheduled to be razed next month for Dancing Stag Tower 2. There goes my ADD again.

Twenty-five minutes of silence from door to door after asking if we are okay as we leave the church parking lot, and then, twenty-five minutes later, "BOMB! GET OUT!" and we all jump from the doors as the car pulls into the garage, and about forty feet later, the car blows up from the rear and slides all the way across the floor of the garage to the other wall and crashes into it. The gas blasts out of the tank, torn open by the bomb, and is immediately vaporized into volatile fumes, which ignite and begin a flash-burning fireball throughout the garage and half way back to us. WHOOM! Bubba, who had been standing in the drive before the blast, is thrown between a pair of cars on the left while Doc and I had exited the right side of the car and were still behind the stairwell wall on the right, just before the car exploded. The bomb detector had sounded and flashed as we entered the parking garage. We see Bubba land and go to where he lay, totally unconscious, with a visibly dislocated shoulder. I grab my phone and press the power button quickly three times. Help will be coming soon. Doc had also managed to hit the red button on the car door on our way out.

Doc lays Bubba out on the floor and, removing her shoes, sits down with his arm between her legs. "Kneel down by his head. Keep it still." It almost seems gentle to watch, partly because he doesn't complain (being unconscious), and partly because she doesn't make any sudden jerking movements, but instead, pressing against his ribs with one foot and his neck and jaw with the other, she carefully pulls and twists, gentle and measured and slow, then, when it is properly aligned – pop – it goes in all on its own. I take the Desert Eagle from his shoulder holster and the Sig ACP from his belt giving it to Doc, and we have to go. This mercy stop has come to an end, because we know that we will soon be out of time . . . and in fact, soon is now.

We hear the rolling rumble of the garage door coming down behind our location, with a clatter and a thud and a final clack to lock it in place, and we have to go. They are trying to lock us into the garage, making us easier targets. There some men coming from the farthest corner of the garage, by the rear exit and fire stairs, as we bolt up the near stairs, half a flight into the lobby. We hear screams as we top the stairs. I suppose someone has tried to open the car and received a little shock. Sounds like two down. As we cross the lobby floor, there are more men getting out of cars, running toward the building, and an elevator door closing, I fire a single shot at the glass front of the lobby in their general direction. I don't know if I hit anyone or not, but all of the people in the lobby begin scurrying like rats, running out the back of the building, away from the shattering glass and running gunmen. We make it to the elevator that is closing, one of four on that side of the lobby, and we go to the third floor. I have pressed 3 and 60 so the car continues to rise at alarming speed since it doesn't have to stop for a while. I would have taken it to my office and then my private elevator to the bunker, but it is not one that is able to reach any of my floors. Doc pulls a fire alarm, and we get into Service Operations HQ with a swipe of my ident card. It will open anything in this building, even your place if you live here. Still, we are far from safe.

The guys from the garage meet with the guys from the front door, and begin running around the lobby and lower offices, trying to find us, some of them are watching the elevators' floor indicators. No one will know all the details of our attack until, by review of security video, their exact actions, how many they are, and where they go can be fully ascertained. For now though, we can only know what we can see and do what is in our grasp to keep ourselves safe. The first order of business is to reduce their numbers, and housekeeping is an excellent place to do that.

We find our way to the maintenance elevator called a dumbwaiter, from days gone by, but it is not really dumb. We force open the doors and wedge them back with some rubber door stops from Guest Services. I look with Doc up the dumbwaiter shaft and find that it is way the hell up there, so finding the power panel for it, I release the power, engaging safe descent mode, and it lowers itself to where it rests on its brakes in between the fourth and fifth floors, as I stop it. "Let's make a bucket bomb," I say to Doc. I go to the laundry area and find a couple of gallons of bleach which I dump into a janitor's mop bucket. The splatters are going to ruin these pants. She finds a couple of maids carts and removes four bottles of toilet bowl cleaner and then to the janitor's cabinets to retrieve three cans of acetone, one gallon each. I set the bucket under a fire sprinkler pipe at one of the joints, and what we need now is that: a ball of string – more accurately, twine for packages. "The bad guys gotta be finding us soon. Take this ball of twine and climb into the bottom hatch of the dumbwaiter and out the top, then, hold onto the end of the string and drop the ball of it to me through the hatches. I gotta MacGyver this thing." She doesn't get the MacGyver comment, but understands the plan. There is a safety ladder that runs the length of the shaft, up one side, but no room to crawl past the car. When she is inside, she reaches down, and I toss her a step ladder, so she can reach the top exit. As she climbs up, I go to the maintenance engineers' corner and get a pipe wrench. I head to the dryers and turn off the gas at the valve and then disconnect the pipe so that when I reopen the valve, the fuel flow will fill the room as quickly as possible. I open that valve fully, and gas begins to stream into the room.

Doc reaches her objective and drops the twine, which I find resting on the floor of the shaft well below me. I use a mop to pull the string to me, not caring if it unwinds below. I take it through the door and over the sprinkler pipes on this side and that, and then I tie it to the necks of the plastic bottles of drain cleaner resting them in the mop wringer of the oversized bucket partially full of bleach. I go to the door again, "Pull it up 'til I say stop." She does, and when it is about a foot above the bucket I tell her, "Hold it right there." I hear voices down the hall, and we're about out of time, so I open the lids to the acetone, normally used to remove scuff marks, glazing, and gum from the marble and terrazzo floors. The gas valve is fully open, flooding the room, and I turn the acetone containers upside down in the mop ringer of the bucket and run, as quickly and quietly as possible, to the dumbwaiter as the mixture in the bucket begins to gurgle and bubble. Up the ladder and through the lower trap I climb. "Drop it!" I yell and slam the trap door as the string disappears. Scurrying to the top, I close that lid, and we lay on our backs on top of the car. Suddenly, this seems like it may be a very bad idea, but we are kind of committed now.

The bottles have fallen into the mixture that is consuming the plastic by the second, the gas is flowing into the room, the door to the hallway crashes open below, and several people stream into Service Operations, racing frantically to the crannies and corners of the place, looking in closets and more. We can barely make out their voices shouting, "What is that stink?" says one voice. "Don't shoot, there's gas," says another.

A third voice yells out, "They're up here I think," and then it happens. My impromptu variation of acetone peroxide has ignited and detonated, along with the gas that has been filling the room, and whoever is in the room dies in the blast, which pushes the entry doors off the wall and down the hallway in two directions but also races up the shaft, driving our dumbwaiter up to between the sixth and seventh floors where it suddenly slams to a stop because, after all, the brakes are still engaged. The force of the blast was more engaging, but still, the brakes work their will. When it stops, Ilyssa and I fly up nearly ten feet and fall back on the top of the car with a thud and a BANG! We each have the presence of mind to hang on to our guns, but when we hit that roof on our way down, I squeeze a bit too tightly, having my finger on the trigger, and fire off a fifty caliber round that smashes into a ladder rung and off the wall, splintering the bullet, some of which comes to graze my forehead.

Doc wipes the blood from my wound with a bit of spit on a rag that used to be part of her slip, "Well, now you'll not only be handsome, but rugged too."

"Thanks?" I say with a question in my voice. "Four more dead!" I am thinking.

We are just below the seventh floor doors, so we wrestle them open and find ourselves in a much smaller version of the room we just left. It doesn't have laundry and maintenance, but it does have some janitor and housekeeping supplies. There's one on every other odd numbered floor.

We are unaware that in one minute the garage door will go up, and three vans of people – field operators – mercenaries – paid ex-soldiers – will launch into the garage – twenty-one in all. One van pulls all the way across the garage, past my smoldering car, driving over one of the dead bodies that tried to open the car, to stop, finally, at my personal elevator. Altogether sixteen men, four women, and Benson! As the rest of them stream out into the garage, a woman jumps out and goes directly to the elevator, checks my elevator call button, and shouts to Benson, "No power, sir."

"Verify" comes his command.

She pulls an electric screwdriver from her left calf pocket and unscrews the panel, she produces a power finder (a non-contact voltage tester) and waves it next to all the connections, shouting, "Dead, sir."

"Thanks, Jacqi! Take the lead. You, Lopez and Sean, secure this garage" Then, "Park those vans," he shouts at someone else – the garage door comes down – "Everyone going up . . . get your masks on!" Benson pulls his smart phone out, taps an icon and opens an app, taps the app a few times, and turns his phone off. As he puts it back in his pocket, a gas is released in the lobby that puts everyone to sleep in less time than it takes for Benson and the team to get there. Everyone carries an MP5 in their hands and has an UMP on their backs, a Ka Bar survival knife on the right calf, unless they are left-handed, and a .45 ACP of their choosing on their non-dominant hip – just in case – they also carry two extra clips for each gun, as well as whatever personal equipment a soldier prefers.

"Medic!" a shout comes from near the front of the garage – it's Bubba. One of the troops runs to him, recognizing his voice. "Gimme a gun!" he says. The medic sets down his shoulder bag and hands him his MP5.

"It's hot," he says, meaning that there is a round in the chamber, safety off. "What's hurt?"

"It's my left shoulder," he grimaces, "sore as hell. Don't know why."

"Can you move it?"

"Just enough to aim a gun." His eyes get big and teary! "Aaaaah!" he groans out loud, "Maybe I should aim with my right."

"Maybe I should leave you a different gun," he says, extending him a pistol.

He turns the gun around and accepts the .45, "I'll be okay, join the rest." And he does.

"Sean, at the garage doors; Lopez, cover in the far corner near the stairs, and I will take this corner." Jacqi barks her orders, which are carried out without a shrug. "And Lopez?"

"Yes, ma'am."

"Drag Bubba out of view." When they get to their positions, each disappears as if they were never there. She is a feisty little Columbian woman, 5'4", 135, tightly packed into her full tactical gear and scarlet red hair, face of a cartoon fairy almost, with freckles. In another environment, different lighting, and civilian duds . . . Wow! At least, that's what I thought when I met her before.

Up on seven, we are still operating under emergency lights. Doc and I crack open the door to the maintenance room and peek out one way, seeing nothing. Then I ease my head around the door frame to look the other way, where I see two men with small machine guns – maybe Uzis or MAC-10's. Can't tell! Easing back in, I close the door as silently as I can and point for Doc to stand behind the door. I lock it. It clicks slightly. I go hunker down behind a shelf of cleaners and paper supplies. There is twisting of the knob. It doesn't yield. There is tinkering of the lock, and the door knob begins to turn.

The door opens slowly, and one man sneaks into the room, followed closely by another. Doc has raised her Sig to where the barrel fits between the door and the jamb, and as if "using the Force," she aims it at the right side of the face on the second man. BANG! She fires. There is a reflexive squeeze of his hand, and four rounds fly from his weapon into the left leg and buttocks of the first man through the door. The man she shot falls dead on the floor, as the wounded man collapses back on top of him, and racing across the room BANG, BANG, I shoot him in the neck and face, and another reflex spray crosses the room puncturing a desk drawer, shattering a coffee pot, and decimating a coffee cup. Someone's "World's Best Dad" mug is a goner.

"Quick," Doc says, "let's drag them in." We lock the door again, and we have gained two machine guns, but our position is a dead giveaway, thanks to the blood and brain stains in the hallway outside. With the doors locked, we glean the ammo, weapons, and flak jackets from the bodies and then put the bodies against the door to slow anyone else from getting in. We put on their body armour; drag the desk to the middle of the room, and behind that we put the shelf, throwing all the paper products, cleaning tools, plungers, toilet brushes, etc. into the open floor, to confuse the footing of any intruders.

As Benson and the men arrive on the lobby floor they find everyone either passed out completely or almost there. One of Benson's team finds a bad guy, not quite resting soundly, and gun-butts his head into La-La Land. He goes down. "Ladies!" he says, pointing at the Martin sisters, "you, Tomas, and Six Four will secure the prisoners, open the doors for airflow, and liaise with the police and fire when they arrive. Also, anyone that comes down, direct them to the rear entrance to wait on the far back lawn. Martins are in charge." He uses his key and disengages the fire alarm.

They call the one guy "Six Four," not for his height – he is only 5'10" – but he is the fourth generation of his family to be part of Seal Team Six – two generations American and two Texican after the migration.

"Six men come with me, six with Terry! Terry, you take the north stair, I take the south, one man from each team at each floor to clear it and then move up the stair to join the rest. If there is any fire on a floor we break up to assist as needed. Everyone stays on comms. No chatter." He pauses, "Jacqi, say something to verify comms."

"Thumbs up if you hear me." Everyone's thumbs are up.

"Thanks, Jack."

The lobby crowd works feverishly to get everyone rolled over and zip-tie their elbows and wrists together behind them. Once they are all zipped, they roll them on their backs and pull their pants down to their ankles, throwing all guns, knives, and ammo they recover against the longest wall in the room. People begin streaming out of the stairs. The ascending teams have told people to "Stay calm, keep going down," and, "Go to the rear lawn for safety," as they come upon them.

"The lobby is secure and venting" is the report from Tomas; six men are already checking floors two, three, and four, then Tomas fires at four men attacking the tower at the front stairs from the outside visitor parking lot. One goes down right away, and one falls wounded inside the doors. The women turn and open up with their weapons and are joined by Six Four, all of whom hit their targets far more than they miss. Thirty-five rounds into those three men and five into some random cars in the lot. Only three in the first guy though; a rising patterned burst into the chest, neck and face. The final shot did the trick though, passing into his mouth, through his teeth, epiglottis, and taking out the lower rear of his brain as it left his head, splattering his brains all over the rest of the people charging up behind him. The others died of more random perforations.

"Secure again," says Tomas.

A plasma torch begins to burn through the garage door, and so Jacqi calls out, "We have someone cutting into the garage from the front." The ladies respond by going to the front where the dead intruders have just gone down.

"We're on it Jacqi," comes the whispered reply. "Keep getting those people out," calls one of the twins, pointing to the civilians.

Tomas is waving people to the rear of the building, "Keep going, out, out, out!" And Six Four is telling them, "All the way to the back of the yard!" Both of them waving frenetically as the girls switch out their guns for the .45 UMP's. They want them for their superior punch. They step quickly through the front door and unload on everything in front of the garage door, emptying their clips. They step back in for brief cover, switch guns, step out, and stand waiting, each staring carefully down their barrels at the van and car that are there. Seven aggressors lay dead, right in front of the door, having had no time to flee when the ladies opened fire. The car's fuel is detonated by a round, burning like an Aggie bonfire, and the van looks like Swiss cheese. "I've got left," says Clara. Some fools jump from the front of the van and the rear at the same time hoping to take the girls by surprise, and each takes a shot to the head from one of these amazing twins.

Claire yells, "Anyone out there who wants to surrender, throw down your guns, walk to the front lawn, and you get to live." She can still see the shadows of feet and legs under the van, so she knows someone is there. "No?" Clara pulls a frag grenade from her belt and looks at her sister, who smiles and shrugs. "Are you absolutely sure? We can see to your safety!" she hollers. A shadow moves but does not come out or say a word that can be heard. Clara pulls the pin and, counting to one, throws it overhand, like a baseball pitcher, skipping it under the van, and it bounces up to bash into the car beyond as the ladies jump back into the building. As it impacts the car, it explodes, throwing the van over on its side with three bloodied bodies pasted to it as it flies, and destroying the plasma cutter. The ladies recheck their objective, "All clear on the front," says Claire.

Floors two, three, and four have been cleared and five, six, and seven are being checked now. Two of the good guys find four of the bad guys on floor six and have them in crossfire where the corridors meet with elevators on each wall. Residents are scurrying like squirrels in a burning tree to get out of the way, down the stairs, anywhere the bullets are not flying. The security office is in the center of the sixth floor, so both teams from the stairs pour into the place. Once the men in the hallway are dead, Benson leads his team to the door of Security. Facing a reinforced steel double door, they get their explosives guy, Guy, to set it up. He pulls out what looks like three tubes of caulk from Home Depot, but it is a new kind of det cord. He squeezes it out around the perimeter of the door and puts a big "X" across the middle, making certain that there are no gaps, and he puts a remote detonator on the crossing point of the X. Everyone stands flat against the wall by the door as Guy drops the stick, and the door shatters into about a dozen smaller parts and flies almost entirely into the security center. Two men toss four flash-bangs into the office, and once they explode, six men and a woman rush in, putting two rounds into every face they find. The room is a mess of smoke and bodies, but there is no longer any resistance . . . only residue. The safety measures of the Security Center kick in, the smoke is sucked out in seconds, but the bodies remain, nine in all, and several bullets lodged in the walls, servers, a monitor, and the glass. The monitors, all but one are still showing what the intruders had been watching; namely, the seventh floor maintenance room.

"Seventh floor! West side! GO!" Benson shouts, as he sees three men converging on a large smear on the floor outside the door. Six armed rescuers fly out of the office.

Up on seven, there is a rattle of the door knob again and then the chink, jiggle, jiggle, click of the lock being finessed open. The knob turns fully, and someone attempts to open the door, but the dead bodies make passage an arduous task. One armored mercenary puts his shoulder into it while another man kicks at it with all his might, and the first one gets through the door just as six guns go off, full auto – MP5's – from the other end of the hallway. Two of them fall like ground meat to the floor as the one closes the door from inside, but his day is not to be much better because as he stands with his hands on the door, Doc puts her gun in his neck, and a puddle forms between his boots. "Keep him," I tell her, "Let them know we don't want anyone in here but Benson. And don't tell them that it's you and me."

We lock the door and strip the prisoner of his clothes – but he can keep his pants, socks, and boots – and we take his weapons, watch, cell phone, and comms. A knock comes at the door. "It's Security, folks. Are you okay?"

"I'm fine," she says, "but I won't speak to anyone but Benson. Is he okay?" She is speaking with an east Texas redneck accent.

"Yes, ma'am, he's fine. I'll get him down right away." Then we can hear him say into his comms, "Mr. Benson, we got to the galley, and there are dead tangos in the hall and a lady that says she will only speak to you." He pauses for response, then, "Roger that, sir," he says into the comms. "He says he will be right here, ma'am."

It is less than a three minute wait before Benson is knocking on the door, "May I come in?"

"Yes," she says, "but only you."

When he sees me, his eyes light up, and I am glad to see that. Still, I put my finger to my lips and wave him over to the other side of the room, away from the door, not wanting anyone else to hear. "Someone on your team is an inside man – has to be – and right now I trust you, Bubba and Stephen, so here is what we are going to do. We are going to contact Mr. Schroyer and back trace everything on this guy's phone and everything we can learn about him. We are going to take him to my bunker and keep him there 'til we're done, and Mr. Schroyer, along with you and I, we're going to find out who sent them, who their contacts are, and then we will decide what to do with them. If Stephen and Bubba are up to it, I would trust them, but right now . . . no more."

Benson taps his comms and says, "Jacqi, the building is secure, but can you get me full power restoration?"

"On it, sir," comes her reply. Benson raises his thumb to me. He pauses a moment and listens again to his comms, which he removes for a moment, "Fire and police are arriving on the scene. You and Doc keep the prisoner locked up here, and in a few minutes, they will have the situation in hand, and I will move you." Using his comms again, "Someone check on the condition of Bubba and see if Stephen is fit to operate." He listens and chuckles a little and says to me, "Bubba says he would be fine if he could have a swig of shine and put his feet up a while."

"Tell him there's a near-full, quart jar in the fridge in my bunker. He's welcome to the whole thing."

Benson's reply is gracefully, "Have Bubba meet me in the bunker. He knows where."

The standard lights come on, and the safety lights go off.

"Okay, Jacqi," Benson says, into his comms, "you liaise with the police and fire and have the lobby group holster up and assist in tending to the civilians in the back yard. Terry, take a team to clear Mr. Danz' office and residence, then return to the lobby to help Jacqi. Look to any medical needs and make certain that anyone needing a phone, or an attorney gets one. Everyone else, pack it up and head to the house after checking to see if the police want our weapons. If they do, give them up, get receipts, and provide ID as requested. We want no personnel onsite in twenty minutes. I have this room under control." She says something we can't hear. "It's just a couple of the rich building residents that wish to remain anonymous. I'll take care of them." Turning back to me, he says, "We will go up to your office and then directly to the bunker. I'm pretty sure that Bubba will already be there."

"I need something from my desk before we go down."

The Basement

We wait about thirty minutes or so as Doc changes into the proper attire for an assault team member – flak jacket, goggles, weapon, peripheral gear – and I strip down to pants, belt, and t-shirt. Benson returns, and we find the corridor clear. The alarms have stopped, and people have begun to meander back to their places. Doc and Benson walk the prisoner and me to the elevator, both of us zip-tied, both of us with a canvas bag over our heads, with me barefoot, being forced along by our collars. The door opens, and we move into an elevator car. Someone must have thought it suspicious for us to be going up because Benson says, "They have to be identified." I can sense several people around us, and the doors open a few more times on the way to the office, but when we arrive, we are alone.

As soon as we are out of the car and the elevator closes going down, Benson snips my zip-tie, then locks the elevators out of this floor, and Doc pulls the bag from my head, kissing me deeply and earnestly. The prisoner doesn't get any of these courtesies. "You look so hot right now!" I tell her.

I reach the desk and remove my cell phone – the disposable one I bought to talk with Doc in secret. I've had Justin reload them about a half dozen times so that we have always had private lines. Cinco has another, but it's forwarded to her tech. I open it, and I access the contacts in my personal cell phone. I find Schroyer's pocket number and dial it from the disposable. He doesn't know this number, so he'll flip it to voice mail. "This is Bill! Call me back on this number." I put both phones in my pockets. We get into my personal elevator, and Doc puts her hand on the pad, and in no time, we are at the range entrance, through the armory, and into the bunker, and yes, Bubba is there waiting, arm in a sling, resting in the leather La-Z-Boy, with a small glass of shine in his hand. Doc heads for one of the back rooms to change out of these combat clothes and freshen up a bit.

"Damn, Josh-you-a, dees some mighty fine ass shine! Where ju get daat?" After the third serving, he seems to get just a bit more Coon-Ass in his speech.

"I've got a cousin – of sorts – in the western Carolinas whose family has been in the shine biz for ten generations or more. They went legal about twenty years ago, but they produce about 300 gallons a year of this paint thinner in homage to the past." I grab the bottle of "Ol' Blitch" and ask, "Does anyone else want a taste?" I pour four glasses. "Cut him loose," I tell Benson.

As the bag comes from his head, he begins looking around, like someone who wants out. He should want out . . . this is a very dangerous place. "Sit down." I point to the couch and hand him a glass. "Speak English?" I ask, and he nods. "I want you to understand a few things right up front. First, I don't have a grudge against you, and I don't want to kill you, unless you force the matter. That being said, I will end your life to protect the people in this room. Second, I will know today who you work for and everyone involved, whether you help or not, but helping is better for you, and easier on me. Third, I am in a position to make you disappear or help you disappear, whichever you prefer and demonstrate according to your actions. Do you understand?" He nods his head and drinks his whiskey. It burns on the way down, so he looks at the glass with a bug-eyed start, and a half a smile, wrapped in a little fear. "I want to be civilized and friendly. Do you want to be my friend?"

Again he nods, "We have someone." He looks around the room but sits still. He looks in my eyes and says, "You have my phone. My quick-dial numbers 2, 3, and 4 are the people I answer to and those numbers reach out to your people that work for us. This is a job for me. It's not a religion or a political ambition. If you are offering me an 'out,' I'm taking it. I got no dog in this fight, and I got no bushido bullshit." Looking at him now is the first time I realize that he is Japanese. Hmm.

Benson gets a comms report that the assault team had detonated the primary transformer for the building, taking out the electricity, but had also disabled the backup generator, which Jacqi had fixed, allowing us to have full power again. "This was a seriously inside operation," he says. "They knew specifics about the building, and details about the car, as well as security protocols for every contingency. I may have to kill someone today."

"Brbrbrbr, brbrbrbr, brbrbrbr," my disposable phone vibrates, "Schroyer?"

"Yeah, what can I do you, big man?" he asks.

"Can you do your work from my location?"

"Sure, as long as there is an UberWeb connection. What do you need?"

"Do me a favor; be at my office in half an hour and bring whatever you need to get the guts of the world to open up to you. And, John? . . . Absolute QT."

"I'll be there," and he is. Twenty minutes later he arrives and meets Benson in my office, and Benson brings him down from there. He isn't carrying anything more than a tablet with a snap on keyboard by ASUS. Benson introduces him to Bubba and the prisoner, whose name is – I kid you not – Tomas Gepherson. "If it's all the same, I'll call you Geff." Geff shrugs. "Okay, Geff, what do you know?"

"I know," says he, "that there are several numbers on my phone that belong to the contractors on this job. I know that I can get you into my bank account, and you can follow the money from there. And I know that she is as much a target as you, because they want to send a message that the associates of the primary are in just as much danger." He looks at Doc intently, "Sorry. And I know they wanted it to be a big production – a statement to the world."

"Well," says Schroyer, "that's a pretty good start. Can I have his phone and use your table?"

"Sure," I glare, "all you need is my table system?" I feel a bit foolish.

"Well, your system and this." He pulls what looks like a jump drive out of his pocket and plugs it into my TV. Opening his tablet, he sets it on the table and turns it on. As it boots up, he takes off his jacket and sets it on the back of a kitchen chair as he heads for the fridge to get a bottle of water. When he gets back, the tablet is fully running, and in a few strokes, he has his tablet connected to the table and TV and to the jump drive looking thing he has plugged in. But it isn't actually a jump drive after all. It connects directly to his server systems at his home office by creating a tunneling protocol that includes the table, the wall extension screen, and the TV as well. He takes the man's phone and sets it on the up/down loading zone of the table, and it brings up all of the information on the table that the phone has to spill. He swipes it with five fingers to the left, and it all goes to the wall. He gets the banking information from Geff and opens his account and starts chasing the money. He finds the deposit for this morning, $250,212.27 US – came from an account that paid it in Kongo Francs, which explains why it is not in even thousands of dollars. There had been an exchange rate bump during the transfer. "Since you have been paid in US Dollars it was only worth about 78,000 Texican Dollars. You were grossly underpaid for this job." John turns his attention to me, "You are going to need Cinco and maybe Ethyl if you are thinking about what we discussed last month." He glares over his glasses at me, "Are you?"

"Yes," I say. "This is it." I get to my burner phone and call Cinco. "I'm going to need you in the bunker, Babe. Are you available?"

"Glad to hear your voice, Boss. I watched over Stephen when you were attacked, just like you said. I went with him, following the ambulance in his car. TV has been alight with news about an attack on the Tower. How are our friends, our girl?" I let her know we are okay, Doc is fine, and I notice there is some noise in the background on her end, hospital noise. I ask her to keep every detail a secret 'til further notice. "Stephen should be released in a just a little while. Twenty stitches and a tetanus shot; he'll be fine soon. Should I bring him along?"

"Yes, Stephen is my hero. Is he really okay though?" She confirms that he should be fine. "No worries," I say as I hang up the phone.

"Worries!" says Schroyer. "Big worries," he continues, with a slightly shocked look on his face. "Look at this." He brings the phone records to their open state and creates a diagram on the wall panel that shows that the three numbers on Geff's phone that are his contractors, have called a few numbers more than the others. There are a few hundred random calls to bad people all over the world, and then there is a concentration of numbers inside Texas, the US, at the Pentagon, the State Department, and to two members on my security team; Terry and Stephen. Then he generates a cross reference of the numbers at the Pentagon and State, and there appears to be frequent, ongoing communication, directly from them to Terry and Stephen as well. "Based on this information, you may want to alter Stephen's travel plans." I scroll to Cinco to not let Stephen know I'm alive – just that they have to get back shortly.

"What do the police know about my attacker at the church this morning?" I ask.

Schroyer types, pecks, swoops, and swipes on his keyboard, and my table, for a few seconds, none of which makes any sense to me. "He's a nobody from Mexico, a hired gun, so to speak, who has done work for several smaller drug companies in the south." He means lesser cartels. He clicks and types a bit more, frantically defying password pages 'til, "Viola! That's what I thought. The CSU people collected all the evidence and look at this." He double taps a photo with his finger, grabbed it with four fingers, and stretches it out, twisting it a little, "This knife has a blade that is less than two inches long. Even if it went in all the way, it couldn't kill anyone without a lot of luck or a lot of skill . . . and Paco, there in the morgue, had neither."

"So, it was all part of a ruse to get you back to the Tower garage, for a more dramatic kill, and Stephen is the backup plan, trying to gain your trust, just in case." Benson grasps it immediately and he looks at Bubba. "Get Sean here, now. We need to slow Stephen down a little bit, just in case."

I can have them do an errand on the way. I scroll to Cinco, "If Stephen is in good enough shape, please stop and get a package for me at Walgreen's in the Medical Center. It will be under your name. Don't let him call anyone."

I get on the wall computer, open a screen for Walgreen's orders and request a package of "Splat!" in "Blue Envy 2.1" and pay for it with Cinco's company credit card and use her name. It will be ready in five minutes, and I check the box marked "discretion required." It will be in a bag with no external labeling except her name.

"That should take them about another ten minutes. Where is Sean?"

"My locator shows him coming out of downtown now. He should be here in five or ten minutes."

"Mr. Danz," Schroyer says, "your package is in my office, complete and ready to go when you are. But there is no one there today." He explains, "With the attack on your tower, we would automatically evacuate our offices so that our own alibis can be established. Everyone would be at their own homes right now, uploading time-stamped photos and videos of their lives to their NuGle, Facebook, and other social media accounts, to give themselves a real-time account of every minute of the day somewhere else. You understand." I do understand. I wish I could have been somewhere else today.

I scroll again, "Cinco, can we talk?"

She replies back, "ping 24.30.1.55:2500." I tell Schroyer and ask, what the hell does that mean. He opens a terminal window on the table and swipes it to the TV. He types in "ping 24.30.1.55:2500" which shows up on the screen in red with a "reply" times four as:

Pinging 24.30.1.55:2500 with 32 bytes of data:
Reply from 24.30.1.55:2500: bytes=32 time=60ms TTL=50
Reply from 24.30.1.55:2500: bytes=32 time=63ms TTL=50
Reply from 24.30.1.55:2500: bytes=32 time=61ms TTL=50
Reply from 24.30.1.55:2500: bytes=32 time=59ms TTL=50

This is followed by a reply in blue, "Thank you!" A few seconds later we are looking at everything she sees and the text is overlaying the image in real time.

"What do you need?" she asks.

"Stephen was in on the attack."

"Are you certain?" she scrolls.

Schroyer uploads the police data to her address. She reviews it as she follows Stephen into the Walgreen's and back to the pharmacy pick up desk. I speak and Schroyer types.

"What do you want me to do?" she asks.

"Are you armed?" I query.

"Always"

"Is he armed?" I ask.

"No, the cops took all the weapons at the scene," she scrolls back.

"When you get into the elevator to come to the bunker can you shoot him in the ass?"

"Would you like me to capture or incapacitate him?"

"Nope! Wait 'til you are in the lift and do it." I am seriously pissed at him.

"Roger, WILCO, sir," she replies, "See you soon, Boss."

"Well," I say, "that takes care of Stephen. What about Terry?"

"My updates say that he is still at the office, helping the others in talking with the police and our company lawyer." He thinks for a moment, "Do we want to let the police in on what we know?"

"Terry and Stephen are partners in the company, aren't they?" Benson nods. "What happens to their shares after this?" I ask.

"I suppose they pass to the rest of us," is Benson's reply.

"What do you suppose your company will be worth when the world learns that I am dead?"

He has an astonished look that is a mix of bewilderment and denial. "But, you ain't dead?"

"Mr. Schroyer? Do we have a retirement plan for Benson and the boys?"

"As per your request, sir, yes we do; with a very attractive severance package for each of them, which I assume can be made larger for some, since two of them will not be enjoying their remunerations." He replies, "I only wish mine was half as good."

"Actually, John, if this all goes without a hitch, yours will be better. I know we're friends, but what you are about to do is going to cost you greatly. You will be compensated even better than the rest. I promise! For now though, I need you to access information about one of the dead guys upstairs and swap my medical history for his. Can you do it?" He nods, confirming that he understands exactly what I want done and why. But he does take a minute to remind me that I don't actually have a medical history – that I am about to have one, though.

In the morning, after the preliminary medical examinations have been done, the finger print reports on one of the dead attackers will come back saying that he is me. It will doubtless be sent again and return the same result – me. Confirmation will be made by verifying my dental records, which will say it is me. Then cross matching my DNA of record, will seal the deal and convince everyone that it is me, according to the fingerprints, dental records and a DNA match, all of which is being changed by Schroyer. The other guy's records – the real dead guy – are about to disappear completely. After all the checks are double checked, and all the double checks confirmed, "Joshua Danz is dead – murdered in a brazen attack on Dancing Stag Tower. Who would do such a thing?" That is what the news will say. And that is what the news is for.

We wait and wait. Sean arrives and sits with Bubba, who gives him some Ol' Blitch, and the skinny on everything we've been through. We leave the door to the armory and its exit open, so we can hear when they arrive. About thirty-five minutes after my last communiqué with Cinco we hear the bell on the elevator.

There is a shout of "Hey, everyone!" followed by, "BANG!" "Aaarrggh!" the shout is Stephen, announcing they're home. "BITCH! What did you do that for?" He clearly doesn't understand that we understand.

She puts her gun away. There is already blood on his jacket from the stabbing, and now his pants have a matching stain from her bullet. She smirks, and Stephen has a crease wound across his buttocks where the bullet passes through at such an angle that it leaves a clean hole, tunneling through little more than a half an inch of ass and a groove along his hip that will pain him for quite a while.

"Hi, honey, we're home," she shouts glibly. We are all running out except Bubba, who doesn't want to run, and Geff, who really isn't encouraged to get close to a door, especially one which just rang out in gunfire. "I didn't want him bleeding in the elevator. This place is easier to clean up." She has a point.

"Get him a chair, a tall one," I say.

Sean goes to the weapons service room and returns with a stool. Benson helps him get settled on his single-shot buttocks, bends him over a bit, and zip-ties his wrists to the top of the legs of the stool. "Just so you know what this is like, I'm going to pull the stool out from under you," Benson tells him; then he does it. Stephen hits hard on his knife wound . . . rough on the ass. "My grandfather learned this in Viet Nam . . . personally. As we proceed, your damage from the impacts will be increased by the same amount the strength of your muscles is reduced as you hit, and that will continually be reduced as we go. The protection of your ribs by your latissimus dorsi will become lesser, begin to falter, and cracks and breaks will begin to occur. The shoulder muscles will give up and the shoulder joints will begin cracking as you pound the floor. Broken ribs may eventually puncture your lungs. Compression may cause your sternum to break and maybe even injure your heart. Let's hope we don't have to go that far. The only question you need to answer for yourself is whether you want to live." We stand the stool up again. "Is there anyone else in this plot to kill Mr. Danz?" He doesn't speak and down goes the stool again. As predicted, it is worse.

"Ladies," I say, "I don't want to watch this happen to a friend of mine. Would you help me make dinner?"

"I could eat," says Cinco, giving me a kiss hello.

"Okay," says Doc, "but I don't mind watching. I kind of like thinking about what I could fix."

"You really do have a darkly practical side," I say, "don't you? You sexy minx."

"I've already had to kill someone today, and I just don't think this is a situation that requires me to maintain my bedside manner and winning personality," she replies, "if you know what I mean."

"Yeah, I do, Chicka," I tell her, putting my hand on her hip, a little swat on the behind, "But let's make dinner anyway. And, if you do the cooking, you don't do the dishes." She likes that. I notice Benson's glance at my swat of Doc's behind and the kiss from Cinco.

We work feverishly . . . okay, not really feverishly, because we have no cause to hurry making dinner. We have eight large chicken breasts, nearly a pound of broccoli and two large cans of green beans. The ladies lay the bottom of the induction heated crock pot with a layer of sliced onions, green peppers, garlic, and two large cans of Crème of Celery soup. I cut each chicken breast into six parts, lay it in the crock, dust them with garlic powder, basil and a little black pepper, and pour the undrained cans of green beans around the chicken, along with a quarter cup of water, a layer of canned mushroom slices, and then we lay in the broccoli on top to steam. I set the temp on high, and it should be ready in a couple of hours. We all then discover that Doc knows how to make a cobbler. Apple and pear together! Strange, but wonderful!

It isn't very long – maybe twenty minutes – before Stephen comes walking into the bunker, followed by Benson and Sean. He has given up Terry and has let us know again, all of what we already knew, and all that we needed to know but didn't. He was after the money. And we have a deal for him, if he wants to avoid death or prison.

"Stephen," I ask, "how much was I worth in your bank account?"

"Terry and I are each to get $10,000,000 Tex in an account in Costa Rica upon completion of the job. We each already have our Tex-Ex Debit cards on those accounts."

"How would you like to keep it?" He looks at me vacantly, "How would you like to live to spend it? All $20,000,000! Move to Costa Rica? Change your name? How would you like to disappear as a wealthy man?" He thinks that I am kidding. "Do you remember church last week?" I look at Cinco, "Were you there?" She nods for him. "Do you recall the message of Peter's denial?" I pause. He nods, sheepishly. "Well, that's where you are now. You have spent your moment on the other side of that decision. You have suffered the guilt of betrayal, and if you are ready to come back to the right side, then, this is me extending you Grace. Take it."

"Joshua," he says, breaking down and almost blubbering, "I just wanted out! I wanted to quit being a hired gun and muscle for money. I wanted your life." By now he is blatantly sobbing. "I wanted to be like you." He is so overcome when I wave him toward me and open my arms, we don't even notice that Terry has come through the door. He turns to run, back into the armory . . .

"Close!" I shout, and WHOOSH! WHOOM! The door to the entry of the armory, and on the far side, both close on my command. Terry's right hand is already through the door when it closes, and the fingers come off without a sound. Nobody runs to get him, no one needs to, because he is caught like a rat in a trap, and in a little while, we will get the last of any missing details we need to know about the attack. We are all strolling toward the door, having just touched the pad to open it, and then, BANG! A single shot rings out before any of us can get into the armory. When we arrive and the door is open far enough for us to look inside, each of us stands dead still in amazement, disgust, and horror. At the far end of the armory, the door, the ammo cabinet, the racks, and shelves of rifles and handguns, all of them, wear a brilliant sheen of blood spatter, skull, scalp, hair, and more, draining down the walls as a mist that is Terry's brains and blood hangs in the air, settling on everything, making the whole place smell and taste sticky sweet. As the far door slides open from my command, Terry's body lays down with his neck bent all the way forward, head leaned against the door, ooze draining off his face. We stand in wretched revulsion and wait for the mist to clear, all the while realizing how Terry had gone from confident to concluded in a very few seconds, really. Sean examines the body, briefly, and sees the clues that tell him exactly what has happened.

When Terry realized that he was out of time and space, he had come to the end of the road, fingers gone from his right hand, he pulled the fifty caliber Desert Eagle out of his jacket holster with his unsteady left. Pressing it to the bottom of his neck, almost positioning it inside the jaw bone, he fired 410 grains of "Eagle Claw" brand, extra power, hollow point round right through his existence. It bore through the edge of the jaw bone on the way in, snagging and splintering the bullet and the bone, which caused the blast to expand much faster than anyone thought hydrostatic shock could go. The exit wound is almost the upper one third of his head.

I look at Stephen and say, "Peter, meet Judas." And I walk back toward the kitchen.

"What are we going to do with this mess?" Benson asks, not being facetious at all, but practical.

Cinco steps forward with a suggestion. "We are going to put the body in a carpet with all the pieces of him we can find, take it to Joshua's apartment, and drop it all down the composting chute for the building, and in a few weeks, it will all be gone. In a few months, he will be a part of every plant and blade of grass in the yard. All of the guns are about to become property of your security company. We will hose them off so that there is no blood or chunks. We will put them all on a cart to be collected upstairs by the people you think would make the best armorers and have them added to the assets of your company, after they are thoroughly cleaned. Then, when you dissolve the company, the spoils can be divided among the employees. I might suggest a raffle, but it's your business.

"Dinner is going to be ready in about an hour, so we better get at it," she says. "My appetite is not very strong right now, but it is likely to increase after a little work." She says flexing her muscles, like a body builder.

"No, Babe, you are watching our houseguest," I point to Geff. "He is looking a little peaked and nervous, and I want him to know that he is safe in our care. Maybe he can help in the kitchen and the table." I look at Geff, "Okay, Geff?"

"Okay!" comes his reply, with a timid nod of the head.

"Sean, get a hose from the range, please," says Benson.

Sean gets to the other end of the armory, disgusted and almost retching, and heads to the janitor closet by the firing range. With blue latex gloves snapped onto their hands, Benson and Stephen, still hobbling from a wound to his buttocks, take the shower curtain from Mike's bathroom and a rug from the middle of the "living" area of the apartment to the edge of the armory and begin to wrap Terry's body up, being careful not to lay the carpet down in any of the mess and putting a one gallon zippy bag on what is left of Terry's head with a zip tie around his neck to keep it contained. He won't mind; he's dead. We don't want a lot of blood on the inside to seep through, and we don't want any blood on the outside of the rug which may smear onto the composting chute.

Benson removes Terry's wallet and hands it to John who removes only the Tex-Ex debit card attached to the account of the blood money and tosses the wallet on top of Terry's body. He will have the card assigned a PIN that agrees with Stephen in just a few minutes. He checks the bank account and the money has already been deposited. Doc and I put the living room furniture back from whence it came. Stephen takes all the cards out of Terry's wallet and puts them into a bag that can be shredded later.

Bubba brings a step stool from the pantry, for Benson to stand on, to look for little bits of Terry up high. All bits having been collected, even the fingers from his right hand, then they close the rug up around him with a hank of twine and put it all on an ammo cart. Benson then opens the ammo cabinet and begins handing boxes of bullets to Doc and me, who then relay them to the kitchen counter. There are over 20,000 rounds of ammo in my kitchen. In a few minutes, Sean returns with a hose from the service closet of the range. He brings it all the way into the apartment and turns back toward the range so that he can stand on one end and spray toward the other. Can any of us blame him? But Stephen is chosen by Benson to spray out the armory as Sean helps Benson with the body, taking it to the elevator, up to my apartment, and down the chute. Then they take the bag of cards and shred them in my office. Terry's buttons, shoes, and zippers will go into the oven or the trash as needed. In a few minutes, the last remnants of Terry are all rinsed down the drain and the room is spotless, down to the stainless steel walls and shelves with dozens of soaking wet weapons. If he keeps spraying a few more minutes, and the sump pump switches on to carry all the liquids from underground up to the top of the composting system; we leave the hose running for a little while longer. Sean checks the barrels of all the weapons to make certain that there is no flesh and blood in them, flushing with a hose as needed.

I call Ethyl to ask, "Are you free?" She tells me she heard about the attack and isn't busy. I ask, "Can you bring a surgical kit to my bunker ASAP? Speak to no one please." She asks what kind of kit, and I tell her we need to patch up a gunshot wound. She's used to not asking questions when answers can come later and better. Besides, if she really must have the answers right away, or if she requires greater precision and accuracy in the info, she can request a playback from Cinco. She is at the church still and has to stop by her office – part of Ilyssa's medical office upstairs to get her supplies.

Ten minutes pass before Benson and Sean return with the cart. They lay it on its side and hose it off for a while. It's wet but looks fresh and new. They let the water run a little longer still.

Benson makes the awaited call. "Jacqi, I want you to bring the twins to get some new guns for our home collection." There is talking on the other end. "Yeah, yeah, these are weapons we've had stored onsite at Dancing Stag Tower." There's some more talking coming from over there. "No, I don't think we will be continuing that contract." There are more cricket words. "Just be there in twenty minutes, and they will all need a thorough cleaning. Be at the executive elevator door, on the far side of the garage. Um-hmm, where you were today." He hangs up before there can be any more questions. "They should be here shortly."

"The twins?" asks Sean. "Why the twins?"

"Because they really are among the toughest people I know, they can keep a secret, and they keep their gear better than any one of you. Hell, they keep it better than I."

"Me," says Sean, "They keep their gear better than me." He is trying to correct Benson's grammar.

"I already said they keep their gear better than YOU," is his reply. "And I meant it. Let's load it up."

The girls come for the guns and ask a lot of questions of Benson and Sean. Their orders are to take them all back to the office/operations center and catalog them into inventory with serial numbers and record the striation patterns for ballistic matching. Then he tells each of them to pick out an assault rifle and a handgun for themselves, five boxes of ammo for each, as a gift, a reward – a bribe, whatever – for not sharing this information with any of the others, ever. They are glad to help – and once they learn about their own personal gains, they are glad to shut up about it all. Sundown is coming, and he wants the ladies to get gone. They only come as far as the garage where Benson and Sean meet them, while I and mine stay in the bunker, waiting for the boys to return. It takes about ten minutes to get all the weaponry and ammo off the elevator and placed safely into the van. It takes two carts, three levels tall, full on all levels with assault rifles, pistols, revolvers, and ammo to clear the armory. "Team meeting; tomorrow at three. Until then, everyone is off – except you three tending these weapons. Savvy? Jacqi gets first pick." They understand that for a little work, without complaint tonight, their Christmas comes early.

Ethyl, Benson, and Sean come back to the bunker together as we have the table set for dinner and the food out for the eating. Ethyl takes Stephen to the guest bathroom, where we hear some screaming from him as she hurriedly cleans out his wound. First, she drops his pants, stands him in the tub, and while his head is turned, she pushes the opening of a bottle of alcohol against the bullet hole in his butt, then she squeezes it to force the burning liquid through to flow out the other end. He turns to slap at her in pain, and out of reflex, she punches him in the temple. He stops flailing. She puts the bottle to the other side of the wound and does it again, flushing the other direction. He screams and flails at her again, and again, she elbow slams him in the head – hard – dropping him to the floor of the shower. He is pretty well addled as she instructs him to kneel, and stay still, as she closes up the crease in his butt with stitches and patches. Some doctors use tape or glue for most topical wounds, but this one is almost round, with a lot of the meat missing from one end, so sutures are needed at one end, gauze pads at the other. Some anesthetic is applied, injected directly into the buttock, and his agitation and aggravation are soon relieved.

Once Stephen is dressed again, and his personality is restored, everyone takes a seat at the table, me at one head with Cinco to my right, Stephen, Geff and John, with Benson at the far end followed by Bubba, Sean, Ethyl, then Doc, and back to me. I reach for Cinco's hand, and she takes Stephen's, and so it goes, until Doc takes mine, and I bow my head to pray, "Thank you, Lord, Our Father, God, for getting us all through this very difficult day, and for keeping each of us as safe as we have been. Thank you, for old friends and new friends and allegiances refreshed. Thank you for the blessings we share and will share, and as this food is beneficial to our bodies, let us be of benefit to one another. Amen."

"Amen! It's been quite a while, Mr. Danz," says Benson, "I'm sad to say, since someone prayed over my meal. Thank you, sir."

"First off, you are welcome. Second off, all that 'sir' stuff comes to an end tonight, okay?" I look around the table to see if anyone has an objection or did not understand. I turn to Cinco, "you can still call me sir."

"What's the plan, Boss," asks Cinco.

"The plan is to eat dinner, send everyone home that wants to go – except for Stephen and Geff, Doc and me – and to re-convene in Gerhardt's office at nine in the morn. Schroyer has already left the bread crumbs, so in the morning, the world will know that I am dead, as is Doc. Sorry, Babe." I say to her, patting her hand. "When you arrive tomorrow, you will want to leave your cell phones and tech on Gerhardt's secretary's desk, I promise. We have to have a secured conference, and John is going to make certain that we get exactly that. Right?" He nods. "And he is arranging for everyone to get a severance package in about a week or so, from Danzig, but your real severance from me will arrive in about ninety days, right?"

"Absolutely, Mister . . . er . . . what do I call you now?" asks John.

I tell him, "Call me Bill."

Call Me Bill

It is two minutes before nine as Cinco, Benson, Sean, and Bubba arrive at Gerhardt's office, along with Schroyer. They'd met up in the lobby and rode the elevator up together. They stop for a moment at Diane's desk, and Benson says to her, "It's time for lunch." She looks at him like he is crazy, then she turns her gaze to Gerhardt, through the glass wall, who nods to her and waves her on. Benson hands her a hundred dollar bill, "Go someplace nice. You should probably come back around one, just in case." Each of the other guys hand her a hundred dollar bill and suggest something else she can do to occupy her time until one; a movie, a drive, a mani-pedi. Schroyer leaves his laptop on Diane's desk. Everyone else puts their tech on top of it. Their phones and such are safe there. Cinco waits outside.

As the men walk into Gerhardt's office, the TV is playing news of my death. The stock market is bouncing up and down, and stocks related to our portfolio are taking a huge hit – "Who will be the hand at the wheel?" – "What can the death of Joshua Danz bring to what has come to be called The Enterprise, and all the giant, but still smaller enterprises that his hands have touched?" – "What will this do to the global economy since his fork was in so many pies around the world?" It keeps going on and on – five channels at a time, rotating the volume between them, and Gerhardt is already booked into a dozen meetings, to put out fires and minimize losses. He is on top of it all. That is, he is, until I walk into the Diane's office with Doc and set a large aluminum briefcase, on the floor by the door. Both of us sporting our new looks. Doc looks totally hot with white blonde hair, but she looks that way to me every day.

"No-o-o-o!" shouts Gerhardt as, BZZT-ZZT-ZZT!!! Schroyer activates his EMP and the TV dies, smoldering into uselessness on the wall. Smoke rises from Gerhardt's jacket pocket as his personal digital recorder retires forever. Everything electronic within about twenty-five feet is now useless. Even the electronic door mechanism, desk clock, emergency defense, and alarms systems in the room are dead. Gerhardt is worried that he may be next. This does not seem an unreasonable consideration. John turns to Cinco, waving for her safe entry, and she brings with her a small unit that John fastens on the window and then activates. It sets off a continuous hum as it vibrates the windows at random multiple frequencies, preventing a laser mic from listening to the surface of the glass.

"Yes!" I whisper as I come in and hug him. Gerhardt removes his smoldering jacket and drops it to the floor in a heap. "It was a hard trail to find and follow, but it was there to be found." Geff and Stephen come in next, and I can swear that Gerhardt is about to slip into apoplexy. "You know Stephen," I gesture with one hand, "and this is my new friend, Geff. He was one of our attackers, just yesterday, and now he is my friend." I put my arm on his shoulder. "You probably want him to be your friend too, trust me." I point at the desk, nodding to Benson, I motion that the chair should be brought out. "Have a seat, Hugo, and I want to tell you a tale of recent history."

As he sits on his chair, Benson and Bubba sit on the edge of his desk, Schroyer and Cinco get the two chairs in front of the desk, and Geff and Stephen take a couch as I push Gerhardt's chair to the center of the room and the center of attention. It rolls like a thousand bucks, but it should. Doc comes over and sits, or more aptly, she seems to lean on the credenza in that tight skirt of hers that barely allows a seat to be had.

"As a starting point, Geff's phone led to some people in the Pentagon, whose bank accounts led us to Kongo, which we helped to liberate not too long ago, remember? And those transfers led to transfers which led us to American bank accounts, which eventually led us back to you. When we knew someone involved in the middle, finding our way to the top and back down was easy. But the fascinating part was learning that, although you intended to kill me, you also intended to allow the world to continue thinking I was still alive, but living the life of a hermit . . . once again. My vacation in Mexico must have been the framework for this thought, eh?" His face reveals that he wonders how I could know this, and he asks, so I answer. "Your texts and call records to the contract originators in the Pentagon were recorded on their end, archived for future use against you, I bet. You didn't think that they were going to just let you start running things your way again. Did you? No, their plan was to keep you around, like a puppet on a string, and use your corporate connections to eventually repatriate the FreeNation back into the Union, as states again."

"I would never do that," he says, defiantly.

"I don't think they were planning to give you a choice," I raise my voice a bit and then whisper in his face, "but I will." I step back, so we can see each other fully. "So, first I'm going to tell you a story, then I will make you an offer, and then . . . well . . . then, you are going to take my deal," I say with complete confidence.

"First: The Story! Sixty plus years ago, a wealthy young man was trying to get his life in order so that he would remain wealthy in his own right, but nothing he tried ever seemed to fit. He had worked at his father's companies, and although he received a salary, most of his co-workers would deny that he'd earned it. He worked for uncles, trying to learn their skills, and although he could learn the mechanics of what they did – buying, selling, trading – he could never manage to get the hang of the when and why of investing. That's when he met a guy that was something of a savant. He was a ministry college graduate with an idea for a new kind of car construction, based almost entirely on some pretty old tech, and a business model based on the poetic books of the Bible. He had also developed his If/Then manual based on those books and some of his own understanding of history, the nature of man, and of what governments have done with, for, and then to people who were successful in recent past. The young millionaire decided to invest in the car idea and even offered to help the guy get his 'If/Then Manual for Business' published. He read it, twice, or thrice, and though it didn't make any sense to him, he had the sense that it would work, could work . . . well, what the hell, it might just work. He reported back to the guy that he was trying to get publishers to take a look at it, but that since it didn't convey any 'tried and true' methods, they wouldn't take it on. This was a ton of crap because he never tried to publish it. Trust me, I remember. He only used it for himself. He borrowed nearly $800,000 from his dad and put half into the car idea and the rest into some of the investments that the If/Then had suggested, and he managed them as it dictated. He followed the instructions carefully, and in two years time, he had multiplied his money about fifty times and then some. Not too bad, eh?" Gerhardt smiles.

"The car project, or the 'Super Hybrid Carryall' as his partner had called it, was working out just fine. And he plowed about 35% of his investing profits into it. They built a Suburban that got well over forty miles to the gallon and were finishing up with a giant Grumman delivery van, like those used by UPS and FedEx. When they were done building and testing it, they drove it from San Antonio to El Paso and back, well over a thousand miles, on just under thirty gallons of gas. That was over thirty-five miles per gallon . . . in a delivery van that usually got between six and nine mpg, depending on the model. The shipping companies went bat shit crazy and started throwing money at them. Well, more accurately, they started throwing money at him because he had forced the idea man out with countless layers of lawyers and court records, showing that the whole enterprise was his, not theirs. He had taken all of the technology, tools, plans, supplies, equipment, and journals, and had it all moved, over the weekend . . . while the rest of them were celebrating . . . to someplace where the others couldn't find it for months. It would be years before anything would actually be done about it, and in the meantime, he had successfully stolen the patents, registered all of the work in the company name, and he was the company . . . according to all the documentation. Among his victims was not just the guy who had the ideas, but also the engineers who helped in making them a reality, and some mechanics, who were expecting to be on the ground floor with shares that everyone had been promised. But suddenly, they were all broke and unemployed, with no record to show for any of their work over the past several years."

"So, now you are telling me that you were the rich kid and that the empire you built was on someone else's stolen ideas and work? Well, that's just too damn bad because that is how business is done a great deal of the time. So, get over your sniveling guilt trip and move on." Gerhardt thinks he is shutting down some sort of sputtering spill of conscience, that I am trying to somehow make amends, but he still isn't getting it.

"Hugo, I thought better of you than that. I hope you haven't treated that battery genius from the bayou like that." I look at Cinco who is shaking her head.

"No, sir," she says, "his contract allowed for you and his dad to work out a percentage of the profits. You – who this time was me, acting on your behalf – remember, you were in Mexico at the time, so I took the meeting – decided that 35% was a fair figure and that the patents should be his and his alone."

"How did that happen?" Hugo blasts, "I had that contact written for seven percent, which was nearly twice what the next fellow would have paid him."

"Thank you, Cinco, for that. In this case, Hugo, I'm not telling you what I did as the kid. I am telling you what the kid did to me. You see, I'm not Russell Anders." Almost everyone but Cinco and Ilyssa has a deer-in-the-headlights look now. "I am the guy with the ideas! For over five years we worked on that project with Russell, and when it was paying off, he stole it, right out from under our noses . . . right from under my nose. The fact that I end up alive . . . in this body . . . where we are today, is sheer poetry, and a miracle of God, nothing less."

"What the hell are you talking about? Of course you're Russell Anders! We spent millions rebuilding you. We would never have done that for anyone else." Gerhardt is certain, but getting a little confused.

"You and your people were playing God – tinkering in things you could not understand, and over which you have less and less control. You were creating and recreating people in such a way that if it failed in any way you could discard them like toys on the island of misfits – you were the misfit toymakers, putting me in this body, building all the Ethyls for your own purposes, all because you haven't made enough billions, but then, when the most natural thing in the world happens – when your plans suffer a hiccough, you can't believe it's happened. Why? Because you knew what you were doing? And it's all because you thought you had the best minds in the world on it? But you had no souls involved."

"That's impossible!" he sputters. "You have to be Anders!"

"I gotta say, what men plan for evil, God is working for good." It's a bad paraphrase, but several people in the room get the reference. "Well, I had just finished saying goodbye to my wife. She died of cancer, and I had no coverage for her beyond the legally required national insurance, and we were both too old for the government to think we were worth a half million dollar treatment program. I was about to turn fifty-nine, and she would be sixty-two in a month or so. Nope. For the government insurance plan, it was a no-brainer; we would never be able to pay that much back into their coffers in taxes and premiums, so they were not about to spend it on her. I buried her a week before the world changed. Tricia was the love of my life . . . THE love of that life."

I am tearful and misting up as Cinco takes my left hand with her left hand, and with her right hand, she scruffles up my cobalt blue hair. "Don't you just love the do?" she says, kissing my cheek.

"Oh, yeah," I say, remembering my place in the story. "This is how my hair looked all the time I was working with Anders. I kept it buzzed to a 'three' all around the sides and back, bleached out the top and coloured it with 'Splat - Blue Envy' on the long top hair. I kept a full beard for the last ten years of my previous life, most of my last thirty years – full and grey – almost white. Cinco had a time helping me get the hair done last night, but it came out pretty good, don'tcha think?" The guys think it is pretty cool, and Doc has already seen it. There are smiles and nods around the room, and John waggles his hand. "Maybe the beard will grow back, too." Cinco doesn't look like she likes the idea or doesn't, but appears as though she is pondering whether she might.

"When I buried Tricia, I decided to take revenge on Russell for her death. Well, not so much 'decided' as 'determined.' I began to experience the stages of grief, but the only one I can recall is anger. It smoldered up shortly after her death, and by the time we put a plan into motion, I was almost living on caffeine and rage. After all, if Russell hadn't screwed me out of everything, I could have been able to afford all the medical care that money could buy. She may not have been able to beat it, but she would have had a chance." I am getting furious now, just thinking about it. "In the end, he had all the money, and I had a dead wife.

"One of the engineers, Mark Carlé, said that he could get Russell's schedule, and then he did. Because Mark had buried himself in the project so completely, and so long, his wife had left him and taken the kids, so he was almost as pissed as me. We thought we were on the verge of a greatness that would pay off for a lifetime. Mrs. Carlé would have been back if he had been right and gotten the big bucks. He was right. We were all right, but Russell had stolen our pay-off, and our futures, my wife, Carlé's family . . . So, I got myself onto the staff of the Limo service that Russell used whenever he came to town, and he used it for that last visit. Carlé hacked the schedule for drivers and put me on the job. Russell never noticed his drivers; that would have been too much like a relationship, so I would not be noticed either. Still, I buzzed off all my hair – no more blue, bald – I shaved the beard I had worn for a decade or more, put on the uniform of a chauffeur and then, unrecognizable behind my Foster Grants, I picked him up at the airport and took him to the Tower Life Building for several hours. There was too much security there.

"Once I knew where we were going, I texted our destination to Carlé, having set my phone to report my GPS location to Carlé, who was waiting with a gun for us to arrive. It was a very simple plan. He sat at the destination, waiting for us to drive up, where he would shoot Anders as many times as he could. Then, when it came down to it, I balked. As I opened the door for Russell to get out of the car, Carlé appeared from the crowd that was at a club opening, and right before Carlé fired, I stepped in the way of the bullets. I just couldn't murder Anders, no matter what kind of bastard he was. This was a crowd of Texans, and Carlé, well he got three rounds off before they quickly attacked him, and began pounding him to the ground, yet not before I took a couple of bullets in the back. Russell, still not knowing who I was or what was actually happening, did the only humane thing I can recall him ever doing. He pushed me into the back seat and began driving toward Santa Rosa Hospital, trying to save me, and then it happened. At the corner of Commerce and St. Mary's, a garbage truck struck the limo and drove it into what used to be called the 'Alamo National Building.' Russell had become a blood stain on the window. I remember spatter on the windshield and steering wheel and a singular crack down the driver's window. The limo began burning, and I awoke just before I was pulled out. The ambulance guys did everything they could, but in the end, I was taken, dead, to the Nix Hospital where your guys took over. The next day I would have been fifty-nine."

"Happy birthday, Bra," says Bubba. "When was this?"

"That was Halloween, 2020," Gerhardt answers. "The accident," and he used air quotes at 'accident' like Doc had before, "was arranged by Russell's father, whom Russell had attempted to have killed six months earlier, but Harold had survived. Russell was hoping to inherit his dad's fortunes. That was one seriously screwed up family. But, with Russell dead, Harold Anders took over his son's enterprises and ran them quite successfully for several years, using the If/Then as his guide. When the elder Anders found out that his son had devised this elaborate plan to freeze himself and recover someday to run things again, he went insane. He tried to discover where the body was. He wanted to foil the plan by destroying everything, but he couldn't get past Mr. Anders' security, and eventually he killed himself for failing, but not before killing Russell's mother for giving him such an evil rat-bastard of a son. It was all quite bizarre and very hush-hush. He left a note for the police, but my predecessors found it first and the deaths were ruled as homicides during a robbery. Of course, the killer was never found."

"What led you to learn who you really are?" asks Stephen.

"Strangely enough, ever since I woke up in the hospital, even soon after the surgery, I have had two sets of memories and had been unable to reconcile a lot of things. A part of the reconstruction process was to have Anders' lifetime of memories reloaded into his brain, which turned out to be my brain. It was supposed to be a safeguard against systematic shock to his recall. But, in all of it, I could not justify the If/Then system of rightly handling every decision with my memories of a lifetime of Russell's actual decisions. The If/Then is a manifesto of historical understanding of founding principles for America, logic processing of business for profit and reason, with a hand of guidance by righteousness via biblical principles, and Russell Anders was a thief and a totally selfish troll in almost every aspect of his life." I point to Doc, "She brought me the first clues I had by showing me the DNA tests of my head, the parts used to reassemble me, and the DNA of Russell Anders from before the accident." Now I use air quotes for "accident." "That's when I gave her a job . . . to keep her close and watch over her."

"That was over three years ago," Hugo says, thinking he is in control of something again, if only for a moment, "how could you have known this and told me nothing for so long?"

"How long did you know that Anders' dad killed him and you didn't tell me? If I were Russell Anders, it may be considered important; knowing that my dad had tried to kill me. I would want to know that!"

"Damn good point, Hugo!" says Benson, glaring at him. Then looking to me, he asks, "So, did everything come to you slowly, or was there like a straw that broke the camel's back?"

"We were in Africa to check in on the sugar business when I got a prophecy from a street preacher who said, 'You're not who they say you are.' That is all he would tell me at first, except that it was God who told him to say it. Since I already knew that much, and no one besides Doc and Cinco knew that much, I had to reach out to learn more. He told me that God knows the answers, and He would show them to me, if I believe." I clap my hands together loudly, "BAM! It happened! I realized that I had gotten saved nearly eighty years ago. I knew that I had been to Bible College and had gotten married when I was twenty-seven to Tricia, who died holding my hand, and I suddenly sat down on the street corner and cried. Cinco was with me, and I asked her to take me somewhere so we could talk, and she did that. We got to a park around the corner, still in the middle of town. On a bench, under a dense shady tree, I explained the simple, basic Gospel to her – I'm a sinful dirt bag; God can't let unpaid sin and dirt into His house; God, in person, as Jesus, paid the price for my sin with his death, and all I can do is accept it – and then a light came on in her eyes, and she realized that, as part of the original Ethyl implant, this message was already there and that she, the original Ethyl, had believed it back in 2013. Cinco believed it too, now. Praise God, we were on the same page personally, spiritually, but the next few days and weeks would still be extremely difficult.

"For starters, we had been practically living together. Our sex life was consistent and persistent, but our spiritual life was void. And I wasn't just seeing Cinco. We knew that we had to do something about all of these realities and get them under control. Over the next week, it was as if my entire life before the crash played back in my head, over and over, at high speed, several dozen times, pausing or slowing down on important moments to burn them into my current consciousness. I didn't get a single night's sleep without awakening from dreams that were memories so profound that they had the same intensity and impact as nightmares even though they were mostly not bad memories at all. One night, I saw my daughter taking her first steps – I woke with an amazing start, a giant smile. I saw my middle son injured from jumping off his bunk-bed and cutting his leg open, having landed on his bicycle. Even though it happened long ago, I was ready to take him to the doctor right away. It took more than a minute to realize that it was a memory and not a current emergency situation. It was all there, immediate and in living colour, with textures, smells, and all the sensations that come with life. And it worked amazingly well. The only thing missing was Scripture. I had been to Bible College and couldn't recall very much of the Scriptures at all, ten or twenty passages, and that's all. But we thought we knew how to make up for that."

Doc pipes up, "That was my job and my joy. Since the Danzig Enterprises portfolio has a strong share in one of the world's best Bible software companies, it was easy to get the raw code and convert it into memory files, which could be uploaded to a server and then downloaded into someone's memory. The software had nearly 2200 volumes of information, including Greek and Hebrew lessons and lexicons, as well as about fifty Bibles in about a dozen different languages, including original Hebrew, Greek and Aramaic. It was a wonderful thing and such an awesomely powerful tool. After we tried it on Joshua, we were so impressed that Cinco and I did it, too. Suddenly, we had the Biblical retention of a thousand year old Born-Again rabbi. And one that was seriously saved! We were as well armed and ready for spiritual bear as Paul the Apostle, or so we thought."

"We didn't have a grip on how everything should apply to everything, and we still don't," says Cinco, "but with each passing day, we talk and pray and work things out, together. Joshua and I were married in Africa a little over two months later in a Methodist-Episcopal church . . . after forty days of purification." She blushes a bit and gives me a smiling glance. "In Africa, there has been some serious revival and a return to old school discipleship, and some of the denominations there aren't nearly as screwed up as they are in America, or even in the FreeNation. Still, we began going to church and have been almost every Sonday since."

"Twenty months later, I married Joshua too, all of it under his real name and my maiden name; John arranged the papers," says Doc, while John waves a small salute as if doffing his hat, "Joshua told me everything about his past; who he was, how everything fit together – his life, the vehicles, the Enterprise, and we plan to live happily ever after, with your help, and by the grace of God."

"How exactly do you plan to do that?" asks Gerhardt. "You're supposed to be dead, or is that the plan?"

"Well, that is part of the plan," I say, "but leaving you in charge is not the plan. We have no intention of rewarding your attempt on our lives. Still, that doesn't mean that you don't have a role to play. You do, unless you would rather face plan B, which involves a lot of prison time and the possible early widowing of Helge, or yourself."

"What is plan A?" he asks.

"Plan A is that Schroyer arranges to have all the evidence indicate that the guilty parties at the Pentagon actually planned the assassination of one of the world's richest men in an evil scheme to topple the empire of the FreeNation, and that you were, indeed, little more than a pawn in the game. Part of that evidence will include the recordings of the meeting which you, Cinco, and I had with young Mr. Gherardi, where he threatened me, in no uncertain terms. It was planted on the web in about two dozen publically available video sites, duplicated, and redistributed, and then the press was notified. The stories should be hammering the news in the next few minutes. You will announce your retirement with Helge, and you will stay out of the business world for the rest of your life. She deserves a vacation, and you have never given her one."

"What will we live on?" he asks.

"Your personal accounts and retirement package are already worth nearly a $150 million, Texican, and you're like a million years old, Dude! No offense, Hugo, but if you can't make that much money last the rest of your short lives, you deserve to die broke." Then I am thinking out loud when I say, "And when you retire, you should retire Bernard as well. That boy works like a dog for you, hell, he worked like a dog for me when I had him. He had gotten things done for both of us that were well beyond most people. You need to give him a severance package that is equal to at least ten years income, no . . . make it twenty years of his current income, deposited wherever he wants it, to be doled out as he sees fit."

"That's nearly $12,000,000!"

"Sounds fair," I reply, as his breath exhausts, and his shoulders slump in resignation.

"What about the Enterprise?" he asks.

"I thought you would never ask," says Cinco. "You are going to interview dozens of people to replace you, and in the end, you are going to settle on two women to do the job together. One is Feather Eagleheart, mother of Dancer Eagleheart-Danz. She was raised and trained to be a royal leader of a tribe, and, I guess, sharing this job could be the closest thing she sees to that goal, and if she wants it, her son can be trained to lead this tribe when he is grown." I pause a moment thinking of my son, whom I have not seen.

The other is Meredith McGill Iselin, who has great insights and instincts, and who truly understands the If/Then. Feather will get 10% share of everything Joshua has in the company, his apartment and other residences will be deeded to her – she is the mother of Dancer – and his car collection will become her property as well, except the vehicles that will be transferred in his will to the ministry mentioned therein, and whose delivery you will arrange. Meredith will get your apartment, and Cinco's, with both renovated to her specifications, rent free for as long as she stays with the company. This is for her family with Ardit, who is quite frankly tired of the whole business world, and ready to be a full time dad. Each will receive a salary of $600,000 a year, not adjusted for inflation, but with the usual performance bonuses and commission structures according to the by-laws. The rest of Joshua's holdings are going to be sold off, liquidating the estate, 66% of which will be transferred into a series of stock packages, to be the possession of a missionary group based in Mexico near the coast, which is us."

"And exactly what are you planning to do, posing as missionaries near the Mexican coast?" asks Hugo, in a slightly mocking tone.

"Well, for starters," says Doc, "we aren't planning to be 'posing' as anything. We are going to work. We are going to be setting up a clinic, since there are two doctors and a nurse among us, we should be useful. Construction has already begun."

"Yes," I interject, "and we have already begun to setup a farm and cash crops to give some peasants work, recycle the economy, and do some reverse laundry on our money if needed. That way we will have a way to explain our incomes without having to go out and drum up support from outside. It's a tent-maker's ministry of sorts, except that the tent makers are already wealthy."

"Also," says Cinco, "we are going to be providing support for some water project mission teams, as well as air support for all of it, and if he wants to, Mike can join us. After all, he does own that Ugly Angel and the Chinook, and Ethyl has the Caribou. Mike, Ethyl, and I can all fly. And you are going to donate the Boss' Super Black Hawk and personal jet."

"Is that it? That's the whole plan?" Gerhardt asks. "And you expect me to go along with it as if my plans didn't matter?"

"Your plans never really mattered anyway, Hugo!" I tell him. "The boys in the five sided loony bin – that's what my dad called the Pentagon – they were never going to allow your plans to become reality. They were going to blackmail you and threaten you and, if need be, kill you or Helge, just to get their will for what they'd call, 'the greater good.' Don't you get it? That is what Socialism always does. It is all about who owns what and who owns who and how they perceive 'the greater good.' And in the neo-American Democratic Socialist way of life, everything belongs to the government; you only get to use it and be used by it. Since you have always been just a pawn in this widow's web of intrigue, the question you have to answer for yourself now is this: 'Are you willing to give up what you were expecting for a life you can enjoy?' Because . . . if you don't make that decision, I don't have to touch you or hurt you in any way. All I have to do is to remove my hand of protection from you. I am the suzerain, keeping you safe from your enemies . . . unless you say it isn't so. In that case, I walk away – I just disappear – never to help or harm you in any way, but your cadre of co-conspirators cannot allow you to live happily ever after outside of their plan. They probably believe that they can't afford to let you live at all, for their greater good. Maybe they will let you keep your position, for a while. Maybe they will just threaten or kill Helge to keep you in line. Maybe they would rather just kill you both tomorrow, in some freak accident, to leave the Enterprise and the FreeNation in a more vulnerable state than they are in already, for their greater good. I don't want that. Maybe, just maybe, you would rather take my offer and make the deal." I step slowly toward him and sit at the edge of the desk. I reach my open hand out to him and ask, "Do we have a deal?"

"Where did I go wrong?" he asks, and I lower my hand.

"You forgot to ask yourself what the other side of an arrangement wants to get and whether you could actually afford it. You mistakenly thought that what they wanted was better prices or the right of first refusal on the products and services, or maybe, they wanted sole access to any new developments for their weapons applications. You thought it would be a business transaction, but these people don't understand business – they don't understand," I have to pause and think, reconstruct my thought, clear my throat, and wag my finger at him. "No, it's not that they don't understand, but they can't understand a symbiotic relationship where two parties make an exchange that is agreeable to both and each is confident that they have gotten good. They only understand using people, companies, assets, none of which has to belong to them, and all of it is fodder for their folly. They have no reason to believe what they believe; they just do."

"Why do you want to spare me?" he asks.

"I have two very good reasons. The first reason, Hugo, is because God spared me." He looks puzzled, and I really want him to get this right. "I'm going to tell you, basically, the same thing that God told me, in almost the exact same words He used nearly eighty years ago. 'This is a limited time offer and a permanent one. When the time is up, the offer of protection and fellowship is gone. But, for now, I am willing to pay your price, in full, for all of it and set you free.' Take the offer, Hugo."

"What is the second reason?"

"Because," I say, "in 1974, ten years before I met and married Tricia, I had an affair with a young woman – a stripper, named Donna – whose stage name was 'Summer.' In about seven or eight months, it ended, as things often do. I never heard from her again. Seventeen years later, a young girl named Saffron showed up at my house and said that she was my child from that affair."

"Oh, no!" says Hugo.

"It was true. Her mother had raised her for four or five years alone, never having told me about the girl, and then she married a man who was not as good to her as he should have been, but he managed to provide."

"You've got to be kidding!" he bleats.

"The young woman was more than a little bright and managed to get into UTSA on academic scholarships, and by 1996, she was getting her BA in business and marrying a man that was getting his MBA named Otto Hugo Gerhardt. Three years later, they had a son, Hugo."

He reaches for the phone, only to find it doesn't work. EMP, remember? "I have to call Helge and tell her that we are retiring. I wonder where she is going to want to move."

"That's an excellent answer for today, but you've got to realize that you will have to answer that same question to God one day, and I hope you answer Him with a loud 'yes!' and someday soon." I extend my hand again, and this time he takes it. "Cinco can accompany you through the upcoming days and help arrange your announcements, appointments, and meetings, but then she has to die, too, if we are all to disappear."

"Don't worry, Gramps, I can handle that for you," are the words from Hugo's mouth. "Well, at least . . . hmmm. Helge will enjoy going a few places and doing a few things, don't you think, Mr. Danz?"

"Call me Bill," I say, "and I'm sure she will have a great time, if you let her. She deserves it, you know."

I take Schroyer aside by the window and say to him, "John, I told you that your severance package would be the best of the bunch, and I hope you agree. That case, which Cinco set down by the door, has $10,000,000 Texican, in cash. Twenty-thousand of it is in twenties and fifties. There is a Tex-Ex card inside connected to an account in Costa Rica with another $25 million – the PIN is 3333. I may never need your services again, but I want to be your friend for life. Stop in and see us sometime." I say to the rest of them, "John will see to your arrangements as we discussed. I am sure that Sean and Benson can make certain you get to your office with the case." They both nod their agreement. For now, Ilyssa and I are headed to Mexico, taking Stephen and Geff. They can each make their way to Costa Rica from there.

Exit Strategy

Everything goes well with Hugo's meetings and announcements, press releases, and conferences all day long. There are more press events over the next few days, and the announcement that he will be interviewing for his replacement goes out, and the resumes begin rolling in. Hundreds of thousands of people apply, 95% are not remotely qualified in any real way, but that still leaves tens of thousands to be sifted, and they are sifted electronically. Cinco makes certain to get in contact with Feather and Meredith to get them to apply as well. Each is certain that they have no chance, but begrudgingly, they apply anyway. Then Cinco and Ethyl die . . . well, sort of.

There is a late night accident where Ethyl's car loses control on the fly-over at 281 and 410. It manages to jump the barrier and fall over 130 feet to the lowest level of the loop and lands with a SMASH and a CRASH, right on the top of the car. It is upside down, smashed, and flattened out, well less than two feet from the top to the bottom. The bodies inside are too badly disfigured to be identified, even by dental records, but the purses with ID and the DNA matching the next day determine that it was Cinco Anders and her twin sister Ethyl. The news reports: "Cinco was the personal assistant and right hand to the recently murdered multibillionaire, industrialist, and philanthropist, Joshua Danz – her twin sister, Ethyl, was his pilot." Ethyl's blood alcohol level is at 0.057 – nearly twice the level of legally drunk. "She must have been terribly distraught, trying to drown her sorrows," people would say.

It seems rather cliché, but, because it is so public, it stops the hounds from investigating more deeply. There is no burning up of the bodies in the car, and no attempt to cover-up evidence, and the DNA match would be made so publically and easily. The local coroner actually took substantial tissue samples on-site, that would be used for the tox-screen and the drunk test, as well as DNA matching. The bodies are buried at Sunset Memorial Park in a public ceremony. If anyone wants to double check the DNA of the corpses, they are welcome to do so. It is a closed casket ceremony.

What really happened is that two of the Ethyl clones that had never been activated were used as the "accident" victims. Once the bodies were dressed as Ethyl and Cinco, hair properly coloured, and the bodies transfused with alcohol in the blood, someone put them into Ethyl's car, rigged so that it could be remotely operated and – with a bird's eye view provided by Cinco flying and Ethyl driving – a well placed pile of rubbish on the fly-over, from a junk collector whose truck had suffered a flat, everything was in place. The junk man emptied much of his truck onto the shoulder to get to his tire and jack. There was a washer and a small fridge and a couple of steel commercial doors in their frame, and some random junk as well. He had the jack under his truck and was lifting it up to change the flat, when a car came racing up the fly-over and, as if using the doors resting on the fridge and washer as a ramp, launched itself over the cement barriers of the concourse and flew, soaring like an eagle as it inverted a couple of times, and landed far below with a cloud of expanding dust like a coyote in one of those old cartoons. At least, that was what he told the police and the news people who were there and setup in about twenty minutes. Every station had tape of him saying, "That bright red hair blazing in the glow of the street lamps on its way down. It was beautiful to watch, but also . . . kinda . . . terrible to see." The police would help him finish changing his tire and load his truck so the flyover could be cleared for morning traffic. Cinco saved the video for me to see later.

The interviews begin for the CEO seat of the Enterprise, and, as if on schedule, a month later it is announced that the CEO position would be converted to a CEO and COO, with CEO belonging to Feather Eagleheart, "one-time heir apparent to the Kickapoo throne" – as if there actually was such a thing, and the COO position going to Meredith Iselin, "young, proven entrepreneur, long time business associate of Joshua Danz, and a visionary philanthropist in her own right." The press is a useful tool today.

Five Years Gone

It seems forever since we left it all behind, and I must confess with a smile that we have all been a lot happier for it. We've made a home for all of us, and there have been a few additions to the tribe. It turned out that Doc got pregnant almost as soon as we breathed Mexican air, and again, and is pregnant now with number three. The first one was a boy named Joshua Dan, and another boy named Levi Thomas, and now there is a girl coming, or so they say, and her name is slated to be Shraddha Ilyssa.

We are expecting some visitors today or tomorrow, and we've had some others here for about three or four weeks already. We have a fairly open house, even for strangers. For the past few weeks, there have been some visitors who read an article in some magazine about the polygynous missionaries, and they want to see what kind of Mormons we are. It is just getting through to them that we are not Mormons at all, but some fairly fundamental Christians that want to live by the Bible. They have toured the whole place and seen what we do in almost every corner, but they keep coming back to the idea of me going to Utah for something, and bishops and elders, and can their missionaries come here. They just don't seem to get it.

We enlighten them with the pig farms, and they marveled at the SPF structures we setup with four layers of pigs living above one another, with the cement floors and running water troughs and the little swine born in the water. We have a five acre facility that keeps a minimum of 700 pigs at a time, and we release about a dozen or so a week to get the attention and friendship of the jungle tribes down south. Really! We take the little bacon balls, when they get to be about a 180 pounds, and we let them loose in the jungles hoping to make more friends of the natives with food that they still have to chase down and kill, but which keeps turning up, week after week. We also sell a couple dozen of them a week to restaurants in Tampico when they get to be about 250 or so in weight. We call it "Programmas Puerco Por Pagans," and it is currently the financial spine of the operation. We have arrangements with dozens of restaurants that we pick up their food waste and pay them a minimal amount for the goods . . . just leftover food and paper stuff. In turn, they put the waste in specially delivered barrels that are ours. We use that to feed the pigs, along with some of our crops, and the pigs turn it all into money. Of course we have our cash reserves, but this is really working for us. We also have over 1200 acres planted with corn, soy, wheat, oats, sorghum, beans, and yes, weed. We employ about seventy locals as farm hands off and on. We have a guest bunkhouse between the houses and the air strip and a circle of bunkhouses for the workers, about a mile away, on the other side of the road.

From the cash, we cleared a lot of land and plowed and planted and have built our homes, our airstrip and hangars, bunkhouses, and the pins and barns for the pigs. Our homes are on a three acre circle of land that has been dug out sixty-five feet deep, and underground we have the common areas of the family complex and the elevators that come up to the individual homes. In the underground Home, there are the library with thousands of old tech, paper page books, the music room with several instruments, the pool hall with – you guessed it – a pair of pool tables. There are two media rooms where someone can watch a seventy-two inch TV without interruption from light or sound from outside, each with an amazing digital playback and sound systems. Up each elevator is a home of about 3500 square foot, with woman-customized everything, or there is an elevator shack, waiting for a house to be put there. The houses have a very large common back yard above the underground complex, with a large swimming pool in the middle, which sits over the common areas underground. There are three houses upstairs so far and five locked-down elevator shacks.

One house belongs to Ilyssa and me, another belongs to Cinco and me, the third belongs to Ethyl who will always be a part of our family.

Today, there has been an occurrence in town, or I should say in a nearby village. There is a very young woman about to give birth, and today is the day. Ethyl is gone in the Cruiser to help deliver, and Doc is giving a hand. It is getting to be late in the day, and I am concerned that everything may not be going well. As it turns out, the baby is breach, and it is especially helpful to have two skilled hands on the child and the mother. They deliver the baby and close the vaginal tearing and all else they can do out there, but a reality is that the mother and child will have a better chance of survival in the clinic compound, so, here they come. Winter is coming on, and though it doesn't get dangerously cold, tonight will probably be seventy-three or four degrees – I often still think in Fahrenheit – it is still chilly for a new born babe in the near coastal breezes.

One of the Mormon girls – her name is Beulah for some reason – she runs along side of me as I go to open the clinic when I see the Cruiser coming down the road, honking. Then we come back to the car, and she helps carry the stretcher onto a gurney and roll the mother and child to a bed. There is no big hurry, and there is no panic though I have to encourage our young FLDS guest to relax a few times and tell her to "let God and the ladies do their work." The child is blanketed and nursing, the mother gets an IV drip, just to get her fluids and electrolytes up, and the ladies begin bathing the two of them to make certain that they don't draw flies and mosquitoes. They finish up by washing her feet thoroughly, dry, and put on a fresh pair of socks then drop the mosquito netting from the ceiling to surround the bed; we are just a mile or so from a major pond. There will be a tray of fruits and fish brought to her in just a bit, but for now, rest is the plan.

"This is really a different p-p-p-place than we were led to expect," says Beulah, wiping her brow after helping in what she considers heat. She is used to the temperatures of someplace about 700 miles north of here. "And you are – um – a – are different from what I thought we would find, too."

"How so?" I ask.

"B, b, better, I think."

"Well, I don't really get to take credit for much of that," I say, trying to remain humble. "But how do you mean?" I am still human and curious.

"Well," she begins, "for the, for the most part, the men back in the compound where we, where we live are considered superior to the, to, to the women, and the women all have to do pretty much what the men, what they say. And sometimes they get, ga, ga get traded if they don't do what they are told, or divorced, or shunned, or, or, or sometimes they are just sent a, sent a, sent away somewhere. And the men pick the wives, or the prophet says which women will be, will be bound to which men, and sometimes the, thu, tha, that changes."

"I don't think I would like living there, as a man or a woman," I say, just as one of her elders comes into the room, followed by another. The first is Hiram, and I can't readily recall the second. Five of them have gone home; three remain to confirm or deny our Mormonism, once and for all.

"Time to head back to the bunkhouse, Beulah," says Hiram. "We will need our rest for the trip home tomorrow." Beulah looks sad.

"Can't go tomorrow." I tell him, "We don't work on Sabbath."

"But tomorrow isn't Sunday," he replies.

"Funny thing," I say, smiling a bit, "neither is Sabbath," and I walk away. I stop for a moment, touching her arm and tell her, "Here, I know that every one of the women here is superior to me, and far more important." I can hear the distant whoomp of the blades of a helicopter at least five miles away. It is a big one. I let the ladies know, and I invite our guests to dinner in the back yard. We are preparing to seat our guests when a Chinook flies overhead, setting down on the dirt beside the airstrip, about a quarter mile away, so, recognizing the bird, I go with Ethyl to meet it. It is Mike's.

We approach that beautiful beast from the rear; the cargo ramp comes down, revealing a black 1977 Firebird and three people. The first ones off the tail are who I had expected to see, and I'm always glad to see them. It is Benson and Jacqi, holding hands and carrying back-packs. They really do make a cute couple. After the events at the tower, the security company broke up, and he was no longer her boss, so they decided to give it a try. Six months later, love had been declared – I think he actually said it first – then six more months would bring marriage. We got an invitation to the wedding, but we thought it best to not go, since we could still be recognized. I let them know that dinner is about to be served and that the wives will be very unhappy if they didn't join us. The other person is the owner of the chopper, Mike. I walk up and shake his hand and hug him and tell him how much I missed his ugly mug, and then I ask Ethyl if she wants me to stay. She declines, so I'll go back to the houses, to the rest of the family and guests. Ethyl would tell me later how it went.

Mike told Ethyl of how he had been almost everywhere he could think that he had always wanted to go, how they were almost all very crowded places, and they were all totally empty without her. He let her know that he was absolutely wrong in the ways that he had treated her after she got saved, and even before, and that he should have never been considering her as something, or someone, for him to enjoy sexually without having made the commitment to have those rights. He explained to her that his missing her was enough to lead him to a little Pentecostal church in SA, where he had gotten saved, and where he had been in discipleship with someone he called Brother David. Then he got down on one knee and asked her if she would forgive him and be his wife, and he opened a box with a very simple and elegant one quarter carat diamond solitaire ring. She said "yes," and they followed us to the house with her legs wrapped around him, kissing all the way. When they arrived, he set her down, and Ethyl shared the news of their engagement and asked if I would marry them.

"When?" is all I ask.

"Tonight!" is Mike's answer, "if you can fit it in."

"Well," I pause, hesitating a bit, and then I say, "first you have to meet everyone. You know Doc and Cinco, Benson and Jacqi, and these are our kids Joshua and Levi, and this is Hiram and Jacob, from Utah, with Beulah, and this is Mickey," I say, pointing to a five year old boy with freckles and blonde hair, covered in dust, "he's . . ."

"He's my son," says Ethyl. She goes to stand behind Mickey, and holding him by his shoulders as he faces Mike, she crouches down and says to Mickey, "Michael Daniel Rollins, this is your father, Mike, and he wants to marry me, if that's okay with you."

It really is a wonderful reunion. We make a call and get a marriage license brought out to the house for the price of a pig. The judge gets to pick her out and take her right away. I even lend him my truck to carry her. We have a few snacks, postponing the big dinner until we have had the ceremony. Then, at about 10:30 that night, the party begins with a roast lamb, cooked luau style – pasted and stuffed with bananas and various spices wrapped with banana leaves, buried in coals. There is plenty of beer and wine and even a little bit of shine for the happy couple, but not too much. In the morning, there is leftover lamb to serve with the eggs and grits. Yes, Mike figured that he might have to smooth things over with me, so he brought me twenty cases of instant grits.

We watch over the new mom and babe all the next day and come Sunday we will return her to her village with a small pig for her father and a couple of boxes of grits – she likes them – and a few days' supplies of dried fruit and fish. They'll be fine.

By the time we are thirty years from the Enterprise, there have been seven wives, including Tricia, and five remain. There are seventeen children, each named by God. Ethyl and Mike have three of their own. After my grandson Hugo died, Mike and Ethyl were somewhere and ran into Helge. She had come to the Lord, and then she came to live with us 'til she went home to be with her Saviour last year. We have built similar family mission complexes in several other countries. We have seen over 170,000 people get saved here and there, and another 5,000,000 or so get treated, healed or fed. There have been hundreds of babies born in our complex, and many people have died, even as I am about to.

I am living with a brain that's been through considerable traumas, and it is well over a hundred years old, and the bottom line is this: as good a pair of doctors as Ilyssa and Ethyl may be, and as much as we have taken pretty good care of ourselves, this brain is about done. It drives every single heartbeat and breath, it tells all the rest of my body what to do, when to do it, and how much, and it is just getting tired. One day soon, I will go home and I will see Tricia again. In the meantime, I think back over the years, of the women I have loved, the children we have raised, and the adventures we all have shared, and I can't help but remember where this adventure began.

Keith T Jenkins

.

Part One: Opening My Door

Keith T Jenkins

.

Opportunity Knocks

It is the week following Christmas in 2015, and we are about to celebrate our first ever wedding anniversary all by ourselves. When we got married, there were three of us because Tricia already had a daughter, Deborah, from a previous marriage. Then we had four more kids, and there were many lean years, hard times, good times, and more. But almost thirty years after the wedding, we have finally settled down, just the two of us, having married off the last child just a few months ago. There is chicken on the table, with collard greens, and zucchini, when a loud knock rings out at the door. We finish our prayers, and I kiss my wife "amen," as is our tradition, before I get up to answer it. As often happens, because I am not in a big enough hurry to answer, the door bell rings – bing-bong – right before I get there. I open the door, and I notice that there is a new Jaguar parked in my drive . . . something uncommon for the near west side of San Antonio.

The man asks, "Are you the guy with the car?"

Keith T Jenkins